THIS LAND OF FLOWERS

THIS LAND OF FLOWERS

Maryhelen Clague

THIS LAND OF FLOWERS

iUniverse books may be ordered through booksellers or by contacting:

iUniverse
1663 Liberty Drive
Bloomington, IN 47403
www.iuniverse.com
844-349-9409

Because of the dynamic nature of the Internet, any web addresses or links contained in this book may have changed since publication and may no longer be valid. The views expressed in this work are solely those of the author and do not necessarily reflect the views of the publisher, and the publisher hereby disclaims any responsibility for them.

Any people depicted in stock imagery provided by Getty Images are models, and such images are being used for illustrative purposes only. Certain stock imagery © Getty Images.

ISBN: 978-0-5953-6468-8 (sc)
ISBN: 978-0-5956-7377-3 (hc)
ISBN: 978-0-5958-0900-4 (e)

Print information available on the last page.

iUniverse rev. date: 10/26/2021

"Land of Flowers. Aim to gather laurels."

Diary of Lt. Henry Prince, 1836

BOOK I

AUGUST, 1835

C H A P T E R   1

▼

Born in the blue reaches of space, the wind floated down out of the expanse of open sky, pushing tall towers of cumulous clouds before it. Below, the great sweep of aqua sea was shattered by a long spit of land, jutting southward in a dense green of forest and swamp, its length broken by twisted silver ribbons of creek, river and bay. Drifting on the wind's breath, a white Wood Ibis floated gracefully above a world both primitive and deceptively tranquil, uncaring that beneath the quiet canopy of ancient trees raged the old, furious struggle of survival, and a newer, fiercer one fueled by greed and grief. Tall oaks with huge black limbs like splayed fingers brushed the earth, standing proud on high hammocks amid moldering swamps thick with cypress and pine. The bird drifted on the current of the wind, oblivious to the roar of alligator and shriek of panther that shattered the primeval quiet below, unconcerned for the beauty of tangled vines weighed with the profusion of brilliant blossoms that led the early Spaniards to call this country *la Florida*, land of flowers. The white sands that cleaved land and Gulf bore small signs of other life—palm thatched houses on stilts clustered on high ground, and nearby, a few whitewashed buildings near a long pier jutting into a wide bay. The wind swelled as it moved on, far out over the still, sea green water that lay empty save for one tiny, bobbing ship on its surface. Circling gracefully down, it touched its breath to the limp sails, puffing them out and lifting the ship's bow amid white, lacy furls.

The calm had broken at last

Leatrice Hammond stood for a moment listening to a whispering luff along the edge of the mainsail, savoring the cool breeze that lightly traced her cheek.

The Gulf waters, for so long like a flat green plate, now parted in glistening emerald waves along the ship's bow, crested with dainty white foam. Overhead she could hear the soft sloughing of the wind on the sails, a sound she had almost given up hope of ever hearing again. After bobbing about for two days in a sultry, unstirring calm, even this gentle wind had the bounty of heaven in it.

"Breeze is finally pickin' up."

Lea turned to see Thomas Wellington, ship's carpenter, coming down the stairs from the quarterdeck, a cedar plank under his arm. "And none too soon," she said grabbing for the rail as the ship gently rolled. "I'd about given up hope."

"Thought ye'd be bobbin' about here forever, did ye?" Thomas settled on the deckhouse box just inside a thin strip of shade. Resting his foot on a coil of thick rope, he propped one end of the wooden plank on his knee. "She's a trim ship, is the Oriana when she has the weather to help 'er along."

"It's so strange to be at the mercy of the wind," Lea said, lifting the woven net confining her hair to let the breeze caress her neck. "No doubt you are accustomed to it, but my sister and I have always lived on Hudson's River in New York and have never before been outside the sight of land. We're 'landlubbers'."

"Pshaw! Hudson's River is nothin' but a mountain stream next to the Gulf here. Why, you almost always have a wind of some kind on the river, fickle as it may be. But on this here Gulf you're more likely to be sittin' in a suffocatin' calm half the time or prayin' your way through some torrential storm the other. Ye'd do well to enjoy this little puff, seein' as how it could well turn into somethin' worse afore you've time to blink an eye."

A storm might almost be welcome now, Lea thought, turning her face full into the refreshing breeze. Closing her eyes, she reveled in its cool breath. She was glad Thomas had joined her. With Rachel feeling ill and the boys underfoot, there had been little leisure on this trip for conversation. The pleasant banter she had shared with this weathered sailor had done much to enliven a long, uncomfortable sail.

She'd been told it could take as little as twelve days to reach Tampa Bay from New York but this trip had been lengthened by stops at Charleston and Key West. Going ashore at Charleston had at least enlivened the tedium of days at sea on a schooner that carried a lot of supplies but few passengers, and Lea and her family had enjoyed their brief exploration of the picturesque port city. The low islands around Savannah, so famous for their Sea Island cotton plantations, appeared mysterious and inviting, and Key West with its low, tropical houses and busy waterside made her long to jump ship and explore. The last leg of the trip up the coast to Fort Brooke was only supposed to take a quick three days but this dreadful calm had lengthened that to over five.

Up on the quarterdeck the Captain leaned over the rail and doffed his hat to her before turning his attention to the sails above where his men scrambled to unfurl them to the wind. The Captain and First Mate had been pleasantly polite, as had all the men who worked the ship. Yet Lea had enjoyed her conversations with this wizened little sailor, and was as much at ease with him as she usually was with only one other man, her brother-in-law, Ben Carson. But then Ben had always been special.

"How much longer till we reach Fort Brooke, Mister Wellington?"

Thomas glanced up at her, his pinched, blue eyes fading to near invisibility against his tanned cheeks. He told her once that he'd been serving on ships of one kind or another since he was twelve years old. Lea thought his thin, graying hair and leathery skin were a testament to the toll that years upon the world's oceans had taken on him.

"Longer! Why, ma'am, we're almost there now."

Lea's eyes widened. "We are? Where?"

He gestured off the bow. "T'islands at the entrance o' Tampa Bay are just over the horizon there. Can't you see 'em?"

For a moment Lea wondered whether he was teasing her. Then, eyes screwed to the edge of the sea, she strained to make out any kind of dark pencil stroke where sky and water merged. She could see nothing but the Gulf, blue in the distance, greenish-yellow on the surface near the ship, glassy jade below. The Oriana slipped with an easy grace along its undulating surface, carried by the strengthening wind.

"I don't see anything but water. Surely you're making fun of me, Thomas, and that's not a kind thing to do to someone so desperate for the sight of land."

The old sailor chuckled silently to himself. "Now, don't take offense. I'm not funnin' you a'tall. There really is land over there and had ye the Captain's eyeglass, you could see it right enough. We been moving alongside of it for a long time now. Trouble is, the land in Floridy's so flat that ye can't make it out till ye've nearly run aground. But it's there all right."

Lea squinted against the glare. "You mean we've actually reached Fort Brooke? That we'll be docking soon?"

Jabbing his knife point between the coils of a rope pile, Thomas laid the plank down and moved to stand beside Lea at the ship's rail. "In a manner of speakin', ma'am." He pointed a bony finger. "Fort Brooke is in that direction but it's still a good ways off. First we have to cross a sizeable bay—'Spiritu Sancto' the Spaniards called it, or some such heathenish name. 'Calusa' it was to the Indians. Now it's just plain Tampa Bay."

Lea grinned at him. "Thomas, 'Spiritu Sancto' is not a heathenish name. On the contrary…"

"Well, you never know with them Spaniards. There's a number of 'em livin' at Spanishtown Creek near the fort so's ye just as well to get used to their peculiar talk. Mostly they raise orange trees and sell fish, but some own cattle too. Down near Charlotte Harbor ye'll find some that run rancheros, sellin' salted fish and beef to Havana. Rumor says they're rich as Midas."

Lea wiped at a thin bead of perspiration that was slowly trailing its way along her neck. The heat was sweltering in spite of the breeze. "Tell me more about Fort Brooke. My brother-in-law has written us a little but I realize, now that we are about to arrive, I don't really know what to expect."

Thomas shrugged. "It's like forts everywhere sittin' on the edge of a wilderness. Rough, at times. Mostly pretty boring."

"It can't be too rough or Captain Carson would surely not have sent for us to join him there. My sister isn't well, you know, and he's very solicitous of her."

Thomas turned to stare at the horizon. "It's not for me to say, ma'am, what makes a man want his family with him, seein' as I have none. But I do know that things is unsettled in Floridy territory right now, what with them Seminoles actin' up and all. Indians is funny creatures. You just don't never know what they're up to."

Lea gave an involuntary shudder. "Indians! I know they're there and we must grow accustomed to them, but I've tried not to think about them too much."

"Ain't you never seen Indians afore? There must still be a few along the North, that is, Hudson's river."

"A few, yes, but they are a sorry lot, half-starved and dirty and no threat to anyone. These Seminoles are very different, or so I've heard. For one thing, there are a lot more of them and they still consider Florida their home in spite of the Army's presence."

Hearing a noise behind her, Lea turned to see her sister's golden head bobbing up the hatchway. "Oh dear," she said, lowering her voice and leaning closer to Thomas. "Rachel is coming up on deck. Be careful what you say. Her nerves are not strong and just the word 'Indian' throws her into a near panic."

Thomas nodded, almost sorry Lea's sister had interrupted their conversation. During the long voyage he had never achieved the comfortable rapport with Mrs. Carson that he had with her sister. Nevertheless, with polite formality he moved to take Rachel's hand to help her up the last of the steps. Breathing heavily, she stood with one hand pressed to her side and the other clasping her straw bonnet, her lovely face flushed with the exertion of her climb. The wide sleeves and voluminous skirt of her dimity dress could not disguise her body's thin frame. There was an air of fragility about Lea's sister, a delicacy hard to distinguish from outright illness. The sun set her golden hair gleaming until she covered it under the wide brim of her bonnet. Struggling to tie the ribbons under her chin, she primly took the seat on the box Thomas had vacated.

Lea gently took the rose colored strings from her sister's hands and tied them in a bow under her chin. "Rachel, you shouldn't have come above deck. You know how susceptible you are to a sudden chill. You ought to have stayed in the cabin."

"Oh, but Leatrice, it's so hot down there. The cabin is smothering. I felt the movement of the ship and I knew there had to be a breeze at last. I was desperate to feel it too. You're not angry with me, are you?"

"Of course I'm not angry, dear. I just don't want you to get sick now when we've almost reached our destination. Here, put my shawl around your shoulders. Mister Wellington has just told me we're outside Tampa Bay. Isn't that great news? Our trip is nearly over and we should be standing on solid ground again by nightfall."

"Hold on now, I didn't say that," Thomas objected. "You don't never know with wind and tide if'n you can make shore that soon. A lot depends on what this little breeze decides to do."

Lea refused to be discouraged. "Well, it can't be any longer than tomorrow if land is that close. Won't it be a relief, Rachel?"

"Such a relief," her sister said, leaning back against the deckhouse and closing her eyes as she tilted her face to the wind. "I only hope Captain Carson will be there to meet us," she added, dabbing at her face with a silk handkerchief.

"Where are the boys?"

"Still in the cabin. Stephen is asleep even in this heat, but Buck as usual, refused to lie down long enough to take a nap. He'll probably be up on deck any minute now though I ordered him to stay below."

Her voice trailed away and Lea went back to trying to spot some sign of land on the horizon. Thomas leaned against the rail and glanced back and forth between the two sisters. Though there was an obvious family resemblance between them, it showed itself in different ways. Both women were of middle height and both had thick, lustrous hair. But while Lea's was a walnut shade of brown, Rachel's golden curls lay in delicate cobweb spins about her lovely face. Both had somewhat prominent cheekbones and delicately slanted eyes, but while in one sister these traits heightened her fragile beauty, in the other they gave her face an odd, dreamy touch. Actually, he thought, Lea was a pretty girl too. She was simply overshadowed by her stunning sister. Except for the eyes. Lea's were large and green as the depth of the gulf in strong sunlight. Rachel's eyes tended toward a washed-out blue-gray, though that might be due to her uncertain health rather than a natural lack of color.

Yet for all Rachel's beauty, Lea's figure was more to his taste. Firm and rounded, it was something a man could get his hands around, a testament to health and vigor. But then he was only a rough sailor. Even he knew that the finely honed planes of Rachel's face were the kind of beauty poets wrote about, like one of those marble statues. Mayhap the warm, mild climate of El Spiritu Sancto Bay would put some color in those pale cheeks, but knowing the area as he did, he rather doubted it.

Turning suddenly, Lea caught the old sailor studying them and instantly knew that familiar sinking feeling of being compared to her sister and found wanting. She looked quickly back to the shimmering horizon. She ought to be used to it by now—it was something she had dealt with all her life, ever since their old aunts used to cluck their tongues and whisper how sad it was that Leatrice got so little of the family's good looks while her younger sister, Rachel, was a child of golden-haired beauty. For a while in those early years she had resented her sister, until Rachel's gentle ways and fragile constitution led her instead to love and watch over her. In the end, Lea made up her mind that none of it really mattered. They were both simply themselves and that was all there was to it. If, as they grew older, the young beaus tended to gravitate around her sister, she learned not to let that bother her either. There had never been one she really cared about anyway. Except, possibly…

He had been Lieutenant Carson when she first met him at a frolic at West Point, across the river from her home. For a short time she hoped he might grow to care for her, but then he met Rachel and that was the end of that. Nearly nineteen then herself, her sister had just turned seventeen and had all the fresh, unfolding bloom of youth to enhance her innate beauty. But that was long ago and long forgotten. When Buck and Stephen came along she doted on them as any loving aunt would. Well, in truth perhaps a bit more because Ben was away so much and Rachel was so often sickly. Her love for her sister's children had filled a void in her life as well as benefiting the boys and their parents.

And now, after almost a year, they would all be together again. She imagined Ben standing tall in his blue uniform, a welcoming smile on his long, tanned face.

The thought brought a flutter of anticipation which she quickly dismissed. She would be glad to see him again, just as any affectionate sister would.

Far off in the distance the gray shroud that was the horizon broke and for a moment Lea thought she saw a thin rise of land. "Are you certain Fort Brooke is over there, Thomas? You're truly not teasing me, are you?"

Rolling a small barrel up by its iron rim, Thomas settled on its lid and picked up his knife and the cedar plank. "Course I'm sure. I've made this trip enough times to know. Another hour or so with this little breeze and you'll make out the islands at the mouth of the bay, and after that, the scrawny trees on Piney Point."

Lea scrutinized him, her green eyes narrowing. "I don't know whether to believe you or not."

Chuckling, he spat a stream of tobacco juice over the rail. "You can believe me all right. With any luck, by tomorry ye'll be eatin' oranges from the trees at Fort Brooke with y'er supper."

CHAPTER 2

▼

"Gawd-damn!"

Captain Ben Carson glared angrily at the soldier crouched near him who was slapping at a mosquito. Cates should know better than to yell out in this country where even the slightest sound could bring the savages down on you. It may have been accidental but by now the men ought to know their Captain had been in Florida territory long enough to have little patience with accidents. Close behind Cates, Ben saw his friend, Abel Meeker, nudge him silently, nodding toward the ragged line of trees ahead. Above them a relentless August sun beat down, searing the men in their pale blue summer uniforms where they crouched among the tall grass and palmetto scrub. Flies and gnats were everywhere, their loud buzzing an ubiquitous obbligato to the constant squawking of the myriad birds. With one ear tuned for the sudden rattle of a snake, Ben eyed the cypress stand nearly fifty yards ahead, its trees standing like silent sentinels in the afternoon heat. At least there would be shade there and, if he remembered right, a small pond with brackish water to wash away some of the stinking sweat that streamed down his back. Most of the men wanted to head right for it but he knew how crucial it was to make sure the glade was empty first. Though he knew he had a reputation for a certain amount of sympathy toward Indians, he still had a lot of caution and respect for their meanness.

"Look!" he heard Meeker whisper.

From the edge of the cypress stand a shadowy form emerged waving one arm, his dark skin almost indistinguishable from the shade beneath the trees. Juan Montes de Oca, their guide, had obviously found the place free of Seminoles.

The grassy plateau was suddenly alive with men in blue coats and tall army caps rising above the waist-high grass to make their way toward the Spaniard. They followed Ben who removed his hat as he walked to wipe at the damp inside brim. Juan leaned on his long rifle and waited for the Captain to approach.

"The grove is clear, *Capitano.*"

"Good. Any signs that the 'Eastu Charties' have been here?" Ben asked.

Juan smiled at the soldiers' familiar mangling of the Seminole word for 'Indian'. "They have been here for certain, but not within the last day or so."

Ben Carson barely broke his stride as he moved into the welcome shade of the trees, as glad as his men to get out of the direct sunlight. The guide fell into step beside him.

"I believe I find your missing courier, *Captaino,*" Juan spoke quietly.

Ben hesitated. "What do you mean?"

Juan nodded toward the water. "In the pond over there. I did not go close enough to see for certain, but the stench—pah! And the shape of it. I believe we discover what become of him."

Ben searched out the sliver of water shimmering underneath the cypress trees. Certainly there was something in the air besides the usual reek of rotting swamp. If it were Dalton's body, that would explain why they had spotted no Indians on their patrol. The Spanish guide was probably right. This shadowy cypress glade had the feel of dark, mysterious evil.

The search party moved slowly into the grove, some of the men forging toward the pond. Ben jammed his hat back on his head. "Well, we'd better have a look."

The canopy of cypress, far from being a cool haven, compressed the afternoon air like a steam boiler. A flurry of wild fowl scattered off the water at the first sound of the soldier's thrashing, and by the time the detail reached the edge of the coffee-colored pond, there was only the occasional flicker of a water insect to ripple its placid surface.

Along the bank the yellow marsh grass grew so thick and tangled that if de Oca had not warned him, Ben would not readily have spotted the shapeless lump floating among the reeds. He fought down an urge to cover his nose, while beside him one of the men stooped to pick up a branch and went to kneel close to the water, prodding at the twisted debris.

"Christ!"

A second man knelt near the first. Ben stepped between them, close enough to make out the bloated mass among the weeds.

"Is it Dalton? You knew him, didn't you, Cates?"

Corporal Cates' face had turned as gray as the moss dangling from the branches over his head. "Yes, sir. We came down together from Fort Drane. It's him. That is, I think it's him. Hard to tell for sure."

The uniform was shredded but there was enough left to identify a United States Army artillaryman. Though the body had grown bloated and grotesque in the water, it still bore the unmistakable signs of an Indian attack. The scalp had been ripped away, and the gray, sodden intestines bobbed aimlessly from the open gash in the torso. He'd been shot and beaten. If one looked closely, Ben thought, they would probably still see the expression of horror on the swollen features of what had been Dalton's face. Across the pond lay the rotting corpse of the courier's mule.

He turned away, the gorge rising in his throat. Behind him he heard some of the men gagging.

"Meeker, go back to my horse and bring a blanket from my saddle bag. This man will have to be buried with some measure of dignity." Abel Meeker went bounding off as if glad to leave the pond behind. The rest of the detail, drawn by some horrible fascination, moved gingerly up to gape at the body while Captain Carson walked back to where the Spaniard stood talking to Lieutenant James Duncan. "Damned savages!" he heard Duncan exclaim under his breath.

"It was surely the Seminoles, Senor *Capitano*," Don Juan said. He pronounced the name in the ancient way—'Seminolas'. Ben noticed it even as he struggled to shut out an image of the ambush Kinsley Dalton must have ridden into.

"They were waiting for him," Duncan said bitterly. "They knew the mail courier from Fort King would come this way and they waited to ambush him. He was probably still alive when they cut him open."

Ben turned away in disgust while Juan shrugged. "It is the Indian way, Senor."

"Yes," Duncan snapped. "And I'd bet anything they were bent on getting even for the death of one of their tribe at that skirmish up at Hog Island in June. It was Dalton's misfortune that he had to pay."

Corporal Cates shuffled up behind them to lean against the trunk of a cypress. "Bloody bastards," he muttered, his face still ashen.

Ben thought Cates and Duncan both very restrained. He also wanted to unleash a string of curses. Everyone knew the Mikasuki sometimes mutilated their enemies in battle—it was a fact of life. Yet every time he came across an example of it he was filled with the same revulsion and incomprehension. He would never understand Indians! He pictured the brown face of old Chief Tsali Emaltha whom he had come to know fairly well during his months at Fort Brooke. 'Charley O'Maltha', the Irish recruits called him. The old man was a familiar sight around the fort because his village at Thonotosassa was not far away. Straight of back, lidded eyes heavy with pride of the ancient Creek nation, the old Chief had often impressed Ben with his quiet dignity. Indian children, for all they ran around naked and smelled of bear grease, played and laughed like children everywhere. Seminole wives ground their *coontie* flour and tended their homes like all women. Yet just when you thought you could treat them like ordinary people, this terrible barbarism that lurked beneath the surface came shrieking forth to curdle your blood.

"Cates," Ben snapped. "We'll need to find Dalton's dispatch bag if it's still here. They probably threw it away somewhere. Take two men and start searching the grass. Meeker, you and Wilson start digging a grave. I want Dalton's body deep enough that the wolves can't get at it and well enough disguised that any Seminoles coming this way won't dig it up again."

As the men moved off, Ben turned to his Lieutenant. "Duncan, take half the patrol and start searching out nearby villages. See if you can learn anything about who did this and why. You're probably right about Hog Island but let's make sure. I'll take the rest of the patrol back to Fort Brooke."

"Right away, sir," Duncan said almost with relief, and began at once to call out the names of the men he wanted with him.

The hottest part of the afternoon had begun to wane when Dalton's body, wrapped in an army blanket, was buried beside the banks of the pond. Ben gathered the men for a brief prayer and made sure the grave was well covered before starting the detail back down the military road that connected Fort Brooke with Fort King, nearly eighty miles to the north. Glad to be going back to the safety of the fort, there was a briskness in their step now, spurred on by the memory of what had happened to a lone soldier in this wilderness.

The state of the road belied its strategic military importance. A twenty foot wide swath of cleared track, rutted with tree stumps and encompassed on every side by wild, empty country, the sand was so deep in places that the men's boots sank with every step. Thickets of gallberry and saw palmetto, the dreaded harbinger of rattlers, threatened to swallow the white thread of road. The noises of the scrub muffled the men's subdued voices, the sound of their shuffling feet, the jingle of harness on Ben's horse. Sharp bird cries, the eternal buzzing of insects, the loud jabbering of tree frogs, and the occasional distant howl of a panther or bobcat played on the soldiers underlying fear, a fear that had been exacerbated by the sight of Dalton's ravaged body. Though little was said, they all cast frequent uneasy glances toward the catbriers and palmetto thickets to the hardwood forests beyond and thought how welcome the sight of Fort Brooke was going to be. By the time they reached the pine barrens around the Government Spring, only a mile or two from the fort, the sun had begun its slow descent and the heat was eased by a cooling breeze off the bay.

Ben Carson rode slowly ahead of his men keeping a sharp watch on the woods. Now and then he allowed his mind to dwell on the pleasant prospect of settling later into a comfortable chair on the shady veranda of his cottage, dragging off his high boots and sipping a whisky while the evening breeze blew away the miasma of this day's work. When he heard someone call his name he pulled sharply up to see an orderly from the fort jogging toward them. He reined in his tired horse. Now what!

"Captain Carson, sir," the soldier called, making straight for Ben. "The Commandant sent me ahead to tell you that a ship has arrived with your family aboard."

Ben came forward in the saddle so abruptly his mount danced sideways in the road. "My wife? Here?"

"Yes, sir. Ship Oriana anchored out in the bay just as I was leaving. Your family's probably ashore by now."

Ben pulled his horse still. He looked behind him at the short column of men, all of them as anxious as he to reach the safety and security of the fort. But he was mounted and a senior officer. And it had been a long, long year since he had last seen his wife. "Corporal, bring in the detail. You're not likely to meet any hostile 'Eastu Charties' this close to camp. I'm going on ahead."

He took off in a cloud of dust, ignoring the quiet chuckles of the men left behind. He heard Cates bark an order to march but was gone too fast to hear the Corporal muttering to himself: "Well, I suppose if I had me a pretty wife waitin' that I'd not seen in many months, I'd hustle off too."

Ben quickly covered the last mile to the fort, hurrying past a few Seminole *chickees*—the palm thatched huts that served as Indian houses and were sometimes used by friendly Seminoles visiting the village—past Judge Steel's house and post office at the edge of the settlement, then along a dusty street dotted with a few ramshackle wooden shacks leading to Saunder's trading post on the outskirts of the Fort. One of the new wooden buildings he noted was a makeshift tavern catering, no doubt, to civilians and soldiers alike. Riding past the pickets, he skirted the grove of live oaks near the barracks, circled the parade ground and made straight for the long pier built along the waters of the bay. As he expected, it was crowded with people and mired in confusion. Much of the ship's cargo of boxes, barrels and crates of supplies had been haphazardly stacked among the usual paraphernalia of coiled fishnets, baskets of redfish, and barrels of oysters, shrimp and mullet brought in by the fishing boats from Spanishtown. The supplies were destined for the sutler's store, though some would no doubt be siphoned off to fill the shelves of Mister Saunder's trading post. Every trooper from the camp who had free time had crowded around the dock, adding to the confusion of ship's passengers and the usual assortment of village civilians—white farmers, a scattering of black slaves, Latin fishermen from Spanishtown Creek, and a few friendly Seminoles. Through the crowd he could just make out the shape of a woman standing on the pier, her wide skirts spreading around her like a bell jar, a feathered bonnet on her head and one hand holding that of a young child. His heart missed a beat as he swung from the saddle and pushed through the crowd to jump easily up on the dock.

"Rachel!"

The woman turned and he recognized Lea Hammond, his wife's sister. Fighting down his disappointment, he forced what he hoped appeared to be a warm smile. "Lea,"

"Ben! Oh Ben, at last a familiar face. I'm so glad to see you again."

Lea extended her free hand which Ben took in his gloves and raised politely to his lips. Her green eyes glittered with excitement, and her face was flushed and a little freckled from the sun. He looked beyond her, searching anxiously for his wife.

"Buck," Lea said, drawing the boy closer. "Say hello to your father."

Ben tore his gaze away from the Oriana lying at anchor in the bay. He knelt beside his son and took the boy's hands. The child still had a northern pallor and looked embarrassed to be dressed in his 'Sunday best'. That was probably Lea's doing, he thought. August in Florida would soon rid him of those clothes.

"Hello, Papa," Buck said formally, trying to remember his mother's drills of what he should say to his father after so long an absence.

"Hello, my 'buckaroo'. I'm very glad to see you again." The familiar nickname Ben had given his son as a baby brought a smile to the boy's lips but it quickly faded under the awkward silence that followed. Under the best of circumstances Ben found it difficult to make small talk with children, and he had been around his own sons so little that he found it hard to know what to say. Now, with his whole attention increasingly focused on the glittering waters beyond the pier, he could hardly be bothered to try. Buck, sensing this, retrieved his hands and edged behind Lea's skirts.

"Rachel is still on board the ship," Lea explained. "And Stephen, too. I'm afraid they both had a difficult voyage and Rachel felt she didn't have the strength to come ashore this afternoon. I thought I would come ahead and prepare our—where you want us to stay." Her voice trailed off.

"Rachel is ill? I thought her health had improved. That was why I insisted she make the trip."

"Oh, it has improved," Lea said quickly. "Wonderfully so. It was the seasickness. You know she's never been much of a sailor. A few days rest back on solid ground and she'll be good as new."

"I should go to her," Ben muttered. And he had a report to file. The thought of seeing Rachel again had briefly driven the horrible image of Dalton's body from his mind yet the army would want to know about it and the sooner the better. Relationships with the Indians were chancy at best and Dalton's murder could signify a new level of hostility. Much would depend on whether or not it was done by a few renegade savages or had been condoned by one of the Chiefs in revenge for that flogging and killing by a party of whites in the skirmish up near Hog Town last June. He was on the verge of taking off when Lea laid her hand on his arm.

"Captain Carson, might I ask that you direct us to our—our quarters before you venture out to the ship? I am a little weary and would welcome a chance to settle in."

Ben gave her a guilty smile. "Forgive me, Lea. Of course you must be tired and anxious to get settled. How could I have been so rude. You probably still have your sea legs as well."

She gave him a shy smile that for a moment brought a resemblance of his own dear Rachel. "As a matter of fact, the ground has not stopped heaving under my feet since I stepped ashore."

"And it won't for a few days at least. Here you, Private! Come over here."

At Ben's call a young trooper who had been kneeling beside an open crate containing bottles of wine jumped to his feet.

"Yes, sir."

"This is my wife's sister, Miss Hammond, and my son, Benjamin. I want you to escort them to my cottage and help them get their boxes inside. Take good care of them and see that they have everything they need to be comfortable."

The soldier took one last glance at the bottles. "Yes, sir, Captain. Please to make your acquaintance, Miss." He gave Lea a smart bow.

"Thank you, Private...?"

"Bell, ma'am. Company A, Second Artillery."

"I'm afraid we have several large boxes, Private Bell. My sister brought some household articles with her for her new home. It will be a lot to carry."

"Commandeer a wagon, Private," Ben ordered. "Miss Hammond will want to ride anyway. She's only just left the ship after a long voyage."

"Oh, no, Ben," Lea said quickly. "I can walk. It will do me good."

Ben's black look sent Private Bell scurrying. "Nonsense, Lea. Give yourself time to get used to being back on solid ground again. Private Bell will take you to my house so if you'll excuse me, I have a rather important report to make before I can be rowed out to the ship. I'm sure you'll find everything you need."

"But Ben…that is, is there any special place you want us to put our things?"

He was already headed toward his horse but he called back over his shoulder. "You can tell which room is mine. You and the children take the other room and help yourself to anything you like. I probably won't be back until late tonight."

Lea looked after him, telling herself it was only natural and right that he should attend to his duties and then to Rachel. All the same, she thought as she looked around, she did wish he could have stayed at least until she was safely aboard the wagon. She had not missed that look of disappointment when he recognized her, yet what else should he have felt. Of course he was looking for Rachel and of course he would hurry to her side. Wasn't that what husbands were supposed to do?

And there really wasn't anything to fear, she told herself, looking around the pier. At her side Buck held tightly to her hand, his eyes fastened on a group of people clustered on the sand below. Over his shoulder Lea could see that one of the dories had been drawn up on the beach, filled to the brim with fish. In front of it a swarthy man in loose cotton trousers and a floppy palm leaf hat was haggling with a Seminole woman dressed in a brightly colored skirt. A jet-black braid of hair hung down her back. She was barefoot and her skin was a deep, walnut bronze. In a string of Spanish broken with a few strange-sounding words which Lea supposed must be Seminole, the fisherman continued to argue over prices. When Lea sensed eyes watching her she turned to the other side of the pier and saw a man standing not twenty feet away on the sand. Neither a soldier or a poor fisherman, he was attired in a linen frock coat and trousers, with a brown straw hat drawn deep over his eyes. They were dark eyes, almost black, and they stared at her with an undisguised interest. He grinned and touched the brim of his hat with long fingers. Lea looked quickly away. She had noticed quite a few of the soldiers looking her over while she waited on the pier for Ben yet there was something unsettling in this man's focused appraisal.

A sickness twisted inside her. She was a stranger in a strange country. The barren flatness of sand and water that spread around her filled her with dismay. Here at the pier the bay merged with the headwaters of a broad river, while the fort in the distance looked little more than a collection of whitewashed, ramshackle buildings and tents. The heat had subsided a little but the merciless glare of the sun still made her eyes ache. The sandy track in front of the pier wandered off toward a patch of coarse grass surrounded by swatches of yellow weeds. In the distance a row of wooden barracks were shaded by a grove of huge towering trees trailing some kind of dead fungus. She had never seen a place so wild and untended.

The confusion around the dock was heightened by the stench of fish mingled with the pungent odors of livestock—scrawny cattle, wandering pigs, chickens and dogs roaming at will. She spotted two other women, one a neat, prim-looking matron holding a parasol, the other a slovenly, pudgy woman in a long dirty skirt and loose man's shirt. Both moved with ease among the hordes of soldiers, merchants and fishermen and both seemed to be treated with equal courtesy.

Buck, his seven year old curiosity growing apace with his aunt's dismay, stretched his arm as far as her grip would allow and stared down at the Indian woman. Lea could tell that for Buck there was no sense of strangeness in this barren Florida landscape. He seemed to be consumed with a growing spirit of adventure and was obviously anxious to begin exploring everything new. When she felt his hand slip away she quickly reached to grab him by the collar of his jacket.

"You stay with me, young man," Lea said more harshly than she meant to.

"But Aunt Lea…"

Her fingers tightened on his collar. "No! You can't go running off yet. First we'll see where we are to live and go about getting a meal. Perhaps then we can explore a little. I'm not turning you loose in this strange place without knowing something about it first."

"I won't go far, I promise. Just down there. I want to see the Indian lady."

"Absolutely not. You're staying with me. You'll have plenty of time later to look at Indians."

We all will, she thought, as she spotted Private Bell drawing up a wagon. It looked like a sturdy vehicle though it would surely not be not a dignified or particularly comfortable ride. But as her knees buckled under her and the dock swayed with the motion of the waves, she decided it was very welcome anyway.

As she stepped to the edge of the pier a hand reached up to help her down. Lea paused and found herself looking into the face of the man who had been studying her so intensely a few moments before. It was a darkly handsome face, lean, with a thin mouth smiling up at her. A friendly smile, she supposed, yet one which she found vaguely disturbing.

"*Buenos dias,* Senora." he said, politely tipping his hat. "Allow me to be of assistance."

"Thank you, sir," Lea murmured. His palm was warm and slightly damp, his grip unusually strong. She stepped quickly down onto the sand, then tried to pull her hand away to grab at Buck who jumped down beside her. The stranger's strong clasp forced her to yank her hand free in order to clutch Buck's jacket before he could run off. With the boy in her grip she started for the wagon but the man stepped in front, barring her way.

"You are just arrived, Senora," he asked, still smiling.

"Yes," Lea said, trying to edge around him.

"Your first trip to Tampa Bay? You are perhaps the wife of the *Capitano* Carson I hear so much about?"

Lea glanced nervously away. "Captain Carson is married to my sister."

His smile grew wider. "Oh, of course. Then please allow me to be the first to welcome you to Fort Brooke. Perhaps I could escort you to your new home."

The stranger was all politeness yet Lea found his frank interest strangely unwelcome. "You're very kind, sir, but…" She broke off, relieved to see Private Bell hurrying toward them.

"I'm escorting the lady, Diego," Private Bell said, taking Lea's arm and forcibly drawing her toward the waiting wagon. With a hurried, "Good day," Lea gratefully allowed herself to be handed up onto the wagon seat then scooted over to make room for Buck when Bell lifted him up.

Clambering up beside them, Private Bell took the reins and slapped them on the mule's rump. "You want to steer clear of that *Senor,*" he muttered to Lea. "He's a great one with the ladies, if you get my meaning."

As they pulled away she glanced back to see the gentleman watching them, an annoyed frown on his face. Yet, as she turned back to the road, she realized she was too weary to care much about appearing rude. There would be time later to mend fences with Senor Diego. All she wanted now was to be settled inside a comfortable house on good old solid earth.

CHAPTER 3

▼

Lea stepped out on the porch of Ben's quarters and opened her parasol, squinting against the glare from the crushed oyster-shell path. What a relief to escape the stuffy cottage! The close rooms and Rachel's underlying melancholia at times grew depressing, though she would cut out her tongue before saying so. Poor Rachel's headaches, aggravated by the constant heat and ubiquitous insects, had already convinced Lea's sister that nothing about Fort Brooke or the Florida Territory was appealing. Lea did not agree, but that was probably because her health was better and she liked to venture out and explore new places. She never felt so free as when she escaped the oppressive gloom of Ben's cottage to roam the Fort and the flat lands around it.

She paused on the porch long enough to drink in the fragrance of a nearby sweet bay tree and admire the Pride of India bush blooming riotously beside the low steps. The huge live oak that shaded the house was dotted with tiny yellow jasmine blooms, like little sunbursts among the dangling fingers of gray moss. No wonder the first Spaniards to discover Florida had called it 'the land of flowers". Yet there was nothing here of the orderly, carefully arranged gardens that name suggested to a northerner. Rather, this was a wild, exotic country, nature run riot in a tangle of vines and creepers, giant trees and rivers the color of bark—so different from all that she had known back home. And yet, unlike her homesick sister, she did not find this strangeness displeasing. She saw a dark beauty in the thick, black oaks, the exotic lime and orange trees, the tall, skinny pines. She had never before seen so many kinds of colorful birds. There was something enchanting about the sight of swirling sea gulls or a heron or ibis toe-dancing along the shore of the sparkling bay. She found it all unique and fascinating.

"Good afternoon, Miss Hammond."

Startled out of her reverie, Lea looked up to see Julia Lattimore, the wife of one of Ben's company Lieutenants standing on the shell path. One of only a few officer's wives at the fort, Julia was one of the first people to welcome Lea and her sister. A Virginian, she was a short, dumpy woman with a ready smile that gave a tinge of beauty to her round, plain face.

"And is Mrs. Carson feeling any better?" Julia asked.

"A little. The heat still bothers her sorely but other than that, I believe her strength is returning."

"I'm glad to hear it. Tell her we've all had difficulty adjusting to the Florida sun, though my husband tells me there are hotter army posts. That's hard to imagine, isn't it."

"Indeed it is."

"She will soon grow accustomed to it, I've no doubt. All of us have."

Would she, Lea wondered as she started across the grass toward the sutler's store. Rachel had never been one to adapt easily to change. She had never had to be. Coddled and pampered from birth, always susceptible to chills and fevers, she had been protected first by her doting parents and sister, later, by her husband. In the first years of her marriage, when Ben was briefly an instructor's aide at West Point, she had gladly stayed near him. Later, she tried to be a willing wife at the various places he was posted but had found most of them so difficult that she didn't stay long, even when Lea came along to help out. Now Fort Brooke was going to be her first experience living so far from the family home overlooking Hudson's River, and what a strange environment she had chosen for it! One could only hope that soon she would regain her strength and begin to take some of the same delight in the place that Lea had.

Yet it is my first time so far away from home too, Lea thought with some surprise. No one is worrying about my ability to adjust—not even me! One does what one has to. But then I've always enjoyed good health.

"Afternoon, Miss Hammond."

This time it was the plump wife of Private Lovis, carrying a basket filled with clean, neatly folded laundry. Ben had told her that several of the enlisted men's wives supplemented their husband's meager salaries by taking in washing. Lea smiled her a greeting and continued on. There was a remarkable egalitarian spirit among the officers and enlisted men and their families at Fort Brooke, probably because their total numbers were so small. The fact that they were all sitting on the edge of an isolated, hostile wilderness probably also had a lot to do with smoothing the edges of the customary class-conscious army life. She had only lived here a few weeks yet already she could name most of the people she met on her daily excursions. The varied backgrounds of the enlisted men amazed her. Irish and German immigrants, laborers and farmers from almost every state, they were mostly rough men who never spoke much about their former lives but were friendly and polite.

She had been surprised to find so few women here. Some, like Rachel and herself, were officer's wives and kinfolk. More were wives of the enlisted men, living in tents on the other side of the old barracks. A scattering of frontier wives and daughters could usually be found visiting the area, dressed in homespun and dragging along wide-eyed, stringy-haired children. The adjoining village of Tampa—if you could call one trading post, a post office, a courthouse, a few log cabins and a saloon a village—had only a scattering of permanent inhabitants. Most days their numbers were augmented by the settlers living far out in the woods who came in for supplies and to exchange gossip around the porch of Saunder's store or Judge Steel's post office.

What had surprised her even more were the number of Negroes who worked around the fort. They were unfailingly polite, touching their foreheads or sweeping off their battered hats as she passed. It made her uncomfortable to know that most were slaves belonging to the army men A few claimed to be freemen— though Ben had told her it was far more likely they were runaways. She had been astonished to learn that even the Seminoles owned Negro slaves. According to Ben one of the main reasons old Chief Micanopy refused to emigrate to the western lands was because he was afraid he would not be allowed to take all his slaves with him. On the other hand, it was common knowledge that runaway slaves from the north often found a haven with the Seminoles where they were accepted and welcomed. The anger of white slave owners over this perceived injustice was probably the reason they were so hostile toward the Indians.

A military wagon swept by, churning up a cloud of dust. Lea hid her face with her parasol and recalled how she must have looked the afternoon they arrived, perched on a wagon seat, wobbling down this same track while Private Bell pointed out commissary buildings, horse sheds, barracks, parade ground, and the old Indian burial mound. It had all seemed so flat and heat-seared then, not to mention shabby. Most of the buildings had been put up after Major George Brooke first established the fort eleven years ago, and they had fallen into disrepair during the two years the fort was all but abandoned eight years later. Now that the post was once again becoming a viable defense against the Seminoles it had begun to take on new life. You could see it in the new buildings of raw pine and cedar, in some of the old ones newly whitewashed, in the new fences and oyster shell paths. Now that she was becoming accustomed to it, everything had taken on a comfortable familiarity.

The bright sky suddenly darkened and Lea looked up to see a huge flock of passenger pigeons flying overhead, turning the sky as black as a thundercloud. They were as familiar a sight in New York as in Florida, yet she much preferred the clouds of chattering, colorful parakeets so common at the fort. Or the egrets with their beautiful feathers so prized by the Seminoles.

"Aunt Lea!"

Lea turned to see Buck come running down the path toward her. She shook her head at his disheveled appearance. Earlier this morning he had started off as clean and prim as Rachel could make him, but there was little left of that now. His jacket had no doubt long since been shed—it would probably take her an hour to track it down later. His shirt was dirty and the hem hung out, and his face was so streaked it would require a hard scrubbing before supper. At least he still wore his boots.

"Aunt Lea, Mister Clarke took us to the river today! You should have been there, Aunt Lea. It was wonderful!"

"The Hillsborough River? Did your mother say you could go? You didn't go into the water, did you? And where is Stephen?"

"We did go in the water. We went swimming, Aunt Lea! The water was warm and I caught a frog but it jumped right out of my hand and then I couldn't find it again. It was so much fun!"

"Oh, Buck," Lea sighed, kneeling to tuck in the boy's shirt. "Look at you. Such a sight! Your Mother will be prostrate when she hears you were swimming in the river. And where is Stephen? You haven't left him alone somewhere, have you?"

"No." Buck squirmed under her hands. "He's at the horse sheds with Private Clarke. He wanted to see the horses. Private Clarke likes Stephen and me. He does nice things for us, and he's from New York too."

"I have not met the gentleman yet. However, I do wish you'd ask your Mother's permission before you go off on excursions like that. You know she doesn't want you running around the fort loose and she's terrified of the river."

"But I know how to swim—a little. And we didn't go into the deep part. There were Indians there, Aunt Lea. And fishermen, too."

"Indians! Oh dear. Now I know your Mother will disapprove."

"Then don't tell her, please. You won't, will you? It was such fun and not a bit scary. You won't say anything, will you? Please."

Lea smoothed back the unruly strand of hair that nearly obscured Buck's big, blue eyes. He never looked like such a cherub as when he was pleading with her to protect him from something he knew he shouldn't have done. Yet she was partial to him. He was the first baby in the family and she rather liked his curiosity and his daring ways. Had she been born a boy instead of a useless girl, she liked to think she would have been just like him.

"Oh, very well," she said, grinning down at him. "I won't mention it this time but you must not go again. At least, not unless I go with you. I'm sure your Mother wouldn't mind then." *And I would love it*, she added to herself.

"You're the best, Aunt Lea," Buck cried, darting from her hands. "I'm going to the stables and tell Mister Clarke that you want to go to the river too."

"Buck! Find your jacket. I don't want to have to search the whole cantonment for it tonight."

He was already disappearing behind a corner of the barracks. I shall have to get to know this Private Clarke, Lea thought as she continued along the walk. Any young man who takes the trouble to make two small boys so happy must be a good fellow.

She was now only a few steps away from the sutler's army store. Lea hesitated, twirling her parasol. Ahead of her lay the scattered buildings of the village, and beyond them, the flat ground was open and beckoning. The pickets leaned on their rifles lazily, half-dozing in the afternoon sun, oblivious to the bustle at the nearby pier. Lea thought about the river, imagining its shady coolness. Well, why not? The afternoon could not be more placid. Ben had told her not to go outside the limits of the fort without an escort but surely this scene looked safe enough. And she could always say she intended to mail a letter at the post office.

The guard nodded and touched his cap as she started up the trail into the village. Farther along she crossed the path to Saunder's trading post and continued on toward the white house with its neat fence that housed Judge Steel's post office and residence. Off to her right there stood a small two-room log courthouse that the Judge had erected once the legislature marked Tampa as the County seat. Scattered nearby, like cast-off toys, sat several log shacks squatting in a sea of sand, and beyond them a few old Indian palm frond 'chickees'. Stray dogs panted in the shade of oaks, and chickens and a few hogs scratched among splotchy patches of weeds.

The usual group of men gossiping around Saunder's post eyed her as she strolled past. She glanced back long enough to spot one among them in a flashy waistcoat and spats. This, she supposed, was one of the gamblers and speculators Ben told her about, men who occasionally came in on the ships in the hope of making money off the soldiers. There were women as well, country housewives and daughters whom she recognized from seeing them at the sutler's store. And one or two whose painted faces and shabby flounces earned only a discrete, guarded glance. It was not hard to guess why they had come. Any military post, even one perched on the edge of a wilderness, always attracted that sort. She knew Rachel would have been appalled, but she found the whole diverse stew rather fascinating.

Beyond the post office a path through the brush led toward the river. Here at the end of the village street the path was narrower, more overgrown with weeds. And here the drone of insects overpowered at last the raucous noises of the fort. Slapping at the ubiquitous mosquitoes, Lea followed the path that wound through palmettos thickets and waist-high scrub to where it emerged into clearing shaded by overhanging branches of hardwoods. And there was the river, not wide by the Hudson's standards, but shimmering in the sun, the color of tree bark, moving lazily toward the bay. One of the tree branches had grown out over the water where it dipped its fingers below the surface. The sandy bank was packed hard, probably by Indians. The far side of the river was sheltered by a wild profusion of trees, sweeping vines, and bright flowers. It was a beautiful place of restful solitude. Lea felt as though she had stepped suddenly amidst the cool stone walls of an ancient country church.

She looked around to make sure no one was about, then sat down and pulled off her hot boots and damp stockings. Bunching up her skirts, she stepped gingerly into the water. It was warm, like tepid tea, and it felt refreshingly fine. She waded back and forth, then stood looking out at the broader stream. Reaching down she splashed her hand in the water, not clear like the crystal waters of the bay, but a dark, coffee color. Ben had told her it was the oak leaves that made the water so dark. So dark, and yet so inviting.

She looked back at the bank where her cast-off boots lay, then again at the water, conscious of the clinging dampness of her chemise and petticoats underneath her blue calico. It was so tempting!

Oh, why not, she muttered, and began pulling off her dress.

Upriver, about half a mile to the north, Captain Carson shifted his weight against the rough trunk of a blackjack oak that stretched its branches out over the dark surface of the Hillsborough. A few feet away, directly across from him, Holata, the brother of Chief Tsali Emaltha, sat cross-legged on the ground, his brown hands resting lightly on his soft leather leggings. Watching that face, with its heavy-lidded eyes and skin the color of old pine, Ben wondered again if any of the words issuing from Holata's stern mouth could be believed Two other men sat in the circle—to his right, Lieutenant Warren, an adjutant to General Clinch, who had arrived from Fort King the day before, and, opposite the Lieutenant, swarthy, sharp-eyed Don Montes de Oca, army scout and long-time resident of Spanishtown.

"Ask him where Charley O'Maltha is now," Lieutenant Warren said snappishly to the Spaniard who was acting as interpreter. Warren's impatience with this meeting had been obvious from the first.

"Senor, I don't think…"

"Just ask him."

Montes spoke to the Indian who answered with a shrug. In the ensuing silence the lilting voices of several Indian children playing on the bank across the river came carrying over. How ironic, Ben thought, that children could laugh and play while their elders sat discussing matters of life and death. The sun glistening on the dark water set patterns dancing on the river's surface. Through gaps in the moss dangling from the tree's branches he could make out the palmetto thatched roofs of Seminole houses on the far bank. A thin thread of smoke rose from a fire in the center of the temporary camp, carrying with it the nut-like smell of *sofkee*, the cornmeal mush staple of Seminole diets.

Holata Elmaltha broke the silence with a sudden burst of guttural sentences. Although he spoke to Montes, his eyes never left Lieutenant Warren's face, and the contempt in them was obvious. Warren glanced a question at the interpreter and worked his jaw over a plug of tobacco.

"Holata says that the place of his brother, Tsali Emaltha, matters nothing," Montes translated. "In fact, he prefers that it not be known. What is important is that the Chief has put his life in danger by honoring his promise to go to the western lands as the White Father demands. While he cares nothing for his own life, he wishes you to know this and protect his people."

Warren waved a gloved hand impatiently. "Tell him that if he really wants our help he will have to tell us where to find Alligator and Sam Jones and Jumper. They are the ones who make life dangerous for his people. If Holata and his brother, Charley, want our protection then they must help us catch these troublemakers. Tell him that, and don't mix it up. I know you interpreters."

Montes glared at the Lieutenant with murder in his eyes. Ben knew he was debating whether or not to get up and leave, and to prevent that he broke in quickly.

"Don Juan is one of the best interpreters we have at Fort Brooke. You can trust him completely."

Somewhat soothed by Ben's words, Montes turned back to Holata and they began a long exchange. Ben only half-listened, catching a few words and knowing that most of what was really meant was not what was being spoken. If Lieutenant Warren had any sense he would recognize that Holata spoke some English by the way the old man bristled every time Warren called his brother 'Charley'. He waved at the flies that buzzed loudly around his head. How he wished this whole thing could be done with. His thoughts drifted for a moment to a pleasurable image—sitting on his piazza enjoying a Cuban seegar as his lovely Rachel moved about inside his quarters, humming a tune. What was the use of all this, anyway.

"Holata says that no one knows where Jumper and Sam Jones are hiding. But he wants you to tell General Clinch that many young braves are angry and would rather fight than take this long journey to a strange country. There is one among them who is especially bitter, a young war Chief called Asi-yaholo. He has made himself the spokesman for those who would rather die than leave their homes."

Ben turned to Warren: "Asceola. Isn't he from North Florida, up your way?"

"Yes. Appalachicola. A half-breed whose mother was Creek and father a Scot. We know him as 'Powel', after his father. Ask this man if he has been seen in any of the villages along the Lockcha-popka-chiska."

Ben listened as the Spaniard rattled off Warren's question, wondering how the Lieutenant had somehow learned the Seminole name for the Hillsborough River. It was probably all of the language he knew and he'd thrown it in to impress Holata. The Indian nodded gravely then, looking directly at the Lieutenant, broke into a stream of sentences thick with feeling. Without understanding one word, the Lieutenant shifted on the ground and sent a stream of tobacco juice into a nearby bush.

"I do not think I get all that," Juan muttered.

"You must have the general idea. What's he complaining about now?"

Montes dark eyes flickered over at Ben. "Our friend, Holata, says that the white-eyes have not been fair to his brother, the Seminole. That he promised them four million of acres in middle Florida…"

"Good God! Here we go again," Warren muttered.

"…where no man would bother them for twenty years. Now many whites come to live on this land and the Indian must move again, this time to a barren country far across the water where he has never been before."

"Remind him that seven Seminole Chiefs signed the agreement after they saw the place for themselves. Does that count for nothing?"

"He said, I believe, that he knew you would say this, and that the treaty of Fort Gibson was a trick, as was the trip also. However, because his brother Chief

Tsali Emaltha is an honorable man, he will abide by the paper on which he put his mark. He says you must do your part by protecting his people."

Clearly Holata had had enough. With an easy grace he rose to his feet, lifting his hand in a gesture of friendship even though nothing of the kind was reflected in his face. Behind him two young braves went running to the water's edge to draw up the hollow palm log canoe that had brought them all across the river. The two officers rose to face the Indian. Though Holata was not a tall man, he looked them over with a regal dignity. There was pride in his stance and the sharp planes of his face. The same pride was reflected in his dress—the soft deerskin leggings, the colorful full-sleeved shirt and the turban topped with one graceful egret feather. Ben was impressed, until he remembered Private Dalton's savagely mutilated body.

"Goodbye," the Indian said easily in English.

Warren blocked his way. "Tell him to take word back to Charley O'Maltha to bring his people into the Fort. We can protect them there. It is impossible to do anything for them if they stay out in the swamps."

Montes spoke to Holata who nodded and walked toward his canoe. As the younger braves pushed it out into the water, Ben and the Lieutenant started up the shallow bank toward the sandy road beyond. A few steps behind them Don Juan de Oca pulled his palm frond hat down over his narrow face.

"I do not think he is reassured," he muttered to Ben.

"I don't think he came here looking for reassurance. Charley knows we don't have much to give anyway."

Warren pulled a plug of tobacco from his shirt pocket and broke off a piece. "Why don't they face up to the fact that they are going to have to leave. They don't have the weapons, the men, or the ingenuity to stand up to the United States Army. They ought to just accept that and go quietly."

"That's wishful thinking, Lieutenant. Would you?"

"All right then, Captain. If you are so wise about the ways of savages, what do you suppose he came here for? Just tell me so I can carry the word back to General Clinch."

The three of them fell in line striding the narrow sandy path the military called 'the trail to the falls'. Ben answered, weighing his words.

"I think that since he was near the fort anyway, Charley sent him over to drop us a few hints and see which way the wind is blowing. More than that, I think he was trying to tell us that we are very close to an all-out war and we'd better keep a sharp lookout."

He half expected Warren to laugh, or perhaps to shrug off the warning. But the Lieutenant continued walking, chewing thoughtfully.

"If that is true—and mind you, I'm not convinced of it—then that is just the kind of information the General sent me here to find. If we don't deport these savages peacefully this whole territory could go up like a powder keg. We know about Powel. His Red Stick Creeks are our main troublemakers. Some of the more isolated settlers have moved closer to Fort Drane because of them."

"A few have moved to Fort Brooke as well," Ben said, "but they are mostly people who live out near Thonotosassa where Charley O'Maltha has his village. What about you, Juan? Have you heard anything?"

"There is some concern among the fish rancheros near Charlotte Harbor, but then we have a different sort of Indian down there. The old Calusas were always more warlike, and the Seminoles who moved south tend to take up their ways."

They were nearing the outskirts of the fort. Far in the distance the usual commotion around the pier told them a ship's tender had arrived. The muted blasts of artillery practice inside the fort vied with the neighing of horses and the calls of the pickets. The sounds were oddly reassuring, Ben thought—civilization on the edge of a wilderness.

"I'd better go write up some kind of report," Warren said, slipping the tobacco plug back in his pocket. "It should go out with the dispatches in the morning. Why don't you join me, Captain. We can have a gill of whisky and go over it together. You know the O'Maltha brothers better than I." He hesitated a moment. "And you too, Juan. Would you like a quick drink?"

"Some other time, thank you, Senor." Though polite, his tone was edged with sharpness. "I must get home. My little daughter was ill with a fever when I was called away and I am anxious for her."

Montes doffed his straw hat and loped down the path toward the village. The officers followed, unhurrying in the afternoon sun. "Don't trust Spaniards any more than I do Indians," Warren muttered.

Ben laughed. "Then poor Juan is really at a disadvantage. Not only is he Spanish but he's married to a Seminole woman. You're wrong about him, though. He's lived at Spanishtown Creek for many years but they say he's from a cultured family back in Spain. He's well educated and one of our best interpreters. I can vouch for that."

"Well, maybe, though it would not be difficult for him to be better than others. Most of them are former slaves who mix up English with African and Seminole. You're a more tolerant man than I am, Captain Carson."

"You get that way living at Fort Brooke. There are more Indians and Span-iards here than Anglos."

"So I've noticed."

Ben was about to agree to join Warren for that drink when his attention was caught by a glimpse of a woman in a blue dress walking toward them in the dis-tance. Almost immediately she veered off the path toward the river and disap-peared into the woods. Something about the color of the dress caught at his memory. It was a deep blue, like one he'd seen Lea wearing. Surely not…

Yet might that not be something a girl like Lea would do, a girl unfamiliar with the dangers of the wilderness? He could hardly believe she'd be so foolish, and yet he ought to make certain. "Lieutenant, I believe I'll save that drink for later if you don't mind. I need to make a stop at the post office first. My wife is expecting letters from home."

"Of course," Warren commented dryly and walked on toward the fort. Ben waited to make sure he didn't look back, then darted into the underbrush. He did not search for a path but waded through the scrub, protected by his tall boots. Once he found the path he moved more cautiously. If it were not Lea he'd seen, he might go blundering into some private assignation at the river's edge and that would be embarrassing for everyone.

It took him some time to find her and when he finally knelt to push aside the fan-shaped palmetto leaves he didn't know whether to be embarrassed or just plain furious. It was indeed his sister-in-law, out in the river and up to her neck in the dark water, gently circling her arms and lifting her face to the sun, a beatific smile on her lips. On the bank her blue dress and parasol lay piled in a heap.

He was about to go striding forth in righteous wrath when he spotted the alli-gator. It was in the middle of the river about sixty feet north of Lea, moving like a sluggish log, its lidded eyes protruding above the calm surface of the water. She had her back to it now but any moment she could turn.

"Lea," he called softly. He heard her intake of breath as she spun around. Ben rose up slowly, just high enough for her to see him. "Don't move or speak!" he said in a deadly hushed voice. "Be still. Absolutely still! Don't move a muscle."

Her cheeks turned bright red but she dutifully froze, only turning her head very slowly until she saw the gator. The crimson blush drained to white as he heard her draw in her breath. Yet she remained still. Ben groped around until he found a long branch thick enough for his purpose. Moving slowly he made his way up the river's shore, a good way above Lea. Reaching out with the pole he splashed the water noisily. At the movement the alligator turned and glided toward him.

"Oh," Lea cried softly.

"Quiet! No matter what I do, don't make a move until I tell you. Then run like hell for the bank. Do you hear?"

She nodded, mesmerized as the gator slipped slowly toward shore. Ben walked farther up the bank, then eased out into the water until it was up around the ankles of his boots. Reaching out with the pole he splashed the water noisily again. Immediately the creature turned toward the sound and glided toward it. Grabbing the pole, Ben heaved it upriver and out into the water as far as he could throw it. At the turmoil in the water, the gator circled around, away from Lea and toward the noise.

"Stay," Ben whispered, though he could tell panic was close to getting the best of her. Her eyes were tightly closed now, and she was hardly breathing. He slipped back down the bank, waited until the gator was far enough away to be safe, then cried, "Now!"

Splashing furiously Lea tore out of the water and up the bank. She would have continued blindly down the path but Ben caught her and pulled her back. Wearing only her shift and petticoat, she was soaking wet and shaking with fear and not the least modest about her lack of apparel though Ben knew that would come later. He took off his coat and laid it around her shoulders, holding her tightly for the few moments it took to calm her down.

"I ought to use that stick on you," he muttered. "Of all the foolish, insane, headstrong things to do!"

"I know," she wailed, pulling the collar of his coat up around her face. He kept his arms around her until her shaking subsided, then he stepped back. Her cheeks flamed crimson as she looked down at her wet underclothes. "Your nice coat—it will get wet…"

"It'll dry. But you—you could have been killed ten times over. Not only are there alligators in that river, there are snakes too, many of them poisonous. Wild bobcats have been seen here, even panthers. Not to mention some lowlife settler or renegade Indian who would be eager to take advantage of a woman alone. What in heaven's name were you thinking of!"

Tears welled in her eyes and she wiped at them with the back of her hand. "But I didn't see anyone."

"Right now I'd wager the Seminoles on the other side of the river are laughing themselves silly. You didn't see them but you can be damned sure they saw you. I *told* you never to leave the fort without an escort."

"I know you did. It was foolish and I'm sorry. I won't do it again."

Because he'd expected her to defend herself, her apology took some of the steam out of his righteous anger and for a moment he did not know how to respond. To be fair, since the arrival of his family at Fort Brooke Lea had spent most of her days indoors taking care of Rachel and the boys. She had not had time to see much of life around the post. "Well," he said grudgingly, "at least it turned out all right. I just want you to be aware of the dangers. Get your clothes on and I'll take you back."

She kept the coat around her shoulders until she could duck behind a tree to pull her dress over her wet underthings. When she emerged Ben thought he had never seen a creature look more bedraggled. He helped her get her shoes on over her damp stockings, then, throwing his coat over his arm, they fell in step along the path to the village.

"I've never seen an alligator before," Lea murmured. "Would it really have gone after me?"

"Possibly, had it been hungry enough. It's very common for them to go after dogs or even children. They're not something you want to fool around with, but I suppose you didn't know that. I must arrange to have one of the soldiers take you and Rachel and the boys on a few excursions to show you something of life here in Florida. Meanwhile, you must promise me never to go out alone again."

"I promise, but somehow I can't see Rachel wanting to take an excursion around the fort. As for the boys, though you might not be aware of it, they have already done a little exploring." They were nearing Augustus Steele's house and post office when she suddenly grew self-conscious about her damp skirts and hair. "Do I look too terrible to go back among civilized people?" she asked, opening her sunshade and pulling it close around her head.

Ben glanced at her. "You'll do. No one worries overmuch about appearances here, as I suppose you've noticed."

"That's true, but there are a few well-bred ladies who might be scandalized. I'll try to get home before they see me." She added hesitantly: "Ben, how did you come to be out in the woods so conveniently? Has anything happened?"

"Only the usual problems. I was at a meeting with Holata Emaltha, Charley's brother. In his roundabout way he warned us that some of the younger braves are dead set against deportation and will probably try to stir up trouble."

"Does that mean they will attack Fort Brooke?"

"Probably not, because it's pretty well protected. They like to hit isolated homesteads and plantations where they can strike fast and disappear back into the woods. We should be safe enough at the cantonment."

"I'm relieved to hear it, for I tell you Ben, nothing worries Rachel more than the idea of these wild savages coming through the door. We heard such terrible stories in New York about the barbaric way they treat their enemies when they are aroused. It was almost enough to discourage her from joining you in Florida."

Ben shifted the coat over his arm. "To tell the truth, Lea, I feel a little chagrined about that since I know she came at my insistence. This Indian problem didn't seem so bad a few months ago, and I was so certain the warm climate would be good for her health. I ought to have remembered how delicate she is."

"You needn't worry about that, Ben. Truly, she wanted to be with you as much as you wanted her here. As for myself and the boys, well, we looked on it as a grand adventure. We still do." She laughed. "Even this escapade, stupid as it was, has helped to enliven my long afternoon."

Though Ben appreciated the way Lea made light of their new situation, all the same he was glad he hadn't told her or his wife about Private Dalton. "As for the Seminoles, Lea, you must remember that they are being dispossessed and forced to move from their homes to a country they know nothing about. Frankly, I don't blame them for wanting to fight to stay here. I wonder how we whites would accept such a thing."

"I don't suppose we would accept it at all when you put it that way. Must they leave?"

"Oh, yes. It is the only solution for this territory and it is one which the government will force upon them one way or another. This country is too valuable, too ripe for settlement. There is good land here, and fortunes to be made. The Seminole stands in the way of all that."

"But it's so inhospitable. So wild, so untamed!"

Ben snapped a salute to the picket as they neared the grounds of the fort. "That will change once new settlers move in. Some crops grow very well here— oranges and limes are exceptional. There are valuable resources of timber and game and huge open tracks for cattle that cannot be equaled anywhere. The land is crying out for cotton and sugar cane cultivation. Even the climate is attractive, once you adjust to the heat. Wait until you've lived through a winter with no ice or snow. Besides, you know how Americans are. Where there is new land they'll take it and the natives be damned."

"Ben," Lea said warily, "you sound terribly convincing. Are you by chance planning to make one of those fortunes yourself?"

Ben yanked the rim of his hat closer down on his forehead. "Lea, you are too clever by half. The truth is, I see a lot of opportunity in Florida territory once hostilities end. Judge Steele tells me there are already plans in the works to develop this Tampa area. William Bunce has established a large, successful fish ranchero to the south on the Manatee, and fishing is only one of the viable commodities this country offers."

Lea waved a hand around. "But doesn't all this belong to the United States government?"

"There is some dispute about that. Richard Hackley claims that thousands of acres, including Tampa Bay, were deeded to him by the Duke of Alagon when Spain sold Florida to the United States. He has yet to prove it, and meanwhile the government isn't about to give up even a teaspoon of sand. But once the ownership's resolved I plan to be the first in line to buy a claim. By the way, I haven't mentioned any of this to Rachel. It might upset her."

Lea smiled. "That's true enough. Right now she wants nothing so much as to go home to New York."

"And yet, well, I recall that even in New York she was not really happy. The poor darling has never been well enough to enjoy herself completely. I had so hoped this Florida climate would rejuvenate her. If only she had some of your strength."

For a moment Lea felt quite guilty for being so healthy. "Perhaps in time," she murmured.

"All the same, I think we'd better not mention my hopes for the future until I find the right time to tell her about them."

Lea looked over at him and grinned. "Let's make a bargain. I won't say anything about your plans if you won't tell her about my excursion this afternoon. Agreed?"

The mischievous sparkle in her eyes restored his good humor after the worries of the afternoon. *Could anyone ask for a more perfectly charming sister than Lea,* he thought. But he said, "Why, Miss Hammond. Are you trying to bribe me?"

They had nearly reached the officer's quarters. Lea closed her sunshade and moved toward the narrow porch. "Yes, I am. I have no wish to add to Rachel's worries, and, frankly, I'm very ashamed."

Ben laughed. "Honesty was always one of your virtues. Very well then, it's a bargain. In a way, though, I'm sorry we can't talk about the gator over supper. Once we got over the fright of it, we would all have a good laugh."

CHAPTER 4

▼

The heat finally broke in late October. Lea could almost fancy she was back home in New York as she stood on the veranda watching the twilight wash smoky shadows over the row of officer's cottages and breathing in the pungent aroma of woodfires that drifted on the air. It was only a passing fancy. One glance at the heavy green of live oak, brightened here and there with splashes of red flame vine, and she knew she was in a country far different from the familiar hills of home. Still, now that the blistering heat of summer had begun to wane, she found she did not long for that old, familiar Hudson Valley so much after all.

It was a fine evening. Rachel was even feeling well enough to accompany Ben to a small supper party at Doctor Heiskell's house. Her sister's unusual sociability had been welcomed by both Lea and Ben, and though Rachel begged Lea to go with them, she declined, feeling that the married couple should have some time together. Heaven knows, there had been few enough opportunities in the weeks since their arrival at Fort Brooke. Besides, Lea was not too fond of the doctor who had a quick temper and a philosophy of healing that emphasized taking a stick to the sufferer. He was also something of a snob and had made it clear that he felt there were only a handful of women at Fort Brooke respectable enough to be friends with his young, pretty wife. Naturally, Rachel stood high on that short list.

Right now Lea actually preferred solitude. On the other hand, it was too nice an evening to stay indoors. She called to the boys and taking them each by the hand, set out to walk to the shore to watch the sunset. For once there was no activity around the pier. They walked beyond it to the edge of the bay where a thin strip of sandy beach gave way to a thick growth of mangroves and cabbage trees. Spreading her shawl, she settled on the sand where she could watch the boys running and playing in the languid waves that lapped lazily at the shore. The bay and sky were like a big blue bowl, sweeping around her in all directions. Over the water to her right lay the shoreline of Spanishtown Creek, while straight ahead, the dark bulge of Rabbitt Island lay like a stain on the glowing water. The sun was a red globe balanced on the horizon, throwing long shafts of gold, blue-gray, rose, and lilac along the shimmering surface of the bay. Piles of cumulus clouds, edged with silver, were already turning grayish-black with the coming night.

Lea loved these sunsets. Never before had she seen anything like their color and sweep. Perhaps it was because Florida was so flat and open, leaving center stage to water and sky. Whatever the reason, they were a nightly display she had come to enjoy in the time she had been at Fort Brooke.

The laughter of the boys made a joyous accompaniment to the raucous cawing of the gulls and terns as they swooped in graceful patterns above the sand. Stephen, waddling on his chubby legs, was busily engaged in trying to capture one of the tiny sandpipers who scurried in the wake of every wave. Buck was searching among the broken clutter of shells for one that had managed to keep its perfect symmetry, one he could take back to his mother. Lea watched them, smiling to herself and thinking how peaceful it all seemed.

Yet she knew it was not peaceful. Since the day Ben first confided in her about the growing Indian problem she had come to realize more and more how tenuous a peace lay between the army and the Seminoles. Just this morning Ben told her that Chief Micanopy had called together all the tribes at a gathering in the Green Swamp where the younger braves, egged on by that trouble-maker, Asceola, had defied their elders and vowed to die rather than submit to deportation. This was the first open break between the older Chiefs and the young warriors, and Ben felt it meant that war was now almost inevitable. Though he didn't say so, Lea knew that the constant patrols that came and went between the fort and the wilderness were growing more dangerous every day. Thank heaven, at least the families in the fort were relatively safe.

Stephen's ebullient laughter called her back to the present and she saw that his chase had led him knee-deep into the water. Jumping up, she hurried to the shoreline, bunched her skirts in her hand and waded in to retrieve him before he went deeper. She dragged him back to the beach and dried his legs with her shawl.

He struggled to stand first on one foot, then the other. "I almost caught one, Aunt Lea. You should'a watched. I scooped up the sand and it was in my hand."

"Yes, but my darling, you got your clothes all wet. You know you must'nt go into the water, Stephen. You can run after them all you want on the shore but don't follow them into the water. All right?"

Buck came running up to where Lea was still holding the struggling Stephen. "Look at this, Aunt Lea," the boy said, turning over a small rose-colored shell in his fingers. "Isn't it pretty? And its not broken anywhere. All the others are."

Lea released Stephen who promptly ran to the water where a wave lapped around his ankles, stopped abruptly and looked back at Lea, grinning. She made sure he had stopped then took the shell in her hand. "It's beautiful, Buck. I think this is the largest one you've found so far."

"I'm going to take it home to Mama. Do you think she'll like it?"

"I'm sure she will. Hurry now. The light's going and we have to go back in a few minutes."

"I don't want to go home," he cried, taking off again. "It's not dark yet. We don't have to hurry, do we?"

"Well, I suppose we don't," Lea answered. And really they didn't. The boys' parents would not be home until well past nine o'clock and certainly this part of the fort was safe enough to walk through in the dark. There was always someone about to help you if you lost your way.

The children running along the water's edge made ever darker silhouettes against the gray sky. An egret swooped over their heads and disappeared toward the river's mouth, spreading its graceful plumage in the twilight.

What a wonderful place this is for children, Lea thought, settling back on the sand. At least it would be if there were no Indians and no war.

Wiley Thompson, the Indian Agent at Fort King, had set January 1, 1836 as the date for the first ships to leave Tampa carrying the Seminoles to New Orleans, the first stop on their long journey to the Arkansas Territory. By late November the fourteen Chiefs who had reluctantly agreed to the U.S. government's demands began to move their people into the area around Fort Brooke and the villages north near Hadley Flats. They came to await deportation with wives and children, bearing what household goods and cattle they could manage.

Lea was at first dismayed to see the hordes of Indians setting up an impromptu camp across the river. Their strange dress, flamboyant feathers, their pungent odors, their angry glares which could not be completely disguised by their impassive faces, were all unsettling, to say the least. But as she grew more accustomed to having them nearby her fear changed to curiosity and she longed to know more about their strange way of life, so different from all she had ever known.

She begged Ben to take her with him when he visited the camp sites—a request he flatly denied. There were far too many of them and they were too dirty to take a respectable white woman among them. Of course, Rachel agreed with him.

Then, during the second week of November, the Carson household was struck by a more frightening concern than fear of Indians. Not for nothing had Hillsborough been originally called 'Mosquito County'. Ubiquitous fleas, flies and pesky mosquitoes were the darker side of the tropical beauty of the place. After a few weeks most of the settlers took them for granted, and in spite of their nuisance Fort Brooke was known as one of the healthier military forts in the army. Most of the time.

It seemed to Lea ironic that they should have all escaped the dreaded summer illnesses only to be struck down just as the cooler weather was coming on. Stephen was the first to get sick. An 'intermittent fever', Dr. Heiskell said, and prescribed heavy blood letting before Lea objected so strongly he settled for bed rest and calomel instead. A few days later Rachel sickened and took to her bed. The dreaded 'camp fever'—that common ailment of military posts—began to take on epidemic proportions as more and more of the fort's residents came down with it. Yet, as December neared and the weather grew more pleasant, Rachel and her son improved enough that Lea was able to breathe a sigh of relief and begin to look forward to the holidays.

"Christmas is going to seem very strange in this place," she said, sitting on the edge of Rachel's bed to place a cool cloth on her forehead. "It won't seem the same without any ice and snow."

"Oh, how I would love to see snow right now," Rachel sighed. "Just to feel the soft, cold flakes on my face…"

"Ben says it never snows in Florida territory. But never mind. We can do other things to make the season festive. We can hang paper chains, and make holly wreathes. We won't have a goose but perhaps the soldiers can shoot a wild turkey. And think of all the oranges we'll have. We'll make it a happy time. You'll see."

"Oh, Lea, you're always so optimistic. You know it's going to be terrible without Mama and Papa or any of the familiar trappings that always made Christmas so happy."

Lea smoothed the limp strands of Rachel's hair away from her warm brow. Much of the luster was gone from her sister's hair now, as from her skin, leaving a yellow, sallow cast. Lea turned away to hide her worried frown. She had thought her sister was improving but today she didn't like the way Rachel looked at all. In some women, Lea knew, delicacy and softness sometimes hid a strong vein of steel underneath. But unlike Ben, she had long ago realized that Rachel had no such strength beneath her ethereal outer shell. Her physical body had always been frail and her spirit never seemed able to rise above that weakness. How unfortunate she had to come down with this debilitating fever just when she was beginning to enjoy life here a little.

"How is my baby?"

"Stephen's a little better today. He has no fever and I'm thinking of letting him up soon." Would Rachel recognize her lie, she wondered. It was true that Stephen's fever had subsided but his strength had not returned. Far from getting back on his little feet, he lay weak and unstirring, almost unable to lift his head. If the fever came back as Dr. Haskiell feared it might, his poor body would have a hard time fending it off.

"And Buck? Why doesn't Buck come to see me?"

"Don't you remember, dearest? We sent Buck to stay with the Lattimores while you and Stephen are ill. There's no need to expose him to this fever. I did tell you."

Rachel sighed, moving her thin hand listlessly on the linen coverlet. "I suppose so. Oh, Lea, I'm so weary of feeling ill. Where is Ben? Why doesn't he come to comfort me? He made me come here to this awful place and then he goes off all the time and leaves me to be sick and alone. Why does he do that?"

"Hush now. You'll only distress yourself with these thoughts. You're not alone, Rachel. I'm here and I'll stay with you." She dipped the wash cloth in a bowl of tepid water and folded it again on her sister's forehead. "You know Ben is always by your side when he's home, and he can't help that he has to be away on patrol a lot. He's very concerned about you."

"You always defend him, don't you." Rachel's pale eyes studied her sister's face. "And you're so good to me. Did you never resent it that he…I mean, I know you fancied him until he met me that evening you brought him home for a visit. Did you never wonder what might have happened if…"

"That was a long time ago," Lea said quickly. "And it's long forgotten. Since you married him, Ben has been the brother I never had and I'm very happy with that." She reached out to smooth the cloth on Rachel's brow. "What matters now is that you get well so you can both enjoy being together."

Rachel pushed her sister's hand away. Her eyes seemed huge above her shrunken cheeks. For a disturbing instant it seemed to Lea they already looked out at the world from some far place.

"Lea, tell me the truth. I'm not going to die, am I?"

"What nonsense," Lea said briskly. "Of course you're not going to die. Not for a long time. Come now, you've just caught a touch of camp fever. Everyone here gets it sometime or other. You'll soon be right as rain and we'll be making plans for our Christmas celebration. Try to think about that and forget all these morbid thoughts."

She picked up the bowl and walked to the door to retrieve more cool water from the kitchen. How she wished she was as certain as she sounded.

While Lea tried to calm her sister's fears, a few miles away Tsali Emaltha, called 'Charley O'Maltha' by the white-eyes, loped silently along the shady path away from Fort Brooke and toward his nearly deserted village at Thonatossassa. Behind him, three of his daughters followed soundlessly, their soft moccasins rustling in the warm sand. Since most of the people of his village had already moved to the new issuing houses beside Tampa Bay, there were only a few odds and ends to be gathered from the abandoned *chickees* near Thonotosassa Lake. He walked unnaturally, head down, deep in thought and ignoring the sounds of the forest around him. He was an old man and he was profoundly unhappy with the way his life was running its course. This very day he had sold most of his cattle to the army at Fort Brooke—the coins clanked heavily inside the leather pouch at his waist—so that he might have money to take with him on the journey west of the Mississippi—money to help his people settle into their new homes.

This might be the last time his eyes ever beheld his village. The white-eye's ships would come soon they said, only a matter of days, and the winds would carry his people from this land forever. The coins bumped against his side as he walked and the sound of them was hateful. He did not want to sell his cattle to the whites. He did not want to leave this good country or ask his people to leave with him. But what else was there to do? There were only two choices—to go, or to fight. The first was to break your heart, but the second, that was to break your spirit and the spirit of the Mikasuki people. That way many would die, not just the young warriors but women and children too. The white-eyes were strong. They had powerful weapons and there were always more of them coming. The Seminole might win a skirmish or even a battle, but they would never win a war against so formidable an enemy. Better to choose the way of peace and hope that your children's children might live.

Absorbed as he was in his thoughts, it was instinct more than any soft rustling on the path ahead that brought him to an abrupt stop. His head jerked forward and he waited, still as death. When a figure materialized out of the green scrub beside the path he was not surprised. He had half-expected it. Behind him his daughters slipped soundlessly into the brush where they could watch their father from the shadows. He did not look around, but he knew they had gone and it satisfied him. This was the confrontation he had been expecting since the day he agreed to make his fateful mark on the white man's treaty, the mark that bound him to a new country.

The young man who faced him stood at nearly the same height. There was an athletic grace about him, as though his body moved easily from a central pivot. Tsali Emaltha noted impassively the long rifle carried in the curve of one arm, the fringed war belt, the bullet pouch and bone powder horn, the bright turban with its two dyed egret feathers. One half of his face, neck and hand was smeared with red ocher. Bright shafts of light reflected from the silver gorget around his neck. The white-eyes called him 'Powel' after his white father. To the Seminoles he was 'Asi-yaholo', a 'black drink crier'.

Tsali Emaltha's head moved forward like a watchful tortoise as he saw four more silent figures step from the shade, each cradling a rifle. He recognized them all. The last time he had seen Asi-yaholo was at the gathering called by Chief Micanopy in the green swamp where he had been loudly brandishing his knife and denouncing all those who, in the interest of peace, would go along with this plan for removal. These other warriors had been there too, along with Alligator, and Jumper and Coaccochee, the Wildcat, the handsome son of King Philip, all egged on to these heroics by the noisy blathering of this young hothead who was not even a chief.

Across the clearing their eyes locked, the watery, squinting eyes of the older man, the bitter, angry blackness of the younger. Tsali Emaltha watched in silence as Asi-Yaholo raised the bright barrel of his rifle. There was no need to speak, the time for argument was over. He had done what he thought was best and now these foolish young men would have their way. He was almost glad to be leaving it all behind.

It was nearly dusk when Holata Emaltha came hurrying into Fort Brooke followed by the grieving daughters of his brother, Tsali. They had hastily covered the body of their father with shallow brush then gone immediately to tell their Uncle what had happened. Now Holata came, angry, fearful, and with a decided air of 'I told you so' to lay the matter at the feet of the white-eyes.

There was never a question of who had ambushed and executed the old chief. Even if his daughters had not recognized Asceola, the soldiers would have known by the coins left scattered over the old man's body. Their message was clear. From now on this would be the fate of those who cooperated with the army. The gauntlet was down, the knife was buried in the treaty as surely as the day Asceola put it there himself. There was no way now to remove the Seminoles from Florida without a war.

Ben hurried along the walk that evening, his head down, his brows drawn in concentration, keenly aware that his wife's illness was made more complicated by today's awful events. For the first time since she arrived he admitted that he wished she were safe and well back in New York. He should never have insisted that she join him here in this dangerous and difficult post. He had let his need for her overrule any reservations he had about life in this wilderness. If only he didn't love her so much, but, of course, he did love her, and had since the first moment he met her. He loved her gentleness and beauty. He had missed her terribly and wanted her near him.

But had he let that love overrule his judgement? He had been so certain the warm, mild climate of Florida would improve her health. Instead, this dreadful camp fever that had already struck so many unsuspecting soldiers had made her even more sickly. She had always been frail, he knew that, and yet he had insisted she come to live in this inhospitable place. Not only was she suffering now but at any moment he might be ordered into the scrub to fight the Seminoles for weeks or even months. Suppose he was killed. How would she ever manage to get home again with their children?

Leatrice! It was a comfort to remember that Rachel had her sister with her. Lea was sensible and capable and if anything happened to him, she would certainly see that his family returned safely to New York.

The light in the window of his cottage flamed like a beacon in the darkness. He thought of the lamplight gleaming on the porcelain face of his cherished wife and quickened his steps.

The shock waves that reverberated through Fort Brooke at the news of Charley O'Maltha's murder quickly radiated out into the surrounding countryside. Within days nearly five hundred Seminoles were camped around Fort Brooke clamoring for protection. Every day saw more come in, women with frightened eyes, black-eyed children whose thin bodies and protruding bellies bore witness to their lack of food, old men who wore an aspect of confused desperation on their solemn faces. Several of the army men who had served in Georgia and Alabama during the removal of the Creeks and Cherokees told Ben they had seen the same lost expression on the faces of those Indians which they now saw on many of the Seminoles.

Adding to the congestion were the hordes of white settlers from the open scrub who lumbered in every day on rickety wagons piled high with their salvageable household goods. Several isolated families had already been attacked by roving savages, their houses and crops burned, their cattle scattered. Some had relatives who had been murdered and scalped when they couldn't hide quickly enough from the marauding Indians.

The first priority was to try to create some sort of order out of all the confusion. Soldiers were detailed to build a stockade for the Indians on Egmont Key, a small island at the entrance to the Bay. While it helped to relieve some of the crowding near the fort, it could never hold all those who were waiting. The rest lived in makeshift camps on the west side of the Hillsborough, in a condition of near-starvation. The white settlers were mostly country people accustomed to rough living. They threw up tents or makeshift enclosures on the grounds of the fort and even beyond, among the few clustered log buildings of the village.

Fear was in the air. Lea could sense it in the silent thoughtfulness with which Ben and his fellow officers refused to discuss the Indian problem with the women, and the wariness with which the pickets refused to allow the older children near the river. It showed in the way the men looked eagerly every day for a sight of the expected ships bearing reinforcements and supplies from Key West and New Orleans. Although she tried to keep calm in front of Rachel, her sister sensed that something was terribly wrong. Lea thought to ease her fear by saying little, not realizing that her silence only added to Rachel's anxiety.

Lea had difficulty being honest with Rachel when she was so concerned about her sister's health. She had been so sure that both Stephen and his mother were growing stronger, that their bodies would eventually throw off the lingering, debilitating effects of the fever. Death and sickness still raged through the camp to the point where the blockhouse had been turned into a hospital but Ben flatly refused to move his wife and son there as long as Lea was willing to care for them at home. Lea spent so much of her time running between the two sickbeds that she almost grew unconcerned about the worsening situation beyond the fort.

Ben was little help. With his time divided between trying to sort out arrangements for the Indians to be deported and going off on forays into the bush he had little leisure to be at home. When he was there he spent most of his time hovering beside Rachel's bed, wordlessly agonizing over her pale, drawn looks. It was almost a relief to Lea when his duties called him away.

Lea was tired, bone-weary, sleeplessly worn out. She sorely missed Buck's bright, laughing presence yet there was nothing to do but keep him away in a safe household while she did her best to make his mother and brother well. The fever was bound to break soon and then at last she would be able to go outside and breathe the clear, salt air of the bay. Maybe then she could finally begin to plan for the holidays. With Rachel and Stephen recuperating, those plans would have to be simpler than she had originally thought, but no matter. They would make up for it next year.

Then suddenly, without warning, both Stephen and his mother began to sink, as though the struggle had finally become just too hard for their wasted bodies to handle. Ben had just returned from a long patrol to take up his constant watch over Rachel, freeing Lea to care for her young nephew. Late on a blessedly cool December afternoon Lea realized Stephen was dying. She stretched out on his bed, holding his slight body in her arms, willing him to stay even as he slipped away. Numb with fatigue and grief, she wrapped him in a white sheet as they used to do in Bible days, dried her tears and went to join Ben in Rachel's room, determined not to let either parent know that their youngest was gone until she felt they could bear the news. She found there was no need, for Rachel had slipped into a deep, merciful sleep. When Julia stopped in Lea asked her to make the arrangements for Stephen's body then set about keeping vigil beside Rachel's bed, quietly praying that her sister would somehow find the will to live, listening to her slight breath fade in soft, shallow whispers. The last, long sigh came in the early hours of the morning as a bronze tint on the dark horizon announced the dawn of the new day Rachel and her son would never see. Heavily, Lea rose from her sister's bedside to stand at the window, watching the light grow, hearing the first sleepy chorus of waking birds, the first stirrings of the fort coming to life.

She had been up all night and she was so tired her weary mind could not take in that they were both gone. They could not be gone! It wasn't possible. She felt as though a part of her heart was shorn off, leaving a torn and bleeding wound. Why should she still live while her sister lay wasted, still beautiful in death? Surely her life had ended as certainly as Rachel's and little Stephen's. It was cruel of fate not to take her in their place, she who had no one. Instead she had to keep going, keep striving, keep living, more alone than ever before.

As she stared out into the darkness all the wild beauty she had striven so hard to find in this Godforsaken Florida wilderness melted away and she saw it with clear eyes as the stark, savage, flea-ridden, heat-seared country it was. Empty, desolate, barren. Just like herself.

She turned to see Ben kneeling beside his wife's bed, still clutching her cold hand. Behind his stricken face was an agony of unshed tears that Lea knew he would never allow to flow. She wanted so much to go to him but she knew he would not want her. He might even resent that she was alive and healthy while his beloved Rachel lay dead. She didn't think she could bear that.

"I must see to Buck," she muttered. "Someone has to tell him and I think perhaps it would be easier coming from me."

Ben did not look around. She was not even sure he heard her, or knew when she left the room.

CHAPTER 5

▼

Fort Brooke was considered a healthy post, yet since its founding in 1823 so many residents had died from the ravages of fevers, dangerous duties and accidents that a shady patch of high ground had been set aside for a burial ground. By the time Rachel and Stephen were laid to rest there it had taken on the look of an established cemetery. A grove of blackjack oaks, alive with the chatter of squirrels and the quarreling of jays, dangled lacy sleeves of spanish moss that swayed gently in the morning breeze. Below their thick arms crude wooden crosses protruded up from the stunted weeds that grew sporadically in the blocked sunlight. Lea stood among the mourners gathered around the new grave and watched numbly as two raw pine coffins were lowered into the sandy soil. Beside her Ben stood in full uniform, the dappled sunlight gleaming on his braided epaulets, his face like a granite sculpture, his eyes focused everywhere but on the gaping hole at his feet. On Lea's other side Buck gripped her hand, standing so close to her she could feel his small body through the folds of her skirt.

Across the open graves Ben's friend and former commanding officer, Brevet Major Zantzinger, intoned the Episcopal burial service with a military briskness. She could sense the deep well of sympathy among the small group of mourners who had joined them, the officers and their wives who respected and liked Ben even though they hadn't got to know Rachel very well. Most of them could empathize with the tragic death of a child since many had known such a loss themselves. Behind them Lea could hear the rustling movement of the guard detail who had escorted them to the cemetery. Everyone half-expected an attack on the fort any day now, and it was not safe to stray too far even to bury the dead.

At last Major Zantzinger had committed the souls of the departed to his satisfaction. He walked around the narrow grave to lay a hand on Ben's shoulder, murmuring a few comforting words. At Ben's impassive, angry silence he turned instead to Lea whose tear-stained cheeks suggested a more receptive ear.

"Have courage, my dear. The ways of the Lord are mysterious and beyond our understanding. But one thing is certain. Your sister and nephew are most assuredly even now in the arms of a Savior who loves them better than we mortals ever could."

"Thank you, sir," Lea broke in quickly. "You are very kind."

"The Lord giveth and the Lord taketh away."

"Yes, yes. Of course."

Perhaps one day she would be able to see the goodness in all this but right now she rather doubted it. Why should the Lord take Rachel who had a husband and son who loved and needed her, instead of herself whose loss would devastate no one? Why Stephen who was too young to have done any harm to anyone, who had his whole life ahead of him? If this were the Lord's doing then His ways were mysterious indeed.

She jammed Buck's cap on his head then laid her fingers under his chin and tipped up his face to look into his sad, confused eyes.

"Can we go back home now, Aunt Lea?" the boy whispered.

"Yes, my love. We're going home now."

The drummer struck up a long, slow roll and the little band turned away from the new graves to move down the sandy path toward the parade ground. Lea, with Buck at her side, fell in step behind Ben who was walking with steady purpose alongside Major Zantzinger and the newly arrived fort commandant, Captain Francis Belton. They were all headed back to Ben's cottage where some of the women had brought food for the mourners and there was plenty of whisky to go along with it. Yet Lea sensed no hurry to get back for a wake. Everyone seemed to be so borne down by the tragedy of losing both a wife and son at one blow that they probably wished they could just go on home and leave the Captain to his terrible grief.

Captain Belton began a low conversation with his two officers. "I was somewhat subdued to view the pitiful state of the fortifications here, Major Zantzinger. Captain Frazier has built up the place as best he could but I suspect we would not be able to fend off a heavy attack by the savages were one to be launched against us."

Lea could tell that Ben seemed relieved to be talking about something other than his loss. "We've never had to face one, Captain. Though I suspect that won't be true much longer. This is the logical place for the hostiles to hit next."

"It certainly is and I intend it as my first priority to make this cantonment many times stronger than it is now. With so many civilians turning to us for protection, and reinforcements from New Orleans expected any day, we've got a lot of work ahead of us."

They paused as Major Zantzinger prepared to veer away from the procession toward the sutler's store. "Put Captain Carson here on it, Belton. He's been at Fort Brooke long enough to know exactly how to get things done."

Ben's eyes took on a glimmer of eagerness. "I could get to it right away, sir. I think, that is, I'd prefer to stay busy."

"I understand," Belton replied. "Well, we've much to do and we'll need your help."

As they neared the officer's quarters Julia Lattimore stepped up to walk beside Lea. "Miss Hammond," she said almost apologetically, "on my husband's last patrol he killed a large buck and brought back several choice cuts of venison. I'd be pleased if you would accept one."

Though at that moment Lea did not care if she ever saw food again she answered politely, "That is most kind of you, Mrs. Lattimore. If you're sure you can spare it. Supplies at the fort right now are so precious."

"I confess I've been keeping this particular bounty to myself. It's all smoked and ready. I'll bring it by in the morning."

In the morning. What did she have to do in the morning now that Rachel and Stephen were past caring for. "Yes, thank you."

"If there is any other way I can be of help…"

"Thank you but we are well looked after by Nora Cates, Corporal Cates's wife. She was a great help to me during my sister's sickness and has agreed to stay on for a while. But you are kind to offer."

Julia Lattimore's plain face was etched with sympathy that Lea could not bear right now. She liked Julia and had hoped they would become friends before family sickness forced her to become a near recluse. She could tell Julia was shocked at the change in her. She knew she was thin and tired and had lost all that bright interest and joy she had felt before Rachel and Stephen's illness. But what did that matter now when she was likely to be gone soon, back to New York.

"Dear Miss Hammond," Julia said, searching for the right words, "I do hope you know you can depend on us for anything you need in the days ahead. Army garrisons are peculiar, exasperating places but there is one thing about them.

When any member is in need the others will always rally around. After all, if we don't help each other in this isolated wilderness, who will?"

The earnestness of Julia's words managed to penetrate the carapace of Lea's heavy grief. They were nearing the house and, to Lea's relief, Ben still led the way. She had been half-afraid he would abandon her to face the sympathy of friends alone. She stopped on the walkway and turned to Julia. "I shall remember your kind words, Mrs. Lattimore, depend on it."

Impulsively Julia reached out and squeezed Lea's hand. With hot tears burning behind her eyes, Lea walked up the steps to the veranda knowing there would be days ahead when she would take solace from Julia's offer. Right now she just hoped she could make it through the rest of this day.

During the long weeks when Rachel and Stephen were ill, Nora Cates, who had begun as a laundress for the Carson family, had been transformed into something approaching a housemaid. She was a buxom Irish farm girl with red cheeks and a ready smile and had more strength in her two arms than any woman Lea had ever known. She had left Ireland to follow her husband first to the States then into the army. Once installed in the Carson household she had decided that these two sisters had not enough practicality between them to fill a needle case and had accordingly made their cause her own. Her easy-going husband did not object that so much of his wife's time was spent with the Captain's family, thinking it might help his prospects as well.

In the days following the funeral Lea came to depend on Nora even more, until she could not imagine getting along without her. Together they swabbed down every surface in the cottage with borax and water until Lea was near collapse and ordered to bed. She went expecting to be up again by supper but instead the effects of grief and fatigue kept her there for two days. Once back on her feet, her most pressing task was to write the letter that would inform her parents of their daughter's and grandson's deaths. It was a chore she dreaded for they were both elderly and unwell, yet it had to be done. Reluctantly she took up her writing desk and forced herself to put the words on paper, struggling to present grim facts in as gentle a way as possible. She was relieved when it was finished. She folded and sealed it, then grabbed her shawl and bonnet for the trip to the post office.

When she opened her front door she was surprised to see Buck sitting quietly on the low porch steps dragging a stick listlessly through the sand. She was suddenly aware of how Buck had changed from the noisy, exuberant boy he had always been. Everything was different for him. He had lost both his mother and his younger brother and, when she took to her bed, probably feared he would lose her as well.

She suggested he walk with her to the post office and was rewarded with a smile like the sun coming from behind a dark cloud. When he still hesitated because he'd been told not to go outside the pickets, she assured him they would take one of the soldiers as a guard.

"Hurry up now, child, I can't wait all day."

Still grinning, he rushed inside the house and came back with his felt cap jammed on his head. He didn't take her hand as they started down the path, but skipped ahead in his old manner. However, Lea noticed he didn't go very far and often looked back to see whether she was still there. Poor little thing. His world had been sorely disrupted.

That previous fall, Captain Frazier had decided to strengthen the fort against attack by erecting a triangular wooden stockade with two blockhouses at the apex along the shore near the bay. As Lea walked toward it, she was suddenly aware of how many other changes had taken place in the cantonment since the onset of Stephen and Rachel's illness. Squat lean-tos and tents thronged the spaces alongside the little fort, spilling over into the nearby parade ground and as far north as the barracks, forcing her to weave her way between them. Many of the newly arrived settlers from the scrub who had moved to Fort Brooke for protection sat grouped around the open flaps or doorways. A small settlement within the pickets had been created, a mixture of campfires, boxes and crates, assorted chairs and tables, laundry drying on strings, chickens and dogs and children scrabbling around, their noise a cacophony of confusion against the orderly routine of the military fort. As Lea and Buck threaded their way among the stacks of stools and household goods Lea recognized one of the recent arrivals. Old Levi Collar, the first white man to settle in the Tampa area, sat on an upturned barrel, puffing on a long clay pipe. Beside him stood his daughter Cordelia and her sister, Nancy, looking fresh in dark blue merino dresses with starched white bibs. Louis Bell and his wife, Eliza—another Collar daughter—sat on a packing crate opposite Levi, and just behind them, a gaunt farmer in a faded brown coat leaned on a long musket. Beside the farmer, nearly eclipsed by the shadow of a half-completed lean-to with a palm frond roof, was a woman Lea supposed to be his wife since she had that worn-out, aged, yellow look of many country women. In the dirt at her feet two young children played. With their ragged clothes and older-than-their-years faces, Lea took them to also be part of the new arrivals from out in the scrub.

"I tell you, sir, that land up around White Sand road is downright worthless," Lea heard Collar exclaim as she drew near the group. "It won't grow cowpeas! A man is a fool to try to farm up that a'way."

"I take exception to that, sir," the farmer said with an air of exaggerated politeness. "Why my land is as good as any in the territory and if it weren't for these blood-thirsty savages, I'd be there right now, provin' it to anyone who cared to look."

"Now, Papa," Eliza said soothingly, "who knows best what land is worth? The man who works it or the man who's never seen it?"

"You hush, daughter. I seen that land long time ago when there weren't nothin' but savages there. I seen all the land around this here territory and I know what I say. Most of it ain't worth a cup of spit!"

Lea remembered hearing how the Collars and another family, the Dixons, were recently forced to flee their farm a few miles north of the fort in the middle of the night with a Seminole raiding party breathing down their necks. They had barely made it out alive, escaping in a boat and watching the glow on the horizon that marked the destruction of their homes.

"Mornin', Miss Hammond," Louis Bell said, doffing his battered felt hat. "You and the boy out for a walk, are you?"

"Good morning, "Lea answered, aware of a sudden self-consciousness among the group in the presence of the bereaved. "Yes, we're on our way to the post office."

Cordelia Collar smiled kindly at her. "It's good to see you out again, Miss Hammond. We was sorry to hear about your sickness an' all. Feelin' better now, are you?"

"Yes, thank you. Much better. Are you and your family all settled?"

"We've got a room at the surgeon's quarters for the present," Cordelia's pretty sister, Nancy, spoke up. "It's crowded, but we're just happy to be safe."

"I don't believe I've had the pleasure, Miss," the gaunt farmer broke in, sweeping off his hat. "I'm Jonas Crompton, from up the White Sand road. This here's my wife, Alvy, and these are our young'uns."

"You're new to Fort Brooke, Mister Crompton?"

"Yes, ma'am, only arrived two days back. Left my farm, my barn, and my sugar mill, cold standin' and skedaddled. I only hope I find 'em there when I go back and not burned to the ground by them Seminolees."

Levi Collar waved his pipe toward Lea. "You tell 'em, Miss Hammond, that I know what I say. Ain't nobody in Floridy that knows the lay of the land any better than old Levi Collar. Didn't Captain Carson tell you that when you first come here?"

Lea laughed. Levi Collar made a lot of noise but she had learned long ago that anyone who knew him well never took his bombast seriously. He might be loud, but he was also brave and resourceful, as one of the first settlers to wrest a living from the Florida wilderness had to be.

"I'm not the one to say, Mister Collar. I probably know less about Florida than anyone here." She turned back to Bell. "Do you know if the post office is closed?"

"No, ma'am. Judge Steele has still got the post office open and swears he will until he sees the first savage waving a hatchet runnin' out of the woods. But I wouldn't recommend you go there without'n an escort. Just to be on the safe side."

Feeling a tug at her skirt, Lea looked down to see Buck trying to whisper something to her.

"Private Clarke is over there talking to the picket, Aunt Lea. Maybe we could ask him to go with us."

She had also spotted Ransome Clarke and intended to ask him to accompany them even before Louis Bell's warning. It would mean a lot to Buck.

"Of course we'll ask him, dear. I'm pleased to have met you Mister Crompton. Good day to you now." As she led Buck away she could hear their quiet remarks behind her.

"Miss Hammond has such nice manners," Cordelia said wistfully before her father's loud voice interrupted her.

"I know what I'm talkin' about and I'm sayin' that Sand road land is so worthless a feller could stand on a sack of fertilizer and he wouldn't be able to raise an umbrella!"

Private Ransome Clarke had just been relieved of guard duty and was quite willing to escort Lea and Buck on their walk to the post office. Young, gregarious and one of Buck's favorite people, he was also a pleasant companion for Lea who found him refreshingly buoyant after so many dark days of mourning. Buck danced ahead of them as they passed beyond the pickets and along the sandy track into the adjacent village. The scattered, haphazard collection of sheds and log buildings that made up the settlement of Tampa were mostly now shuttered and deserted, their owners having moved into the cantonment. The whole place looked shabbier than ever in the hazy afternoon sun.

"Do you think the Indians will attack our fort, Private Clarke," Lea asked when Buck was far enough ahead to be out of earshot.

"I don't know ma'am, but nobody wants to take the chance they will. There's terrible fierce things happening out there in the territory. Last night Mr. Skinner came in leavin' his plantation burned behind him. And a horse and some cattle were stolen right here within sight of the fort itself. But it's my opinion that there are too many soldiers and too many guns in Tampa Bay for old Powel or Jumper to try their tricks here."

"I hope you are right. I can understand why all these people would want to move into the safety of the fort. An Indian attack is so terrible."

As near as Lea could tell, the only place still open for business beyond the busy pier and Saunder's trading post a raw pine lean-to that dispensed oysters from barrels brought in each day by the fishermen in Spanishtown Creek. Only by promising Buck they would stop there on their way back was she able to drag him away to the framed house near the end of the sandy road where Judge Augustus Steele kept the post office. She knew Judge Steele as one of Tampa's most enthusiastic entrepreneurs. As Deputy Collector of Customs at Fort Brooke, it was he who had convinced the Legislature in Tallahassee to change the county name from 'Mosquito County' to the more fashionable 'Hillsborough', a name which was far more likely to attract new settlers once the Indian problem was resolved. Just a year ago he had seen that Tampa was made the County seat, and had supervised the construction of a two-room log courthouse, now tightly shuttered.

"Afternoon, Miss Hammond," he greeted Lea as she and Buck stepped into the darkened interior of his house. "Fine day, ain't it, for December."

"It doesn't seem like December at all, Judge. Back home we'd be wearing our wool cloaks and gloves by now, not to mention huddling around the stove."

"You can't beat this climate, can you? Here it is almost Christmas and the weather's like a June day up north. I always said it's a gold dollar climate. Now, what can I do for you today?"

"I'm so glad you're still open, Judge Steele. I have a letter to send to New York, if you please. That is, if any mail is getting through in these troubled times."

"As long as the ships still come and go the mail will go with them. That Powel, he ain't goin' to hit Fort Brooke, not if he knows what's good for him. And I'm not closin' down a government post until I see the egret feathers comin' through that door. Even then, not without a fight."

"You're very brave, Judge. I don't think I'd want to stay here alone."

Steele leaned forward over the counter and spoke in a lowered voice. "I got me an army issue carbine right here underneath this counter. If any of them savages come at me there's goin' to be a pile of them on their way to the Great Spirit. Judge Steele don't aim to lose his scalp-lock!"

Lea pulled at the drawstring of her reticule. "Well, if you will let me know what it will cost to frank my letter—oh, and would you have anything special for children today?. My nephew has earned a little treat to lift his spirits."

Judge Steele reached under the counter and pulled out one short whitish stalk. "How about a peeled sugar cane stick, young fellow. I was up to the grinding at Mister Diego's mill yesterday and brought back a few leavings. There's not likely to be any more for a while now, so enjoy it." His smile faded as he turned to Lea. "I was right sorry to hear about your loss, Miss Hammond. It's hard to see why these things happen but I suppose the Good Lord has His reasons."

Lea concentrated on the coins in her hands. "Thank you. You're very kind."

"By the way, Miss, would you do me a favor on your way back to the Fort?" This letter came in with the last shipment and was never picked up. I don't read German much but near as I can tell it's for that Sergeant Cooper, Company C. It's from Coburg, Germany, I can tell that much and I'm pretty sure the name is Kruper, which probably was turned into Cooper by the army. Anyway, if you'd drop it off at headquarters for me I'd be obliged."

"Of course. Either Private Clarke or I will see that he gets it. And here is my letter."

Steele took her letter, glanced at the address and murmured, "So sad...so sad..."

Lea was relieved to walk back out into the bright sunshine after the Judge's gloomy sympathy. Clarke, who had been sitting on the front step, jumped up and the three of them set off for the fort with the boy chewing happily on the sugar cane stick. They made a brief stop at an oyster lean-to where Lea picked up a dozen oysters for their supper.

"Did you know that oysters in Florida grow on trees, Miss Hammond?" Clarke asked as they neared the fort. Lea caught the glint of mischief in his eyes.

"Oh, no, you won't catch me on that one, Mister Clarke," she said, smiling. "I had not been here two days before Private Bell tried to trick me with it."

"But it's true."

"Yes, I saw them myself clinging to the roots of those mangrove trees growing around the shoreline. But its stretching the truth to claim they grow on trees."

"Well, it makes a good tale. Like those schools of fish that take two days to pass by. And..."

"Oh, my goodness…" Lea had slowed to observe a Seminole family resting by the side of the road near the path to the river. They appeared to be one of a small group of friendly Indians who had taken up squatters rights outside the fort hoping to garner enough food from the soldiers to stay alive. The women were thin and gaunt but it was the children that caught at Lea's heart. Their bellies swollen, their huge impassive dark eyes looking starkly out at the world, they sat listlessly in the dirt, showing none of the childish exuberance she was accustomed to seeing. Several old men sat nearby wrapped in dirty blankets. There were no young men at all.

"It's hard enough dealing with reality around here, Private Clarke. Forget about tall tales."

That evening, after reading Buck a story and tucking him in bed, Lea returned to the front room of the cottage feeling restless and bored. Through the doorway she could see Ben in his bedroom going through some of Rachel's things spread out on the bed. He had been so reticent since the funeral that Lea was reluctant to approach him in the hope of making conversation. When she saw him pull out his watch to study the little portrait of his wife in the lid, she grabbed her shawl and walked out on to the porch.

It was a beautiful night, cool and pleasant, with the heady fragrance of wild pennyroyal in the air. A round cheese of a moon cast an amber glow over the shrubs, so bright it seemed she might read by it. Lea walked absently down the path along the row of officer's cottages toward the old Indian mound where the breeze off the bay gave a salt tinge to the air. There were lights twinkling inside the windows of the other houses and shadows moving around inside. She could hear voices, some laughing, some speaking softly, in counterpoint to the military 'all's well' of the soldiers on guard. Everything came from a distance—the bark of a dog, the whinny of a horse, the mingled noises of the squatters in the tents at the other end of the parade ground, even the distant, chilling howl of a wolf out in the scrub.

The Indian mound was a huge shadow blocking the ghostly light of the moon. Lea had been amazed to learn it was actually an ancient burial ground, so old that it predated the Seminoles and probably belonged to the Timicuans, the aborigines who greeted the Spaniards when they first waded ashore in Tampa Bay. The Anglos, ever anxious to civilize and neaten, had built a short picket fence to enclose the mound. Even the dome of the mound had been cultivated with a thick layer of carefully cropped grass. It was amazing to think that this great hill should represent the oldest object in this place where everything else was so new.

One thought of Florida as having no history at all when, in fact, Indians had probably danced and worshipped, and perhaps grieved around this hill for centuries back. Perhaps the Conquistadors in their plumed helmets and short capes had wondered at it. Only the English would be so cavalier as to dismiss the legacy of other peoples. 'I can say that because I'm English stock', she smiled to herself. Yet, as she remembered that she would never lay eyes on her sister or nephew again in this life, she could feel a spiritual bond with the people who had sat by this mound hurting for the same reason.

She ambled slowly back to the house, dreading to go to bed only to toss and turn long into the night. The moon by now had hidden itself behind a bank of clouds and threw elongated shadows across the path and the piazza. She was nearly to the front door when a muffled sound at the porch railing made her stop and peer into the darkness.

"Why, Ben. Is that you?" When he didn't answer she wondered if perhaps she shouldn't just pretend she hadn't heard and go on inside.

"Yes, it's me," he finally responded before she could move. "Where have you been?"

"For a walk down to the old Indian mound. It's such a beautiful night, so peaceful and cool. I hated to stay indoors."

"I saw you leave. I thought perhaps that was what you had in mind."

Lea took a tentative step in his direction. She could see now that he was sitting on the railing, still in his shirtsleeves, looking pensive and lonely. She did not want to join him unasked, thinking he might not want her there. Perhaps he needed to be alone. Still, he had noticed when she left.

"I was trying to sort out some of Rachel's things," he said. Lea, taking this as an indication he wanted to talk, sat down on the edge of a chair near him. "But I can't seem to make any sense of it. Perhaps you'd better just take what you want to keep, and give the rest away. Or, rather, what you wish to carry back to New York. There must be some keepsakes and other things your parents might want."

She struggled to find an answer. "Yes, I suppose I'd better be thinking about that. Going back to New York, I mean." It was the subject she wanted most to avoid but knew she had to face. Until now he had not mentioned it and she had not had the courage to bring it up. "Do you have any idea when?"

His voice was matter-of-fact. "Yes, there's a ship bringing reinforcements due in from Key West any day now and another one or two coming from New Orleans. If one of them returns to Key West after Christmas you should take it. There may be some other women leaving, what with all this Indian business, so you'll have company part of the way. You should easily be able to find a ship up the East Coast from the Keys."

"And Buck?" Her voice sounded strangled, so fearful was she of his answer. If she had to leave Buck here alone with his father she did not think she could go.

There was a long pause. "I think it's best that he go with you. This is no place right now for young children. Oh, he loves it, I know. For him, Fort Brooke is a great adventure. But it's not safe. He'll be better off growing up with you and Mother and Father Hammond in New York. When he's old enough, if he wants to join me I'll be happy to have him."

After Christmas. So soon. But at least she would be taking Buck with her. Ben would be left with no one.

"I shall feel some sadness at leaving Florida. I've found it interesting, even fascinating at times."

"I don't know why you should!" Ben exclaimed, his voice edged with bitterness. "It has brought you nothing but sorrow, just as it has me. I wish to God I had never insisted that Rachel and the children come here."

"You mustn't say that, Ben. Rachel wanted to come. She always wanted to be with you. You had every right to want your family. How could you—how could anyone know this would happen."

"I might have known! Might have realized! There's always risk in a Godforsaken wilderness like this. I just wanted her with me. And my boys. Can you imagine seeing her, lying there dead and knowing I brought her to it. Now I don't know how I'm going to live with the guilt..."

His voice broke. Lea sat, helpless, watching him struggle to regain control. Then on a sudden impulse, she moved to his side and laid her arm around his shoulders. For a brief moment he leaned against her and allowed her to cradle his head with her hand, together in their shared pain.

But it was quickly over. From their common grief, Ben quickly moved to self-conscious embarrassment. "I'm sorry," he muttered, stepping away and absently running his hand through his hair.

"I cry too," she whispered, turning away from him. The words she wanted to say stayed strangled in her throat. *Cry, Ben. Go ahead and rage and storm and shriek if it will help you live again. Let me comfort you. Comfort me!* Yet she could not speak. The familiar dread that he might resent her sympathy kept her silent.

"It's difficult," he went on, as though anxious to defend his sudden release of emotion. "I blame myself, you see. Only myself."

"She wanted to come. Try to remember that."

"Yes, I'll try." He straightened his shoulders. "Perhaps I'll take a walk too. Lattimore's a good fellow and he always has a bottle of something strong about. You'll be all right?"

"Of course. I'm just going along to bed."

"Right. Well, try to get some rest."

He was off down the path before she could ask him again when the boat was leaving for Key West. Yet she did not really need reminding. Right after Christmas, he had said. So soon.

CHAPTER 6

▼

After that unguarded moment on the porch Lea saw Ben clamp an even tighter control over his feelings. It was as though he felt nothing anymore—sorrow, loss, grief, all were hidden under a self-contained silence that shut out everyone around him. It was fortunate, Lea thought, that he was so involved in the busy work of shoring up the fort's defenses for the attack everyone expected to come at any moment. At least his preoccupation with the growing hostility between the army and the Seminoles left him little time for grieving. Events seemed to be tumbling more out of control every day as the soldiers and civilians in the cantonment grew increasingly anxious.

Everyone at Fort Brooke was aware that when Major Belton arrived on the 11th of December he had found a directive waiting for him from General Clinch ordering that two companies be sent north immediately to reinforce the garrison at Fort King. That meant a six-day march straight through Indian territory. Belton was loathe to comply with the order until ships carrying an expected two hundred new troops arrived in Tampa Bay. The column would march, but not until the fort was strengthened. If Lea could have seen Ben pleading with Belton to let him go with them, she would not have worried so about him hiding his feelings. In truth, Ben was so anxious to get away from Fort Brooke, from the sadness and emptiness of his house and from his overwhelming guilt, that he all but pleaded on his knees to be allowed to accompany the march to Fort King.

Most people felt that General Clinch was crazy to order troops up that dangerous road right now, that it was as good as issuing Aseola an invitation to attack. Yet for that very reason Ben wanted to be there. Death seemed an honorable and welcome release from sorrow and an empty life. And it was for just that reason that Belton refused to send him. A reckless and grieving commander was not the best person to be in control of other men's lives. Besides, General Clinch had specified that Captain Gardiner's and Major Frazier's companies be sent and that was the way it would be. Captain Carson would stay in camp.

On December 21st the schooner Motto lowered sail in Tampa Bay. On board were thirty-eight men under the command of a handsome career soldier, Major Francis Dade. In a different time Lea might have wanted to get to know the Major better. He had been stationed at Fort Brooke nearly ten years before, knew the area well, and was serenely confident that the trip through Indian territory to Fort King could be handled without difficulty. With his black beard, courtly air, Virginia manners, curved saber, and silver spurs, the Major cut a dashing figure. Though he had a wife and child in Pensacola, he had always been a favorite with the ladies and his presence at Fort Brooke promised to add a lift to the holiday season nearly at hand.

The column was set to march on the morning of December 23rd with seven officers, ninety-nine enlisted men, and one six-pound canon. Lea spent most of the preceding night with several other women at the fort sewing cartridge pouches and powder bags for the men to hang on their belts. With the dawn coming fitfully in, she stood beside the other civilians to watch as the column moved out. She was surprised to see that Major Dade rode ahead in the advance guard, not Captain Gardiner, until Julia Lattimore explained that at the last moment Gardiner had been persuaded to stay behind with his seriously ill wife while Dade himself volunteered to lead the march. There was an undercurrent of anxiety in the onlookers, for everyone knew the men were facing a march of nearly one hundred miles through dangerous territory. Yet Dade looked so gallant and brave that it helped to lessen the crowd's unspoken fear. Lea waved to Private Clarke as he marched past with his comrades to the beat of the drum and he touched his cap in reply. She wished them Godspeed but she thanked the Lord that Ben was not among them.

She learned later that day that Belton was sending the Motto immediately back to Key West. Frances Gardiner would be aboard, relieving her husband to gallop north to catch up with Dade's column and resume what he felt was his duty to his men. Lea knew Ben had briefly debated whether to seek permission to ride with Gardiner and was relieved when he gave it up as a hopeless request. Of more import was whether or not he would send her and Buck on the Motto. She was ready to start packing when he told her he had second thoughts. It was too sudden, there was no time to prepare. Though he didn't say so, she wondered whether he was unable and unwilling to face the loss of his only remaining child so soon after losing Rachel and Stephen. There would be other ships headed to Key West.

Two days later one of the transports carrying reinforcements from New Orleans finally sailed into Tampa Bay. It was such a welcome sight that Lea began to believe Christmas day was not going to be so bad after all. Her worst fear had been that everyone around her would be festive and happy while her family mourned, but as it turned out, so many others were conscious of husbands and friends somewhere out there in the dangerous wilderness that there was a sense of shared trouble among them all.

Though most of the gifts exchanged were for Buck, still Lea managed to finish a crimson sash for Ben she had been working on since their arrival last August. To her surprise he had a gift for her—a set of lace handkerchiefs, made in Spain, and ordered by way of Key West, probably months before. In a kind of off-hand gesture, he also gave her a beautiful flowered silk shawl with a long white fringe that had been intended for his wife. Though grateful, she carefully re-wrapped it in its gray paper and put it at the bottom of her chest. To wear it now would only awaken sad memories for them both.

Ben had also commissioned one of the regimental carpenters to make a perfect toy replica of the Forsythe artillery musket for his son, and the joy with which it was received gave a lift to all their spirits. About noon, when the transport began unloading men and supplies, activity at the fort became almost frenetic. The extra rations meant a decent meal for everyone with even enough left over for the poorest of the settlers and the bedraggled, starving Indians across the river.

The following day Lea began sorting through Rachel's belongings and airing their trunks in preparation for the trip back to New York. It was depressing work and she was glad to drop it when Buck came to her complaining that his head hurt. An icy chill crept down her back as she felt his warm brow and inspected his flushed face.

"Dear God, no," she breathed as she quickly packed him off to bed and went running for Dr. Heiskell. "Not surprising he should come down with the same thing that carried off his mother and brother," the doctor said after a quick inspection of the boy. "You'd best be mindful yourself, Miss Hammond. I've got nearly a third of the garrison in my hospital right now with fevers and complaints."

"What should I do? I don't want to keep him here. I'm half convinced this house is unhealthy."

"Then bring him along to the hospital. I'll make room for him somehow. At least he'll be where we can watch him closely. What's one more patient to my weary orderlies."

"I'll take him there if I can go too and stay with him."

"A military hospital is no place for a woman. Certainly not a respectable woman. I'm sure Captain Carson won't allow it."

"I don't care. I want this child to get well. And I won't have him thinking his family has deserted him."

It took some convincing but finally the doctor agreed that Buck could be moved into a corner of the hospital where Lea could care for him. Lea made sure Ben wasn't aware of it until Buck was safely ensconced on a cot in one of the hospital's two rooms, as far away as possible from the other patients. When Ben finally learned that Buck had come down with the same fever that killed his wife and youngest son, like Lea, his fear for the boy overrode every other concern. Every minute he could get away from seeing new recruits housed in tents and supplies safely stored, was spent by his son's bedside

Buck did not appear to Lea to be as sick as his mother and brother when they first came down with the fever. Still, she stayed by his side, keeping him cool, or warm as the weather required, feeding him doses of calomel, wiping his hot little face, and encouraging him always that she was there. Because he seemed so fearful that she would leave him, she ended up going home only to sleep.

He had been in the hospital three days when one of the men from Major Dade's column came limping into camp. Sitting beside Buck's bed, Lea watched as Private John Thomas was shepherded into the hospital with a badly sprained back which he had injured while helping to ford the canon over the Big Hillsborough River. He was able to reassure the worried people at the fort that when he left the column on Christmas day they were all safe. With some surprise, Lea realized she had almost forgotten about the dangerous march in her concern over Buck's illness.

The next day the boy seemed to improve but the day after that, to grow more ill. That afternoon as she tried to force a little broth down his throat she was startled by a woman's high-pitched scream. Through the open window she could see a confused commotion of people huddled together, talking excitedly and moving as one body toward the long building. The crowd was parted by a group of soldiers running toward the hospital carrying a bundle of bloodied rags that Lea only realized was a man when they swept into the ward in front of her. The crowd jammed up at the entrance to follow but the orderly quickly shut the doors against them. Some hurried to the windows while others pounded angrily on the door to be let in.

The man on the cot yelled and cursed weakly as the doctors and orderlies ran to bend over him. Lea tried to shield Buck from the commotion but when one of the orderlies came rushing into the second ward to retrieve a bundle of lint bandages, she couldn't resist grabbing his arm. "What is it? What's happened?"

"It's one of the soldiers from the column. Private Clarke, I think."

Her skin went cold. "Ransome Clarke? But that didn't look like…"

"Like Clarke? It didn't look like a human being at all. You ought to have seen him crawling on his knees up the road."

"But what does it mean? Surely not…"

"I don't know," he broke in, cutting her off. "No one knows yet. They've sent for Commandant Belton. Maybe he'll be able to tell us."

The crowd outside the hospital was growing more noisy and anxious. By now word had spread that the soldier who had come dragging in gravely wounded was part of Dade's column, and so many of them had relatives in that command that their resentment at being kept in the dark was growing fast. When Captain Belton appeared he tried to calm them with promises to explain everything as soon as he could. He then pushed his way inside the hospital accompanied by several officers. Lea met Ben's eyes briefly as they all disappeared into the other end of the building.

From her place in the second ward she could glimpse the group around Clarke's bed as Dr. Heiskell worked over him. His screams were fearful and frequently interspersed with curses. He must be near out of his mind with the pain, Lea thought. She was relieved when Ben finally left the group and came toward his son's cot. She could tell by his distraught face that something horrific had occurred.

"The column was attacked about twenty-five miles south of Fort King," he muttered quietly, trying not to disturb Buck. "There were hundreds of Indians—Alligator., Jumper, Micanopy, all the important chiefs. Dade never had a chance. According to Clarke he went down in the first fuselage, along with most of the other officers."

"Are there…any others?"

Ben frowned. "Survivors, you mean? We don't know. Frankly, I don't see how this man ever made it back. He has a ball in the arm and the thigh and three in the shoulder which Heiskell thinks almost certain punctured a lung. How he managed to crawl sixty miles back here to Fort Brooke is beyond comprehension.

Still, he's lucky to have his scalp. Evidently the Indians and their Negroes butchered the rest of the men where they fell."

Lea felt her knees give way and she sat gingerly down at the foot of Buck's bed. It was too much. Dashing, handsome Major Dade, Captain Gardiner, Lieutenant Bassinger, all those soldiers—all this death on the heels of her own searing family loss.

"You're not going to swoon on me, Leatrice," Ben snapped. "That's not what's needed now! We've got to be strong."

He was right, of course and she quickly got herself under control. There had been one hundred and six officers and men in that command. If the slaughter was really as bad as Clarke said, there would not be a family at Fort Brooke who was not affected by it. She must keep her head and her courage.

"Maybe Private Clarke exaggerates," Lea said softly. "After all, he might have only seen one part of the battle and may not be aware that others got away as he did. And he's so terribly hurt that perhaps his mind is not clear."

In the sudden silence they realized Ransome Clarke had finally fainted, as though having made it this far he could now give up the care of his tortured body to others. Ben rubbed his chin thoughtfully. "His mind is certainly not clear but we won't know how much of this is delusion and how much fact until other survivors come in. If there are other survivors." Buck stirred fretfully as his father reached down and smoothed his hair. "I've got to get back. You really ought not to be here, Lea. It's no place for a woman, especially an unmarried one."

"Don't be concerned about me, Ben. If what that poor young man says is true, we've all got a lot more to worry about than my reputation."

The following day another soldier from Dade's column came staggering down the sandy road out of the scrub, cradling a shattered arm and confirming Ransome Clarke's story of the massacre in even more lurid detail. It was now clear there would be no more survivors, that every other man who had marched so bravely away from Fort Brooke on the morning of December 23rd had died either in the first terrible ambush, or in the second furious attack, or in the slaughter of the wounded that followed. The shock waves of grief and horror that swept through the fort seemed to Lea to be almost unbearable. Nor was Dade's massacre an isolated event, they soon learned. The week before a concentrated series of raids on the sugar plantations had cut a swath of death and devastation through central Florida. And on the very day of Dade's attack, Asceola and a smaller band attacked Fort King, beheading the Indian agent Willey Thompson and killing three of the men who were with him. A week later a second force of

Seminoles attacked a column of regulars and militia under the command of General Clinch at the Withlacoochee, though neither side could claim a victory. It was now obvious that a full-fledged Indian war had erupted in Florida territory.

To the stunned inhabitants of Fort Brooke, that war was now brought home with a vengeance. Captain Belton, convinced that the Seminoles hordes who attacked Dade's column would make Fort Brooke their next target, began increasing the defenses with a single-minded determination. His first step was to build up and reinforce the small redoubt Captain Frazier had thrown up last fall along the edge of the bay. He then forced all the inhabitants who lived or camped nearby to move inside its walls. The triangular shaped stockade had a long wall facing the bay and two others that met in an apex with blockhouses on each side supported with canon. Inside the walls were several log buildings—a makeshift hospital ward, store room, officer's room, and ammunition house, with every space in between jammed with tents that housed enlisted men, villagers, settlers and their families A long ditch was dug outside the stockade walls and sharp stakes laid down within it.

Belton's last and most drastic order was that all log buildings in the village and the outlying areas be burned to the ground. Lea was afraid that all Rachel's precious items of furniture would go up in flames along with Ben's house until, at the last moment, the Captain decided to spare most of the old officer's quarters that stood outside the palisade walls. But she had to move into the redoubt along with the others, and Buck was still very weak. She was grateful when they were given space in one of the rooms allowed to officer's families instead of having to cram into the tiny, crowded hospital ward.

In early January another schooner sailed out of Tampa Bay bound for New Orleans with fifty women and children on board, the widows and families of the men who had died in Dade's command. Lea was not among them only because her fear of losing Buck was so great that she flatly refused to consider moving him until he was better. To her surprise, Ben agreed. He had no wish now to lose his one remaining child, or the woman whose companionable sympathy had filled some of the emptiness left by Rachel's death. So it was that once again a ship bearing its sad cargo left Tampa Bay without her.

Throughout the rest of January while Buck slowly improved, news of the increasing ferocity of the Seminoles continued to spread through Florida and as far north as Washington City. More ships arrived every day bringing troops and supplies to swell the crowded conditions of the little redoubt. From behind the palisade walls Indians could be seen stalking the outlying scrub, even venturing close enough to steal horses and cattle. Inside, the settlers living in makeshift tents suffered far more than Lea and Buck, who at least shared a room with some of the other officer's families. Food was in very short supply and the short rations only exacerbated the crowded conditions and the overwhelming sense of fear. By mid January enough ships lay at anchor in the bay that some of the settlers were taken to live aboard them, making life in the little redoubt more tolerable. Lea focused her whole attention on keeping Buck quiet and away from the others as much as possible, and to her relief, while he wasn't much better, at least he wasn't much worse.

At President Jackson's order, General Gaines, then in New Orleans, hastily assembled a force of eleven hundred troops and sailed for Tampa Bay, arriving there the first week of February. His first order of business was to confirm the details of the Dade massacre, including a decent burial for the victims, and to this effect he ordered a detachment of troops to prepare to march up the military road to Fort King. Ransome Clarke had recovered enough by now that he begged to go along. And finally, after Ben's insistent pleading, Captain Belton agreed to allow him to accompany the column.

Lea was dismayed to hear of yet another march through the dangerous, Indian-infested wilderness, and one in which this time Ben would take part, even if it was vastly larger and better armed than Dade's had been. She knew how he longed for action of any kind yet there was something disturbing about his enthusiasm for this march. She was due to sail with Buck for Key West on the Motto at the end of February, and it was entirely possible that he would not return to Fort Brooke before she had to leave. To think that she would have to tell him goodbye, perhaps forever, then watch him march out as the Dade column had done, came close to breaking her heart.

The day before the column was set to march Ben was so pensive and withdrawn Lea hoped that perhaps he was feeling some sadness at their imminent separation. More likely he was just too busy. Once Buck was asleep she turned her attention to packing their trunk until Ben, who had barely spoken during their supper meal, called to her from the doorway of the room, asking her to walk along the battlements with him. He spoke without looking at her, his words so serious they filled her with apprehension. She closed the lid to the trunk and reached for her shawl.

Captain Belton had forbidden campfires but the courtyard was crammed with small groups of settlers sitting around as though they had them. The strong moonlight threw deep shadows on the makeshift tents that, along with the people, filled nearly every space inside the palisade walls. Threading their way between the groups, Lea followed Ben up the steps to the platform along the inside palisade, nodding to a soldier standing guard and wondering why he had asked her here. Did she dare hope that he was going to suggest she wait until he got back from the march before leaving with Buck for New York? For a moment she allowed herself a tiny shard of optimism but when he stopped at a shadowed, empty corner and turned to face her, his frown was so dark and forbidding that feeble hope quickly died. She stood, clenching her hands and bracing for the worst.

Ben gave a nervous cough and turned to focus on the distant scrub. "Lea, what I have to say is not going to be easy."

Her thoughts raced, each more dreadful than the last. Worst of all was the possibility that he had decided to keep Buck with him and send her on alone, without even the solace of the child to comfort her. She braced for his words and willed herself against tears. More than anything she did not want him to see her cry.

He spoke so softly she had to bend toward him to hear. "You know I am leaving tomorrow morning for Fort King. General Clinch wants us ready to march at sunup."

"I know."

"I've been thinking quite seriously about...about the future. Buck's future. Your future."

Her head came up in surprise. "Mine?"

"Yes. What I've been thinking, that is, it involves your future as well as the boy's, especially since you are probably the closest relative Buck has."

"Not closer than you. You're his father."

"Yes, but you see, my own life means very little to me at the moment. I'm leaving in the morning on a mission that might very well involve death for some, perhaps all of us. I'm not afraid of it, in fact I would welcome death as a friend right now. Especially a soldier's honorable death. But that's not the point."

He paused, then with a brisk gesture, turned and leaned his back against the wall, folding his arms across his chest. "Then again, perhaps it is. Because, you see, it is Buck's future that really concerns me. If I should be killed, with his mother gone too, you will be the only relative he has to turn to. Now you don't know this—no one does—but I have some money set aside from the sale of my father's property in South Carolina. To this legacy from my father I've also managed to add some savings from my army pay. It's a considerable sum which I had hoped to use to buy land here in Florida once I retire from the army. As you know, I believe there will be advantages in settling this territory, advantages that will draw new people by the wagonload once the Indians are out of the way. I've always had a dream of establishing a plantation like those I grew up around in South Carolina, and I've been trying to accumulate the means to make that dream come true once this war winds down."

"I knew you felt strongly about this country, but not that strongly."

"Well, it doesn't matter anymore. What matters is that I want to make certain this money goes to my son, for his future."

He paused again, frowning. His long face was in shadow, the gaunt cheeks dark against the moonlit planes of his face. She couldn't see his eyes but the emotion in his voice told her how much this conversation was costing him.

"I'll be frank with you, Lea," he went on. "You have been part of my family since Rachel and I were first married and I feel I would rather entrust Buck's future to you than to anyone I know. I have a strong feeling—a premonition, if you like—that I will not survive the fights we are certain to have with the Indians on this march."

"Oh, Ben."

"No, it doesn't matter. My life is not as dear to me as it used to be. I don't care about myself but I do care deeply about my son and his future. My father is dead, I have no other close relatives other than an old aunt to whom I would never entrust the care of any child, much less my own son. So, it occurred to me that one way to 'tidy up my life', to leave everything I have accumulated in the most capable hands I know, is to…"

Again he paused, as if the words were strangling in his throat. "…is if we two should marry. That way," he rushed on, "everything I have would be legally yours—the money, Buck, whatever few possessions we've managed to save against Captain Belton's pine torches. You would be well provided for and I could die knowing that I had left the people closest to me the better for having known me. For having existed."

She stood in stunned silence, staring at him. Nothing, nothing in her life had prepared her for what she was hearing. She wondered if she had even heard it correctly. Wondered at her own stupidity.

"I realize," he went on relentlessly, "That such a marriage would involve a sacrifice for you."

"Sacrifice!"

"Handfasting yourself to a widower. It's too soon, of course. There would be nothing proper about it. But expediency does not always allow us such luxuries. I just feel, deep in my bones, that I won't survive this march, and it would mean so much to me to know that everything had been left in good order."

Finally he ceased speaking and silence fell between them, heavy as sound. He was waiting for an answer but the words tumbled in her brain, refusing to take a sensible form. When she finally spoke her voice sounded strange, as though it belonged to someone else. "You do me a great honor, Ben. I'm very sensible of that. But there are so many questions. Have you thought what might happen if you are not killed? Do you have any feelings for me at all? You might come to regret such an impulsive step."

"I've thought it through very carefully. I've known you for years, Lea, and I have a great…respect and…affection for you. I don't ask you to take Rachel's place, no one can ever do that. But certainly many marriages are built on a foundation of less respect and affection. Still, none of this will probably matter. You will no doubt be a widow almost as quickly as you are a bride. But at least you will be in a secure financial position and free to marry someone more compatible. And Buck will always have a home."

Lea stared out over the parapet into the darkness, struggling to get control of her churning thoughts. The black scrub gave way to the sweeping velvet of the bay, sequined by the silvery moonlight. Far off in the pine scrub the low, mournful howl of a wolf broke the silence that lay so heavy between them. These were certainly not the words she had hoped one day to hear from a suitor, and certainly not words she had ever expected to hear from Ben. If she accepted him and he did return from the war it would mean that she might never know a real love. She might never have a husband who would love her for herself alone. Might she not come to regret this 'impulsive step' as much as he?

"I don't know what to say."

"Is there someone else? Am I unattractive to you?"

"Of course not. It's just…"

She could not go on. The thought of becoming Ben's wife ought to be the happiest moment of her life. How long had she loved him, forcing herself to think of him as a brother when he fell in love with her sister? Yet under these circumstances she wondered if she should even consider this marriage. All she represented to him was the knowledge that his property and his child would be secure in her hands.

Something of her distress got through to him and he spoke more warmly, more softly: "I would be honored if you would marry me, Lea, even under such unusual circumstances. It would give me great happiness as well as peace of mind. And, if you will accept me, I pledge to you my unfailing loyalty, support and…affection for as long as my life runs its course."

This was the first time he had asked anything of her, and what a request! Yet, to be Ben's wife! To know she belonged to him and he to her. To know that someday he would return to her home and her bed. Surely then there would be time to make of their relationship something new and fine, all that she hoped it would become. Time to ease Rachel's memory and his great grief over her death. If she refused him there would be nothing.

Down below in the courtyard one of the settlers began singing the soft refrain of an old revival hymn, '*I'm just a poor, wayfaring stranger, a-travelin' through this world of woe…*'. Quietly a few other voices joined in the tune, sweetly harmonizing against the percussive chatter of the tree frogs from the oak groove. '*And there's no sickness, toil or danger, in that fair land to which I go*'…

"All right, Ben, I'll marry you. On one condition."

"And that is…?"

"That you allow me to stay here at Fort Brooke with Buck." She hurried on before he could speak. "There's nothing for me back in New York and I've come to like the…the excitement and promise of this wild place. Then too, I believe in family. If I leave now how could we ever begin to forge a family from such a hasty marriage. If I stay, at least we'll have a chance."

Her voice trailed away and in the ensuing silence the singing down below grew louder as more of the people sitting around the courtyard joined in: '*I'm going there to see my Saviour, I'm going there no more to roam…*'.

Lea could almost hear the thoughts turning over in his mind. What did he want with another family after losing his beloved Rachel and Stephen. All he really wanted was to feel that Buck was secure. Yet as much as she loved Ben, she knew in her soul that this was the only way she'd agree to marry him.

"Lea," he finally spoke, "consider the danger. The sickness. Look what this place did to Rachel and little Stephen. How could I live with myself if this wilderness killed you too."

"I'm healthier than Rachel ever was. And I don't mind the danger. It's the only way, Ben."

'*I'm just a-going over Jordan, I'm just a-going over home…*'

She waited with her heart in her throat as he stayed silent, staring out over the courtyard to watch Captain Belton emerge from the storehouse and warn the singers to lower their voices. At length he sighed and reached out to take her hand. "All right, I agree. Thank you, Lea."

Just as quickly he pulled away and they stood like two self-conscious strangers, neither making a move toward the other. "I thought the ceremony might take place in the morning before the column moves out. Will that be all right?"

"I suppose so." Her thoughts raced. There would be no fuss, but he didn't want it. Rachel's veil was packed away in gray paper in the press, but no, that would raise too many memories. This was a purely legal ceremony, one that called for no ornaments.

"I'll go along then and speak to Captain Belton."

He turned stiffly and started for the stairs. On an impulse he turned back, lifted her hand and brushed it with his lips. Lea, standing in confusion, watched him leave, then raised the hand he had kissed and laid it against her cheek.

Ben and Lea were married by Commandant Belton the next morning just as the gray night was beginning to be streaked by dawn. Standing next to Buck's bed, Lea wore her best gown, a cream-colored satin, and the Spanish shawl Ben gave her for Christmas, hastily drawn from its place in the press. In her hair she pinned a white Moon Flower from a wild vine just outside the fort.

The ceremony was witnessed by the Lattimores who, though not strictly approving of such a hasty marriage, were too full of the sadness of their impending separation to much care. Though Ben had Rachel's wedding ring put away he had no desire to use it for her sister, and had managed to pick up a plain gold band among what was left of the stocks of the sutler's store. He placed it on Lea's finger, forcing himself not to remember the youthful joy with which he had once before made this same gesture. When the brief ceremony was over he took his new wife in his arms, giving her a quick hug and a perfunctory kiss on the cheek. Lea's arms went around his neck and she gave him a lingering kiss on the mouth, surprising in its sweetness and softness. Reluctantly he broke away then turned to give Buck, who was sitting up in his bed yawning, a long embrace. Reaching for his hat and gloves, he was out the door and down the steps where his orderly was holding the reins of his horse.

She followed him out of the quarters and watched as he mounted. Most of the soldiers in the huge column had already moved out to the parade ground beyond the gates. Those who were still inside the palisade quickly formed up behind Ben. He gave her a thin smile before turning his mount and falling in with his command, his mind already on the business of the army. After a brief prayer, the Chaplain began intoning the eighty-ninth psalm in ringing tones as the column began moving out: *"My hand will hold him fast and my arm will make him strong"*. Julia Lattimore, after giving her a half-hearted embrace, followed her husband, walking beside his mount through the palisade gates. With a heart growing ever heavier Lea struggled to make sense of the confusion—the incessant beat of the drum, the rattle of iron and leather, the thunder of hoof and boot, and above them all, the Chaplain's voice growing dimmer: *"I will crush his foes before him and strike down those who hate him."* She waved to Ben as he rode across the bridge over the ditch. She turned the shiny new band on her finger. The Chaplain's voice was almost lost now but she knew the words. *"My faithfulness and love shall be with him and he shall be victorious in my Name."*

She watched until Ben was completely lost in the crowd of soldiers on the parade ground. Lea had decided earlier that she would not follow Ben outside the pallisade walls though everything in her wanted to. But she knew that would not be wise. Her feelings were too confused and she was certain his were as well. Besides, she had watched Major Dade's column march off on a morning like this one and she had an almost superstitious dread of seeing Ben leave the same way.

He was her husband now, not her brother-in-law. Inside her room, well hidden in the clothes trunk, was a locked box with a fortune of over six hundred dollars in various Spanish and American coins, mostly old ten-dollar Eagles. She was Buck's mother now, in name as well as in fact.

Yet was Ben really her husband? This ceremony had been timed so that there was no possibility of consummating the marriage. It might never be consummated. She was a virgin bride—would she also be a virgin widow? Had she done the right thing to agree to such a bizarre relationship?

Yet, Ben's wife! As she walked back inside her little room the reality of it made her heart sing with happiness. He might come back. And if he did, he would forget Rachel and want her for his true wife.

She pulled the flower from her hair and folded the Spanish shawl back inside the press. Let the future take care of itself.

CHAPTER 7

▼

Her wedding day! All the more astounding because Lea had long ago stopped thinking about marriage. When it did cross her mind she assumed she would have the traditional celebration with a beautiful dress, a feast, and friends and family rejoicing with her. Best of all there would be someone at her side holding her hand, smiling down at her with the light of love in his eyes. Once she had briefly imagined that someone might be Ben Carson but that dream faded when he met Rachel.

Now that dream was reality, without any of the love, light or rejoicing. Now she must force that image of an imaginary wedding from her mind. She watched the palisade walls close on Ben's column, shutting out the wilderness and enclosing her inside a tiny, safe cocoon alongside people who more than ever seemed like strangers. Fleeing to her small room, she carefully removed her gown and folded it away with the Spanish shawl, tied her hair beneath a large towel, drew on the oldest, most utilitarian dress she owned then followed it with a large apron and went to work. For the rest of the morning and into the afternoon, when she wasn't caring for Buck she swept, scrubbed, scoured, polished and rubbed down every surface in the crowded officer's quarters. Soap, carbolic acid, and oil each had their turn on the wooden surfaces of floors, walls and furniture.

By late afternoon Lea's back screamed in protest when she rose from her knees to look around the room. There was nothing that hadn't been done at least once. Her legs groaned, her hands were red and swollen from the harsh soap, and every muscle in her body ached. She was tired, tired to her bones, but wasn't that what she wanted? Well, it had worked. She had managed to keep her mind as busy as her hands. Perhaps now she should rest.

Sinking into the nearest chair, she pulled off her kerchief and shook out her hair. It was time to go search out something from the quartermaster for their supper.

A short time later she returned with two bowls of thin stew scrounged from the communal pot. Lea gave Buck his supper then stood in the doorway wondering what to do with herself. She didn't want to be around people tonight any more than she had during the day. She imagined them whispering behind their hands, pitying the newly married woman who would spend her wedding night alone. She couldn't face that.

Yet in this crowded redoubt, with its cowering inhabitants clinging together against an hostile outside world, what could she do? Where could she go to be alone?

Swinging a shawl around her shoulders, she walked out into the busy yard, keeping to the darkening shadows as she made her way to the palisade gates, still open to accommodate the new rows of tents set up outside for the latest troop reinforcements. She slipped through the gates, crossed the bridge over the abatis, and made her way around the pine log walls to the back of the fort where she could sit on the sand and look out over the bay. The chilly evening kept most of the soldiers and residents inside the stockade, allowing her a solitary spot on the low dunes. Lea wrapped her shawl around her head and turned her face to the wind, letting it blow away her weariness and anxiety as she watched the colors across the broad expanse of sky meld from rose-tinged blue to soft slate gray. The last of the terns hopped about on the sand before her, while gulls swooped and screamed until the light was nearly gone. At length the blowing sand and chill wind forced her to scrunch down against the raw pine wall, willing her tired body to relax and, for the first time that day, allowing her thoughts to drift freely.

Of course he had to leave. Of course he had married her only to keep his home intact. She knew the facts, she had faced them from the beginning. But oh, how she wished he were here with her. She longed with a physical ache to feel his arms around her, his lips on her throat, to hear him breathe how together they would make this the most wonderful of nights.

Ridiculous! Foolish! They were not going to have that kind of marriage. Ben had never intended it. He had loved Rachel so deeply and for so long that he could never turn to her sister so soon after her death. She even admired him for that loyalty and devotion.

No, her only hope was time, time for Rachel's memory to slip away as surely it must. She too still mourned her sister, yet the truth could not be denied. Rachel was dead, while she, Lea, was here, vibrant, healthy and alive. In time Ben would relinquish his hold on the past and turn to her. She had only to be patient. They had years ahead to work out their future, to build a new home, perhaps even to have their own children together. Patience!

The slow rhythm of the waves increased. The wind picked up, forcing Lea to draw her shawl tighter. On the bay she could hear mullet slapping the surface of the water like scattered applause. One of the last of the gulls, hoping for a hand-out, swooped down on the sand a few feet away, tilting its head at her. When Lea opened her empty palm it squawked and flew off, seeking its roost.

It was time for her to go back inside the crowded fort. No use catching cold now when Buck needed her more than ever. How she wished she could return to Ben's house and sleep in Ben's bed for the first time. She would stretch out her arm over the cool, empty sheets and pretend he was lying there beside her.

Tears stung her eyes, tears as bitter and stinging as the salt spray off the water. She forced them back. While the soldiers and residents of Fort Brooke lived in this terrible fear of an imminent Indian attack there was nothing to do but make the best of conditions inside the redoubt. Soon perhaps, maybe even before Ben returned, she and Buck would be able to move back to Ben's cottage and she could begin to make it a home for the three of them. Time was on her side. She had only to be patient.

It was growing dark and a slim, buttery sliver of moon began to appear against the blackness of the eastern sky. Above her, on the palisade platform, she could hear the guards calling to one another. Soon the gates would be closed. She stood to shake the sand from her skirts then made her way back inside the safety of the fort.

There was a faint odor of something unpleasant on the wind—the first indication they were nearing the site of the massacre. The stench increased as they advanced, an appalling miasma of rotting flesh that lay like a suffocating pall over the woods and grasses. Ben pulled his mount up, covered his nose with his gloved hand and turned to look back at the column. All told, it was made up of eleven hundred men, comprised mostly of the troops who had arrived with General Gaines from New Orleans, augmented by volunteer units and regulars from Fort Brooke, plus over seventy Creek Indians to act as scouts and hunters. The companies stretched behind him, four abreast, like some giant insect weaving its way along the white, sandy trail.

Ransome Clarke had insisted on coming along, though he was not yet fully recovered. Ben wondered whether he was driven by some necessity to prove that the horror of his experience on December 28th had really happened. Would he himself have returned, he wondered? Perhaps so, for even now he was drawn toward the site of the massacre by some terrible fascination that even the rotten smell borne on the wind could not discourage.

As the mounted advance neared the infamous pine barren an officer in the van reined in his mount and lifted his hand, bringing the column to a halt. Ben peered around him, confused by the scene ahead. The full length of the road as well as a breastwork of logs close by were totally black, an undulating, living pall laid over everything. When one of the men in the advance gave a shout the pall came alive with a whirling rush of wings.

"Gracious God, what a sight!" Ben heard the officer behind him gasp. "Vultures! Buzzards! Hundreds of them!"

The men behind him took up the cry as the disturbed birds rose in clouds, some to settle in the trees, others hovering over the column. Ben felt the hairs on the back of his neck come alive as he fought to hold his restive horse. Several minutes elapsed until the horses and the men were calm enough to take up their march again. With order restored the column moved cautiously ahead. A little farther along they began to see indications of what they were going to find—discarded shoes, pieces of clothing, and, finally, two bodies, partially stripped, lying in the marsh grass.

Ben thought he knew what to expect from having heard reports of the massacre from Privates Clarke and Sprague. He recognized the pine woods, the trees cut by cannon ball and grapeshot, the high grass savanna framing the pond, the tiny, hastily thrown up log breastwork. Yet nothing had prepared him for the actual horror of decaying corpses and scorched earth. Stunned, he sat on his horse staring down at the tangle of bodies slumped against the breastwork walls. Then he realized General Gaines had ridden up and was speaking to him.

Look alive there, Captain. We'll need some help identifying these men before we can give them a decent burial. Do you recognize any?"

"Yes, sir. I do."

"Very good. You and Belton and McCall pick a detail and separate the officers from the regulars. I want a guard posted around the entire site, two mass graves dug and a fitting service held so we can get out of here and on to Fort King."

"Yes, sir." Ben wheeled his horse out of the line. Up ahead Captain Belton had dismounted and was kneeling beside a soldier's body. With a lurch of his stomach Ben recognized the dark hair and beard of Major Francis Dade. *"No time for that now,"* he thought and forced himself to get to work.

And what work it was! Major Dade and Captain Frazer lay with the advance guard along the trail where they died in the first terrible fuselage, a good two hundred yards ahead of the main body. Behind them the bodies of men killed in the first fire lay scattered in the road where they had fallen. Inside the hastily assembled redoubt of long pine logs piled three feet high and arranged in a tight triangle shape, lay the bodies of the officers and men killed in the second onslaught, many of them resting on the upper log where they had died. The decaying shapes of the oxen that had dragged the canon lay still harnessed to the caisson. The caisson itself, stripped of its cannon, lay burned and black outside the redoubt. Beyond it long rows of pine trees stood shattered by musket balls, evidence of the soldiers shooting at Indians hiding behind them. So many dead, so much death! Even the stillness of the forest around them had an unnatural solemnity as the silent column broke apart to explore the carnage.

Many of the men were still lying in the grotesque positions where they fell. Some were little more than skeletons while the sky blue of their military trousers had scarcely faded. Others, though the flesh had shrunk, still retained their skin, smooth, dried and hard as parchment. Hair and beards helped to identify many, including Major Dade himself. Dade clearly had a bullet through the side while many of the men in the breastwork were shot in the forehead or neck where they fired from behind the logs. Some throats were cut and a few skulls bashed, evidence of the work of the Negroes belonging to the Seminoles who had been let loose to plunder and wreak vengeance after the battle. Most of the bodies had been stripped of shoes, coats, and shirts but left with other valuables. A few men had fallen back inside the breastwork and Gardiner himself lay near the center where he had probably directed the fight. Ben recognized the body of Lieutenant Keais still propped against a pine log, his broken arms tied in a sling to his chest, his head slumped forward. He appeared to be asleep.

After identifying the men, as many valuables as could be found were gathered to return to relatives—Lieutenant Bassinger's red money belt and handkerchief, Captain Fraser's breastpin with a painted miniature of himself, Lieutenant Mudge's cap and ring. Watches, pins, brooches, rings and silver buttons were gathered along with nearly three hundred dollars of paper and gold and silver coins that lay scattered the length of the site. The bodies were then placed in their graves and decently covered. The six-pound cannon was retrieved from the pond where the Indians had thrown it, and placed muzzle-down on the officers' grave. A Scottish dirge was played by the band of the 4th Regiment, followed by "The Death March" while the troops formed in columns of companies to march at a slow pace around the entire ground with arms reversed.

All in all, Ben considered it was a fitting tribute to a gallant sacrifice. But, like everyone there, he was never so glad to leave a place in his life.

By the first of March there were over one hundred and fifty soldiers—regular army as well as Alabama and Louisiana volunteers—posted at Fort Brooke, with more arriving on ships in the Bay every day. Across the river nearly three hundred Florida volunteers lived in tents when they weren't drilling and marching. In the Army's wake came the usual civilian hangers-on, 'whiskey gentry', gamblers, ladies of dubious virtue, even a few entrepreneurs anxious to make a quick dollar off the soldiers. The fort was now so well defended that the threat of an Indian attack seemed less and less likely and the civilians who had been packed into the small redoubt were allowed to spill out once more into the surrounding grounds. Many of the outlying buildings of the fort and the village which Captain Belton had burned to the ground began to be rebuilt. And Lea and Buck went home to Ben's cottage.

It was her house now too. She felt a twinge of panic as she moved her things into Ben's bedroom, forcing herself to do it even though she felt like an intruder. They were married, even if he had ridden away right after the ceremony, and something must reflect the reality of her wedding. She took a moment to look around the cottage then got to work. Walls had to be whitewashed, surfaces scoured, scrubbed, and wiped down, perhaps even a garden started out back. Thank the Lord, there was much to keep her busy.

During her first week back in the officer's quarters Lea was so occupied with her house that she managed to avoid the people of Fort Brooke. The increasingly hectic life of the fort—new troops constantly arriving, more settlers seeking refuge dragging in every day— all went on as usual while she stayed withdrawn in her cottage. She refused to bring Nora back to help, while visitors who came to call got a short, polite and chilly welcome. She turned down all invitations from friends and avoided any social gatherings. The pall of bereavement left by the recent disasters near Fort King and the Withlacoochee still lingered over the cantonment, and the deaths in her own family gave her a good excuse to stay home and mourn.

But that was not the true reason and she knew it. She sensed underneath the pleasantness of the women in the camp a disturbing uneasiness about her position. She was Mrs. Captain Carson now, yet somehow that other Mrs. Carson was too fresh in people's memories to make the transition. It was hard to dispel her old status as the 'wife's sister', not to mention the 'maiden Aunt'. They did not quite know who she was, and neither did she. As the days dragged on it was easier to work in her house and yard and avoid people altogether.

She knew embarrassment was a large part of her reluctance to face people. How they must pity her—a wife whose husband had ridden off immediately after the ceremony, leaving her to face the fort on her own. It did no good to tell herself that both she and Ben had accepted this arrangement when they agreed to marry. She still felt like an abandoned wife.

The only friend she welcomed with some sincerity was Julia Lattimore. But even though Julia pleaded with her to give up her self-enforced exile, she would not give in.

"So many of the families have gone back north that there are only a few respectable women here now and you're one of them," Julia argued. "We need you. We're planning a little frolic for the officers as soon as a soldier who can play the fiddle arrives. Just a simple thing with a few country dances. Won't you help us? It would do you good."

"I just can't, Julia. Not yet. Give me a little time."

"But Lea, you need to get out. You can't keep yourself cooped up inside this house until Ben comes back. It's not right. Nor is it healthy. When I think of how lighthearted you used to be..."

"I will be again someday. Give me a little time."

Julia threw up her hands in exasperation. "Time! You are determined to hide between these four walls until Ben comes back, Lea, and who knows how long that will be? If this is the result of your marriage I'm almost sorry I had a part in it."

At the sharp, poignant shadow that fluttered over Lea's face Julia's irritation was overcome by remorse. She reached out and took Lea's hands. "I didn't mean that. Truly I'm happy for you, my dear friend, and I know that once Ben returns you are going to be happy too. I just hate seeing this great change in you since your wedding."

"I'll be all right in time. That's what I hold on to."

A few days after this conversation Buck came running into the house calling for Lea. His face was flushed and his eyes bright and big with news. "Indians, Aunt Lea! Miles and miles of them. A whole camp full. You've got to come see."

He grabbed her hands away from her mending to tug her out of the rocker. For an instant Lea felt a surge of panic. "Not an attack…?"

"No. They're just sitting on the ground, all over the village and down by the river. Just sitting there. Come see, please Aunt Lea. I can go if you go with me."

"We shouldn't go outside the fort grounds, Buck. And you must not even think of going out there alone." She tried to remember. Hadn't she heard even before they moved from the redoubt that the friendly Indians who would be repatriated to the west would leave from Fort Brooke? Maybe they were starting to come into the village.

"That's why you have to go with me. Please come, Aunt Lea. I want to see them."

Had the Seminoles finally agreed to deportation, Lea wondered, her panic giving way to hopeful pleasure. That would explain such a large gathering. And that would mean the war might soon be over!

"Wait a moment, Buck. Let me think. I suppose we could try to go out but there's a good chance the pickets won't allow us to. You'd better be prepared for that. Are the Seminoles so close to the fort?"

"They're almost in it. They're everywhere. It must be all the Indians in Florida!"

"I doubt that. All right. Give me a moment to get my bonnet and parasol."

There was dust on her bonnet, it hadn't been used in so many days. She tied the ribbons under her chin, surprised at her willingness to be drawn out after so long a time. Yet she must know why all these Indians had come to Fort Brooke. If it meant the war might be ending it would be worth facing her neighbors.

Lea had to hold tightly to Buck's hand as they made their way past the redoubt, then northward toward Saunder's trading post. She recognized the Private standing picket as one of the soldiers who sometimes served as Ben's orderly.

"Mornin', Miss Hammond," the young man said, touching his tall leather cap. Lea did not correct him. If he knew of her marriage he had probably forgotten it by now.

"Buck tells me we have an influx of Seminoles, Private. Why have they come? There's no danger of an attack is there?"

"Oh, no, ma'am. Them savages have come in to be carried off to Arkansas territory and they were probably chased here by their own people who don't want them to leave. I never saw so many of 'em in one place afore in my life and never hope to again. A sorry lot, that's what they are."

From where they stood Lea was able to see clearly into the village. She was astounded at the number of Indians squatting in the village's main street. They stretched back surely beyond Augustus Steel's house, with more spilling down on each side toward the woods and the river and out into the pine barrens beyond the few scattered log buildings that had been rebuilt since Captain Belton's fire.

Private Larson leaned on the long barrel of his musket. "We're goin' to move 'em back later this afternoon, toward the woods where they won't be so close. Makes the whites uneasy to have 'em so near. And they don't smell so good neither. Don't you worry about it none, Miss Hammond. They'll all be gone soon enough, and they don't dare bother us long as they wants to sail."

Buck tugged at her hand. "Come on, Aunt Lea. Let's go see them up close."

"I...I don't know, Buck. Perhaps we shouldn't."

"Good afternoon, Mrs. Carson."

At the cultured voice behind her, Lea turned to see Lieutenant Stowe, one of the officers she vaguely recalled meeting at Dr. Haskell's house. Stowe was from Alabama and had all the cultural graces of a Southern gentleman. All the prejudices, too, she recalled, which was why she hadn't bothered to get to know him better. Now he gave her a graceful bow. "I'm pleased to see you abroad, Mrs. Carson. We heard of your indisposition and we missed you."

So that was the story, no doubt given out by Julia. She decided to go along. "Yes, I'm feeling much better, thank you. I'm curious about this sudden influx of Seminoles. Can you explain it?"

"It appears that some of the more enlightened among the savages have finally bowed to the inevitable. Over a hundred have already arrived and more come trickling in every day. They will be shipped out as soon as we can arrange transport. In the meantime, there is nothing we can do but let them camp on our doorstep. Its an inconvenience, but a temporary one. They shouldn't bother us."

"And is this all of them?"

"In Florida? Oh, by no means. How we wish it were."

"Aunt Lea, come on," Buck cried, tugging her toward the village. Lea turned to the Lieutenant. "Can we walk among them?"

"Do you really want a closer look? They're none too presentable, you know. But if you wish it, then I'll escort you."

"Thank you, Lieutenant Stowe. I appreciate it, and Buck appreciates it even more."

The Lieutenant reached out to grab Buck by the collar and pull him back. "You stay right beside your Aunt, young man. That's an order."

Buck obediently fell in beside Lea as they started up the village street. The last time she had been here Lea remembered that most of the buildings had been closed and boarded up before they were burnt on Captain Belton's orders. Now, not only had they been rebuilt but more had been added, most of them open for business. Either their owners were not as worried about an attack as before, or couldn't pass up the opportunity to serve the influx of soldiers arriving at the fort. The village looked just as seedy as she remembered, and the noise and rowdiness, if anything, had increased. There were one or two new taverns with gamblers in stripped waistcoats and hard-looking women lounging around the doorsteps.

But the biggest change was all these Indians. Though a space had been designated for them behind the main street, they had spilled over into every accessible spot where a camp could be set up. Most of them just sat among their bundles, the children hovering close to women, their scrawny dogs digging at the sand beside them. As Lieutenant Stowe pushed his way through them, thrusting any obstruction out of his way, Lea followed, tightly grasping Buck's hand and growing more disturbed by the minute. She could not believe such abject poverty. It was beyond anything she had ever seen and the deeper they went into the crowds of native people, the worse it grew.

They had obviously come here with just what they could carry, a few jars, woven baskets, and blankets tightly bundled. Scattered among them were a few scrawny cows and an occasional chicken, none of which seemed to have any more energy than their owners. There were a few mature men but no younger ones, and only a few young boys. Women, children, and old men with lined faces and blank eyes made up most of group. The children did not run about as most children would but sat near their families, lethargic and brooding. Their eyes appeared sunken and their stomachs were distended and swollen, so out of size with their small bodies and thin limbs as to appear almost deformed. As Lea neared the river one of the old men came hobbling up to Lieutenant Stowe, speaking in his guttural language and gesturing with his arm. The Lieutenant asked him a question in Mikisuki then turned to Lea.

"Would you excuse me for just a moment, Mrs. Carson? There seems to be a dispute here about who owns that brown and white cow. Frankly, its so skinny I don't know why anyone would want to claim it, but I'd better see if I can solve the problem."

"Of course. We'll just wait here for you. You won't be out of sight, will you?"

"No, no. Now don't wander off."

"No fear of that, Lieutenant. I'll watch you the whole time."

Yet the Lieutenant had barely left her before Lea's eye was caught by a child lying in its mother's lap ten feet in the opposite direction. Holding tightly to Buck, she ventured over to peer down at the child. He was obviously very ill.

Open sores near his eyes oozed a milky fluid that attracted the flies that half-covered his face. Lea bent closer.

"What is wrong with your baby?" she said to the woman who stared back at her with uncomprehending, black eyes. "Sick? Sick?" Lea added, making what she hoped was a gesture of illness. When all she got in return was a blank stare she began to turn away. Then the woman lifted her arm to her lips, opening her mouth and shaking her head. As comprehension dawned, Lea looked closer at the child.

"Food?" she asked. The women shook her head. "You mean you have no food?"

This time the woman nodded. Lea looked around at the crowd of Indians sitting and staring up at her with fixed gazes. For the first time she saw in close detail things she had missed before. The jars scattered around held very little beside parched corn. There were no fires. No carcasses of animals. No stacks of coontie roots or baskets of peas. She stepped to some of the other women close by. "Food?" she repeated. Most shook their heads. A few picked up their half-empty baskets to hold up to her.

It dawned on her then that these children were not deformed by disease, they were starving. She stood consumed with dismay as Lieutenant Stowe came striding back.

"Well, that's settled for the moment. Not that I could do much but refer them to the Colonel, if they don't take a hatchet to each other in the meantime."

"Lieutenant Stowe, there's a child over there who is seriously ill. Has Doctor Heiskell seen him?"

"Doctor Heiskell? I doubt it. He's kept busy enough with sick soldiers. He certainly has no time or inclination for Indians. Besides, they have their own remedies."

"But Lieutenant, this child is hungry. And so are all these others. There are signs here of starvation. Can't we do something? Shouldn't we do something?"

"Why it's not our place..."

Lea swung around to face him. "Not our place! Who brought these people here? Who decided that they should leave their homes to be shipped to the Arkansas territory? They didn't ask for this."

Stowe stepped back, frowning. "These people came here willingly."

"At the insistence of the United States government. Don't we have a responsibility for them since we are forcing them to leave? I know supplies at the fort are limited but surely we can at least spare something for the children."

Stowe's handsome face darkened. "Really, Mrs. Carson. It is not my place to make such a suggestion. Nor yours either, I respectfully point out. They're only savages."

Lea caught back the stinging reply she longed to hurl at this unfeeling officer. Instead she said coolly, "A hungry child suffers the same, Lieutenant, no matter what his race."

Stowe frowned in annoyance at being put on the spot like this but Lea gave him no time for rebuttal. Starting back along the path she asked, "Who would decide whether or not we might share our food with these people?"

"I suppose the Post sutler. Though he couldn't do anything without the approval of General Scott."

"But General Scott is at Fort Drane, is he not?"

"Yes, ma'am. Right now Major Sands stands as commandant of Fort Brooke until the General returns. However, the Major is not one to be sympathetic towards Indians. Especially not since..."

"I know. The deaths of Major Dade and his men have made us all a little hardhearted."

"I'm relieved you understand that, ma'am."

Lea forced herself to make polite conversation with the Lieutenant until they were back inside the fort and she could thank him for escorting them outside. He had made Buck very happy, she assured him, and had given her much to think about. The Lieutenant smiled and bowed over her hand, relieved she had abandoned the question of feeding the Indians. He was already at his desk trying to decide whether or not to approve a request from one of his Private's to marry a local girl when Lea went hurrying into Julia Lattimore's front room.

"Julia, whatever you're doing, drop it and come with me."

Julia stared with amazement at the animation on Lea's face, a face she had grown used to seeing brooding and lethargic. "What on earth...?"

"Don't ask questions," Lea said, grabbing her hand and pulling her up. "Just come with me. We're going to call on the Post sutler." Lea grabbed Julia's bonnet from a peg behind the door and shoved it on her head.

"James Lynch? But why?"

"Nevermind why. Just come."

Though the walk to the sutler's store was a short one, Lea was too obsessed with her purpose to explain what she had in mind to her friend. When they finally stood before the sutler, Julia was as taken aback as James Lynch when Lea blurted out her demands.

"Those people are starving. I know that a supply ship arrived last week and we have enough rations set aside that we could afford to distribute some of them to these Seminoles before they embark. All I need is for you to approve the order."

Lynch stared at Lea, trying to remember whose wife she was. Oh yes, Captain Carson's sister-in-law, now his wife. He had only recently arrived but already he had heard about this peculiar marriage, so indecently soon after the death of the first Mrs.Carson. "Madam, what makes you think the army can spare food intended for its troops to feed these hostiles? There are ten times as many men here now as there were two months ago. They must be our first concern."

"Are there not more supplies, too? Surely we can afford to spare some for hungry children, Mister Lynch. As Christians we can afford to do nothing less. If we don't, some of them might not live to take those ships to Arkansas territory."

Lynch's face darkened at this pushy woman's implied criticism. "You are mistaken in thinking we have extra supplies. Indeed, look around you at these empty shelves. Until new stocks arrive from New Orleans what we have is very sparse and is needed for our troops. In any case, I am not the one to allow this authorization, Mrs. Carson. You would have to get that from General Scott."

Lea stepped back, her lips pursed. How like the army! "And General Scott is off in the bush looking for Alligator and Jumper. Very well, what about Major Sands? I understand he is the Commanding Officer at the moment. Cannot he order you to authorize a food distribution?"

"I suppose he could. But you won't find much sympathy there. He had close friends among Major Dade's column."

"I know. Come along, Julia. We're going to see Major Sands."

Gripping Julia's hand, Lea pulled her across the porch and down the path. Though Julia longed to argue her friend out of this foolish business, she was too happy to see something of the old Lea to even try. Besides, perhaps Lea was right. If the need was so great, why shouldn't they share.

Major Richard M. Sands was not motivated by any similar sympathy. "Let them starve!" he snapped when the two women stood before him.

"That's a shameful remark, Major," Lea exploded while Julia cringed behind her. "Unworthy of an officer and a Christian."

"And I suppose that fearful slaughter near Fort King was Christian! You saw Ransome Clarke. You heard his story. How can you even think of giving part of the little food we have, which incidentally is earmarked for our fighting men, to those murderous heathens? The sooner they're all gone from this territory, the better."

Lea laid her hands on the Major's table and leaned into his face. "For heaven's sake, Major Sands, we're talking about women and children and old men. The warriors who led the Dade massacre aren't out there. They're in the bush fighting General Gaines and my...my husband. These people are innocent victims."

"The wives and children of murderers."

"Children, Major. They didn't ask to be born Seminole. We can't just stand by and let them die of hunger. I appeal to your sense of charity, of justice."

Back and forth they went while Julia watched, half appalled, half amused at Lea's stubborn resistance. She would not give in, and her determination eventually overcame the Major's opposition. Though Lea did not know it, Major Sands had been entreated before to send food out to the Indians, not just by some of the women but by some of the soldiers as well. This implacable woman was simply the last straw.

"Very well, Mrs. Carson. I will make this concession in the light of the faith we are called to, though it goes against my every instinct. I will give up a little corn and rice for each family unit. But you women will have to work out the distribution. I won't assign a single soldier to help you."

Lea frowned as she remembered the sea of people squatting on the ground outside the village, all the way to the river. "What about the men who are off duty and willing to help?"

The Colonel hesitated. "That's their own concern."

He drew a paper from a drawer and began writing on it. "And I won't have any amount of stores removed that would threaten the military personnel or the settlers in this fort." The scowl on his face was black as thunder as he handed her the paper. Yet as the women hurried to the door he called after them, "Try to get the Indians to boil the corn, not parch it. That way it'll go farther."

Lea could not hold back a radiant smile as she walked out of the building with the paper in her hand and Julia in tow. "I never knew it would be so difficult."

"Lea, are you sure you want to face this? It's going to be awfully hard. So many people..."

"I'm sure. If you could have seen them, Julia. The suffering, and the hopelessness in their eyes. But you're right. We're going to need a lot of help. We'll start with the officer's wives, those who are still here—you know them better so you can round up the ones who are willing. Then the enlisted men's wives, I'm sure some of them would pitch in. Nora can help with that. And perhaps I can get Lieutenant Stowe to identify the soldiers who are off duty and would be willing to assist us." She stopped in the middle of the path, turning to her friend. "Here.

First thing, you take this order to the sutler so he can get the process moving, then start on the officer's wives. I'll join you in a few minutes."

"Where are you going now?"

Lea had already started across the parade ground but she called back over her shoulder, "To see Doctor Heiskell about a sick child."

In spite of anything the doctor could do, the sick Indian child died during the early hours of the next morning while Lea was sound asleep in Ben's bed. It was the first deep and restful sleep she had enjoyed since the day of her wedding.

CHAPTER 8

▼

Nearly four weeks later, early on a drizzling morning in late March, Lea stepped onto the veranda of Mr. Saunder's store and found her attention drawn to a commotion at the nearby pier. A government tender from a newly arrived cutter moored out in the bay had been dragged up on the sand and surrounded by several soldiers who were helping out its occupants. As the soldiers herded the new arrivals into a line, Lea stepped closer and saw that the group was made up of women and children, accompanied by a few men in civilian clothes. One of the men looked familiar.

Just beyond the porch steps she spotted Private Randy Cates leaning on his rifle and watching the activity on the pier. "Mornin', Miz Carson," he said, pulling on the brim of his tall leather cap as Lea made her way to stand beside him. "That's a group of Spaniards that escaped from Charlotte Harbor just ahead of a war-party," he said when Lea looked a question at him. "They was lucky to get out alive. We got a troop of Louisiana volunteers all set to march down there tomorrow to give the white folks some protection."

The familiar man was rudely shoved ahead of the soldiers. "It doesn't look as though they're getting much of a welcome," Lea commented dryly. Where had she seen that fellow before?

"That there's the Spaniard they believe's been selling arms to the Indians," Cates replied. "He'll probably be looking at time in the guardhouse unless he can clear his name."

Pushing the man ahead of him, the soldiers marched toward Lea and Cates. The Spaniard was tall with a tanned skin, high brow, prominent cheekbones, and dark lively eyes. An amused smile played about his thin lips. He stared at Lea as he passed, paused, lifted his straw hat and bowed politely. "Good day to you, *senorita*," he remarked, before the soldier shoved him on down the path. Lea nodded her head, then suddenly remembered where she had seen him. Surely he was the man on the pier who had studied her so intently the day she arrived last August.

"Who is that man?" she asked Cates as they started back toward the parade ground.

"Ramon de Diego. He owns a piece of Bunche's trading post down on the Manatee as well as a sugar mill and a big fishing ranchero on Charlottle Harbour. Got a lot of money, so they say, and some of it for sure was got selling whisky to the Seminoles, and probably other things too."

"Like guns?"

"He says supplies but for the army that means them Spanish rifles from Cuba. And munitions too. Now if they can just prove it."

She knew nothing about the man yet somehow Lea could believe he would deal in illegal contraband with the Indians. On the surface he seemed polite, even ingratiating, yet there was something there that did not feel right. As they neared the flagpole Cates paused and touched his cap. "Well, I'll be gettin' off to the storehouse, Miz Carson. Nora wants me to bring home some salt, if'n I can find any. Good day to you."

"And to you, Private Cates." She walked on down the path to the officer's cottages, thinking how accustomed she'd grown to being called 'Mrs.Carson'. Even Cates had finally learned to use her married name. Her work with the Indians had given her the strength not to care any longer what people thought of her. If anyone now looked at her with pity because her husband had left her at the marriage altar to ride away, she was too busy to notice.

As she walked back across Fort Brooke she was amazed to realize how much everything had once again changed during the time she had been so overwhelmed with her private concerns. For one thing, the number of troops at the fort had continued to swell since Ben left. There were soldiers everywhere, all over the fort and spilling out into the village. New barracks had been thrown up along with rows and rows of small white tents. Most of the trees in the old orange and lime groves had been cut down to make room for them, as well as some of the beautiful old oaks.

There was another, more subtle change—a feeling of assurance in the air. It differed strongly from those first dismal days after Ransome Clarke crawled in with the disastrous news of Major Dade's defeat. Then everyone had expected an Indian attack at any moment. Now most of the white settlers who had taken refuge in the fort had moved back to the village or to some of the ships in the harbor. The flimsy shacks clustered around the stockade were almost gone now, making more room for new barracks and tents.

She knew the village of Tampa was inundated with new arrivals as well. Farmers and their families still rolled in from the interior nearly every day. With every ship that arrived came more gamblers, camp followers, prospective settlers, and entrepreneurs, hoping to cash in on the horde of new soldiers. Though a new holding area had been built on Egmont Key for the Indians who were awaiting removal, more came in all the time to camp around the village.

Lea felt some consolation at the way the army was now caring for the desperately needy Seminoles. It was now acceptable government policy to feed the so-called 'friendlys' who camped within the village boundaries and Lea allowed herself some credit for that change. She still spent most of her day organizing the supplies and seeing that they were fairly distributed, and it pleased her that her authority was accepted. It was 'see Miz Carson' all the time now and she heard it with pride and confidence. Surely Ben would be impressed when he returned and learned about her work.

That she had not received a letter from him was a disappointment yet what else could she expect. After all, he was off fighting a war. Rumors floated around the camp on the winds of each new day and Lea grasped at them as avidly as all the other wives. When Colonel Lindsay arrived with a group of Alabama volunteers in early March and left at once for Fort Drane, there was wild talk that he was joining Generals Clinch and Scott in a campaign to wipe out Asceola and Chiefs Miconopy and Alligator. It was said that there had been a battle but no word arrived on casualties or the outcome. Yet Lea felt in her heart that Ben could not be hurt or killed. Surely God would not be so cruel as to destroy her hopes for happiness before they even had a chance to grow.

She entered the welcome coolness of her front hall, removed her sunhat, and adjusted the two long pins in the tight knot of hair atop her head. A quick change into something more plain and cool and then she would head for the quartermaster sheds. She had just unbuttoned the top of her dress when she heard a loud pounding on her front door. Quickly refastening the button, she stepped into the hall and looked up in surprise to see Lieutenant Stowe firmly grasping Buck by the collar of his shirt.

"Mrs.Carson, good day, ma'am," the Lieutenant said, tightening his grip on the squirming child.

"Lieutenant Stowe. Buck What's wrong? Please, come in."

The officer was already inside, dragging Buck with him as he stalked into the front room and half-threw the boy into the nearest chair. With one hand firmly pressing Buck against the cushion he faced Lea, his eyes dark with anger.

"I take it Buck is in some kind of trouble," Lea said cautiously, suppressing an urge to run to the child. She struggled to remember where he had gone after their brief session at his books that morning.

"It is my painful duty, ma'am, to tell you that this lad here is in need of a strong hiding. I've watched him for many a day now, getting into scrapes, looking for fights, using every chance he gets to pummel and attack other boys. Today was just one step too far."

"Lieutenant Stowe, he's only a small boy..."

"Small he may be, but his temper would suit a lad many years his elder."

"What exactly has he done?" Lea asked, dreading to hear the answer.

Stowe glowered at the top of Buck's head. "He beat up a boy smaller than himself. Not that he won't take on the bigger boys as well. But this was uncalled for and unsporting. Beat him up bad, too. If that lad's nose isn't broken, I'll miss my guess."

Lea's heart sank. "Is this true, Buck?"

Buck stared down at his hands without answering. Lea waited, wishing Ben were here. It was obvious Lieutenant Stowe expected her to be horrified and outraged but somehow she was not. Buck looked too much the young, eager child she knew him to be, and she could not see him suddenly transformed into a bully, even over a broken nose. Yet Stowe was an officer known to be fair. There must be something here she was not seeing.

She leaned closer to the boy, speaking softly. "Tell me the truth, Buck. Were you fighting?"

He nodded, still not speaking. "Why? What was the reason? Did the boy taunt you or hit you first?" Buck shook his head.

"Well," Stowe intoned, "at least he has the grace to tell the truth. I saw them together minutes before the fight broke out, and though they were yelling at each other, it was Buck here that threw the first blow. Went at the other boy something fierce, he did, and that smaller boy being the blacksmith's son too."

"Ballard's son? The blacksmith in the village?"

"That's right. It'll be some ruckus when the smithy sees his boy."

"Oh, Buck," Lea sighed. "Georgie Ballard couldn't whip a fly. What on earth were you thinking of?" Buck stared numbly off into space, his lips tightly pressed together. He was never going to explain or defend himself while Stowe stood there watching. Lea turned to the officer.

"Thank you for bringing Buck home, Lieutenant. I'll handle the matter now. I'll walk over and see Mr. Ballard later this afternoon."

"That boy needs a firm hand, Mrs. Carson, if I may be allowed to speak. I've watched him. He's bossy and feisty and much too quick to use his fists. He needs a man's strong hand on his backside."

"He's only a young boy, Lieutenant. I'm sure you are aware that his mother died just a few months ago and his father has been away for some weeks now."

Her cheeks flamed as she realized how her comment reflected on her own position. The officer, sensing her embarrassment, glanced quickly away.

"Yes, ma'am. I know that. And I'm truly sorry to have to lay this problem on your shoulders. But I know Captain Carson would not want to see his boy growing up to be a bully and a wastrel."

Lea gently but firmly pushed Stowe toward the door. "I feel the same. I promise you that is not going to happen. Thank you again."

Stowe lingered for a moment, looking as though he had a lot more he wanted to say. He had barely stalked down the porch steps before Lea was back in the front room kneeling by Buck's chair and gripping his arms so tightly he squirmed with pain.

"All right, Buck. Are you going to tell me what happened or am I going to have to use a strap on you as your father most certainly would if he were here?"

Buck glared at her from under his glowering brows. "Papa is never here."

"That can't be helped and you know it. I don't want to punish you, Buck, but you can't go around beating up other boys, especially ones from the village. Perhaps I have allowed you too much freedom but if you cannot be responsible…"

"He shouldn't have said it!"

Lea stopped, staring at this child she thought of as almost her own. She saw no tears, no suppressed sobs, nothing but fury and outrage.

"He deserved it," Buck went on. "I stopped his mouth for him and I'll do it again!"

She sat back on her heels, gloom slowly growing in her chest. This kind of anger was not something she had dealt with before or ever expected to. Buck had always been such a good, cheerful boy.

"What did Georgie Ballard say?"

"Nothing."

"Come now, Buck, he said something that offended you and it must have been pretty bad for you to beat him up. Can't you tell me?"

"No, ma'am."

"You know I can't deal with this if I don't know what it's all about. If it was something about your mother or your father…"

"It was about you," he blurted out. "He said bad things about you and he shouldn't of, and I hit him for it."

Lea felt her stomach turn over. "Me?" she whispered, her mind racing. Of course. Georgie would have heard his parents discussing her hasty marriage, so sudden and scandalous. Marrying her sister's husband almost before that sister's body was cold in the grave. Without realizing it, her hand flew to her throat.

"He said you were an Indian-lover! That you were probably part Indian yourself. And he said you were ugly!"

From deep within Lea a tiny, effervescent bubble of relief bounded and began to spread. She sat back, letting out her breath. "Was that all he said?"

"Yes," Buck mumbled, aware that somehow the insults which had outraged him in the village did not seem so horrible here in the front parlor. And it didn't help that his Aunt Lea was trying so hard not to smile.

Lea reached out and pulled the boy to her, squeezing him in her embrace. Then she laid her hands on his shoulders and pushed him away.

"Buck, I'm proud and grateful to you for defending me. But you must understand that you cannot go around beating up everybody who makes you angry. That's the way savages act and we are supposed to be civilized people. You'll have to be punished. You know that."

Buck nodded, though in fact he did not see why he should be punished for defending his family's honor.

"And you will have to go with me to apologize to Georgie Ballard."

"Oh Aunt Lea, do I have to?"

"Yes. But for now, you'll spend the rest of the morning in your room. It will give me time to think about ways to keep you busy and out of trouble. Go along now."

She watched him drag off across the hall and slam the door to the bedroom. Only then did she sit in the chair he had left, wondering at his words. It had been such a relief to know that she was not being accused of being some kind of scarlet woman that she hadn't really considered the other accusations. Of course her work with the Indians invited name-calling, and the Ballards were known to be prejudiced, self-righteous people. But ugly?

Like a moth to a flame she was drawn to the tin mirror on the wall. She stood, confronting her image in the wavering surface, staring at this person, this stranger who was her and yet not her.

All she could see was Rachel. Rachel, the beautiful, delicate sister whose classic cheeks, wide, startled eyes, and pale, creamy skin were in such contrast to the face that looked back at her. She traced her wide mouth with her finger, her high cheekbones, the slightly upturned eyes, the dark brows starkly drawn against a forehead spotted with pale brown freckles. This was Lea. She laid her palms against her cheeks and peered closer. She was not delicate or beautiful and she never would be. She could not compete with Rachel's angelic perfection.

"Get hold of yourself, Leatrice Hammond," she whispered sternly. "Leatrice Hammond *Carson!* You don't have to be Rachel. Rachel is dead and I am alive. I am Ben's wife now. I have to be myself."

And yet…

Reaching up, Lea pulled the pins from the knot on top of her head and allowed her thick hair to fall around her face. It did help. The severity of that tightly tied bun had done nothing to enhance the angular planes of her face which were softened by the falling waves around her shoulders. She twisted the long strands of hair into a loose rope around her head, draping tendrils over her ears in a fashion that was much prettier. Then she looked down at her dress, running her hands along her sides. She was more full-figured than her sister whose thin frame had always suggested an ethereal waif. Why hide her good health under drab, ill fitting dresses that, no matter how comfortable, made her look like one of the country women who rattled in on wagons from the interior.

"I could do more to make myself look presentable," Lea commented to the air as she fluffed her hair around her face. "I'll never be as beautiful as Rachel, but I don't have to make myself deliberately ugly. Ben certainly would not want to come back to a plain wife. At the very least, I might save Buck from a few more fist-fights."

In the days that followed Lea worked hard to implement that promise to herself. She decided one of her best features was her thick healthy hair that reached almost to her waist, and while it was a burden at times to bear its weight, she took to tying it back in a handsome chenille net which was flattering to her face, or braiding it in a halo around her head. She wore attractive dresses and made certain they were decorated with some small piece of jewelry or bit of lace. Her efforts made her feel feminine and pretty and she was pleased at times to notice the admiring glances she received. Some of the young soldiers even began casually flirting with her.

More to the point, she increased Buck's time for schooling and took him with her even when she was working at distributing food to the Indians. He could always do something to help and she made sure he was too busy working to get into trouble. It had not been easy to face Mister Ballard and his self-righteous wife, but Lea, with Buck firmly in hand, had apologized and discussed the problem so amicably that they generously forgave the fight. Georgie Ballard, on the other hand, whose nose was bruised but not broken, was so smugly pleased at the way Buck had gotten himself into trouble that Lea left feeling almost glad Buck had beaten him up.

The fist-fight was almost forgotten when, on the afternoon of April the fourth, Colonel Lindsey and his weary, dusty column came straggling into Fort Brooke. Everyone in the cantonment went running to greet the men and learn what had happened on their march. Lea, Julia, and several other women surrounded the officer almost as soon as his boots left the stirrups.

"It was all pretty futile," Lindsey commented as he lifted off his saddlebags. "We never fought more than a skirmish. The hostiles faded into the bush before we could get at them properly."

"You mean there was no fighting at all?" one of the women asked hopefully.

Lindsay threw his leather dispatch bag over his arm and started toward headquarters, his audience crowding around him. "Yes, we had a few small battles but not the big one we were hoping for. Please, ladies, I have a report to make."

Julia grabbed his arm. "But Colonel, can't you tell us how many were hurt? Was anyone killed? Are there many wounded?"

"No serious casualties in my group," Lindsay answered. "Most of the injured are with the other columns."

"What other columns," Lea asked.

Lindsay stepped up on the porch of the building he was so eager to enter. He stopped and faced the women clustered around the steps, holding up his hand. "You will hear the whole story after I make my report. As far as I know, none of you are widows. Generals Scott and Clinch are about a day's ride behind me, camped in a pine barren near two ponds about fifteen miles to the north. They should arrive tomorrow, barring any unforeseen trouble. And now, please, I need to make my report, wash away some of this grime and find a good stiff drink of whisky."

The women's babble of voices around Lea faded into a blur of sound as she stood, alone and stricken. Tomorrow! General Scott had taken over General Gaines command and Ben with it, and they were only a day's ride behind Lindsay. Tomorrow, April the fifth, he should come riding back through those gates, back to his home, back to his wife, back to her!

She couldn't move. Her feet had grown leaden, frozen to the ground. There would be no more waiting, no more worrying whether he was safe or even alive, no more concentrating on how to make herself compete with Rachel's memory. He would be here with her, his wife, and for the first time she was not sure if she was glad or terrified at the thought of facing him.

"Lea?"

Julia's hand on her arm brought her back. "Are you all right?" she heard her friend ask as she peered into Lea's white face.

"Yes, yes, of course."

"Isn't it wonderful, Lea! They'll be back tomorrow, Laurence and Ben. They made it through the campaign all right."

"Yes, it's wonderful. I...I ought to go get ready. There must be a lot to do, a lot to clean..."

"Lea, that house has been scrubbed down to the raw wood already. You can't do anything more. Why don't you and Buck come and take supper with me. Maybe I can get some of the bachelor officers to join us and we can learn more about what happened on the march."

Lea shook her head, not even tempted. "No, I don't think so. I think I'd rather be alone, if you don't mind."

Julia watched with dismay as the Lea of weeks before returned before her eyes, the same distance, the same inward focus, the same sadness. "Are you sure? It might be better for you to be around other people. Take your mind off..."

"No, I think I'll just go along home," Lea answered, turning away. She did not want to offend her kind friend but this was one night she wanted to be by herself. Tomorrow, for the first time since their wedding, she and Ben would be alone together. She had to think. To plan.

At noon the next day the vanguard of General Clinch's grimy column began straggling into Fort Brooke. Lea had been dressed and waiting since early that morning, keeping Buck near her to try to keep his white shirt and nankeen trousers clean. The day was very hot with intimations of the coming summer in its sticky, steamy breath, and she could not help remembering the cool April days on the Hudson. Deliberately she made herself remain calm, all the while trying not to picture herself clasped in her husband's arms, overjoyed to see and hold him again.

Nonsense, she grumbled to herself. It won't be like that. We haven't had time to grow into so passionate a response. A gentle embrace and chaste kiss was as much as she could expect.

When she heard the first commotion signaling the arrival of the column she clasped Buck's hand and hurried toward the pickets to wait with the other women. Almost at once it began to seem there would not be enough room in Fort Brooke to hold all the incoming soldiers. General Scott's column had not even arrived yet and already there were troops everywhere, some of them collapsing on the grassy parade ground, too weary to march any longer, many piled in the wagons carrying the wounded and sick. After an hour of watching anxiously she gave up trying to keep Buck in hand and took him back to the cottage for his dinner. Most of Clinch's battalion had arrived by now but Scott's and Gaines' were still no where in sight. The day dragged on into afternoon while Lea grew weary with her expectations. So many images of Ben's arrival and the welcome between them crowded her mind that she was exhausted from trying not to hope for too much. For the tenth time she checked the kitchen, making sure everything was ready for Ben's supper that evening. Once more she went around the house straightening, dusting, wiping surfaces that already gleamed back at her. When, finally, there was nothing more to do and the heat had grown unbearable, she closed the curtains of her bedroom and stretched out on the bed, hoping to keep cool by keeping still, certain she was too anxious to fall asleep.

An hour later Julia woke her up shaking her shoulder.

"Lea, they're here. Wake up!"

Groggily Lea looked up at her friend, realized what she was saying and bounded off the bed. "Oh, no. Ben's come back and I'm asleep?"

"He was in one of the columns behind Laurence so he should be coming in about now. When I didn't see you turn out I thought I'd better check. Let's go. We'll catch him as he rides in."

"Oh, Julia, my dress is all wrinkled. And my hair…"

"You look fine. Just a quick brush."

"And my eyes are all puffy."

"Nonsense, Lea. After all this time out in the scrub do you really think Ben will care if your eyes look puffy? Hurry up!"

Casting around for Buck who was nowhere in sight, Lea let Julia pull her through the house and out on to the walk. They were nearly past the quartermaster sheds when Lea spotted Buck near the hospital building. She detoured long enough to grab his hand, trying not to notice that his clean clothes were considerably more grimy than earlier, and dragged him toward the road.

She almost ran right past Ben. It was Julia who pulled her up when she spotted him standing near headquarters, his horse grazing nearby. Lea stopped, staring at her husband, for a minute not even recognizing him, he was so much thinner and wore an unaccustomed stubble of beard. He stood deep in conversation with a very large man wearing a fringed buckskin shirt, smiling at something the man was saying. Lea's hand went to her heart to still its pounding, then with Buck firmly in tow, she walked over to the two men.

"Hello, Ben," she said. He looked up quickly and something fell across his face, a shadow, an alteration. A barrier silently settled between them, something she could not see or name yet strong enough to hold her where she stood. She froze, her arms pinned to her sides, arms which should have been flung around his neck. Embarrassment draped around her like the folds of a blanket.

"Why, hello Lea," Ben said awkwardly. "And Buck, my boy." He knelt beside the child, clasping the boy's shoulders in his gloved hands. "How are you, son? You've grown a bit just since I left. You look fine. Fine."

"Hello, Papa," Buck mumbled.

"I brought you something. Wait, here it is." Rising, Ben dug in his saddlebags and produced a Seminole hatchet decorated with two tattered feathers. "I thought you might like to have a souvenir."

Buck reached eagerly for the hatchet. "Was it from a battle?" he asked, fingering it lovingly.

"As a matter of fact, it was. Left behind by one of Jumper's men who probably planned to use it on your Papa. Luckily he never got the chance."

"You will be careful with it, Buck, won't you?" Lea said, remembering Georgie Ballard.

The boy swung the blade through the air out of range of harm. "I will, Aunt Lea. Can I go show it to the other boys?"

"Of course. Run along but make sure you're back for supper."

He scampered off, leaving Lea to face Ben, awkwardness growing between them.

"Oh, Lea, excuse me. This is Clay Madrapore, one of the scouts who accompanied the column. Clay, my…my…wife, Lea."

His voice fell on the word yet Lea was relieved that at least he had spoken it. She had wondered for a moment if he would.

"Your servant, ma'am," the large man replied, lifting his battered army hat to reveal a shock of sun-bleached hair. Though Ben was a tall man, Clay Madrapore topped him by nearly two inches. He had a strong face, tanned and weather-worn, with light blue eyes that held depths of kindness but, Lea suspected, could turn to steel when provoked. She was always a little uneasy around these wilderness men who seemed as untamed and wild as the scrub country they made their home. Yet now, with Ben standing beside her, awkward and obviously uneasy, she was glad of the chance to focus on someone else.

"I'm pleased to meet you, Mister Madrapore. We're all so happy to see the column return safely. I hope it wasn't too difficult out there."

She heard herself babbling on while Clay looked from her to Ben and back again, his knowing eyes taking everything in.

"It could have been a lot worse," he said quietly. "There's not one of us but is glad to be back here with his hair intact."

Lea rocked slightly on her heels. "Ben, you must want to get out of those dusty clothes and wash up. I have supper all ready for you— rabbit stew, fresh blackberry cobbler—the things you like."

Ben pulled off his hat and ran his fingers through his hair. It had grown long on the campaign, falling almost to his shoulders. It was also grimy with dust, like the rest of him—so different, Lea thought, from his usually careful grooming.

"That sounds delicious. I've quite a bit to do first though before I can allow myself such luxuries. These men have to be quartered and a report has to be made. But I'll come along as soon as I'm through. Why don't you join us, Clay? A home-cooked meal would be a treat for you, I should think."

The scout looked between them again, somewhat embarrassed. "Oh, I'm sure you'll want to be alone with your wife and family this first night home. I wouldn't want to intrude."

"You'd be most welcome, Mister Madrapore," Lea said, with as much graciousness as she could muster. Things were not going at all as she had pictured and there was the nagging thought that with company in the house, she and Ben might put off facing each other a while longer. She was certain her husband had invited the scout because he felt the same way.

"Well, if you're sure, ma'am."

"Of course. Have Ben bring you along when he gets through. It'll be a pleasure to have you."

"I thank you most graciously, ma'am. Truth is, I would enjoy a family supper for a change."

"That's settled, then," Ben said, pulling his saddlebags off his horse's back. "We'll be along when we can."

Lea watched Ben walk up the low steps to the porch of the headquarters building and stand aside to hold the door for the scout. Before following Clay inside, he glanced back at her and she caught a quick glimpse of his face. She smiled and lifted her hand but he was gone before she could wave. That glimpse haunted her as she walked back to the cottage.

What had she seen? Not welcome, not joy. Fear! Fear and something else. Dislike? Perhaps that was too strong a word. But regret. Yes, certainly regret.

"*Oh, God,*" she thought, clenching her hands into tight fists within the folds of her skirt. *What have we done?*

CHAPTER 9

▼

"Every soldier in the army knows those three Generals—Scott, Gaines and Clinch—can't stand each other. That's why Scott is taking such delight in packing Gaines back off to Louisiana."

Ben lifted the bottle of brandy over Clay's glass. Its deep green color glinted in the soft lamplight. When Clay nodded he filled his glass then replenished his own.

"I thought I detected a higher level of malice than was warranted at Fort Drane," the scout drawled.

"Of course Scott had good reason. General Gaines came roaring down here on his own initiative. Scott, being the President's official appointee, naturally resented his attempts to interfere, no matter how well intentioned they were. But now that Scott is here and in charge we ought to see an end to this Indian trouble very soon."

Clay wiped at his lips and pushed his chair away from the table. "I wouldn't be too optimistic if I were you. Not many of you West Pointers are adept at dealing with Indians. My, this was a tasty dinner, ma'am. I seldom get a home-cooked meal, especially one this good."

Lea lifted her eyes from her plate where they had been fastened through much of the evening and smiled gratefully at Clay Madrapore. She had been excluded from most of the conversation except for Clay's polite attempts to draw her in. They helped but did not quite alleviate her embarrassment over the way Ben had ignored her all evening.

"The cobbler was my mother's recipe. An old one from the Hudson Valley."

"Oh, you're from New York then. Mister Irving's country."

"Yes. He lives south of us, in neighboring Westchester County. I met him once when he visited our neighborhood."

"I admire his work. What is he like? I always picture him as Rip Van Winkle incarnate with a long beard and shaggy eyebrows."

Lea laughed. "He's nothing like that. He's short, portly, rather fussy. But he has such a keen wit and is so entertaining you don't think about his looks at all. Where do you come from, Mister Madrapore?"

"Please, call me Clay. Everyone does." For the first time that evening Clay Madrapore looked ill at ease. He made such a pointed effort of folding his napkin and laying it beside his plate that Lea began to wonder whether he was going to answer her question.

"I'm from all over," he finally said. "But I suppose if I had to name a place of origin, it would be Virginia. Though I haven't lived there for quite some years."

Lea rested her elbows on the table and set her chin in her hands, regarding him more closely. "Forgive me, but you're very unlike…"

"Most army scouts? I know. I've heard that before. But it's a misconception to assume all scouts are backwoodsmen."

"Perhaps, but I do not think many of them have read Mister Irving's books."

"Or any other writer's," Clay laughed. "If they can read at all it's usually only maps and such. Yet I never subscribed to the premise all learning had to be practical in nature. A good officer should be schooled in more than the army rule book. Isn't that so, Captain?"

"Oh, yes. Of course," Ben mumbled, reaching again for the brandy bottle. Lea studied him a moment then rose from her chair. "Perhaps you will excuse me, Clay. I'll just clear up a few dishes and leave you men to enjoy the rest of your drink. That must be the last bottle of brandy in the whole of Fort Brooke. I hoarded it for just such an occasion as this."

Clay jumped to his feet. "Would you like some help?"

"No, thank you. Please, just continue your conversation. I'm sure you both have things to talk over. Ben, why don't you and Clay move to the parlor where you can be more comfortable."

Ben refilled his glass, not meeting her eyes. "We'll just stay here, I think."

Lea piled up the plates and carried the stack into the kitchen, closing the door behind her. She sat them on the dry sink, then collapsed into a nearby chair, twisting her hands in her lap and trying to calm her turbulent emotions.

It had been a terrible evening! Ben had not come to the house until just before supper, along with their guest who had washed and put on a clean shirt and long leather vest. Lea had been forced to make conversation with Clay in the parlor while Ben freshened up. By the time he emerged, clean and combed but wearing an unalterable weariness along with his brushed uniform, it was time to serve their supper. The unspoken barriers between husband and wife were strong enough to be felt by their guest throughout the meal, adding even more stiffness to the conversation. It was only when Clay engaged Ben in a one-sided discussion of the war, or got her talking about her home in New York, that there had been any relaxation at the table.

Lea rose wearily to wash up the dishes. She felt drained and weak and too tired to worry about the rest of the evening. She hated the thought of putting Ben to some kind of test, of making demands on him that he would find offensive. Perhaps they could make a fresh effort tomorrow when they were more used to each other again. With a quiet determination she finished up the kitchen chores and went back to the front room, declaring she was tired and excusing herself for bed.

Later, lying alone in the double bed, she could hear the muffled voices of the men in the parlor like a soft obbligato to the noisy insects outside her window. She turned on her side and pulled the covers around her, fighting tears of disappointment. Though afraid her churning emotions might keep her awake, she fell at once into a fitful, exhausted sleep. She woke once in the night to reach out her arm and feel the emptiness of the space beside her.

By the next morning Lea's disappointment, confusion and indecision followed her around like a stray dog nipping at her heels. She was too busy to sit quietly and look them in the face since much of the distribution of food and medical care for the hordes of Seminoles still outside the fort rested on her shoulders. She went through the motions of the day's chores like someone who had taken too heavy a dose of laudanum the night before but in her capable way she still managed to get everything done. If she noticed Julia watching her out of the corner of her eye or studying her face with a mixture of curiosity and pity, she deliberately ignored it. She wore her misery bravely, pulling it around her like a cloak. Secretly she might know her life was in shambles but she would die before admitting it to another living creature. Whatever the problems of her marriage, they lay only between Ben and herself.

When Lea returned home in the early afternoon she found Ben there, washed and wearing a clean uniform. He was strapping on his short artillery sword as she walked into their bedroom and sat gingerly on the edge of the bed. Everything in her screamed 'where were you last night?' but she refused to speak the words.

"Where is Buck?" she finally asked in as matter-of-fact voice as possible.

"At the stables as usual," he replied, fussing with his sash and avoiding her eyes. "I gather that is where he spends most of his time."

His tone implied criticism and she foolishly leaped to the defense. "He enjoys it so and the men don't mind. They tell me he's going to be a first-rate horseman."

Ben arranged the folds of his military sash. "It's as good a place as any, I suppose, and he must learn to ride sometime. But it might be better if he put more of his energy into his schooling."

"I've added time to his instruction and I intend to add more as soon as this business with the Seminoles is finished. That's kept me pretty busy of late."

"Yes, I've heard about the good job you've been doing. Everyone brags about it. God knows those wretched people need someone to help them."

Lea took some comfort his words, implying as they did pride at all she had accomplished. "Your strong-box is safe, too," she blurted out. "I mean, we haven't had time to talk but I want you to know it's quite safe. I check it now and then just to make sure it's all there. Naturally, I haven't mentioned it to anyone else."

The color rose in Ben's tanned face. "I knew you wouldn't."

"Would you like to count it for yourself?"

"No, no. That isn't necessary. I know it's safe with you."

He picked up his military hat and set it on his head, running his fingers along the brim. It was only then that it dawned on Lea he was getting ready to go out. Tentatively she rose to her feet, as though to hold him there.

"Ben, you'll be back for supper, won't you? I thought we might have…"

"No, no, that's quite impossible," he broke in. "Colonel Lindsay has asked me to take a few of the regulars up to join a group of Alabama volunteers on the Little Hillsborough. He wants to shore up the stockade there that protects the crossing and he thinks I'm the best man for the job."

She stared at him, not believing what she had heard. "But Ben, you've only just got back from fighting in the bush. Must you go back out into danger again? Can't someone else go?"

"Lindsay thinks I'm the best choice. I know the area well, I've been here the longest, and I'm on better terms with the Seminoles than most of these new officers who are not on any terms with them at all."

He was already into the hall, talking to her over his shoulder. Lea followed him, her frustration swelling.

"But I'd hoped, that is, we really need to sit down together. Ben, we need to talk about…"

Ben hurried even faster. "Now, Lea, there will be plenty of time for that when this trouble has simmered down. Right now this is where my duty lies and I must meet it. I trust you to care for Buck and, well, everything else while I am gone. That is your duty."

He stood in the doorway, glancing back at her. For an instant their eyes met then he quickly looked away. "Tell Buck goodbye for me," he said in that strained formal tone she was beginning to hate.

Lea fought to keep control. "How long will you be gone this time?"

He shrugged. "Hard to say. A week. Two, maybe. Perhaps more."

She bit back all the bitter words she wanted to hurl at him. "Take care of yourself."

"I always do," he said, with the faintest touch of a smile. Lightly he touched his fingers to his hat brim and stepped on to the porch, closing the door behind him. Through the window Lea watched him trip down the steps and stride along the walk. Then she turned, grabbed up a cushion from the nearest chair and threw it with all her strength at the door.

The following afternoon she had a visitor. Staring at the slight, stooped figure standing on her porch, it took Lea a moment to recognize Ransome Clarke, he had aged so much from the boyish, smiling youth who had marched away so proudly last Christmas. With a cry of pleasure she welcomed him inside and sat him in the best parlor chair while she fussed over him.

"I'm so sorry I have no coffee or tea to offer you." she said, taking the opposite chair. "Supplies have been so meager lately. Our last bottle of wine has been watered to make it go farther but it's still pretty tasty if you'd like some."

"No matter, ma'am. I don't care for nothin' anyway."

"It's grand to see you doing so well, Private Clarke. You look, well, I won't say wonderful, but considering what you went through…"

Clarke laughed. "I appreciate your candor, Mrs. Carson. The truth is, I ain't never goin' to be the man I was and I know it, and when those well-meanin' biddies tell me I look as good as before it's all I can do not to shake my fist in their faces."

"They mean well. And it is truly a miracle that you are so fit after the terrible injuries you suffered."

"That's true enough. The doctors patched me up pretty good considering I was just about knocking on the pearly gates. I came by to see Buck, to say goodbye before I left. He's a special little friend to me."

"You're leaving? I'm sorry to hear it."

"Yeah, I finally figured to turn in my blue coat for civilian black. I'm goin' to New York to watch the dear old Hudson roll to the sea. I figure I can get my health back quicker there. Then too, I've been told I can make a little money putting my experiences in a book or goin' around the country talking about the massacre. There's this fellow wants to line me up some speeches. Imagine, a poor spoken fellow like me giving lectures!"

"What you endured was very special," Lea said quietly.

"I suppose," Ransome answered, a hand going automatically to his shattered shoulder. "And I had my chance at revenge. There's nothing now can happen that will ever wash those pictures from my mind. I found that out on this last campaign. Now all I want is to see the backs of them Seminole savages forever."

Lea pursed her lips to keep from commenting that the Seminoles were also suffering from this war. "You deserve some good luck," she said instead.

"And how is Captain Carson?" Clarke asked, brightening. "Has he about recovered from the campaign?"

"Why, yes." Deliberately Lea fastened her eyes on her lap. "He's very fit. He's gone off again, you know, up the Little Hillsborough to work on the defenses there."

"I heard that. It's too bad he had to go back out into the scrub after all he went through. But then nobody gets to rest long. Men march a hundred miles to get to Fort Brooke then have to turn around and march out again the next day."

Lea glanced up in surprise. "All he went through? He didn't say much about the campaign."

"I don't suppose he would, being the kind of man he is. But it was bad for Gaines and the Captain and the column they were with. Real bad. Probably he just wants to forget it all, kind of like I do."

"Forget what? What happened?"

"Didn't he tell you? They got pinned down on the Withlacoochee by a great party of 'Eastu Charties' under Powel, Jumper and Alligator. For nearly a week they was cut off from the rest of the column, tryin' to hold out in a breastwork they threw up and called 'Fort Izard' after the Lieutenant who got hisself killed there. When the rest of the army finally came along they was out of supplies and so close to starv'in they was eatin' their horses and mules. I suppose they had about decided they was going the same way as Major Dade. At least this ambush turned out better."

Lea gripped her hands in her lap. And Ben had never said anything about it. "I didn't realize it had been so bad," she said lamely.

"It was bad right enough. I saw those fellows when they was led out. It wasn't only how thin and dirty they looked—it was the fear in their eyes. It reminded me right stark of what I saw in the faces of those men last December inside that pine barricade. They knew they was going to die, you see, and it showed in their eyes. That same look. It haunt's a soldier."

His voice trailed away and Lea saw something of the expression he was describing briefly touch his thin, white face. "Are you sure you won't have some wine, Private," she said quickly, bringing him back from some far, haunted place.

Clarke gave a small shudder. "No, thank you, ma'am. I really ought to go now. I just wanted to pay my respects to you and say good-by to little Buck. We was always good friends, Buck and me."

"He'll want to see you, I'm sure. I imagine you can find him hanging around the stables. That seems to be his favorite place these days."

Clarke's smile lightened up his thin face. "Just like always." Rising, he extended his hand to Lea. "All the best to you, ma'am, and the Captain, too. He's a lucky man, the Captain is."

"Thank you, Private Clarke. And may God go with you."

She walked with him to the door and watched as he limped down the walk, remembering the youthful spring that used to be in his step. Now that she thought of it, there was a similarity between Ransome Clarke and Ben, both in the droop of their walk and in the quiet desperation in their faces. There was that distance too, that they seemed to want to keep between themselves and the world. Did that come from the dreadful experiences they had shared, she wondered? Yet Clarke had been horribly wounded, while Ben...

How would I know, she thought bitterly. She had seen so little of Ben while he was home, and spoken of nothing private or personal. He hadn't mentioned he was involved in bitter fighting and a desperate siege. In fact he hadn't mentioned anything at all except that he had to go away again.

She turned from the door looking frantically around for something to clean.

Two nights later Lea was sitting in a chair by the lamp mending one of Buck's shirts when she heard heavy footsteps on the porch followed by a knock at the door.

"Anybody home?" said a cheerful voice.

Recognizing Clay Madrapore's deep base, she laid aside her sewing and welcomed him into the sitting room.

"I've come to fetch you," Clay said after declining her offer to sit. "We've discovered a talented fiddler among the regulars and he's been put to work down at the parade ground. The listeners just couldn't sit still and have taken to dancing some reels and country dances to his accompaniment. Everybody's joining in and it's gotten pretty frisky down there. I thought you might enjoy it too, so I've come to bring you along."

"Oh, Clay," Lea exclaimed, pinning up a loose strand of her hair. "I couldn't. It's been a long day…"

"Nonsense, it's just the kind of brightening up you need."

"But I look terrible. This old dress…and Buck is already asleep."

"You look fine. I'm not talking about a fancy ball, just a few high spirits in the bleakness of war-time. And Buck will be fine."

It was on the tip of her tongue to say that Ben might object but she caught that back. He probably wouldn't care and if he did, well, too bad. "All right. Just give me a minute to change my dress."

They could hear the laughter and the music as they walked along the path to the parade ground. Several lanterns had been hung around the perimeter and someone had brought out a large keg—probably whisky, Lea thought. Though food had been in scarce supply around the fort for the last four months there always seemed to be plenty of grog. Whatever it was, it had obviously served to lubricate the spirits of those on the sidelines who were enthusiastically clapping and stomping to the rhythm of the dancing.

"It's a regular frolic, isn't it," Lea exclaimed as they worked their way into the crowd.

"And all the better for being spontaneous," Clay shouted above the noise. Glancing around, Lea was surprised to see how many people had gathered for the fun. Officers and coremen as well as hordes of civilians had been drawn to the festivities. On one side of the open dancing space tall General Scott stood talking to James Gadson, the man who above all others, Lea knew, had dreams of developing Florida. Across from them, General Clinch, Colonel Lindsay and Commandant Sands smiled and clapped in time with the fiddle. Among the civilian families Lea recognized William Saunders talking with the Dixons and Kennedys, as well as Levi Collar who looked on proudly as his pretty daughters danced. Surprisingly, there were also a few of the denizens of Spanishtown Creek, one or two with their wives. Though most of the women members of the fort were present there were still so few of them that some of the men had partnered each other. Lea spotted Julia prancing happily as the reel came to a close, but not with her husband who was away on yet another march to the Withlacoochee. "If Julia can, so can I," she thought and let Clay lead her into the line as they formed for a new dance.

By now a drummer and piper from the army band had joined the fiddler who was as talented as Clay had said.

The lanterns around the parade ground sparkled like stars against the gathering dusk but Lea barely noticed as she threw herself into a country jig. Her skirts whirling, her smile growing broader, she lost all other concerns in the sheer joy of bouncy rhythms and busy feet. She soon lost Clay who bowed out after the first dance to give way to a joyous private whose huge steps and powerful spins sent her head reeling. The next dance was a more sedate quadrille followed by a schottische and another jig more spirited than the first. By that time Lea had to stop to catch her breath. Spotting Clay in a nearby group, she hurried over to take the glass he held out to her.

"It's not whisky, is it?" she said breathlessly, knowing her weak head for strong alcoholic spirits.

"No, it's water and molasses." At her horrified gasp, he laughed. "Just joking. It's diluted wine from General Scott's supply. He sent some over in honor of the festivities. It seems there has been so little to enjoy lately what with this war and all that he wanted to make sure this was a pleasant evening. Drink up."

Lea sipped her wine and enjoyed the cooling breeze off the bay. She spotted a few chairs someone had set up for General Scott and a few of the older women and moved over to take one. She was barely seated when Mister Gadson walked up to her.

"It is very pleasant to see you again, Mrs. Carson," he said, gallantly kissing her hand. "Is your husband here?"

"No, unfortunately he is at the outpost on the Little Hillsborough. I hope he'll be back soon."

"Too bad. He is missing quite a pleasant diversion."

Lea recalled meeting James Gadson on only one or two occasions and was surprised he even remembered her. But then he did know Ben. In fact, she remembered, it was Gadson's dream of developing the Fort Brooke area which had so intrigued Ben before Rachel got sick.

"And have you met Senora Costa de Diego," Gadson asked, indicating the woman sitting next to Lea. "The Senora is a recent arrival to our fair shores."

For the first time Lea looked over at the woman beside her and into one of the most classically lovely faces she had ever seen. For an instant her breath caught in her throat as she recognized something of Rachel in the pale skin and perfect features. And yet the two women were very different. Rachel had been all delicacy and softness, like a flower just unfolding. Costa de Diego was fire and ice, dark flashing eyes under sculptured black brows, perfectly formed lips, red against her white skin, ebony hair swept up and piled around an exquisite comb that pinned a black lacy veil falling around her shoulders.

"I'm pleased to meet you, Senora," Lea said politely. The woman's lips lifted in a slight smile. "I also," she answered in a cultured voice. Accustomed to the dumpy slovenness and broken English of the Latin ladies of Spanishtown Creek, it took Lea a moment to realize that Senora de Diego was a proud aristocrat who looked on her with something barely above contempt.

Gadson went on. "The Senora has only recently arrived from Cuba in order to join her husband who has a ranchero on the Manatee. I've convinced them this village will be a growing and important area once the Indian problem is settled."

"I haven't been here so very long myself," Lea said to Senora de Diego. "Yet I find that I have come to like Florida very much."

"Perhaps in time I will be able to share your enthusiasm," Costa answered, fanning herself vigorously with a brilliantly painted fan. "But for now, no, I do not care for *la Florida*. Too many…mosquitoes."

"They can be rather daunting," Lea said lamely.

"I prefer Cuba. So much happening there. So lively and energetic. And not so many Indians. I do not care for these Seminoles."

"And this is the Senora's husband," Gadson broke in, drawing a man forward. The man bowing over Lea's hand was carefully dressed and very familiar. When he lifted his head to smile at her, she recognized him as the man at the pier she had encountered twice before and cautiously withdrew her hand. Seen close up, Ramon de Diego was handsome in a swarthy way with strong cheekbones and a long, wide chin. His eyes were black and as flashing as his wife's. His dark hair was combed straight back and gleamed against his skull. Yet there was something about him that made her shudder. Perhaps it was the way he ogled her, as though with only a little encouragement he would bend and lick her neck. Lea inched back in her chair.

"Good evening, Senor," she said as politely as she could.

"I am charmed to meet such a brilliant flower of Florida gracing this primitive fort, Senorita," he said, smiling broadly. Lea, embarrassed, glanced at the man's wife sitting only a few feet away, her beautiful eyes fastened on the dancers whirling around the parade ground.

"It's *Senora* Carson, Ramon," Gadson broke in. "Mrs. Carson's husband is an army Captain, away at the moment guarding a fort on the Little Hillsborough."

"I apologize, Senora," Ramon replied graciously. "That must be very difficult for you. If I can be of any help while the Captain is away, you must not hesitate to call on me."

Over Ramon's shoulder Lea glimpsed Clay Madrapore advancing toward her. Hoping she could draw him to her side, she searched for his glance and smiled, bringing him straight to her.

Taking in the situation, Clay pushed in front of Diego. "I wonder if you would favor me with this next reel, Mrs. Carson," he said, reaching for her hand. "I was always fond of a country dance."

"I'd love to, Mister Madrapore," Lea said brightly. "You will excuse me, Senor, Senora."

"You'd better watch out for those two," Clay whispered as he led her out on the floor. "I've heard about Ramon Diego. Not only is he rumored to be selling arms to the Seminoles but he also goes after every pretty girl within five miles, if not ten."

"Even married ladies?" Lea said, glancing back over her shoulder to see Ramon's eyes following her.

"If they're willing. And many are."

"But his wife is so beautiful. I don't think I've ever seen anyone with more perfect features save my sister, Rachel."

"There are some men for whom one woman is never enough. Be careful of him. It might be wiser not to let him know that Captain Carson is away."

Lea blushed in spite of herself. "Mister Gadson already told him. Besides, surely by now you know there are no secrets inside this fort. Senor de Diego can find out anything he wants by asking around. However, I don't believe you need to worry. I cannot imagine he would bother with me."

Clay's hand tightened on her waist. "Do not sell yourself short, Mrs. Carson," he said, bending to whisper in her ear.

Lea laughed. She realized she was enjoying herself in a way she had not since Rachel fell ill back in December, another world away. The guilt she had briefly felt about coming here without her husband was long gone. Ben had not said ten words to her while he was home and had chosen to leave again right away. She might as well take advantage of what pleasure she could without worrying about what he would think.

And enjoy herself she did. During the rest of the evening she took part in every dance except when she was sitting on the sidelines trying to catch her breath. With a start she realized she had forgotten for a little while that she was a married woman. Clay's comfortable solicitousness soon gave way to the other soldiers who showered attention on her as though to make up for the fact that Ben was not there. She even stood up for one quadrille with Ramon de Diego after he asked her so often she was embarrassed to refuse him again.

The night was wearing on toward midnight when Lea finally realized how weary she was. For a little while she had forgotten the confusing problems of her marriage but now they all came rushing back. All at once she wanted nothing so much as to go home to the solitude of her bed. No matter how pleasant a diversion the evening had been, it did nothing to solve the shambles of her marriage. All that still lay waiting for her.

Wrapping her shawl around her shoulders, Lea made her way to the edge of the grassy parade ground to take the walkway back to her cottage. As she stepped away from the lights she felt a hand on her elbow.

"I would be honored to escort you to your door, Senora Carson," said Ramon de Diego, bending and smiling into her face. "I thought you began to look a trifle weary and might be leaving soon."

Ramon's company was the last thing Lea wanted. Pulling her arm away she stammered, "That's not really necessary, Senor. I'm sure you would rather stay and accompany your wife."

Ramon moved closer to her, gripping her arm. "My wife would never forgive me for allowing a lady to leave unescorted."

"Excuse me, Senor," Clay's voice broke in, "but I promised Mrs. Carson earlier I would see her home and I wouldn't dream of taking you away from your lovely wife. Why didn't you tell me you were ready to go, Lea. I've been waiting for you."

Lea looked gratefully up into Clay Madrapore's pale blue eyes as he gently disengaged her arm from Ramon's grip. "Thank you, Clay," she answered, moving closer to him. "I looked for you but you seemed busy and I hated to interrupt."

"No interruption," Clay drawled, pulling her arm through his. "Good evening, Senor."

Ramon did not try to hide his irritation. "Of course, if you promised earlier…"

"Good evening, Senor," Lea smiled over her shoulder. "Please say goodnight for me to your wife."

Ramon bowed. "I shall indeed."

They walked out of the circle of the lanterns and into the darkness of the graveled walk where the only light was the bronze moonlight glazing the grass. "Thanks for rescuing me," Lea said quietly. "He's terribly forceful and I do so hate to be rude."

"I'm glad I saw you leaving. I thought he might pull something like that and was watching. You appear to have made a conquest tonight. But it would be wiser to stay out of his way."

"I will if he will allow me. Believe me, this is a 'conquest' I never wanted. If his wife wasn't so proud and cold I would try to make her a friend. That would put him off."

Clay's lips were grim. "I wouldn't count on it."

They walked on in silence while the music and laughter faded behind them. Lea expected to go straight home and was surprised when Clay suggested that they first walk down to the bay to have a look at the beautiful water and the star-filled night. She only hesitated a moment before agreeing for she too felt drawn to the water's sequined expanse by the beauty of the night. How often had she gone to the bay alone? It would be pleasant to share its loveliness with this protective friend.

They walked in comfortable silence toward the quiet, sloping sands of the bay. The water stretched out to the horizon like a great, dark silver bowl. Moonlight shimmered on the gentle waves, brightening the night sky to a deep slate gray.

"It's so very peaceful, isn't it," Lea said, spreading her shawl on the sand and sitting on it. She pulled her skirt over her knees and clasped her hands around them.

Clay stretched beside her. "It seems peaceful when its like this. We all know how deceiving that can be."

"Costa Diego called this place *la Florida* tonight. It's an apt name, isn't it. A wild, exotic tropical country of sand, scrub and wonderful water. Flowers, palm trees, wide-spreading oaks, spanish moss..."

"Wildcats, alligators, snakes, Indians, mosquitoes, fleas..."

"Clay Madrapore! You certainly know how to dash cold water on poetic sentiments."

"I'm simply a realist," he said, laughing. "I have to be in this place if I want to keep my hair."

"Yes, but you don't need to destroy all my illusions."

Clay reached down and grabbed handful of white said, letting it drift slowly through his fingers. "Some illusions are better destroyed."

Lea looked at him sharply. "Why do I think you mean more by that remark than the merits of Florida?"

"Forgive me, Lea," he said, looking into her face cast in shadows by the moonlight. "I feel I must speak because I like Ben Carson very much and I admire you. I think maybe your illusions about Ben have hurt you and I hate to see it. They may even hurt him as well."

Lea made an effort to rise and got tangled in her skirts. All the beauty of the night had suddenly grown dark and murky. "I don't think that is any of your business," she said sharply. Clay reached out and gripped her arm, pinning her in place.

"Perhaps it isn't, but I will speak even though you might hate me for it. I was there the night Ben came home, remember. I saw the two of you together, and, God forgive me, I put up with him when he demanded my company the rest of the night, drinking and gaming to keep from returning to your bed."

Tears stung her eyes. "That's a cruel thing to say."

"But it's true, Lea. I told you I'm a realist."

His tight grip hurt her arm and she tried to pull away. "You don't understand. Ben loved my sister Rachel so much. She was…she was delicate and beautiful and from the first time he saw her she was the only thing in his life that mattered. Not even his children meant as much. He cannot simply turn away from that and come to me. There hasn't been time."

Clay's fingers eased on her arm. "But I suspect it wasn't like that to you. I saw the hurt he caused you that evening and I cursed him for a fool."

"He married me as a convenience. Nothing more."

"But it wasn't just a convenience to you, was it?" His voice was so gentle Lea slumped back on the sand, trying not to cry. "My dear girl," he went on, "I only want to say that if you want to be happy with Ben—and I believe you can be—you must force him to face reality too. Don't allow him to treat you like a house-keeper. Make him be a husband to you. Let him know that you are there and he must deal with you as his wife."

"But you don't understand. He thought he would be killed—he wanted to be killed. He needed someone to care for Buck and…and for his estate."

"Well, he wasn't killed. And if he could survive that terrible siege at the With-lacoochee, it isn't likely he will be. Julia Lattimore told me you have always been more of a mother to Buck than Rachel because she was sick so much of the time. As for any 'estate', how much could a Captain's pay produce? No, he married you for his own selfish reasons even though he'd never admit it. He'd be crazy to let a woman like you get away. He knew you'd be grabbed up quickly and then where would he be."

Lea shook her head in amazement. "You don't know what you're talking about. Ben's never seen me as anything but a sister or a maiden aunt."

"If you think that then you haven't seen the truth. But it's there, my girl. I know it. You've only to make him see it."

"But how? I don't even know where to begin."

Clay threw up his hands. "What do I know about 'how'? That's women's ways and women's business. You'll find a way. You must, if you want any kind of life with Ben Carson. And you do, don't you?"

She stared out at the water. "I've always wanted it, since the first time I met him." Her voice was no more than a whisper he had to strain to hear. Then suddenly, shuddering, she shook her head and jumped to her feet. "I want to go home. Please take me back."

Slowly Clay rose to stand beside her, brushing the sand from his legs. She knew how obvious the turmoil seething inside her must be and was relieved when he reached for her shawl, shook it out and laid it around her shoulders, waiting while she grew calmer.

"Do you really think he didn't want me to get away?" Lea said quietly. "How could that be? There has never been a word between us to indicate it, even when he asked me to marry him."

Clay hesitated, then stepped closer, turned her to face him and laid his hands on her shoulders. "I know it is true because I am a man. I know I would never have let you go."

She caught her breath, looking up into his strong face. "But..."

"No," he said, laying a finger on her lips. "Forget what a beauty Rachel was, and how much Ben loved her. If you really want him, fight for him. You are here and your sister is dead. All his life with her is past, all your life with him lies ahead. I saw you tonight, smiling, your eyes dancing, your face alive with joy. You're healthy and wonderfully alive. And you're beautiful."

"Me? No, Rachel was beautiful."

"To hell with Rachel," Clay answered grimly, and bent to kiss her. His arms slid easily around her, pressing her body into his. His lips were hard and demanding and Lea felt herself drawn to him along a great surge of warmth. She fell forward and he supported her, pressing his lips on hers as if to drink from some sweet, fragrant fountain. She was swept along in her response.

Then, just as suddenly, he broke away, dropping his hands and turning his face toward the dark sea.

"That's what you deserve, Lea," he said in a choked voice. "A man who will take you and hold you and love you for the woman you are. Don't let Ben give you anything less."

She fought to get her breath. "Clay. I...oh, dear..."

He laughed, bringing her back to her senses. "Forgive me. I meant to lecture you, not kiss you like that. I humbly apologize. Blame the stars and the sea and the way you looked with the moonlight reflecting in your eyes. Come along now, I'd better take you home."

"I...I don't know what to say."

Deliberately he took her arm and propelled her back toward the walk. "There's nothing more to say. Try to remember my advice and please ignore the way I took advantage of you. It won't happen again. Merciful God, I protected you from Ramon Diego only to assault you myself. What a baggage I am!"

"No," Lea replied, laying her hand on his arm. "I'm not offended. In fact, it was rather nice."

"Don't tempt me, madam, or I might try it again. Tell me we are still friends, even though that wasn't a friendship kind of kiss."

"Of course. Always friends."

She was grateful when he squeezed her hand then moved away, keeping a distance between them as they set off down the sandy path toward her cottage. Somehow it seemed safer that way.

CHAPTER 10

▼

The panther's scream cut through the rattle of the scrub like the screech of a banshee. Ben pulled his mount to a stop while behind him his patrol lumbered to a halt, nervously unshouldering their rifles as they peered through the tangled underbrush. Quietly Ben scanned right and left, trying to see behind the leafy wall of thickets, tree trunks, vines and creepers that nearly obliterated the last stretch of Federal road winding toward the new bridge.

How had that one sharp cry pierced the incessant din of insects and birds so noisily familiar on these treks into the deep woods outside Fort Alabama? A panther's scream was common out here but Ben easily recognized this one as not the usual predatory howl of an animal but the dreaded signal of a Seminole scout. The hairs on the back of his neck came alive as he strained for some further sound inconsistent with the racket of the woods around him. Not a whisper was heard from the volunteers waiting patiently behind. Though usually a contentious bunch, these men from the Alabama farms had learned well during their month in Indian territory. None of them felt really safe, even inside the stockade. Out here, mired in the unknown depths of thick scrub, all but buried among the overhanging branches of hickory and oak, sweltering in the steamy heat made even more stagnant by their fear, out here they could only draw furtive breaths and pray that an ambush would not be concealed in the short stretch of woods leading to the new bridge over the Hillsborough.

Cautiously Ben inched his horse forward. Not much farther now, he thought, scanning the thick trees. The main thing was not to panic.

With a sudden cutting swish an arrow shot across his face, missing his nose by inches before thudding into the trunk of a tree to his right. Ben reared back in the saddle, yanking on the reins. "Run for it!" he yelled, as he pulled his mount as far out of the path as possible. His men needed no encouragement. Pounding past him, they streaked for the bridge, tearing aside straggling branches and ignoring the clutching sand. Ben held back until the last one passed, trying to control his nervous mount and every second expecting a deadly hail of arrows. Once his patrol reached the bridge he plunged after, all of them shouting to the sentries at the gate. By the time the first man reached the log wall the gates were opening. The last man was barely through before Ben dashed after him, swinging out of the saddle as the heavy wooden doors were slammed shut.

Lieutenant Turner came running from the blockhouse, pulling on his blue tunic as he ran. "What happened?" he cried as Ben threw the reins to a private who ran up to lead his horse away.

"Seminoles. Alert the sentries. The devils may be up in those pine trees any minute trying to pick us off."

"A war party?"

Ben started toward the blockhouse as the Lieutenant fell in beside him.

"I don't think so. There was only one arrow. Probably a small, isolated group. But I heard their signal and I'd stake my life there will be more coming."

As they climbed up the low steps to the darkened interior of the blockhouse the alarm drum began to rattle behind them. Ben paused in the doorway, looking up at the crown of trees that ranged like sentinels above the pointed ramparts of the stockade wall. "They've attacked this fort twice trying to drive us out. It's only a matter of time before they try again."

He eased into a chair while Lieutenant Turner perched a hip on one end of the plank table, both men watching the frenzied activity in the yard through the open door. The troops had long ago learned what to do when they heard that drum roll. No one was going to stay in the open areas of the stockade while there was danger from snipers. The tall pines nearest the fort had all been cleared away but the forest beyond made a perfect perch for patient braves eager to pick off a few of the enemy.

"Maybe they'll just try to burn the bridge again," Turner commented. "Even though we gave them a good thrashing the last time, it's still the weakest point in our defense."

"I don't think they'll be so foolish." Ben slammed his hand on the table. "The truth is this fort is in an untenable position. Isolated skirmishes are one thing but should they ever decide to throw a whole force against us, how long could we hold out? We'll have to abandon this place soon."

"Why not tell that to Colonel Lindsay, Captain? We're sending a dispatch to Fort Brooke tomorrow. It can't hurt to try."

Ben gave a grim laugh. "One more time? I've been saying the same thing with every report since I got here. But you're right. It can't hurt to try again."

He walked to the open doorway and scanned the treetops. Everything seemed quiet but with Indians that was likely to be just the time disaster struck. It was a lesson most white men needed to learn only once in this wilderness.

"I'm going to wash off some of this grime, Turner. Tell those sentries to keep a close watch until sundown."

"They know," Turner replied. "Only too well."

The entire garrison was relieved when the expected attack never came. By supper time, with the sun a crimson ball hovering over the forest and the deepening darkness illuminated by the campfires in the yard, things had returned almost to normal. Though dawn might still bring a horde of Seminole arrows speeding sudden death from the trees, at least for tonight all was quiet. A kind of lazy calm settled over Fort Alabama. They had made it through one more day.

Ben ate his supper beside one of the fires, chatting with a few of the regulars. They were seasoned troopers now, these men who had left their plows and cabins in the backwoods of the country to earn their fifteen dollars a month with the United States Army. Along with the volunteers from Alabama, they had hacked this fort from the wilderness, wresting log walls from the pine trees, throwing up crude blockhouses and a powder magazine, erecting barracks and storehouses. It was not an uncomfortable place when you forgot the constant threat of the wilderness outside. Rough it certainly was, but livable for all that. Ben was amazed at the way troopers could turn the crudest of camps into a home. Almost as amazing was the way they could develop a camaraderie among themselves in spite of their divergent backgrounds.

They laughed now as they scraped their plates and set up card games on upended barrels. Ben sat back, pulled out his tobacco pouch and filled his pipe. The night creatures were going full blast outside the stockade walls, a noisy accompaniment to the laughter and banter of the men.

Yet in spite of the serenity, he could not shake off the memory of that arrow whizzing past his face earlier that afternoon. Even the quiet in this camp had a kind of terror underneath it, waiting to erupt. He supposed he ought to be thankful he had made it to another evening with his scalp-lock intact, but it had been close.

"Look at that, will you, Capt'n!"

Private Meeker, sitting beside Ben, nudged his shoulders. "Nobody gets cards like that by chance. Silas Jones, you're either a cheat or you got a pipeline to the devil."

Ben leaned over to examine the cards spread fanlike on the barrel.

"Hold on there, Meeker," Jones cried. "Don't accuse me of cheatin' lessen you can prove it Not lessen you want a knife in yo're belly."

"But Capt'n, he wins all the time. That can't be luck."

Jones swept up the cards. "Yo're daft, Meeker. I always been lucky at cards and you knowed it since the first time we played. Next time you accuse me of cheatin', yo're gonna lose some of them pearly white teeth yo're so proud of."

Ben laughed. He knew both men well enough to realize most of their argument was bombast. "Try another hand," he suggested. "Maybe your luck will improve, Private."

Meeker grumbled but took the deck Jones handed him and began to shuffle the cards. When two other men ambled over to watch the game Ben rose and walked up the steps to the narrow platform built along the ramparts. He spoke briefly to the sentry, a private from the western reaches of North Carolina who had never been able to shake his fear of Indians. Ben had never understood why he had volunteered to come to Florida and fight Seminoles, but then he had long ago given up trying to determine what motivated men to join the army. Their reasons were as varied and complicated as the soldiers themselves.

"All well, Simons?" he asked, moving silently alongside the boy.

The private leaned on his rifle and touched his cap. "Peers to be, Capt'n. For now, leastways."

The whites of the boy's eyes glimmered in the dim light. He had a small face narrowing to a point, with thin cheeks and a permanently pursed mouth. He looked to Ben like a boy raised on slim rations in his childhood. That may have had something to do with what brought him here.

Ben leaned against the rough bark of the wall and pulled on his pipe. In the square below the flaring light from the fires reflected on the squat tents and log buildings. It was getting really dark now and all the terrifying music of the night was tuning up—the roar of gators down by the river, the screech of owls over the low palmettos, and, most unsettling of all, the howling of wolves out in the forest. Ben saw Simons shudder.

"It's chilling, isn't it," Ben commented softly. "But not so chilling as the sound I heard out there this afternoon. I'd bet my life that was one of Miconopy's braves."

"You ought to know, Capt'n. You been here longer than anyone."

"Yes," Ben sighed, quietly adding, "Sometimes I wonder if I haven't been here too long."

"Well, sir, I can only say it's a comfort to us to think how well you know these woods. And these savages, too."

Ben smiled. "Thank you, Simons. Keep a close watch now."

"Yes, sir. I will."

Ben walked away, leaving the private a little less apprehensive. In all likelihood there was nothing to fear now, not until dawn or later tomorrow on patrol in the forest. He shuddered again remembering the arrow. At the juncture of two walls he stopped apart from the sentries and hidden by the shadows. His pipe had gone out but he sucked on the empty stem, enjoying the solitude so rare in the close confines of the fort.

Sinking down, he rested his elbows on his knees and leaned back against the wall, reflecting on how a few inches made the difference between living and dying. Yet why should that unnerve him—he who had so often lately thought to welcome death? By now, in this place where a life was worth no more than a dried leaf, he ought to be immune to fear and the terror of dying. Not for him the insane clinging to life at any cost. Men who felt that way had something to live for.

Yet to his surprise he realized he was relieved that arrow had missed him. He was glad to be sitting here, lost in the darkness, still part of this mysterious, wild and untamed world. He recalled how once he had felt such enthusiasm for this Florida territory. It was going to make his future, a heritage he could leave his sons. But that was before Rachel died. And Stephen. He had only one son left now, and no wife.

Lea! Yes, he did have a wife even though he could barely think of her that way. He fought to remember Rachel's perfect features but they grew shadowy and thin, merging from a bloodless mist into the rosy image of her sister.

What on earth was he going to do about Lea? He had hurt her terribly when he was home, he could see it in her eyes and her expressive face. He'd never expected to have this problem. He had wanted so much to leave an orderly situation behind him that he had acted impulsively, hastily. He should have died on the Withlacoochee instead of Lieutenant Izard, in that siege where they were pinned down for days waiting for a last deadly ambush, so hungry they were forced to eat their horses. Why didn't God take him then? Why not this afternoon? It would have been no more than he expected.

But it hadn't happened. And now, here he sat, mired in the scrub, defending a fragile outpost of civilization in the middle of a barbaric wilderness, hoping he would not be called back to Fort Brooke where he would have to deal with the woman he had married in such haste.

For of course that was the real reason he had come here and would gladly stay until the order came recalling him. The army had offered him a legitimate way to put off a confrontation with Lea. He had no idea how he could resolve his hasty marriage but as long as he was here in Fort Alabama he could postpone the need to find an answer.

Yet it would have to be faced someday. What was he going to do? Send her away? Divorce her? Both solutions would be cruel and the second one scandalous, besides ruining his career. Lea was a good, kind girl and a member of his family. If only he hadn't been so hasty.

"Captain Carson."

Lieutenant Turner's voice. Ben jumped to his feet and saw the Lieutenant climbing halfway up the platform stairs.

"Excuse me, sir, but I've just broken out a bottle of porter I've been sequestering since we came to this Godforsaken spot. A few of the others were wondering if you'd like to join us."

Ben slipped his pipe inside his shirt pocket. "I'd like that, Lieutenant. Thank you," His dreary thoughts were already slipping away.

Near the middle of May the first large contingent of Seminoles gathered around the pier to board ships for their relocation to the west. Lea went down to watch and to say farewell to a few of the women and their children she had come to know. Not that a white woman could ever know them really well, she thought—these quiet, self-contained creatures from an alien culture with their impassive faces, heavy silences and stoic suffering.

From the moment she arrived at the crowded wharf she realized this was not going to be the simple leave-taking she had imagined. Huddling with their pitiful belongings, they set up a strange wailing as they were pushed into the tenders to be ferried to the ships. The older men moved back among the trees, laying their palms along the rough trunks of live oaks and gently touching their leaves in a poignant gesture of farewell while the watching soldiers laughed. There were tears on many brown cheeks, angry defiance on others. A few of the more aggressive squaws laughed and threw parting taunts at the soldiers for their notable lack of success against Seminole warriors. Frightened children cowered near their mothers, some of whom who knelt to sift the Florida sand through their fingers before they were forced into the boats.

One tall Indian, wrapped in a ceremonial blanket, stopped at the shore, turned, and began to recite a farewell speech to his hereditary home with words that were wrung from his heart. Another sat resolutely on the sand and refused to go. Lea watched as long as she could but when the dogs belonging to the people in the boats began to run back and forth along the shore piteously whimpering and howling, it was more than she could take. She fled back to her house in confusion.

It was not supposed to be like this. The army had focused for so long on removing the Seminoles from Florida that it had become an accepted fact. She knew it would be difficult for them but somehow she never realized how difficult, how wrenching, how emotional an upheaval. For the first time it was driven home to her that this territory was *their* native land, going back generations. She, who had so willingly left her native home to follow her sister into the wilderness, had never imagined the grief it would cause native tribes to relocate. No wonder they fought against leaving. For the first time she wondered if the United States Army was doing the right thing in Florida.

At Fort Alabama a column of marching troops finally arrived with the long awaited orders. The stockade, it had been decided, was too precariously placed to risk so many men. They were all ordered back to Fort Brooke, leaving the isolated Alabama fort abandoned until a decision could be made about its future.

They did not leave without one parting shot. One of the gunners rigged the door to the powder magazine with a trip wire attached to the trigger of a musket. The men had not marched six miles south before, to their great merriment, they heard the explosion. As expected, the Indians had slipped into the fort almost as quickly as it was abandoned and one of them tried to force the door to the magazine. It was weeks later that Ben learned three Seminoles had died in the blast.

This time she was not expecting him. The news had not yet spread through Fort Brooke that the Alabama volunteers were coming home so Lea was completely unprepared for the shock of seeing Ben coming up the veranda steps, then his tall form filling the doorway. She walked out of the kitchen to stand staring at him, her eyes wide and her face drained of color.

Ben gave a relaxed laugh. "For God's sake, Lea. I'm not an apparition."

She was suddenly aware of how shabby she looked. "I didn't know...I didn't expect..." Great heavens, how confused, how stupid she sounded!

Unbuckling his small sword, Ben walked toward the bedroom. "You'll have to excuse the grit," he said. "I'm covered with dirt and sand and I'm too exhausted to care. All I want is to sleep for three days in a real bed."

Finally able to move, Lea threw her washcloth in the dry sink and followed him. He had taken off his coat and sat on the edge of the bed in his shirtsleeves, pulling at his boots. They were grimy with dirt, his uniform trousers were white with sand, and she could smell the pungent sweaty odor of his body from the doorway. She forgot her own careless appearance in wonder at his own, it was so unlike him.

"Here, let me help you," she said, kneeling to tug at his tall leather boots. An uneasy silence fell between them which Lea finally broke. "What happened? I mean, what brought you back?"

"We've abandoned Fort Alabama. It was never much of a go anyway, too isolated and too deep in the wilderness. I suppose I should be happy they sent us back before we were all massacred. That is certainly what would have happened otherwise."

Lea glanced up at him, noticing the dark smudges under his eyes, the way his hair fell forward over his brow. She had never seen him look so tired or so discouraged. She tried to smile. "You don't seem very happy about it."

"That's because I'm too weary to feel anything. I didn't realize how draining that outpost was until I rode into Fort Brooke and remembered what a safe, ordinary life is like."

Lea gave a yank and worked his boot free. Ben leaned back until she got the second one off, then stretched on the bed, his arms out, his legs splayed. He hadn't meant to come home this way. He had planned to clean up and think through what he was going to say. But somehow none of that mattered. All he wanted was to lie down and sleep.

Still on her knees, Lea watched as he drifted off. She had never seen anyone go to sleep so quickly, she thought, smiling. Her freshly scrubbed coverlet would get wrinkled and dirty, but no matter. Her husband was home again. Even more miraculous, he was sleeping on her—their bed. This was not the way she might have planned it, but she was grateful all the same. In fact, she was glad she hadn't known he was coming and had been spared the hours of agonizing over what to say and what to expect.

She rose and pulled a light quilt from the chest at the foot of the bed, drawing it over his stocking feet. Time enough to talk later.

By suppertime Lea was transformed—hair brushed until it gleamed, her prettiest dress, little pearl earrings dangling from her lobes, a ribbon around her throat. These days the sutler's shelves were more empty than ever but she had managed to get a little flour and lard, and along with the last onions from the garden she stewed up a few slices of her hoarded smoked beef, adding a thin pastry on top. Her nervousness had grown in proportion to her fussing, yet she was happy. She had thought hard this afternoon as she worked around the house, readying it for Ben when he woke. Clay's words still hammered in her mind, challenging her. She still felt uncertain of the best way to proceed, but one thing was clear. Ben would not be allowed to turn his back on her this time. He would face the fact of their marriage even if it meant sending her away.

A cold chill went through her heart at that thought but she faced it resolutely. If nothing lay ahead but separation and heartbreak, very well then. Better to get it over with than go on in this limbo of not knowing.

By eight o'clock her resolutions were beginning to falter. Ben still lay in an exhausted sleep in the darkened bedroom. Lea and Buck had eaten half the dinner and saved the rest for the Captain when he awoke. Lea refused to call him, convinced that he needed the rest. Buck had come in more excited over an invitation to spend the night with a young friend than the knowledge that his father had returned. At first Lea thought to keep him home since it might not be seemly to let him stay out the first night Ben was back. Then a little voice at the back of her mind thought better of it and she sent him happily off at dusk, hoping she was doing the right thing. Nora left a little later after cleaning up the kitchen and laying out the Captain's supper.

Lea sat in the rocker in the parlor listening to the soft sighs of the evening around her. Once she almost got up to light a lamp against the darkness but her mood was such that the darkened room suited it better. Besides, a resolution was forming in her mind which she felt would not survive any light.

She sat for a long time listening to the creak of the rocker and an occasional sleepy murmur from the bedroom. Once in a while she heard him give a soft snore, a homey sound that brought joy to her heart. After an hour of facing her fears and inhibitions, her resolve formed and she left the parlor to lock the front door. Carefully she put away the food in the kitchen, made sure the back door was also locked, then entered her bedroom. A soft breeze lifted the curtains at the bedroom window while moonlight poured through it to bronze the floorboards. Deliberately Lea pulled the curtains across, making the room even darker.

In the soft darkness she unbuttoned her dress and slipped it and her petticoats off around her feet. Stepping out of them she reached for her nightrobe but thought better of it. No, if she was going to be a wanton she would go all the way. Modesty, inhibitions, all must be put aside if she was going to go through with this. Besides, they were married, weren't they?

The cool air gently caressed her bare skin. Other than taking a bath Lea could count on her fingers the times she had ever stood completely naked before the world, but now it gave her a feeling of freedom and release. Something almost primitive stirred in her as she crossed to the bed and sat down. Ben was facing her, curled toward her, his breathing deep, his face peaceful.

"Dear Lord, forgive me," Lea murmured. "Darling Rachel, forgive…"

No! This had nothing to do with Rachel. This was her life and her future. Ben was here, he was hers and she wanted him. She pulled the quilt up over both of them and very gently eased her lithe, warm body down against his. How amazing the way her curves fit his. How surprising they melded so naturally. She laid her palms against his cheek and lowered her face, her hair spilling over his shoulders and her breast. Then she began to kiss him, draining all her longing and love into his lips..

Ben stirred, coming up out of slumber, growing conscious of the soft petal kisses on his face. Dimly he became aware that he was lying on a bed and someone had their arms around him, that their lips were drifting across his own. His hand moved lethargically to touch soft flesh, tantalizing in its hollows and curves. With a start he realized his fingers had closed around the full symmetry of a woman's breast.

With a groan he rolled over against the yearning body next to him. His hands drifted along the gentle flesh, downy and delicate as a cloud. Urgent fingers pulled away his shirt, slipped beneath to wander over his chest, easing him out of his clothes. He lay, bemused, a languorous warmth spreading within him, dreams of sirens ringing in his ears, carried along on the increasing current. There was a wondrous body against his own, rounded, alive, tantalizing in its curves and smooth undulating surfaces. His blood began to sing and swell. An urgency grew within him and in a swift reversal of roles, he took over the searching, the desperate yearning. His arms closed about this woman's naked body and he melded into it. Dimly he heard his own voice—"Oh Rachel, my love…"

Lea lay like a flame in his embrace, her chin resting against his head as he bent over her breasts, her arms gripping his strong back. She heard his murmured words and pursed her lips tightly together, never answering for fear he might recognize her voice and the enchantment would be shattered.

*   *   *   *

When she woke the next morning the place beside her was empty. She turned over, stretching full length, reveling in the feel of her taut body, smiling to herself in satisfaction. Now she was truly married. Like it or not, Ben was her husband, her partner in a fully consummated marriage. Now she was truly his wife.

Her ecstasy did not last any longer than it took for second thoughts to come flooding in. She sat up in bed, hugging her knees, fighting a nameless fear. Lea knew well enough that joy in the dark of night could look quite different in the light of day. Ben might have at first murmured Rachel's name but she knew with certainty he had eventually realized who was there with him. How could he not when it grew obvious he was making love to a virgin. Yet he had not broken it off and sent her away. On the contrary, he had drifted back to sleep cradling her in his arms. Of course by the time he realized it was Lea he was making love to, it would have required more than weak flesh was capable of to turn away. That was how she had planned it.

Would he hate her for seducing him now that he could look at it dispassionately? Was it a mean, callous trick, preying on him when he was weak, tired and vulnerable? Would his pride be so wounded that their relationship might never be repaired?

Shaking herself, she jumped from the bed. She would have to wait and see. In the meantime, she would keep busy—her never-failing antidote to anxiety. The bedsheets which bore the telltale signs of her wedding night must be taken away and washed at once. Nothing must be allowed to tarnish the wild abandonment and utter joy of those hours in the dark.

Pulling a nightrobe over her shoulders, she stood at the wash stand and splashed cold water over her face. After toweling her cheeks, she reached for the brush and began to pull it through the long hair cascading around her shoulders. Then she heard a noise and turned to see Ben standing in the doorway.

Her hand stopped in midair. He was fully dressed, washed and combed and showing none of the grit of yesterday. His hand rested on his wide leather belt, his booted feet were set wide apart. The look on his face was difficult to read, part scowl, part embarrassment. Glancing down, Lea saw that her robe barely covered her breasts and she pulled it closer around her, refusing to look away. She knew all her hopes and longing were mirrored in her eyes.

"I've made coffee," Ben said quietly. "In the kitchen."

"Oh. I'll be right there."

He turned away, leaving her to clutch at the hope that at least he had not sounded angry. Hurriedly she threw on her clothes and swept up her hair. For good measure she splashed some lavender water on her temples and pinched her cheek to put some color in her pale face.

When she walked into the kitchen he was sitting at the table, a cup between his fingers. Lea poured herself some coffee then sat down opposite him, afraid to speak before he did. As he continued to stare down at the steaming cup, she wondered what was going on behind that impassive face.

She couldn't know the demons that plagued him or how he had risen that morning full of a determination to be firm with her. He would apologize then set her free. It was the best solution.

But that was before he saw her standing at the washstand, her hair falling down her back, her white breasts gleaming above the edge of her robe, her face so radiant and full of promise, her lithe, healthy body so enticing. In that single moment of hesitation he had lost forever the ability to send her away.

Ben coughed nervously. "I think I took advantage of you last night," he said quietly. "I'm sorry."

"You did. But you needn't apologize. It wasn't your doing at all. It was mine."

He looked up quickly and there was a flash of something in his eyes Lea recognized as amusement. It encouraged her to go on.

"I deliberately went to you. I couldn't tell you how much I wanted us to be truly married so I decided to show you. You don't hate me for it, do you?"

He gave a short laugh. "Hardly. I'm sure you're aware you didn't have to force me. In fact I'm a little embarrassed at how much I enjoyed it."

Impulsively Lea reached across the table for his hand. "We have to face this, Ben. I know you can never feel for me all that you felt for Rachel. And I know when you married me it was more from convenience than wanting me as your wife. But I love you, Ben. I've always loved you. I want to be your true wife more than anything in the world. I want to care for you and keep your family for you and follow you anywhere."

She hesitated, almost afraid to go on. "Do you think we can have a life together? If you really, truly don't, then say so now and I'll go back to New York or anywhere else you want to send me. Just tell me."

Ben forced himself to look deeply into her soft eyes, so hopeful yet so afraid. How could he be so cruel as to pack her off, especially after last night? He was committed to her now. She said she loved him. Well, in truth, he loved her too, perhaps not quite as he had loved Rachel, but deeply all the same. How could he not when she had been so much a part of his family for so many years. She was a good woman and she had given herself to him, trusted him. He wasn't a cad. Nor was he one to ever turn his back on duty and responsibility.

He spoke on a long sigh. "Lea, I could never send you away. What kind of life would that be for you? If there is someone else, of course I would set you free."

"There's no one else, Ben."

Abruptly he rose and moved to stare out of the window before turning back to her. His voice was level but resonant with feeling.

"It's true that when we married I did not expect to live long enough to make a life with you. But God has seen fit to keep me in this world, for some purpose I hope. There's no reason why we can't search for it together. I'm a poor bet as a husband, Lea. You know my faults as well as anyone, having lived with Rachel and me so long. And you know how much I cared for her. I will always think of her as the great love of my life. Yet I have always had an affection for you. If you still want me, poor a choice as I am, then I'm willing to try to make a go of it."

Her body sagged with relief. All the tautness, rigidity and fear lifted from her heart. She rose and walked over to stand before him, slipping her arms around his waist.

"We will make a go of it, Ben. I promise you all that I can give."

His expression lightened and for the first time he smiled, then bent to kiss her lightly on the lips. His arms went around her and she leaned against his hard body, resting her head in the hollow of his neck.

Everything was all right at last. Everything would be all right from now on.

CHAPTER 11

▼

A thin sunlight was just beginning to break through the shroud of dawn as Lea stepped from her kitchen door into the yard behind the house. She could sense it was going to be a hot day later on but for now these early morning hours held a deliciously cool freshness too enticing to resist.

It was the time of day she loved best. All around her she could hear the sounds of the camp coming to life, the sharp snap of wood being chopped, the cries of sentries, the drums calling assembly. Along the row of officer's cottages she could make out spirals of smoke from her neighbor's kitchens. She ought to be at her stove too, she thought, lifting her arms over her head to stretch full length. But she could not face the day's activities yet. She was usually an extremely conscientious housewife but this glorious morning was too precious to spend indoors. Ben was already gone and Buck still asleep. Another half hour and Nora would be fussing around the kitchen. Why waste the best part of a summer day over a hot, smoky stove? She would do something different, something invigorating and delightful. She would go for a ride!

Quickly she changed her dress to a full-skirted one suitable for straddling a horse, pinned up her hair under a wide-brimmed straw bonnet and went striding toward the stables. Although not a frequent rider, it was by no means unusual for her to order one of the stable hands to saddle a quiet animal for her. She had never gone out this early, however and it made her feel daring and adventurous.

The young soldier led out an amiable mare. Lea climbed on its back, adjusted her skirts and took the reins in her hands as though she was accustomed to riding out every morning of the world.

"You'd better take this along," the private said handing her a leather riding crop.

"But you said she was gentle."

"Well, ma'am, she is, but even with the best of horses you sometimes have to show them who's in charge."

Lea smiled her thanks and touched the crop to her hat brim before turning her horse toward the bay. She rode along drinking in all the changes that had created yet another transformation at Fort Brooke in the months since Ben's return. Back in early spring the camp had swelled with men. They poured in because General Scott was setting out on his ambitious plan to break the back of Seminole resistance, a plan everyone now knew had failed miserably. At least eleven hundred new soldiers had arrived, setting up long rows of white tents, enlarging barns, erecting new storehouses and other outbuildings. During those two or three months Fort Brooke had been a bustling place, crowded with troops and their officers including no less than three Generals! She had enjoyed the excitement of it even when her energies were occupied with worry over her marriage and her work with the Seminole refugees.

And then, as suddenly as it happened, it all changed.

Many of the friendly Indians had been shipped off to the western territories. The volunteers and most of the Regulars had marched away to tramp the vast scrub country of the reservation. General Scott was recalled north to face a government inquiry as to why his plan failed so badly. A new commander, General Jessup, had recently been appointed but he was currently so occupied in Georgia that authority for the Fort had been temporarily handed over to the territorial Governor, Richard Call.

But the biggest change, she thought as her mare walked sedately along the shore, was the way alarm and fear had evaporated. Lea remembered well the terrible trepidation everyone felt last January when it seemed a full-scale Indian attack might come at any moment. Almost no one now thought that would happen because the fort was considered too well defended.

"Indians like to fight their way," Ben had said just the night before. "They choose places where they have cover and can get out safely if the battle goes against them. They don't like to make war in the open."

Ben is right, she thought, leaning forward to stroke the mare's sleek neck. By now many of the white settlers had packed up to return to their homes while more and more of the new arrivals who came on every ship had chosen to settle in the village. Tampa was beginning to grow again though it was still a long way from a busy, thriving town.

The gulls came swooping around her hoping she had brought food. Lea loved to watch them glide and dive but she refused to feed them for fear of being swamped. Her horse grew a little skittish at their antics and she reined her in to stand and watch the growing sun gild the low expanse of bay and the small, shaggy islands out in the water. A few moments later she moved on, heading away from the fort. The vegetation here was short and scruffy. Sea oats bobbed gracefully in the slight wind near the water and farther back, jagged palmettos fought with thickets and a few scraggly pines for space to grow in the sand. They were primitive plants yet Lea admired them. They had none of the lush beauty so common in her Hudson valley yet she loved their wildness, their thorny determination to survive in heat and an inhospitable soil.

At the shore up ahead she could see two fishing boats pushing out into the bay. She remembered Ben saying when the white man first came to this long, flat bay, the fish were so thick you could almost walk across the water on them. Even today there were so many varieties that after all these months Lea could still only name a few.

She had thought the shore deserted but as her mare ambled on she saw the man who had pushed off the fishing boats still standing by the water. She could tell he wore a white straw hat, a long vest over shirtsleeves, and high boots but she was too far away to make out his face. Looking around, she realized she had wandered farther from the fort than she intended. She was, in fact, not far from the well called Government Spring that furnished the fort with most of its fresh water. The man saw her and waved, striding forward. To turn back now would seem impolite so she rode on. She would just say 'good morning' then go back the way she came.

Her heart fell as she recognized Ramon de Diego, his tanned face under the brim of his hat lit with pleasure.

"*Buenos dias,* Senora," he called as Lea pulled up her mare. "A nice morning for a canter, eh?"

"Good morning, Senor Diego," Lea replied formally. "Yes, it is very pleasant."

Ramon stopped close beside her. "I had no idea you liked to ride in the early hours. I've never seen you before when I was out to see my men off."

"I've never come this far before," Lea answered. "In fact I seldom ride at all. It just seemed such an ideal morning for it."

There was a familiar light in Ramon's eyes as he looked her over. She resisted a shiver, it reminded her so of the way a predator might lick its lips at the sight of its hapless dinner. She tried to pull her horse around but Ramon reached out and grabbed the bridle, holding the mare's head close to his body. Rather than yank it out of his hands she decided to keep up the pretense of a polite exchange.

"I shall have to look for you after this, Senora." Ramon reached out long fingers to stroke the mare's neck. "Perhaps you would like a walk along the beach to rest your horse. Come, I'll help you dismount."

Lea looked back where the trees and roofs of the officer's quarters were barely visible above the dunes. They were quite alone except for the fishing smacks gliding away on the silver waters of the bay.

"No, thank you. I must get back. My young stepson will be awake soon and wonder where I've gone."

Surely she was foolish being afraid of this man. Then his fingers inched along the mare's neck toward her leg. His voice was low and friendly as he allowed his big palm to lightly rest on her knee.

"Your horse might graze while we enjoy the cool morning. Would that not be…pleasurable?"

There was no mistaking the suggestion in his voice or the way his dark eyes looked up at her from under long lashes. His fingers slid smoothly along her leg, inching up under the hem of her skirt. She grew speechless with outrage. He was not inviting her to enjoy the morning, of that she was sure.

"Please loosen my bridle, Senor de Diego," Lea said in a steely cold voice. "I must go back now."

He smiled up at her, undaunted by her anger. "You mistake my intentions, Senora. I mean you no disrespect." His polite tone was belied by the soft strokes of his fingers as they worked their way along her calf, lightly rubbing her leg just above her boot.

"Really, Senor," Lea cried, yanking her horse around to loosen his grip on the bridle. "You go too far." Kicking her mare, she backed away, struggling to control her horse. "If my husband knew…"

Ramon laughed and stepped back. "A woman with spirit," he said, smiling up at her. Lea raised her crop to strike him then thought better of it. "Good bye," she snapped, turning her mare to go thundering back down the beach toward the fort. His laughter followed her.

She was still shaking even after returning the mare and walking home. Had she been mistaken? On the surface his words were innocent enough. Yet the look in his eyes, his fingers stroking her leg and the suggestion in his tone belied everything he said. Surely she was not mistaken in that.

She was so accustomed to polite respect from both soldiers and civilians that she hardly knew what to think of a man so brazen and obvious as Diego. What kind of woman was he used to dealing with? Did he imagine all the women of Tampa were like those painted harlots in the saloons of the village? Did he suppose officer's wives were desperate for the attention of any man after weeks and weeks of their husband's absence? He had a beautiful, aristocratic wife. Why wasn't he satisfied with her?

"Lea!"

A familiar voice broke her concentration and she realized someone had been calling her name. She turned at the gate of her house to see Clay Madrapore coming down the walk. His fringed shirt and high boots were covered with a thick layer of yellow dust. It lay so thick on his head that his shoulder-length hair appeared to have been bleached by the sun.

"You must have just ridden in," she said, managing a thin laugh.

"That's right. I only arrived from Newnansville moments ago. I was hoping you'd rustle up some breakfast for me. I don't think I can look at another piece of jerked beef."

"Of course," Lea said, opening the gate. "Come on in. Ben's not here but Buck and I haven't had breakfast yet so you can join us. How were things up in the north country?"

"Too much sickness and as unsettled as you might expect," he said, following her up the walk and into the house. "Governor Call is just waiting on the arrival of a Tennessee volunteer brigade to start a new offensive. Meantime, old Sam Jones and Powel jump on any whites they can reach."

They met Nora in the kitchen just taking biscuits from the oven. Lea added some thin slices of army bacon and the last jar of her home-made preserves. She chatted amiably with Clay while Buck came running in to gobble down his food and then dart out the door. When Nora moved outside to work in the garden, Lea and Clay sat at the table enjoying a second cup of coffee. Lea studied the lines of hard riding on Clay's face. His shoulders, usually so ram-rod straight, sagged a little and there were dark lines along his cheeks which suggested he must have been in the saddle most of the night. She was gratified to see how he gradually relaxed in the peacefulness of the kitchen.

She was conscious of the way Clay studied her between sips of the strong coffee and felt sure her anger and anxiety were easy to read. She did not guess that he read them as proof conditions in her marriage had not changed and was surprised when he reached to lay his hand over hers on the table.

"No better?"

Lea looked up in surprise. "What? Oh, you mean with Ben." Her face took on a softness and sweetness that gave Clay a sudden pang. "Oh my yes, it's much better. I'm so grateful to you for the things you told me that night of the dance. They made a real difference. We've worked out our problems and I feel now that we are truly married. I'm very happy, Clay."

He could read the truth in her shinning eyes. "I'm glad to hear it, Lea, but you sure had me fooled. When I saw you standing at the gate I figured things were still as bad as could be."

Lea studied her cup in her hand. She knew it would not be wise to tell anyone about her encounter with Diego this morning even though it would help her to speak of it. But surely she could trust Clay. Very guardedly she told him of the incident, not mentioning Ramon by name but venting her outrage and her anger.

"You don't have to tell me who it was. I can guess. The scoundrel! If he ever bothers you again, Lea, just let me know. I'll teach him a lesson he won't forget."

"And wouldn't that be wonderful! Why do you think I don't want Ben to know about this? I don't want to be the cause of any fights. Please, forget it, as I intend to. I won't have anything to do with Senor de Diego ever again, and I don't want you or Ben 'teaching' him any lessons on my behalf. Promise me you won't speak of this to anyone."

Clay muttered something she took for an assent, and she rose to set her cup in the dry sink. It was only later, after he had gone, that she realized he had not actually given her his promise.

Clay had not returned to Fort Brooke alone. He was accompanied by two of Miconopy's warriors who were entrusted with a message for Ben from Ote Emathla, a man the whites called 'Jumper', the Chief's son-in-law and one of his most important headmen. They refused to go directly into the fort, preferring to stay at the squatters camp outside the village with the women and old men who waited for the daily dispensation of food.

Ben was both surprised and curious to learn that two of Miconopy's braves were waiting outside the village to see him. Just after dawn the following day he walked out of the fort with Clay to make his way past the ramshackle buildings of the village—it seemed there were more of them every day—into the shaded oaks bordering the river. As always, it dismayed him to see the pitiful Indians huddled around their fires. From what Lea said, things had improved now that there were better supplies and a dispensary but the problems still seemed enormous. For every group of Seminoles who melted back into the scrub, ten new ones arrived every day to take their place. After the first large shipment west the round-up for emigration had been put on hold and now it seemed it would never happen before Tampa was overrun.

Ben noted the two Indians who were waiting for him were as thin and gaunt as the refugees hovering near the Fort. Though their impassive faces showed no hint of pleasure, they assured him they came in peace to tell him Ote Emathla wished to speak with him. Their polite words were in contrast to the burning hostility in their eyes.

"The taller one says Jumper is near Charlie O'Malley's old camp in Thonotassassa," Clay translated.

"I understood him," Ben said quietly. "I'm just wondering if they can be trusted. Perhaps it's a trick."

"Why would they want you instead of one of the commanding officers? Does Miconopy or Jumper carry a personal grudge against you?"

"Not that I know of. As a matter of fact, I had some dealings with Jumper after the failure of the treaty of Fort Gibson. I tried to be fair and I figured he respected me, if it could be said he respects any white man. But I could be wrong. It's difficult to tell with Indians."

"Then you must go. You might learn something of value for the rest of us. I'll go with you if they'll allow it."

"I'll need my horse," Ben said, turning to the Indian.

"No horse," he replied. "Go now."

Clay leaned near Ben to whisper, "You're not going to be allowed to go back to camp and tell them where Jumper is. I'm ready now if you are."

Already the Indians were headed for the woods. Damn! Ben thought. He hadn't any weapon with him except a scouting knife and no canteen. His uniform was wool and not one he would have chosen for a march but he had no choice. His curiosity about why Jumper wanted to speak with him made him determined to go, dangerous or not. The two Seminoles were fast disappearing behind a fringe of palmetto scrub. Only a black-tipped feather bobbed above the fronds.

"Come on," Ben said to Clay as he waded into the palmettos. "If we don't move fast we'll lose them."

The dense underbrush almost obliterated a barely visible trail. They walked for what seemed hours, the palmetto trail interspersed with hardwood hammocks so thick the sun could barely penetrate. Clay, Ben knew, would have easily kept up with the braves had he not held back for his sake. They waded through swampy creeks where mud clutched at their boots and slogged, sweaty and tired, beneath the scrub pines until Ben was certain Lake Thonotassassa must be directly ahead. Yet the lake was nowhere in sight when at last they pushed through into a clearing and found a group of ten or twelve Seminole warriors grouped before a moldering *chickee*. A quick look round told Ben this was no camp, abandoned or otherwise. The wily Jumper had evidently picked this spot only because it was more open than the woods around it and had no intention of bringing white men into a real camp.

Though he had seen Jumper from a distance at the Withlocoochee siege, Ben hadn't been this close to him since before the outbreak of the war when the Seminole headman served as a spokesman for Miconopy and the other Chiefs who gathered at Fort Gibson to protest the deportation. He had to hide his shock at how the Indian had changed. Always an imposing figure, Jumper had become hardened by the war. Gaunt and leathery, his protruding nose and sloping forehead were more prominent than ever. There was a steely contempt in his small, deadly eyes as he watched the white men approach yet his voice when he spoke was polite, like the exchanges Ben remembered.

Ben was even more surprised to recognize the tall young man standing next to Jumper. Cooachocee, the 'Wildcat', was the son of King Phillip and just beginning to attain a distinctive reputation among the ranks of Seminole warriors. He was extremely handsome, with regular, almost Grecian features. Decoratively dressed in feathers and colored cloths, his presence already exuded an authority and determination that made one take notice. What a coup it would be to bring these two in, Ben thought with regret.

"Hie la! ay-it-liepts-e-chez?" Ote Emathla said, politely inquiring after Ben's health.

"Hin-cla; good," Ben replied and shook the Indian's hand.

Jumper motioned them to sit beside him and offered them food, a formal courtesy since there was none in sight that Ben could see. He and Clay both politely declined and the Seminole came directly to the point.

"The Captain will know a Spaniard at Fort Brooke called Diego?" he said in Seminole, obviously trusting Clay to translate.

This was the last thing Ben expected to hear. He was primed for some kind of dialogue on the progress of the war, something he could carry back to his superiors at the fort. Hiding his surprise, he nodded. "I've met him. He is one of the partners with William Bunce on the Manatee river."

"This man, Diego, he is very bad. My people need guns and bullets to protect them from being carried away to a far country. I had much trade with this man. The rifles he gave us were old and worthless, though he promised they would be new. The bullets were less than he promised. The crates were mostly straw. I would kill this man myself but for the wrath of the soldiers upon my people. I tell you this, Ben Carson, because you will know how to deal with Ramon Diego."

Ben's interest picked up. William Bunce had long been suspected of dealing arms to the Indians but so far no one could prove it. It might be to his advantage if he could. "The Chief knows it is against our law to sell guns to your people. I will certainly see that Bunce and this Diego are punished."

"No, no. Bunce he is friend to the Indian but does not break your law. Diego, he is not friend."

So much for catching out Bunce. Ben chose his words carefully. "I cannot help but wonder why the great Chief tells me this. I have not been able to prevent the suffering and deportation of your people. And Ote Emathla knows well that when we face each other in battle, I must fight against him and his warriors, even to death."

Jumper's grim mouth almost softened. "I know that, Ben Carson. In battle I would kill you as well. Yet Chief Miconopy says to you in this moment of peace between us. My people have little hope here. But your woman brought food to my women and children when they starved outside the Fort Brooke. It is for her also I speak. This man, Diego, has insulted your wife. You should know this."

It took Ben a few seconds to realize Jumper was talking about Lea, not Rachel. "Insulted my wife? How?"

"She will tell you. I warn you so you watch and not let harm come to her. This man, Diego, must pay for his wickedness. You see to this, Ben Carson."

Jumper gave a slight motion of his hand, bringing one of his braves running up to hand him a rolled up strip of leather. When he smoothed it out Ben saw that it was covered with crude pictures and odd figures. Ote Emathla ran his finger down one wavy line.

"Here is the trail you call White Sand. Here, Fort Brooke, and here, Arriaga trail, Seminole land. From the tree split by lightening, to the shores of the crooked water to the ancient oak near Holata Emaltha's old camp ground. When my people are carried across the great water, you take this land. Chief Miconopy gives it to you."

He paused, assuming Ben knew exactly what he meant when actually all Ben could tell was that the land appeared to be north of the fort. Yet Ben's heart missed a beat. Could this possibly be the beginning of his hoped for plantation? "How large is this land?" he asked cautiously.

"Enough for grazing and fattening many cattle."

Getting a grip on his soaring hopes, Ben reminded himself that Miconopy and his Chiefs had no right to transfer any part of Florida to anyone except the United States government. Besides, the concept of owning and transferring land was incomprehensible to an Indian. Did the wily old Chief hope that by encouraging ownership he could get the white men fighting among themselves? He glanced at Wildcat sitting with folded arms, watching intently, his dark, handsome eyes every bit as deceitful and wily as Jumper's.

"Ask him if the Great Chief Miconopy give Ramon de Diego the same map as this?"

The headman's evident surprise told Ben he had guessed correctly. "Chief Miconopy gave his mark on a paper Diego made. It is not the same."

Maybe not. But it opened the door to one hell of a dispute.

"The Chief does me great honor," Ben said as Jumper rolled up the scroll and handed it to him. Ben slipped it inside his tunic. "I thank Chief Miconopy and his true headman, Ote Emathla. In return, I tell him that a new white father will soon come to this country to deal with the Seminoles. His name is General Jessup. He is known to be a soldier of the first merit. If the Chief will work with him, perhaps there can be an end to the spilling of blood."

The faintest trace of a smile hovered over Jumper's slash of a mouth. "I do not think any white man will let our people live in peace," he said, reverting to English. "But I remember your words, Ben Carson."

"The whites have deceived us!"

It was Coacoochee's voice. Ben looked sharply at the figure of King Philip's young son who spoke as though he could no longer contain himself. The young Seminole rose to his feet and went on while Clay softly translated. "I love this land. My body is made of its sands. The Great Spirit gave me legs to walk over it, eyes to see its ponds, rivers, forest and game. The sun shines to warm us and bring forth our crops, and the moon brings back the spirits of our warriors."

Ben glanced at Clay who was staring at the youth, as mesmerized as himself at his eloquence. Jumper also watched without interrupting, nodding his approval.

"The white man comes," Wildcat went on. "We could live in peace but he steals our cattle and horses, cheats us and takes our lands. The white-eyes are as thick as the leaves in the hammocks and grow thicker every year. They may shoot us, they may chain our hands and feet, but the red man's heart will always be free."

In the ensuing silence Ben hardly knew how to reply. Everything this young warrior said was true but how to explain the complexities, the tragic necessities behind it all?

"Coacoochee speaks truth," he said quietly. "I have no answer."

Jumper stood up. "Go back to your camp now. My warriors will show the way. You will go in peace as far as the river where one crosses to eat acorns, the Lockha-popka-chiska."

The interview was ended. Ben rose, Clay beside him. He knew he must leave yet he could not bring himself to walk away from so precious an opportunity to talk face to face with these two implacable foes and esteemed leaders of the Seminole nation.

"Is there no way Miconopy and his brothers would meet with us to end this war? If Wildcat could persuade his father and the other chiefs…"

The subdued hostility in Jumper's eyes flared like blazing coals against his swarthy skin. "It is too late for talk. Like Coacoochee says, the white-eyes come more all the time to take our hunting grounds and drive us to starve. Your ships would carry us across the water far from our homes so the whites might take our land for their own. We will fight for what is ours until the last warrior lies dead, my brothers and I, though we may not win. That is why we give you this land, Ben Carson. We will go to the hunting grounds beyond and this country will fill with your people. But we wish to choose who holds what was once ours. Keep it, watch over it, and remember Chief Miconopy and Jumper when it is yours."

Ben glanced over at Clay. Both men knew the meeting was over. "May the Great Father protect and guide you both," he said, and turned away, Clay following him.

They had eaten nothing all day but they dared not stop for fear Jumper's protection might crumble before the hatred of his warriors. Much later, when they finally reached the white strip of the Federal road and were near enough to the Government Spring to feel safe, both men dropped on the sand to rest and reflect on what had happened.

"Now what do you suppose that was all about?" Ben asked, wiping his sweaty brow with his sleeve.

Clay pulled off a boot and dumped the sand out of it. "I've been mulling it over all the way back. The map seems genuine but I doubt the idea originated with Miconopy. This sounds more like a sneaky plan to pit two white men against each other in their hunger for land. The old Chief's not smart enough or sly enough for that kind of a scheme. Indians might not understand the idea of owning land but they've certainly seen enough of white people to know how greedy they are for it. Jumper is just clever and devious enough to come up with a plot like this and convince his Chief to go along."

"And Wildcat, too, I suspect. There's a young man to be reckoned with. He's going to be a formidable foe unless Jessup can bring this war to an end soon."

"And that's not likely," Clay said, pulling on his boot, "given the hostility we've seen today and the enemy we face. Wildcat is a rising star and Powel already wields great influence. Sam Jones is wily and hates the whites but he's old.

The main Chief, Miconopy, is fat and lazy but easily swayed by warriors like Jumper and Alligator who will never give in until they're forced to do so. You know, don't you that Jumper was most certainly among the horde of warriors who massacred Major Dade's column. I was surprised you could talk with him so calmly."

"I tried not to think about it." Ben took the scroll Jumper had given him from his coat and unrolled it on the sand. "I can't make anything of this. Do you recognize these boundaries?"

"No, but I do know the trail called the Arriaga Springs. It shouldn't be too difficult to figure out once it's safe enough to go up there and explore."

"I can't even tell how large it is. At least fifty acres, wouldn't you say?"

"It meant so much to him it's probably more. Possibly hundreds."

Hundreds! Ben could barely contain his excitement. Surely this could be the beginning of the homestead he hoped to carve out once the war was over. Visions of rolling acres and a great plantation house rose in his mind.

Clay's level voice took some of the steam out of his soaring expectations. "You know, of course, that the United States government will never recognize this as legal."

"Yes, I know. But I intend to fight for it anyway."

"How, for heaven's sake?"

Ben rubbed his hand against his chin. "I'll take the first step the next time Robert Hackley visits this area. I intend to purchase as much of this land as I can afford from him. Then I'll have two claims to my credit."

Clay gave a soft chuckle. "The United States is probably no more ready to recognize Hackley's claim than they are Miconopy's map. Do you really think they'd give up this valuable Florida territory simply because back in 1819 the Spanish Duke of Alagon gave a deed for half of it to Hackley's father? But I suppose as long as the question hasn't been settled, it's worth a try."

"I think so. Now all I have to figure out is how to get that other paper off Ramon de Diego. It'll probably mean a fight but I suppose that is what Jumper had in mind. It's the only thing that would have brought him and Coacoochee this close to Fort Brooke right now. They must know about Governor Call's plans to raise a campaign against the tribes that he hopes will end the war."

"Oh, they know. They probably figure it will be as big a failure as all the others."

"What do you suppose," Ben said casually, "Jumper meant by an insult to Lea?"

Clay thought a moment, wondering if he should pass on what Lea had told him. That he decided to do so was more because of his dislike of Diego than concern over Lea's pride. He was surprised at Ben's volatile reaction. The Captain was furious, outraged, ready to take on Ramon the moment he reached camp.

"Don't go leaping into anything crazy," Clay warned. Beneath that oily charm Diego is as ambitious as he is mean. He'd as soon shoot you in the back as look at you."

"Don't worry," Ben snapped as he rolled up the scroll and tucked it back into his tunic. "I won't give him the advantage of knowing I'm after him until it's too late. But I'll make him pay for this. Lea is Rachel's sister and no one is going to insult her while I know about it!"

CHAPTER 12

▼

May 7, 1837

"Dearest Mama and Papa:

It has been so long since I last wrote that I feel I must begin with an apology. So much has happened in the intervening time."

Lea dipped her quill in the ink pot beside her wooden writing case. She paused, holding the pen over the paper and watched, wondering how to continue, as a tiny black blot fell to the surface. Her parents were growing old and frail while she lingered in this hot, hostile territory. How to say that she worried and knew they worried too. That she regretted all this time apart, that she longed so much to see them and be with them again.

"You'll be glad to know the primers arrived safely. I was very glad to get them since all the teaching I've been able to give Buck has come from the few books I brought with me or from newspapers that arrive infrequently and often in bad shape. Some of the other women and their older daughters are going to help me teach the younger children now that we have the proper books. We dearly wish for a proper teacher as well and occasionally we find one of the soldiers who might suit. But the Army allows them so little time in camp before they are marched off again that it is not practical to use them. Captain Carson fares as badly. He has tracked up and down this 'vile country' as the soldiers call it, often wading through water for days at a time, in heat, rain..."

Enough of that. She should not continue with this line of thought even though it was all too true. Ben never came home but he had a tale of woe to tell—endless marching, camping out in all kinds of blistering or wet weather, fighting his way through swamps and bogs, eaten alive by insects, living for days in damp clothes and boots, often without any army rations of rice or pork and having to rely on what they could hunt and kill. Then when he did come home, it was only to rest up briefly before heading out again.

"*Two months ago General Jessup declared the war over. He forged a truce with several of the hostile chiefs who agreed to bring their people into Fort Brooke for deportation to the west. We now have nearly four hundred Indians waiting and more coming in every day. Captain Carson is convinced the fighting is nearly over and he is seriously thinking of leaving the army and settling down here.*"

Should she write that? It would grieve her parents to know she'd be making her home so far from them and so permanently. Yet it was Ben's dream to start his cotton plantation once the war was done. She might as well be truthful.

"*My hope is that once it is safe to travel and things settle down, perhaps Buck and I can sail back to New York for a visit.*"

This was not going to happen anytime soon of course, but it wouldn't hurt to give her parents something to look forward to. And who knew but it might be possible, once the fighting was done and this new country began to build.

"*You'll be glad to know we are all well even though there has been a lot of sickness in this place over the last year. Last week Robert Jackson, the Surgeon's assistant, told me there are several hundred sick soldiers in the hospital and infirmary. It's even worse for the civilians. In one family, the Collars, four of their younger children have died. But Buck has remained in good health and I seem to grow stronger all the time. Many of the illnesses which bring down others I have avoided altogether. God has been good to us.*"

Lea paused to dip her quill in the inkwell. Indeed, last spring and summer Fort Brooke had suffered more sickness than anytime since she arrived here. It was strange how some of the soldiers felt this station was one of the healthiest they had ever been posted to while others suffered so badly from the mosquitoes, flies, vermin and fevers. It was true that the climate had carried off Rachel and Stephen very quickly but they were among the most vulnerable, the frail and the very young. She and Buck seemed to thrive in it. Even Ben stayed strong in spite of the hardships he and his soldiers had to endure.

The little village of Tampa is beginning to grow, albeit slowly. We even had elections recently. We now have a Judge, a Justice of the Peace and a City clerk. There are plans to build a new courthouse and, I'm told, in Tallahassee even talk of statehood. I find it rather exciting to be in on the birth-throes of a new state.

And what conflict this talk of statehood had spawned, even in her own home! She found the idea interesting enough but Ben had grown almost obsessed with the opportunities that lay in opening up the Florida territory. Unfortunately, his enthusiasm was putting his career in jeopardy, something she was constantly warning him about. For when Judge Steele, one of Tampa's oldest and most prominent residents, decided to lay out a town on land outside Fort Brooke— land that still actually belonged to the government—the military became very upset. For a time it looked as though Ben would be forced to choose between the army and the town. To her dismay, he even toyed with the possibility of resigning his commission in order to run in the elections. Thankfully he decided instead to wait and see if the war was really over before doing anything so drastic. But no need to go into all that in her letter. It would only worry her parents.

I will close for now as I have no other news of interest. The schooner Althea put into port yesterday with supplies for the fort, and she plans to leave tonight again for Pensacola with, I hope, this letter aboard. I trust it will not take too long to reach you from there. I send you my love and all my prayers and good wishes for your continued good health. Please write to me, your letters are always so dearly welcome. Your loving daughter, Leatrice.

She folded the paper thinking of all she had not said and hoping they would read between the lines. Don't worry about me, I'll be fine. I love you both so much and miss you terribly. Will God ever let me see you again in this world, to enfold you in my arms and kiss your dear faces?

And yet…and yet, even given that opportunity she knew she would never choose to leave this place where her life was so closely entwined with her husband and stepson. Where death, sickness and danger waited to strike daily. Where a new kind of living was slowly being forged out of a wilderness Eden. This was her life now and she could never go back.

To no one's surprise, General Jessup's truce fell apart in early June. The Seminole war-chiefs, Asceola and Sam Jones with over a hundred warriors sneaked into camp one night and led nearly 700 waiting Indians back into the forest, among them such notables as Micanopy, Jumper, Cloud and Alligator. It was a terrible blow to General Jessup's hopes as well as to his reputation and it made him more determined than ever to rid Florida of these hostiles by any means necessary. Ben watched the gradual build-up of more troops with growing unease over where he fit into the General's plans, yet he consoled himself with what he felt was the one good result from the aborted truce. Jessup had got the Seminoles to agree to a new reservation boundary south of the Hillsborough River, thus opening up all the land north of Fort Brooke to settlement. He intended to make his own claim there as soon as possible.

The following month Ben was encouraged to hear that the Hackleys had finally filed claim to half of Florida, a claim based on Richard Hackley's grant from the Spanish Duke of Alagon back in 1819. At the same time Judge Steele filed for the village of Tampa and began formulating plans to sell lots. Ben then began to make his own plans—to meet with Robert Hackley, Richard's son, in Tallahassee to purchase the acres on Miconopy's map and, while there, to also file a claim under the preemption act as a second precaution. But first he had to see the land for himself. And after that he must find a way to nullify Ramon de Diego's competing claim, in case he made one.

Ramon de Diego. It hadn't taken Ben long to lock horns with this gentleman after his encounter with Ote Emathla and the young Wildcat. Not long after that meeting he was asked to serve on the military Garrison Court where Diego had a petition to establish a trading post on the Alafia River. Ben jumped at the chance. He was somewhat surprised when he walked in the room and saw Diego lounging easily in one of the chairs facing the table where the three officers were to hold court. Being aware of Ramon's business interests with the fishermen of Spanishtown creek, Ben expected to see someone much like them. To his surprise, Diego was as different as could be. Well formed, meticulously dressed in frock coat and felt hat, with a charming smile and polite manners, he seemed more like a Spanish aristocrat than a fish rancher. He also exuded confidence, as though his approval had already been bought and sold. Well, thought Ben, as he took his seat behind the table, he's in for a surprise.

The court weighed in on several other cases before Diego's petition came up. They included the usual camp mishaps—ruling on an officer who had struck a private for refusing duty, two incidents of soldiers drunk at their posts, and a shooting between two regulars that appeared to be the result of a quarrel rather than an accident. During all these procedures Ben quietly studied Ramon sitting politely in the background, legs crossed, long fingers drumming softly against his knee. A very self-assured gentleman, Ben thought. If he hadn't known of his insulting behavior toward Lea and his scheming traffic with the Indians, he might even have been tempted to admire him.

"Next, the petition of Senor Ramon de Diego to establish a trading post comes before us for consideration," Lieutenant Reeve droned, picking a paper from the top of the pile before him. "Senor, would you like to explain your proposal?"

"Of course, Lieutenant," Diego replied, rising easily to his feet. "As you gentleman probably know, I have been associated for some years with William Bunce and Manuel Olivella in a large ranchero on the Manatee. I also have a ranchero of my own in Charlotte Harbor and connections in Key West and Havana. Thus, I assure you I have the wherewithal to support a small trading post on the Alafia river which might also suit the purposes of the military establishment."

"I fail to see how," Lieutenant Clary spoke up. "The Alafia is only fifteen miles or so from the fort and the Indians often camp there. Aren't you worried about raids?"

"I respectfully suggest that for these very reasons a post where information might be 'overheard' concerning plans for future attacks could be of great use. As for raids on my post, I have for some years maintained friendly relations with the Indians and I believe they would respect that."

On one side of Ben Lt. Reeve shuffled restlessly through the remaining papers in front of him, mentally tallying how much longer these proceedings would take. On Ben's other side, Lt. Clary lounged back in his chair and smiled at the petitioner. "If you think that, Senor Diego, you are more sanguine than most men with knowledge of the hostiles. I suppose there is something to be said for a listening post, but nevertheless…"

"We need to move on," Reeve broke in. "This is a simple request which I believe would cost the military little. Senor de Diego takes all the risk. I therefore…"

"Just a moment," Ben interrupted. "Senor Diego suggests he could be the 'ears' for the military. I suggest that he might just as well serve as a spy for the Indians. After all, we know little of where his loyalties lie."

For the first time Ramon focused his black eyes on Captain Carson, giving him a long appraising stare. All the good humor of a moment before faded under his cold scrutiny. "Would the *Capitano* care to elaborate on his very unkind comment?"

Ben gave him a thin smile. "Gladly, Senor. It is well known that William Bunce is sympathetic to the Indian claims for Florida. I suggest that the same might be said of you. Like Bunce, you have been known to unlawfully trade grog to the Seminoles and even worse, guns and ammunition. If they do not attack your proposed post that could well be the reason."

Diego almost visibly swelled. "Those are serious accusations, *Capitano* Carson."

"Nevertheless, they are true. Were you not once jailed here at this fort for these very reasons?"

"It was never proved and I was quickly set free."

Lt. Reeve leaned toward Ben and whispered, "Do we really need to make an issue of this, Captain? Let him run the risks. Perhaps his post will prove useful in the long run."

Ben turned back to Diego. "I believe Ramon de Diego to be a rogue and a spy who is simply desirous of another station from which to supply the Indians with guns, whisky and ammunition. I will never approve the establishment of this post."

"I concur with Captain Carson," Clary spoke up.

"The military," Ben went on, fixing his eyes on Ramon, "is more inclined to furnish traitors with 'iron ornaments' for hands and legs than to set them up in a business which would serve to enhance their malicious activities."

"Well," Reeve broke in, anxious to turn the conversation from the dangerous turn Ben had taken, "we are not dealing here with traitorous activities but with the petition to establish a trading post. I suppose we might as well make it unanimous. Petition denied."

Diego gave them all a cold appraising stare, focusing finally on Ben with naked anger darkening his aristocratic features. "I can go over your heads to the Commandant."

"Go ahead," Ben answered. "But I believe you will find that Captain Munroe will abide by the ruling of this court. Good day, Senor de Diego."

As Ramon turned and stalked out the door Lt. Clary muttered under his breath, "There goes an angry man. I hope this was wise."

"I believe he is more surprised than angry," Ben said dryly. "He was so sure we would accommodate him. With what reason, I wonder?"

"Next," Reeve commented briskly.

Two hours later as Ben walked down the low steps of the headquarters he was surprised to see Ramon de Diego move from a post he had been leaning against and walk toward him.

"*Capitano*," Diego said stepping in front of Ben.

"Excuse me." Ben tried to move around him but Diego blocked his way.

"It was unkind of you, *Capitano*, to refuse my petition. I'm sure you know I am a bad man to make an enemy of."

"Senor, I do not care whether you are an enemy or not. I know of your traitorous activity from the very lips of those you sought to cheat. I suggest you leave this area and go back to Havana where your 'business dealings' will be met with more accommodation. We do not need your kind in Florida."

With a sudden shove Ben pushed Diego aside and went striding on. '*And let that be for Lea,*' he thought with satisfaction.

Behind Ben, his handsome lips tightly pursed, Diego watched the Captain's retreating back. "You will come to care, *Capitano*," he muttered. This arrogant *gringo* with the prissy wife did not know how he had thwarted his, Ramon de Diego's, carefully laid plans. This trading post was to be his first step toward breaking away from William Bunce, the first brick in the edifice that would make his fortune. The prejudice of one smug, self-serving officer had created a galling setback, but it would be overcome. William Bunce was not going to last much longer. Like a fool he was preparing to throw in his lot with the Hackleys and Augustus Steele. Anyone with an ounce of sense should know the U.S. government was never going to recognize Hackley's claim to half of Florida, and as for Steele, he was a man with far more ambition than acumen. He, Ramon, on the other hand, was neither foolish nor stupid. He knew how to play the Indians against the Anglos and he was just getting started.

Diego angled his fine Spanish hat on his handsome head and flicked the brim with a long finger. "You have injured Diego, *Capitano,* and the spirit of a Spaniard calls for vengeance. Oh yes, you will come to care."

Ben had plenty of leisure to think about his encounter with Diego during the months before he was finally able to take a week's leave and ride north to scout out his claim in Central Florida. Though he had never been able to meet with Robert Hackley, he'd heard a rumor that Diego was trying to purchase vast acres in that same area from him. However, Ramon had not been seen around Fort Brooke in almost a year and Ben supposed he might have given up and gone back to Havana after all. Good riddance!

So much had happened since that angry encounter with Diego. Last winter he decided to get serious about making plans to leave the army and start building a new life in Florida. As the number of troops and officers swelled again, taxing the resources of the fort, he joined three other army men in an ambitious scheme to invest in real estate and set up a merchandising store in the village of Tampa. Captain John Munroe, the fort Commander, paymaster Donald Fraser, and sutler Henry Lindsay purchased 55 acres on the west side of the river and laid plans to plot their own City of Tampa there. Ben invested as a silent partner with them in a venture to open a store on the east side near the water. At this point all these plans were only on paper but he and his co-investors were excited about the possibilities. The previous July Augustus Steele, who had sold them the land, had sailed north to visit Richard Hackley on Staten Island, probably to clarify his own deeds to the village outside the Fort. Ben himself bought two of Steele's lots on the east side of the Hillsborough, near the river on what was to become Water street and began erecting a small log house there. Lea and Buck were not too enthusiastic about moving into it—it was still very primitive—but he felt sure they would do so when he made his resignation official.

He was increasingly anxious to do just that, especially with the discouraging turns the war was taking. Just last fall General Jessup, convinced he had the right to take any means necessary to end the hostilities, arrested Powel, Coacoochee, and Coa Hadjo when they came to a parley under a flag of truce. Wildcat eventually managed to escape but Powel died in captivity and Jessup's reputation was tarnished by the treachery. Later General Zachery Taylor arrived and by Christmas had fought a large indecisive battle against a sizable force of Indians at Lake Okeechobee. Men and supplies kept pouring into Florida but the Indians seemed more determined than ever to die fighting rather than be deported to the west.

The worst of the fighting had become confined to South Florida when Ben finally got away to scout the area where he hoped to build his future. The land he picked for his plantation, as near as he could place it to the map Jumper had given him, turned out to be perfect for his plans.

"It's easy, rolling country, Lea" he eagerly reported to his wife on his return. "Not flat pine barrens like around Tampa. And lakes! They're everywhere. Very beautiful. There are very few settlers in the area right now but that won't last and it only tells me I've got to move quickly with my claim. A lot of clearing will have to be done but once that's accomplished, it should be perfect for growing cotton."

"So you're still set on a cotton farm?"

"I am. And I think this will be an ideal place for one. You know, General Clinch has a plantation up near Fort Drane where he was able to grow cotton rather successfully before the war. I hope to emulate that."

He grew silent as he caught her studying him. He knew she dreaded giving up the stability of his army career, yet she had never discouraged him in his dreams for the future. "But why cotton?" she asked. "Why not sugar cane or cattle?"

Ben thought for a moment before answering. "I suppose because it's what I learned growing up in South Carolina." Though he knew that much was true, he didn't add that this burning ambition for a successful plantation was based more on his desire to be like the wealthy aristocrats he had admired in his youth than on any love for cotton itself. His own father, with his dusty apothecary shop, had always been looked down on by the young blades who rode through town. Even as a child Ben had longed to be one of them. Though it was probably too late for him, he could damn sure still make it possible for Buck.

Lea tilted her head thoughtfully, pursing her lips. "What about the Seminoles? Are they not still in the area?"

"Oh, a few, I suppose. There's bound to be some risk involved but I believe it will be worth it in the end. And I won't move you and Buck there until I have a house and outbuildings up and ready."

"And we are to live in the village until then?"

"Yes. You won't mind too much, will you?"

He could almost see her mentally sizing up the proposition. The new log house would not be nearly as comfortable as the officer's quarters where they had lived for so long but the village itself was infinitely better than two years ago when it had consisted of little more than a post office surrounded by a few scattered shacks. Now there were several substantial houses, a two-room courthouse, a boat repair, harness and cobbler's shop, a laundress' and a second blacksmith's establishment, even a theater. Yes, there were several saloons as well, to say nothing of the questionable huts up the river where some unsavory women plied their trade. But more people arrived with every ship and Steele continued to sell lots to enterprising entrepreneurs.

All the same he was relieved when Lea finally smiled. "Well, I always wondered what it would be like to be a pioneer."

Dear Lea. Thinking about it later, Ben pulled out his watch, flicked open the lid and focused on the fragile, lovely face of his dead first wife. It had been a while since he had done that, he realized, having been so busy of late. Rachel would have found all this too hard to bear, he thought. She was made to be cosseted and pampered and oh, how he had delighted in doing just that for her. But there was other work to be done now and certainly Lea with her hardy good health was more suited to it. Perhaps that was what God had intended when he took Rachel away. But it was still hard. So hard.

During the autumn of 1838 a Constitutional Convention met in Tallahassee to begin the push for statehood for Florida. In December an amendment was passed rejecting any claims to land titles in the territory based on the Alagon grant, assuming Congress granted statehood to Florida. The Hackleys' claim was thus effectively nullified. By the time word of the decision reached Fort Brooke Ben had already tendered his resignation from the army.

BOOK II

1842

CHAPTER 13

▼

Lea stepped out on to the breezeway of her log house, squinting against the glare and shielding her eyes with her hand. In the distance, above the sloping fields bordered by a narrow line of trees, smoky piles of great, brooding clouds hovered over the horizon. The wind had picked up, shuddering the branches in the grove of oaks near the house. One of those sudden summer storms coming, she thought. Another violent tirade to break the hot monotony of the day. At least it might cool things down a bit.

She picked up her basket of ever-present mending and eased into a pine rocking chair, absently plying her needle and gently rocking back and forth. She ought to be writing a letter to her parents, it had been so long since the last. But mailing a letter meant a trip into Tampa and since she'd been too busy to send one with Ben when he left a few days ago, it would be a while now until the next opportunity.

Besides, it was difficult to tell them about all the changes in her life. She didn't understand them all herself. Nothing had been the same since Ben resigned from the army four years ago and staked out his new claim in this wild countryside. Of course he wasn't the only man in the army to leave the military and pin his hopes on the empty land that had suddenly become available in Florida territory. A real estate boom of sorts had lured quite a few military men into investing in land around the village of Tampa as well as out in the scrub even though it was still a very chancy business. The fifty-eight acres on the west Hillsborough that Lindsay, Fraser and Munroe had tried to turn into Tampa City had not worked out but the store Lindsay and William Lovelace established in the village, and in which Ben had invested part of his capital, was still doing business.

Neither she nor Ben had been surprised when the courts ruled that Hackley's original deeds, purchased long ago from the Spanish Duke of Alagon, were invalid and the two hundred and fifty-six acres of land surrounding and including Fort Brooke belonged to the United States government. Hackley's star had been falling since December of 1838. Her enterprising husband just gave up that plan and began working on others to get what he wanted. Ben was nothing if not resourceful when it came to making his dreams a reality, Lea mused, thrusting her needle into one of Buck's oft-mended cotton shirts.

Ben had improved the house he'd built on his two lots in the village, then turned his attention northward to the land Chief Miconopy had given him. Deciding his best claim to the land lay in developing it, he and an army of hired hands came north to clear fields and build a primitive log house. She and Buck had joined him when the dreaded Yellow Fever struck the fort and the village.

Lea smiled remembering her first sight of this homestead. They had traveled up the White Sand road dragging a wagon loaded with supplies and their household goods, and it had been slow going. Several times they camped at night around the wagons, a bit of rustic domesticity she had never experienced before though Ben's army training had served them well. The last night they stopped at their nearest neighbors, the Turners's, twelve miles away. How she had looked forward to sleeping in a real bed again until it turned out to be so infested with fleas she could barely rest.

In fact, the primitive state of the Turner household had filled her with dismay. She had known many 'cracker' families at Fort Brooke but had never before experienced their life style close up. She'd often heard the officers at the fort criticize these hardy settlers for their ropy-haired children and ignorant ways, yet Lea had always felt a grudging admiration for their ability to forge a home out of a stubborn, relentless wilderness. And certainly they were hospitable, sharing their meager provisions with a uncommon generosity.

At least the Turner's poor settlement had helped prepare her for the first sight of her own home. That one room log house, primitive horse shed and outdoor scaffold stove with its makeshift roof were a long way from all that she saw around her now. Her needle rested as she gazed lovingly at Ben's plantation—the two room log house with a narrow breezeway down the middle leading to a large detached kitchen at the rear, the substantial barn, the two fenced cowpens, the smokehouse and cabins where their Negro workers, Tom, Primo, Josie and Rafe lived, the carefully tended gardens stretching away to the long, rolling fields— and her heart swelled with pride for Ben and the men who had helped him build all this. It was a magnificent accomplishment.

And she had helped too. She had learned all manner of new ways to sustain her household with only her own two hands and the help of Primo's wife, Josie. Together they prepared the food, made soap and candles, sewed the clothes on their backs, kept a garden going, and, using liberal powders of borax to keep roaches at bay, maintained a level of cleanliness considerably higher than that of her neighbor's, the Turners. Of course, any settler in this country had to wage an ongoing battle against Florida's tropical pests. Smudge pots in the yard and cotton mesh nets over the beds helped deter the mosquitoes, but only the advent of cold weather controlled the flies and fleas. Still, she had never worked so hard or been so satisfied.

Lea frowned as she remembered the only disappointment of these last four years. By now she had expected to have two or three children of her own running around this log house. None had come. Whether God was withholding them for a reason or she had simply been born barren, she couldn't tell. Either way, it was a bitter, painful loss, the only real failure of her marriage. Buck was more like her own son every day but how she wished she could give Ben more sons and maybe a daughter or two. Had she done so, she felt certain it would have lessened the frequent arguments between father and son as well as the times her husband snapped open his watch to study that old portrait of Rachel in the lid. That happened less now than it used to yet still often enough to remind her she had not yet completely replaced her sister in his heart.

Enough daydreaming! The gray clouds were growing nearer and blacker now. Lea threw aside her mending basket, rose to grab her sunbonnet from a peg near the door, tied it under her chin and went striding down the steps to look over the vegetable plots. The newly planted peas and greens were still young and tender but the second corn crop was tall and nearly ripe. They would have to be on their guard to protect those tender new plants from the hordes of wild turkey and deer who took for granted they had been put there for their benefit. Even if they managed to keep the predators at bay there were still the summer rains. If there was one thing she had learned about farming since becoming a homesteader, it was that too much rain could be as disastrous as too little.

She was almost past the split-rail fence enclosing the garden when she saw Primo coming toward her. His bare toes dug into the raw earth while one hand clamped his round straw hat to his head against the wind.

"Primo," Lea called, "there's a hard rain coming. Would you tell Tom to get everybody inside?"

Primo answered her in that musical hybrid of English and 'gulla' she had come to enjoy. "He already done it, Miz Carson," he yelled back. "Dey's comin' in now. I hopes dat rain don't hurt dem cotton plants none."

Lea gripped the fence rail against a burst of wind that melded her skirts to her legs. "I hope so, too. There's not much we can do about it though. Have you seen Buck?"

"He down by the crick las' I see he," Primo answered. "Dat were about noon."

How like Buck to run off without doing his work. But she refused to reveal her irritation with the boy. She would not criticize Buck to the hands no matter how angry she got with him.

"Well, send Rafe to look for him. I don't want him outside in this storm."

Primo grabbed at his hat as a gust of wind nearly whisked it off his head. "Massa Buck, he can take care of hisself, Miz Carson. He done know dem woods better'n anybody."

"I know. But do it anyway."

Primo bobbed assent and turned back down the road toward the fields. In the distance Lea could see the dark forms of the workers coming in pulling the slow oxen behind them. Satisfied, she hurried over to the barn to make sure the pigs were safely penned and the chicken coop fastened then walked back to the house. One of the wild tabbies that had recently given birth to a litter of kittens ran across her path to duck under the porch, headed for her nest. Once the rain was over, Lea thought, she must remember to put out some milk for her.

A gust of wind clutched at her skirt and sent it billowing. The tin tub hanging on a nail against the breezeway wall began to wobble crazily, banging against the wooden frame. Lea grabbed it and ducked inside the kitchen, the door slamming on its leather hinges behind her.

"Where is Josie when I need her?" she said absently to herself. As she set the tub on the floor the rain began to clatter on the shingled roof of the house. It swelled in intensity, like a swarm of insects clanging with a million tiny hammers. She pulled off her bonnet and shook it out then stood listening to the clatter over her head.

It was strange this sound of rain on a roof. There was none of the gentle patter she remembered at her parent's Hudson home. Even the storms in this Southern wilderness were different. They swept in out of a clear sky, turning the day to night, declaring with a primeval violence that this land would not be subdued. The rain came in thick sheets and the lightening shattered the sky as it must have in the early days of creation. Thunder rolled on booming blasts that went on for-ever while the wind whipped the trees and sometimes even shook the house.

It was frightening. It was exhilarating. And she loved it.

She also loved that they were usually quickly over, leaving the world washed and clean and a little cooler.

Picking up a bowl of field peas to be shelled, Lea walked over to the wide hearth and lit an oil lamp standing on a table near her rocker. There were a few blood-red embers in the fireplace waiting for revival when supper was to be heated. She pulled the rocker away so as not to be near their faint warmth and sat, slowly rocking back and forth, stripping the pods and wondering where Buck had got to. She hoped that child had sense enough to seek shelter from the rain somewhere.

It had been hard on Buck, moving out here to this wilderness. With no nearby neighbors the enforced isolation had been almost as grim and lonely for Buck as it had for her. Her thoughts again wandered back to the long months before when, full of hope and plans, she sat between Ben and his son as they drove their team up to the one room house where they would begin the process of transforming Ben's dreams into reality.

That house was little more than a log box formed of raw wooden logs with mud and daub between the cracks, with a plank floor so unfinished she got splinters when she walked across it in her bare feet. The barn had been given more attention than the house and provided a better home at first for the oxen, the horses, and the milkcow. That was also true of the chicken coops, cow pens and long length of fences separating the area near the house where the gardens would go.

Nothing had been done carelessly. Ben had talked to every pioneer family he could find before he began building. He'd cleared the oak hammock first to put up the house and plant the gardens. The cedar shingled roof was his idea. It was so much more practical and sturdy than those palm frond roofs common to Florida homesteaders. The scaffold stove had soon been replaced with a spacious chimney and its roof enlarged to form the kitchen. The ample hearth and even this oil lamp were luxuries he had been able to afford because of the capital he had saved.

The breezeway was another of the practical ideas he got from the pioneers. Two years ago Ben added a second room to the original one with a porch across the front, and an extended walkway through the middle leading back to the spacious kitchen. The breezeway helped cool the bedrooms and parlor while the detached kitchen kept most of the heat from the house. And heat was a constant problem. The big oaks he left near the front of the house helped to shadow it most of the year and the kitchen facing east made it a little cooler on summer afternoons. Once Lea moved in her rugs and furniture the raw plain house had seemed almost civilized.

Of course they talked constantly of the great sprawling mansion that would someday replace it, even though that was no closer now than when they moved here. Yet she had already planned it clearly in her mind, down to the furniture and the flowered Wilton carpet in the front parlor. Her fingers grew still and she laid her head against the high back of the rocker, picturing it—a two-story white house with wide columns along the porch, a long graveled road leading to the outer buildings and sweeping away to fields dotted with cotton bolls like newly fallen snow over their lush greenery.

A sudden gust of wind sent the window shutters slamming back against the wall, allowing waves of rain in to drench the floor. Lea jumped up to close the hinges, brought out of her idle day-dreaming by the reality of the storm. A banging on the porch told her she ought to bring in some of the hanging tubs and baskets on the breezeway which were certain to be blown away in the wind. Then she realized the banging was actually the stomping of feet on the boards of the porch.

Must be Josie finally getting back. She had just managed to get the shutters fastened when the kitchen door flew open carrying a squall of rain with it. Lea ran to shove the door closed against the wind but stopped when the frame was suddenly filled with the tall form of a man. A moment's panic gave way to pleasure as she recognized Clay Madapore standing in the doorway. She pulled him inside and together they pushed the door shut and locked down its leather strap.

Clay stood there dripping wet and smiling down at her. "Sorry I brought the rain in with me but I couldn't find a way to get in without it." His oilskin jacket dripped rivulets on the straw mat near the door. She reached up to help him remove it then took his soaked hat.

"You gave me a start. Goodness, even your shirt is damp. Hang up that wet coat and come sit by the fire."

"You don't need to ask twice," Clay commented as he threw his coat on a peg beside the door. He walked toward the hearth. "I knew I'd find refuge here."

Lea shoveled the coals in the fireplace into life then grabbed the handle of a pot standing on a trivet near the hearth. "I can heat up some coffee if you'd like. It won't take long. It was made this morning and should still be fresh."

"I would like some, thank you." He reached out his long hands over the low flames. "Half an hour ago I never thought a fire would be so welcome. One things about a storm—it cools things off some."

"Until the sun comes out again and steams up the place. What are you doing way out here so far from town? If you came to see Ben you're out of luck. He's been down at Fort Brooke buying supplies for the last week."

She handed him a tin cup which he filled from the pot over the fire. Easing into a chair opposite her, he removed a flask from his hip pocket and poured a healthy dollop of whisky into the cup. Lea resumed her seat and picked up her bowl of peas and watched him as he blew on the hot liquid, then raised it to his lips. His wet hair lay plastered across his high forehead like a sandy colored cap. His thick brows furrowed over his deeply set eyes as he frowned at the coffee. Those eyes looked tired, she thought, even though there was a glimmer of a twinkle in them as he glanced up and caught her studying him.

"I must look like something the cat dragged in," he said, grinning at her.

"You look good to me. I'm very glad to see you, Clay. I get a little crazy for company sometimes when Ben is away so long. Not that there isn't plenty to keep me busy. But conversations with Josie and Primo often leave something to be desired, Tom keeps pretty much to himself and Buck is still only a boy."

Clay sat back, sighed, and stretched his long legs toward the fire, resting the cup on his stomach. "It's a lonely life, isn't it, Lea."

A flush crept up her cheeks as she realized she had revealed too much. "No, no. I've got too much work to be lonely. And though our neighbors live a long way off we try to keep aware of each other and help out when needed." She sighed. "So much depends on this place doing well. It's all Ben and I think about."

"But sometimes you miss the village and the fort?"

She looked away from his penetrating gaze. "I suppose so. I'd be lying to say I didn't. Now and then I long to stand at the counter of Saunder's store and pick out some frivolous gee-gaw to buy. Or dress up and go to a dance social. Or just sit and gossip with Julia Lattimore about the latest news from New Orleans. But there, it's silly to think about those things when there is so much to be done here." She laughed. "Besides, Saunder's store is now Lindsay and Lovelace, and Julia and her Lieutenant are posted in Pensacola.

"I declare, Clay, I never realized how much work it takes to provide the basic necessities of life when there isn't a store nearby. We raise all our meat, kill, dress and smoke everything. We grow crops from seed, hoe, weed, harvest and store them; we make bricks and cut logs for every building and fence. About the only thing we don't do to keep ourselves going is grow our own cloth. Sewing and mending I can manage, but if I had to spin and card and run a loom I think we'd all be running around naked!"

Clay laughed. "What about all that cotton I passed as I rode in?"

Lea shrugged. "That's our money crop, as you well know. The first time Ben suggests I turn it into cloth myself is the day I set out walking for Fort Brooke."

He watched her strip a long yellow pod and took a sip from his cup to keep himself from saying things he knew he shouldn't. He could see the signs of hard work that strained Lea's lovely face. Her cheeks were thinner, her mouth more tight. Her once creamy complexion was dotted with freckles and blotched with reddish streaks from sunburn. Her hair, usually so carefully brushed and shining, was pulled back in a careless bun at the nape of her neck like any country woman's, though a few tendrils of curls refused to be constrained and fell grace-fully over her brow. Damn Ben anyway! Lea was a lady, not a pioneer. She belonged in pretty drawing rooms reading books and playing a spinet. This hard life would soon make her older than her years.

Lea laughed, reading his thoughts. "Now Clay, don't go feeling sorry for me. I've never worked so hard in my life but I've never been more healthy or felt bet-ter. Of course it's lonely at times but it's wonderful, too. There is something very satisfying about creating a successful plantation from a virgin country."

He waved a hand carelessly. "I won't deny it. And from what I could see through the rain as I rode up it seems the place is coming along very well. The last time I was here the ground had just been broken for the cotton fields."

She laid the bowl of vegetables aside, studying his brown face. "It's been too long. I'm glad to see you again, Clay. We've missed you."

"I've been up in the panhandle around Tallahassee trying to pick up news and now I'm headed back to Fort Brooke. This Indian war is all but over, Lea. Last winter two hundred and thirty Seminoles were shipped west and Colonel Worth thinks only about three hundred are left. There's a rumor he's asked President Tyler to approve a non-pursuit policy and move those that remain to a reserva-tion in South Florida. It's unlikely that the Seminoles could mount a concen-trated offensive anywhere in the territory anymore."

"What about Coacoochee?"

"The Wildcat has gone west into the setting sun." Clay laughed. "The last time I saw him he was all decked out in a Shakespearean costume he took off a troop of actors his tribe waylaid and killed up near the St. John's River. 'Hamlet' I think. It was a sight to behold."

"I'm glad he's gone. Maybe now we'll have more new settlers come into this area. Right now our closest neighbors, the Turners, are so far away we barely ever see them."

"You'll get some new people eventually but not right away. In fact one of the reasons I stopped by was to warn you and Ben that there are still isolated incidents of Indian raids across the middle territories and recently they have been on the increase. You want to take care."

Lea frowned. "But Clay, I don't think I've seen a Seminole since we moved here."

"You might not see them but you can be sure they know you're here. They're probably keeping clear of you because Ben is a former officer and they're not sure he won't bring the army against them. But they're getting desperate, Lea. They don't have a chance in hell of avoiding deportation and they know it. I just think you ought to be extra careful for a while."

Lea stared at the glowing coals, fighting down an old panic. The fear of Indian raids at Fort Brooke was bad enough but at least one could feel well protected there. Out here in the open wilderness an attack by desperate, angry savages was the worst catastrophe imaginable. She shivered, remembering the haunted eyes of the white settlers who straggled into Fort Brooke when the war first broke out.

"You're right. I'll talk it over with Primo this very evening and we'll figure out the best way to proceed if something does happen. But for now, tell me about Tallahassee. What's it like? Has the town grown much?"

Clay smiled at her enthusiasm. "It's spreading in all directions like a field of mushrooms. I never saw such traffic—so thick you can hardly cross a street for all the wagons and carriages. New houses being built right and left, each one more grand than the last. There're too many people there for me. I got out as quick as I could."

"Ben wants to make a trip up there as soon as he feels he can leave the crops. I told him he can't go without me, not even if the cotton is ready for picking."

"You should go with him, Lea. You'd enjoy it." He reached to refill his cup thinking how characteristic it was of her to put aside the rumors of Indian attacks for a more pleasant topic. Ever the optimist, Lea. Yet he knew she would heed his warning, though what good it would do without Ben there he couldn't imagine.

"And how is the cotton coming?" he asked, settling back.

Lea hesitated. "Not badly though Primo says it ought to be higher by now. Primo used to work on a farm in north Georgia and he knows more about raising cotton than either Ben or me."

"Does it worry him?"

Lea rocked back and forth. "He says Florida is too wet for raising large cotton crops. And the soil too sandy."

"Primo may be right. I tried to tell Ben Florida wasn't right for the kind of huge plantings you find in other Southern States but he seemed to have his heart set on making money with cotton. I don't know why. Cotton requires a lot of hoeing just to grow the plants. It takes workers to bring in a cotton crop and you know Ben won't own slaves. Unfortunately there're few laborers available in the South except for slaves."

"He'll never go that way. It's a principle with him. He believes he can hire enough free men to do the work."

"There aren't that many free Negroes in Florida and picking cotton's hard work for white men. You really ought to try to get him to consider other possibilities. He should have several money crops instead of focusing on one."

"Several? Like what?"

"Sugar cane, food-stuffs, cattle. Especially cattle. The market for beef can only grow. It's not just Cuba and the army wanting beef—now the whole north east is opening up. And fortunes can be made in sugar cane if you're careful enough."

"But aren't Florida longhorns more risky than cotton? I was told there aren't any markets close enough to make big herds pay. The cattle around here are mostly wild. They're scrawny and diseased and mean and their meat is tough and stringy. Tick fever is a constant hazard."

"Then bring in a good…" Clay sought for a euphemism since one did not use the word 'bull' in polite company. "…a 'seed-ox' to raise the level of the stock. A Hereford or better yet, a Brahman. They're from South America and better suited to the heat. I've been up and down the Florida peninsula and I think this middle country is ideal for raising steers. And until the army leaves—if it ever does—there's always Jacksonville. It's not close but it's a good market town."

"Oh dear," Lea sighed. "I know less about raising cattle than I do about growing cotton." Yet she did not take Clay's words lightly. Ben had so much riding on this cotton crop and it just made good sense not to put all your eggs in one basket.

All at once she realized the wind had died and the rain eased to a gentle patter on the roof. Lea rose to open the kitchen door then moved to the hearth to poke the dying fire into life. "You're going to stay for supper and the night, aren't you, Clay? We've got some fine pork in the smokehouse and with the usual swamp cabbage, sweet potatoes and field peas it's quite tasty. I've even learned to make cornbread. Besides, Buck will be thrilled to see you."

Clay watched her, knowing he ought to be on his way yet so contented for the moment that her invitation was too enticing. "I'd be grateful to," he said. "Thanks for the offer. What can I do in return?"

Lea stood with her hands on her waist. "Not a thing. Unless…well, we are getting a little low on firewood. But only if you feel like it."

"As soon as the rain's over."

He sat back staring at the fire as Lea rummaged around the room getting the table laid. "I declare, Lea, you almost make me long to be domesticated," he said with a sigh.

She grinned at him from across the table. "Almost?"

"Well, tonight anyway. By tomorrow I'll be restless again and out looking for new adventures, as you well know."

The sudden banging of the door brought him straight up in the chair. Josie, Lea's Negro cook, came bustling in, shaking out her shawl and mumbling about a strange colored man sitting on the porch.

"An' he done et a slice of dat ham in the smok'house", she said in disgust.

"Oh, my God," Clay exclaimed, jumping up. "I forgot about my gift."

Lea looked up, a question in her eyes. "Gift?"

"Yes. Come on. I left him on the porch."

"Him?" She followed Clay to the door. What on earth could he mean by 'him?' All sorts of possibilities raced through her mind. An animal? Maybe a breeding cow, or even better, a horse. But then, he wouldn't leave a cow or a horse on the porch. Maybe a hunting dog. Yes, a new hunter would be nice.

The porch was empty. "Now, carnsarn it," Clay exclaimed. "Where'd he get to?"

Josie peered through the door, wiping her hands on a rag. "Rafe done took 'im to his cabin. Go look there."

"Point the way, Mrs. Carson," Clay said, stepping back to allow Lea to go down the porch steps. The rain was only a light mist now and small vapors of steam dotted the sandy yard. Still wondering, Lea struck off with Clay close behind her, pulling the hem of her skirts up against the damp grass as she headed for a line of small wooden cabins below the barn.

They found Clay's gift sitting at a table in Rafe's shack shoveling down a plate of beans. He looked up as they entered the low, dark room then slowly rose. Lea stifled a gasp.

"Lea, this is Ulysses," Clay said with obvious pride. "But I call him 'Ulee'. Ulysses sounds too formal for a former slave."

Lea looked at Clay. "He's free? You're sure of that?"

"Yes. He's got papers." Clay dug in the pocket of his jacket and handed her a dog-eared paper folded over several times and smeared with dirt. "It looks all correct. He once belonged to a Jonas White in Tallahassee who manumitted him in his will. White's widow signed the paper."

Lea scanned the document and handed it back. "My husband won't own slaves," she said to its owner. "All our Negro hands are free and earn wages. Not much, but something."

If she expected her kind words to elicit a smile she was disappointed. Ulee stared at her, his dark face impassive and frozen. He was the largest Negro she had ever seen, tall, with a powerful chest and muscular arms. There was no doubt in her mind that his strength would be a great asset to the farm but his manner was so cold and almost hostile, that she hesitated to take him on. There was something in the dark eyes staring at her that suggested depths of caution if not outright anger. An image sprang to her mind, a memory of the faces of two slaves sold at an auction she once witnessed in front of Saunder's store soon after she first arrived at Fort Brooke. This man might be free now but she suspected he had been hurt sometime in the past. Badly hurt.

"My husband is not here right now, Ulee, but I expect him back very soon. He'll be the one to make the decision about keeping you on. In the meantime you can stay here. Rafe, introduce him to Primo then see that he gets a bed and proper food."

Rafe gave Ulee a suspicious glance, then nodded. "Yes, missus."

Taking Lea's arm, Clay directed her through the door. "You behave yourself, Ulee, you hear," he called over his shoulder. "If you want to stay with Mrs. Carson that's what you've got to do."

Lea glanced back to see Ulee give a barely perceptible nod before resuming his place at the table. Outside, she pulled her shawl tightly around her shoulders as they ambled back toward the house. "I don't know, Clay. He looks like a good worker but there's something about him that worries me. Will he run off, do you think? What's his background?"

"You already know as much as I do. He appeared in Tallahassee with those papers in his pocket. They were signed seven years ago and he told me he had worked jobs around St. Augustine until recently. I tried to trace the widow White but she'd died and her family moved on. Next time I get to St. Augustine I'll check out his story."

Clay sat on the wooden step of the porch while Lea leaned one hip on the nearby railing. "I had an idea he could be a big help to you so I brought him down. If you're worried about having him here I can always take him back to Tallahassee."

"No, no. We can use someone that big and strong. Besides," she smiled at him, "I think you had an ulterior motive in bringing him out here. I suspect you wanted to get him away from Tallahassee. A big, strapping man like Ulee would fetch a good price at a slave auction and I'm told those dealers aren't very scrupulous about papers found on free blacks."

Clay pulled out his pipe and knocked out the ashes on the step. "You know me too well, woman. Let's just say that if Ulee wasn't sitting in Rafe's cabin right now he'd probably be on his way to Mississippi with an iron ring around his neck." He took a long draught on the pipe. "And for all his quiet ways, I believe he's grateful. He'll be a big help to you."

Lea stared out at the steaming yard a moment before starting for the kitchen. "Dear Clay. You always seem to be helping us out. Ulee is not the only one who is grateful. You rest here and smoke your pipe. Josie and I will have supper on the table by the time you've finished."

CHAPTER 14

▼

Clay's words proved prophetic. Ulee never said much nor showed any emotion in response to a kindness. But he threw himself into the work of the farm with such enthusiasm and ability that Lea could only marvel. In a week he had cleared an additional half acre of land and plowed two others waiting for the furrows. He was obviously accustomed to hard work. He was up with the sun every morning, in the fields until sunset, and somehow still found time to begin to put together a tiny cabin of his own. Lea was amazed at all he had achieved in the week since Clay brought him.

She was aware of how he kept aloof from the other workers and that there was a constraint between them—not quite hostility but not camaraderie either. "Tha's a strange black man," Josie said while she and Lea worked in the kitchen at shucking corn for supper. "He don't say nothin', he keep to hisself all the time. Rafe an' Primo, dey tries to talk to him but he don't answer. Won't say nothin' 'bout where he be afore he come here."

"He certainly works hard. Already I feel we can't do without him."

Josie nodded. "Tha's true, missy, but I don't trust no man what won't talk or be friend-like. He be strange and tha's all there is."

Josie's sentiments were echoed by Buck late one afternoon when he suddenly stomped into the kitchen after being gone since morning. "I don't like that Ulee," the boy cried, heaving his hunting bag at a peg on the wall. "He's ornery and he won't teach me nothin'."

Lea straightened from bending over the hearth, too annoyed to suppress her anger. "Buck, where have you been all day? You know you were supposed to help Ulee seed those new fields. I told you two days ago."

"He don't want me. He can do it better by himself. He told me so this morning."

"Then you should have done something else. You have chores to do, just like the rest of us. What's your Papa going to say when he gets back?"

Buck grabbed a biscuit from a plate on the table then threw his wiry body in a chair, slouching down as he bit off half. "I went hunting. We need meat, don't we."

"No, we don't. We've got plenty of supplies at the moment. What we need is for you to pull your share of the load around here."

Buck glared up at her. "Oh, Aunt Lea. Choppin' wood and throwing seed, that's boring. I like the woods. I like to track and hunt. And I'm good at it, I don't care what that black nigger says."

"Buck! That's enough." She lifted the end of her long apron to wipe her damp brow then stood studying this boy she loved like her own son, a boy who grew more restless and unmanageable every year. How old was he now? Thirteen? Fourteen? Surely not that much time had passed since Rachel's death.

Lea walked to Buck's chair and laid her hand on his shoulder. "Listen to me, Buck. If we want to make a go of this place we all have to pull together. Your Pa knows that and so do I."

"He's told me enough times."

"Then pay attention. He wants this place to be successful for you because someday it will be yours."

Buck looked up at her, his eyes darkening. "No he doesn't. He wants it so he'll be a big man. A rich man."

"So? And who do you think will get those riches when he's gone? Use your intelligence, Buck. You're smart enough to know that everything we do here is as much for your future as ours. And you're old enough to do a decent day's work."

"But…" The boy jumped up from the chair. "I hate farm work. Let the hired men do all that. That's why Papa took them on, isn't it."

"You're not asked to do much. You still have plenty of time for the woods. And it would please your Father so much to see you take responsibility."

Buck stalked across the room to the open door. "I'd do it for you, Aunt Lea. But Pa—he's just like Ulee. They both think I'm not good for nothin'. Someday I'll show 'em both."

She watched him stomp across the porch and down the stairs. Shaking her head she took the chair Buck had left, her shoulders sagging with weariness. They'd had this conversation before and always to no avail. Buck grew wilder every year and his resentment of his father grew along with his wild ways. She could not understand it and nothing she could say seemed to lessen it. And his father was just as bad. She knew that Ben had a fierce love for his only son yet he seemed mystified, even confused about what that son wanted from him. Whatever it was he was unable to give it and his frustration too often exploded into anger when Buck left things half-done or not done at all. Buck was so different from his father. Ben had to go out and make his own way in life at a young age and he had done so with a dogged devotion to duty and responsibility. His son was being given so much and wasn't even grateful enough to do his share. The solution seemed so simple to Lea. 'Just do what your father asks as well as you can'. But that was a solution Buck deliberately refused to try. He seemed to resent even being asked to try it.

Still, it was curious that the boy's distrust of Ulee was as deep as Josie's.

Ben shifted his weight on the hard wagon seat and thought how glad he was that home was only a few more miles away. He never made this trip without feeling some satisfaction that he had chosen to settle this large track miles east of the White Sand road. Even wiser was his decision to build his homestead farther east near a small L-shaped lake which had served their need for water until the well was built closer to the house. Best of all there were already large tracks of open land cleared by wildfires and left fallow, which meant they hadn't had to chop down so many thick hammocks of cypress, pine and oaks to clear fields for cotton planting. While he was in the village he had heard rumors that huge Hillsborough County would soon be divided to the north. Thankfully his land would still be in Hillsborough, thus making him eligible to serve in some political capacity someday after his farm was established. Yes, all in all, he had chosen well.

The sandy road narrowed between hammocks of cypress and the ever present pine barrens then grew wider as he moved into the open fields of his homestead. He felt the usual glow of satisfaction to see them appear out of the forest even though his pleasure was still tinged with the anxiety of possibly losing them. Thanks to his service in the Army he'd been able to stake a claim to this land with Colonel Worth last year but that was so tenuous he wondered if it would ever stand up to a challenge. And on this trip he'd learned the challenge had already been made.

His jaw clenched as he thought of the reason why. Ramon de Diego had lost no time trying to buy this whole parcel for himself. Since the first day he learned of the deed Chief Miconopy had given Ben, Diego had vowed to fight him for the land. Colonel Worth was anxious to establish civilian communities in the areas the Seminole had vacated when the reservation was moved south and though everyone knew it was the United States government, not the Army, who had the authority to sell or give away open land, the Colonel encouraged settlement even when it was not sure the claims were valid.

But Ben knew this war was drawing to a close. In fact the Colonel had already declared it all but over but that was a moot point as long as there were still Seminoles in Florida. Still, he'd seen the northern newspapers while he was in Tampa. Already they were crowing about the wonderful new country up for grabs in Florida—rich lands in a climate where the sun shone year round and all you had to do to grow anything was to stick it in the ground. While he knew how untrue that was, he did not doubt that soon there would be hordes of new settlers pouring into the region ready to grab what they could. Open land, cheap land drew new settlers like flies to a dead hog.

Well, he had done everything he could to get ahead of the pack. In spite of the Judge Steele boondoggle several years back, he still had claim to two lots in Tampa village and his silent partnership in the Lindsay and Lovelace store paid pretty fair returns. He'd paid hard cash for that land on the Hillsborough River in the village and as soon as his plantation was well established he would make some further improvements to the simple house he'd built on them.

Ben smiled as he thought of the way Judge Steele had platted streets and lots in the 'town' of Tampa where only oaks and weeds now stood. That plat hadn't worked out but another one would. Once this war was over the place should grow, if, that is, the United States Army allowed it to. Technically, the village of Tampa was sitting on federal land belonging to the Fort Brooke army post, land that included 240 acres stretching north and east. Even now the grumbling between the post and the village was growing so contentious that Augustus Steele was threatening to pull up and leave the area. Yet surely things could be resolved and both could exist together. It was the only way of progress.

As he came closer to his homestead he recognized his numbered brand on some of the cattle roaming the woods. His tired horses pulled into the road skirting the first of the long, green cotton fields, their plants now nearly grown and dotted with yellow buds. Come fall and they would look like they were covered with snow as the white bolls burst from their pods. Ben imagined workers strewn across them, bending to pluck the thready bolls, worth their weight in gold. He visualized stacks of bales covered with burlap and tied with rope waiting to be transported to the ships at the Tampa docks. He could almost hear the money jingling into his coffers.

Nearing the house, he passed the fields he had helped to plant himself—corn, beans, melons, peas, and even a small section devoted solely to tobacco.

His horses picked up a little speed as they plodded toward the outbuildings and knew they were nearing their stable. The saw pit lay idle now but it had been crucial when they first started cutting logs for barn, house, sheds, and workers' cabins. The small brick-oven was cold but newly made bricks lay stacked around it drying in the sun. It was comforting to see the pens near the house where the milk cow and her calf grazed. The barking of Tom's two scrawny curs alerted his arrival while three pigs rooting beside the road scurried out of his way into the weeds.

They entered the yard and Ben saw Rafe coming from the barn to take charge of the wagon while Josie paused on the porch of the house to watch. He looked over at one of the far fields where someone was plowing with the oxen and wondered who it could be.

"Evenin', sur," Rafe said, smiling at Ben. "We is sho glad to see you back safe."

"Thank you, Rafe. See that they get a good rub down, will you. It's been a long ride." Wearily Ben heaved himself off the wagon just as Lea appeared in the kitchen doorway wiping her hands on her apron. "Rafe, who is that working in the field? I don't expect any new men for several days."

"Thas' Ulee. He come with Mista Clay."

Ben frowned but he knew Lea would explain. He started toward the house, every muscle in his body complaining as he walked. Lea came flying down the steps to throw her arms around his neck and give him a crushing hug.

"I'm so glad you're home! You don't know how I worry about you being on the road by yourself."

Ben put his arm around her shoulder as they walked toward the house. "I'm glad to be safely home myself. But I was lucky. No trouble anywhere. All I want now is to wash some of this dirt off and pull up to the table. I hope you saved me some supper."

Her arm tightened around his waist and she lifted her face for his quick kiss. "I've been saving some every day for a week hoping you'd get here. And the water for a wash is already hot."

"What a perfect wife you are."

He said it lightly, without noticing the color his compliment brought to her cheeks or the delighted smile on her lips.

By the time the sun slipped over the horizon and night began to fall Ben had washed, changed his shirt and enjoyed Josie's good cooking. He filled his pipe and sat in the rocker on the kitchen breezeway while Lea picked up her mending basket and took the opposite chair, pleased to make a little progress on the never ending sewing while there was some daylight left. She was so content that her husband was safely back and sitting beside her that even the huge pile of clothes to be mended couldn't daunt her happiness.

Yet she feared something about the trip had not gone well. Ben usually returned from these excursions full of gossip about the events of the village, the fort and the war but tonight he was preoccupied and quiet. She was very much afraid she knew why.

"Did you have any luck verifying the claim you made with Colonel Worth?" she asked guardedly once all the lesser things had been discussed.

"Yes, but I heard rumors that Diego will be contesting our land anyway. For one thing, he got to Hackley when I wasn't able to. I'll probably have to go back down there again before the matter is settled."

Lea frowned when she thought of Ramon de Diego. She still detested the man for the way he'd treated her on the beach long ago. But lately there was something more about him that worried her. Over the last few years he seemed to have taken an obsessive animosity toward Ben that created nothing but conflict.

"It seems that man is always after the same things you are. What has he got against you, anyway?"

Ben shrugged. "I once prevented him from establishing a trading post on the Alafia river." No need to mention the other irritants—how Diego had cheated the Seminole and made advances to Lea. In fact, if Jumper's intention so long ago had been to create bad blood between them, it looked as though the plan was succeeding famously.

Lea sighed and tried to put thoughts of Diego out of her mind. "The next time you go into town, Buck and I might go along with you, if you don't mind. He would love a trip and I could use some things from the store—sewing thread, a few yards of calico—things like that. Tom and Primo seem able to run things pretty smoothly and Ulee is a big help. If we were only gone a few days I'm sure they could manage."

"Ulee? Oh, yes. The new man. Rafe said Clay brought him by."

"Yes, a few days after you left. Of course you'll have to talk with him and see if you want him to stay on. But I've been impressed with his hard work and he seems to be intelligent as well. I think he could be a real asset."

"Clay must have thought so or he wouldn't have brought him. What's his background?"

"He's got manumission papers from some big farm up in Tallahassee. He says he worked for several people in St. Augustine before turning up back in Tallahas-

see where Clay rescued him from the slavers. Clay was on his way to St. Augustine and he said he'd check out his story."

Ben gave Lea a wry smile. "Clay seems very interested in our welfare."

"Now Ben, you know he is a true friend. He was yours before he was mine."

Ben nodded. "I know. I'm getting suspicious of everyone these days trying to
deal with this problem of a valid deed. There's talk that a new proposition is
going to come out of Washington City very soon. The government is promising
160 acres, free food, seed and weapons to every family who agrees to build on the
land and work it for five years. When that happens we'll be overrun. We have to
have a secure claim before then."

Lea dug her needle into the heel of a thick sock. "It would be nice to have
nearer neighbors. Maybe you can file one of those claims."

"Lea, you know 160 acres isn't even a fifth of what we have here. No, I already
have squatter's rights but I want this farm to be absolutely mine before anyone
comes around trying to homestead on it. And I will, even if I have to kill Diego."

Her fingers paused and she fought down the cold stab of ice in her chest.
"Spoken like a soldier. But let's hope it won't come to that," she added casually.
"By the way. I want you to speak to Buck. He's not done half of what you told
him before you left. All he wants is to run in the woods and hunt all day. Nothing I say has any effect."

"Buck!" Ben exclaimed in disgust. "Why am I not surprised. That boy is hopeless. Well, he has to learn to carry his share of the load and he will if I have to beat
it into him."

Lea smiled to herself. Ben was hard on his son and had threatened him with
beatings before. Yet she remembered how reluctant Captain Carson had been to
use corporal punishment on the young army privates under his command. And
the accepted use of the whip was one of the reasons he refused to own slaves.
"Beating doesn't help, Ben. You know that. Try talking to him. Better still,
promise him a reward. Something he wants."

"A waste of time. I'm sure you've already tried all those tricks and nothing has
worked."

"I do try to make him see that everything you do is for all our sakes but it
doesn't seem to make an impression. He thinks you just want to be a rich
planter."

She was relieved when he smiled, leaning back against the rocker and drawing
on his pipe. "There's some truth in that, you know," Ben said quietly. "I remember when I was a boy, watching the wealthy planter's sons ride in on their fine
horses with their fine airs, then seeing my father toiling away in his dingy apothe-

cary shop. I was ashamed of his…well, his poverty. It's taken me a long time to realize he was a better man than they would ever be—decent, honest, Godfearing, unfailingly kind."

Lea's rocker creaked as she moved back and forth. "Surely you must have known some decent planters."

"Oh yes. The Castlemans became my benefactors, saw that I had schooling and got me my appointment to West Point. They were good, caring people, and rich with it. I guess in some way I've always wanted to be like them."

"They must have owned slaves."

"They did. They believed there was no other way to run a large scale plantation. Their slaves were part of their wealth. Like most planters they were mortgaged to the hilt against the value of their land, crops and slaves."

"I suppose that will be our fate someday as well."

"It already is to an extent. Though not from slaves, of course. I figure what little I pay Primo, Rafe and Josie more than makes up for the price I'd have to shell out to buy them."

Lea laughed. "Well that's certainly true of Ulee as well. Clay snatched him away from bounty hunters who were itching to put him on the market. He'd easily bring five hundred dollars, Clay thought."

Ben leaned forward in his chair to knock his pipe against the rail, spilling ashes flecked with bright cinders on the ground. "From the looks of him probably more. Where is Buck now?"

"I don't know. He didn't come in for supper. He's probably down in Rafe's cabin. He likes talking to him."

Ben dragged himself up from the chair. "Well, I have to go speak to Tom and this Ulee fellow. I'll look in on Rafe on the way back. Oh, by the way, I brought you something."

Lea looked up in surprise, smiling with delight. "You did?"

"Yes. Wait a minute, it's here in my saddlebag." He rummaged through the leather bag hanging on a wooden peg inside the door and pulled out a package wrapped in gray paper. Handing it to Lea, he stood back and watched as she opened it, exclaiming in delight.

"Ben…it's beautiful…" She held up a large square of rose colored shot-silk cloth embroidered with tiny white flowers. "I've never had anything so pretty," she exclaimed holding the shimmering silk to her chest.

"It was a remnant, probably not enough for a whole dress but I thought you could make a skirt or one of those little shoulder capes you women wear. Do you really like it?"

Lea rose and kissed him on the cheek. "I love it. Thank you, Ben."

He gave her a quick hug and started for the steps. "I brought a new rifle for Buck but I won't give it to him until I see he's grown more responsible. Don't say anything to him about it."

He started across the yard, grateful for the cooling breeze that curled the smoke upward from one of the smudge pots put out against the mosquitoes. The night creatures were roaring their usual frenzied songs and a new moon cast a thin bronze light along the sandy path to the workers cabins. Ben stopped to stare up at it as a thin, dark cloud drifted across its surface. He thought about the piece of pink silk and how pleased it had made his wife. Of course, it wasn't the right color for Lea. It didn't complement her complexion or the red lights in her hair. When he saw it in the store his first thought was that it would have been perfect for Rachel. How beautiful it would have been against her white skin and golden hair.

Rachel! He tried to conjure up her face in his memory but it wouldn't come clear. Yet he knew well enough how he felt. The adoration, the admiration, the pride that she belonged to him was still there, sometimes stronger than ever. And the pain over losing her was there too. Still hurting, like the thrust of a knife. Most of the time he could keep it at bay with all the work and the planning it took to get his plantation off and running. But there were times when it came back, striking like a bayonet thrust in his belly. Would that ever ease, he wondered.

Useless thoughts! He shook them off and started briskly down the path toward Ulee's half-built cabin. Ah well. Lea was a good girl and a good wife. She deserved a nice present.

CHAPTER 15

▼

Two days later the men Ben hired in Tampa showed up. Lea worried that the number of hired workers might soon outgrow their space to keep them, yet there was no question that Ben needed more help if he were to produce the kind of money crop he wanted. Everything she had heard about growing cotton said it needed many workers in order to be successful. Certainly that was the impetus for the burgeoning slave trade on the large plantations in other Southern States. Right now the small Carson homestead was nowhere near as extensive as the huge plantations to the north yet one good crop could well lead to another, and another, and then, who knows? Someday Central Florida might be in a position to equal or even surpass its neighbors.

She mentally chided herself for catching Ben's wild dreams. They had both worked so hard to get this place started and now that it was growing and expanding they needed more hands and more strong backs. They would just have to make room for them.

When she found a few minutes to herself late one morning she decided to ride out to the cotton fields and see how things were going. Ben and the other men were all there so she took a canteen of cool water with her. It was a hot day and she knew they could use it.

Her old mare ambled along the road sedately. Even Lea's kicks couldn't get the animal to go faster. When they neared the fields she pulled her grateful mount to a stop and sat looking over the scene, drinking in the emerald green of the fields bordered with a distant line of the forest turned bluish-green by the startling light. In the great blue bowl of sky above billows of high chalky clouds clustered in fantastic shapes and swirls. The tiny forms of the men working in the fields seemed small and insignificant against the glory of earth and sky around them.

Ulee, as usual, was working by himself. Rafe and Primo were nearby, their backs bent over their hoes. The two new workers, both white men, worked closely together, chatting and laughing. Ben was wielding a hoe alongside Tom, his wide-brimmed straw hat bobbing between the green rows.

Lea paused to look out over the neat rows of plants. They appeared very small for having been growing so long. There were lots of yellow buds but not as many as she had expected by now. Perhaps it was too early.

Ben straightened, saw her and waved. Her mare ambled over to him, swishing her tail and snorting with displeasure at having to move again.

"I brought you some water," Lea said, slipping down off her horse. Ben's face was red with exertion and sweat dampened his shirt front and back. He took the canteen gratefully and put it to his lips, taking long swallows.

"That was good," he said, wiping his mouth with his sleeve. "Leave it here and I'll share it with the other men." He pulled off his hat. "What do you think?" he asked, looking around proudly.

"It looks wonderful, Ben. All your hard work has paid off."

"It's coming along but its not there yet. Another month and this field will be ready for picking. We've managed to escape insect damage and the rain's been just right. It should be a good crop."

"I'm glad." His enthusiasm was so strong she didn't have the heart to dampen it. Yet something about the plants worried her. She knelt down to inspect one, drawing the leaves between her fingers. The edges were dried, almost withered. They probably just needed another good rain.

"How is Ulee doing?" she asked, rising and brushing the dirt from her skirts.

"I wish I had three like him. He's worth more than those two men I brought in put together. I think they only came to scout out the area for their own homesteads."

"I see he's working apart. Does he always do that?"

"Always. Of course the two white men wouldn't have it any other way. They already told me they won't do 'negra' work. I think the next time I hire more workers they'll be black."

Lea watched Ulee walking the rows alone and silent, intent on his work. "What about Rafe? I thought by now they'd be friends."

Ben took another swig from the canteen. "Ulee isn't interested in being friends with anyone. He likes to be by himself and that's all right with me. As long as he does his work he can live like he wants."

Lea rode back to the house thinking about Ben's words. The big Negro hadn't unbent at all from the silent, withdrawn man he was when Clay brought him even though nearly a month had passed. She had made several efforts to be kind to him but though he was always polite, he never responded. Josie's disgust with him had reached the point where she no longer complained about it. If he wanted to be left alone and that was fine with her. But Lea wondered what was behind that impassive facade. One heard tales of slaves turning against their white masters, murdering them in the night. Ulee was no slave but he was so big and strong if he decided to wreck mayhem on the farm no one could stop him. She didn't really believe he was that angry but then she didn't really know anything about him. All the same, it was a relief to know that Ben kept his rifle near the bed at night.

The following afternoon Rafe came running up to the porch calling for her. When she hurried outside, drying her wet hands on a towel, she could see by the look on his face that something bad had happened.

"Missus, come quick…" Rafe stammered, clambering up the steps.

"What's is it, Rafe? Not Captain Carson?"

"No, missus, not Capt'n. It be Ulee. He hurt bad."

"Hurt? Where? How?"

"He step on a snake. He foot, him swell up big already. Hurry, Missus."

"I'll be right there." Snakes! They were so frequent and such a danger that Lea kept a basket with the implements she needed just for this kind of accident. She ran back to the kitchen and grabbed the basket, yanked a half-full bottle of whisky from a cabinet, and flew down the porch steps, racing toward Ulee's cabin, Josie right behind her. By the time she got there Ben and Rafe had brought Ulee in from the field and laid him on the layer of sacking he used for a mattress.

Lea knelt beside the pallet. Ulee's ankle was already twice its usual size with dark black streaks against the brown skin snaking up his leg. She eased away a large wad of tobacco from atop the wound and saw that someone had used a knife to make two cross-cuts over the punctures. Dark blood oozed from them.

Rafe leaned down to whisper, "Ulee done tole' us to use t'baccy like the Injuns do."

Ben moved away to allow her a closer look at the ankle. "I tied a tourniquet around that leg and Primo sucked out some of the poison. I hope we did enough. I'd sure hate to lose this man."

Lea worked frantically, pouring whiskey over the wound then applying a poultice laced with precious alum. Ulee gasped and twisted but he didn't cry out. "Did you see the snake?" she asked her husband.

"Yes, I killed it. It was a rattler. Not as large as some though. Had it been one of those monsters near the lake he'd already be dead."

"The size might save his life." There was more hope than conviction in her words. Still Ulee was such a large man himself, perhaps the smallish snake had not injected enough poison to kill him. "Ulee, does it hurt?" she asked.

The Negro nodded. "Him hurt." His face was already puffy and there was a grayish cast to his brown skin, as though someone had smeared it with ashes. The whites of his eyes contrasted starkly with his dilated pupils. Lea recognized not exactly fear there but grave concern.

"Here, drink some of this," she said, handing the bottle to him. He looked a question at Ben, who nodded.

"If it helps you get through this you can have the rest of it," Ben said, staring at the inflamed leg. Ulee took a long slug of whiskey, then handed the bottle back. After dressing the wound and watching the whiskey relax the man, Lea stood up and pulled Ben to the door.

"That's all we can do for now, Ben. He's going to be pretty sick. Josie and I can take turns staying with him until we see whether or not he'll pull out of it. And you'd better keep a close eye on Primo. If he has any kind of sore in his mouth, the poison can affect him as well."

Ben nodded. "Primo knows that. It was all I could do to prevent him from bringing you the dead snake. His remedy for snakebite is to put pieces of the body on the wound until it's all used up. The poison is supposed to prefer snake flesh to human."

"If I thought it would work I'd try anything."

"Do everything you can for Ulee, Lea. I don't care how long it takes for him to recover, as long as he does. He's the best worker I've got and I need him if I'm going to bring in that cotton."

"I know. We'll do our best."

Ben squeezed her shoulder and left to go back to the fields where he had a pretty good idea the new men were slacking off with no one to watch them.

It was two days before they knew Ulee would pull through. In the beginning between bouts of retching he tossed feverishly on his bed, mumbling words that Lea could not understand. Once or twice he cried out in nightmarish fear or struggled to get up, flailing his arms wildly. It took Lea, Josie and Rafe to restrain him that first night but by the morning he lay in an unconscious stupor which was even more frightening to Lea than the violence had been. She was certain he was dying.

That afternoon, when she wearily went to the cabin to relieve Josie, she was stunned to see Ulee turn his head and look at her, his eyes dull but lucid. A faint smile played about his lips.

"Well," Lea said, her hands on her hips as she stared down at him. "Well, I think you are going be all right after all. Captain Carson will be glad to see it. Are you hungry?"

Ulee nodded weakly and she hurried back up to the kitchen to bring him a little broth. He tried to take the spoon himself but was too weak and finally submitted to allowing her to put it to his lips. Afterward he slept again, much more peacefully than at any time since the accident. By evening Lea felt they could leave him alone, just looking in from time to time.

Yet over the next few days she often found she was drawn to Ulee's cabin to sit beside the patient. She told herself it was because she wanted to be certain he would recover for Ben's sake but the real reason was because Ulee was finally beginning to talk to her. Not a lot, not anything very revealing, but enough to encourage her to be there in case he said more.

A week after the accident she found him sitting in front of his cabin enjoying the shade of a nearby blackjack oak. She pulled up a stool to sit and have a look at his leg stretched out before him. A gnarled oak limb he had begun to use for a cane was propped near the door.

Lea removed the poultice and sprinkled the wound lightly with a powder of lime to slough off the dead skin. "That leg is healing well, Ulee. How is the strength? Have you tried standing on it yet?"

Ulee shook his head. "Him still hurt."

"I know. But you've got to use it to make it stronger. Not too much at first, just little steps. One day soon it won't hurt at all." She watched him nod his head. "We've got to get your strength back. Captain Carson says you'll be needed to help bring in the cotton crop very soon now."

Ulee looked at her, his dark eyes boring into her face. "Ain't gonna be no crop worth bringin' in."

Lea's heart sank. "What do you mean?"

"That lan', she ain't no good for cotton. Oh, maybe some, nuff so's to make clothes for de fambly. But de big bales for to ship out, don't think so, missus. Cotton plant, he need dark soil, not much water. Him not gonna grow in sand and hard rain."

It was more words than he had ever spoken at one time to her. Lea sat back, wanting to argue, to tell him he didn't know what he was talking about. But she knew it was wiser to let him talk. "How do you know that?" she asked. "Have you worked cotton fields before?"

Ulee nodded. "Masta Jonas, he grow Sea-Isle cotton up near Tall'hasee. Big fields, long as you can see. I work in 'em when I old enuff to carry a sack. I knows cotton, missus. This here ain't cotton lan'."

Lea caught her lower lip in her teeth. She did not doubt the truth of Ulee's words—the man probably did know cotton far better than either she or Ben. But his words cut like a knife. "What is this land good for then, if not for cotton?"

Ulee's dark eyes stared out at the tall stand of slash pines beyond the split rail fence. He shrugged. "Corn, crops, 'baccy. Not cotton. Leastways not such a lot of it like de Capt'n want."

Lea's gaze followed Ulee's. Near the trees a group of brown and white cattle grazed on the thin grass. Two half-grown stoats followed her brood sow to root beside the fence. The old mare bent to crop grass inside one of the pens.

"What about cattle?"

Ulee looked sharply at her. He nodded. "Cattle grow good here, ceptin' when dey gets de tick fevers."

She already knew that. The native cattle were small and prone to disease. But what if, as Clay had mentioned, they were bred with imported stock more resistant to those diseases? It might make all the difference. "What about orange trees?" she asked.

Ulee shrugged again. "Don't know nothin' 'bout oranges, missus."

There used to be orange trees at Fort Brooke, a whole grove of them. Limes too. She'd heard that Odet Philippe had established some successful groves before he left the Fort Brooke area. That might bear looking into. It might offer another choice for Ben if Ulee was right and this land was not suited to cotton.

But perhaps Ulee was wrong and Ben would bring in a good cash crop this year. She rose, setting the stool against the wall. "We'll talk more about this, Ulee. You rest now and get your strength back. And try out that leg."

He looked up at her and actually gave her a real grin! It left her with a feeling of satisfaction that not even his discouraging words could dispel as she walked back to the house.

By early fall there were ten hands working the fields and Lea and Josie were hard put to keep up with feeding them three meals a day. One of the Negroes brought his wife with him, a surly, sloe-eyed girl named Nattie, but she turned out to be no help at all. The girl had such a seductive way of making eyes at the other black men that Lea feared she was going to eventually cause a lot of trouble. Lea watched with amusement as Nattie even swiveled up to Ben one afternoon but she got nothing from him but a harsh command to keep her place. Ben might not be the most devoted of husbands but Lea had long ago learned that was because he still held obsessively to his idealized vision of Rachel, not because he had a wandering eye.

Her thoughts seldom went back to Rachel when she was hoeing beans, shelling peas, or had her arms elbow deep in a washtub. But rocking on the porch with her sewing or lying beside Ben at night listening to the deafening clatter of the night creatures, a vision of her sister was all too likely to intrude and crowd her thoughts. Those were the times she felt guilty that Rachel was dead and she was living with Ben, as though it was in some part her fault that her sister had died. But that was nonsense, she told herself. It just happened. It had nothing to do with her.

Yet how thankful she was things had worked out that way. She loved her husband more with every passing year. If he couldn't quite return that love as much as she wished because he still clung to his obsessive grief, well, she would just live with it, no matter how it sometimes hurt. Time would eventually change things.

She sat late one afternoon in the kitchen when the heat made work slow and lethargic in spite of the fall day, and let her thoughts wander. Closing her eyes she tried to recall her sister's face but the image refused to come, like smoke changing shape. What was left now of all that loveliness? What had her sister's brief life accomplished except to produce a wonderful young boy and leave a husband mired in grief? But then, what do any of us accomplish, she thought. Clay, for instance. Restless, always on the go, who never spoke of where he came from or what had brought him to this life, hiding every semblance of his former self behind incessant activity. Ben, a man of character, ability and integrity, pouring his life's blood into building up this farm yet whose stubborn loyalty would not allow him to set aside the love he had felt for his dead wife. Oh, yes, he was a good husband—an ardent lover, a family provider, a rock in this unsettled world. Yet there was always that sad longing for something gone, something that prevented him from fully accepting the heart she offered him. Would any amount of time ever change that? And she herself. What was it in her that made her willing to accept second best and never demand he put her first…

Such thoughts!

She realized her fingers were gripping the arms of the chair. "For heaven's sake, Lea," she muttered. "Stop being so morbid!"

The kitchen door crashed open and Buck stormed into the room jarring her out of her reverie. "I hate Pa! I hate him!" He slammed his palmleaf hat on the table and threw himself into the chair opposite her. Josie looked up from banking the embers of an earlier cook fire and clucked her tongue.

"What now?" Lea asked wearily as she took up a handful of cow peas from the bowl lying in her lap.

"He's so unfair. I can never do anything right. Even when I try to do things to please him it's always wrong. I don't even know why I try. I wish I could leave this place. I hate farming!"

"Josie get the boy a glass of buttermilk. Maybe it will help calm him down."

Buck folded his arms across his chest and stared sullenly at the hearth. "I don't want any buttermilk. And I don't want to calm down. I hate him."

"That's no way to talk about your Father, Buck, and you know I won't stand for it. Now slow down and tell me what's wrong."

She was relieved when Buck's tantrum turned out to be, as usual, over some chore not done as well as Ben thought it should be. It was difficult to know how to handle these problems. She knew she ought to side with Ben because Buck's work usually was sloppy and half-done. It was one of the reasons she had almost given up trying to school him. Yet, she knew too that the boy's resentment of his father grew stronger every day and she hated to see it. They never seemed to be able to reach any common ground and the result was almost every discussion ended up in an angry confrontation.

"Why don't you try to do the things your father asks, Buck. You know it would please him and then you wouldn't have these scenes. He only wants you to carry your share of the load around here."

The boy's lips pursed tightly. "Why bother? Nothing I do pleases him."

"Now that's not true. He's trying to help you grow up to be a mature, responsible man. Remember, he was an army officer. He is used to dealing with young men in ways that get them to shape up."

"Well, I'm not one of his army privates. And if he only wants me to grow up his way, he has a hell of a way of going about it."

"Don't curse. I don't like to hear it." Lea sighed and set her bowl on the floor. She walked over to Buck and laid her hand on his thin shoulder. The boy was growing taller every day, and his loose, angular frame seemed to thrust its way out of the clothes she made for him. She tried to smooth back the lanky hair from his forehead but he brushed her hand away.

"All right, stay mad then," she said. "But when you take this attitude don't be surprised that your Papa gets annoyed."

"I don't care how annoyed he gets. I'm going riding."

She watched helplessly as he stalked out of the door and headed for the fields beyond the house where his pony grazed. His hunting dog, Cracker, bounded off the porch after him. He would be gone the rest of the day now and Ben would be even angrier, and with just cause.

As it turned out, she had never seen Ben so furious with his son as he was later that evening. "The boy is hopeless," he snapped when she tried to approach the subject. "I can't do anything with him. He's useless around this place."

"Perhaps if you complimented him now and then. Encouraged him. He feels he can't please you in any way."

"He can't! He doesn't even try. I wish there was a military school nearby, I'd bundle him off so fast he wouldn't know what was happening. Maybe the army is the answer. He's old enough to be a drummer boy or something."

"Ben! You wouldn't want him part of such a dangerous life, surely."

"It might make a man of him. God knows, I can't."

"He loves riding that pony. In fact, horses are the one thing he seems to excel at. Why not give him more responsibility with them?"

Ben knocked his pipe against the hearth, clicking his tongue. "Let him ride around all day just because he enjoys it? For God's sake, Lea. This is a working plantation, not a cowherd ranch. No, he had better learn now that he has to obey orders and do what he's told or he'll be out of here."

His words raised a thin chill of dread in her chest. She pushed it aside and sought for something to change the subject. There was just too much to do to spend her limited energy on Buck's relationship with his father. They'd have to work it out themselves.

Then she glanced up to see Ben pulling his gold watch from his pocket, fingering it in his hand. "I worry about the boy," Ben said more calmly, his fingers stroking the gleaming gold lid. "If only his mother had lived."

Lea caught back the angry words that sprang to her lips. She focused on her needle while the quiet peace of the room settled around them both. Yet she was anything but peaceful inside. She knew Ben still carried that small miniature portrait of Rachel inside his watch. And she knew when his fingers stroked it he was thinking of her sister, longing for her still, after all this time. It was so unfair. Did he really believe sickly, self-centered Rachel would have been able to control Buck's wild ways? Why, even when Buck and Stephen were young Rachel had left most of their care to her. Why couldn't Ben see that?

Yet to point that out would only make her sound jealous and spiteful. She knew how much he would resent it and so she said nothing and bore the hurt in her heart, hoping someday enough time would pass to dim Rachel's memory and allow Ben to love her. After all, she reminded herself, he had only married her out of need. Love would come later—if it ever came at all.

To Lea's surprise, Buck became unusually cooperative in the days following this latest quarrel with his father. He made a real effort to do the chores Ben gave him and he volunteered for a few when he wasn't asked. He even offered to help Lea hoe the rows of sweet potatoes near the house one afternoon when the warmth of the day made the cool of the woods far more attractive. Pleased, she quickly accepted and the two of them worked steadily, talking now and then of mundane things and carefully avoiding the subject of Ben.

They were nearly half way through the patch when Lea heard Josie yelling from the house. Glancing up she saw her servant standing on the front porch hopping up and down and screeching as though in pain. Lea turned to look where Josie was pointing and gasped.

On the rim of a low hill where the trees began stood a row of men. They were close enough for her to recognize their bright colored turbans with their high standing egret feathers. Each had a long shotgun resting in the crook of his arm.

"Aunt Lea!" Buck breathed. "Indians."

Lea fought to keep her voice steady though her heart was pounding. "Buck, get your pony and go find your Pa."

"What do they want, Aunt Lea? Are they going to hurt us?"

She laid a reassuring hand on his thin shoulder. "I don't think so. They wouldn't be just standing there if they were. And not in the middle of the morning. Hurry now. Ben's with the men in the east field, working the cotton."

Buck hesitated. "But suppose they shoot at me?"

"Slip around behind the house. They can't see the barn from there. Hurry now."

Buck gave her a long look as though reluctant to leave then, as agile as a young rabbit, stooped to run at a crouch along the fence until he could dart behind the house. Lea kept her gaze on the Indians who just as doggedly kept their focus on her. If one raised his weapon she would yell at Buck to stop but none did. They just stood there watching her without moving. Once she knew Buck was out of sight she picked up her hoe and walked at a slow, steady pace toward the porch.

Josie was already hiding inside the house. She peeked around the door frame at Lea muttering, "O ma'Gawd! Oh ma Gawd!" shaking with fright.

"Get hold of yourself, Josie," Lea said quietly. "We can't show them we're afraid."

"But Miz Lea…they's savages. They's gonna kill us all…"

"I don't think so. Not right now anyway. We have to see what they want." *But please, Ben, get here quickly*, she added to herself. She wondered if she should have Josie bring her Ben's rifle from inside the house. Yet that might be all the provocation they needed to point their guns at her. And besides, she was a terrible shot. She decided to stand at the top of the porch steps keeping an eye on the line of men instead.

Her resolution faltered when she saw the Indians start forward. They proceeded at an even pace, almost casually as though they had all the time in the world. There were seven of them and as they drew near the house Lea noted that they all looked as though they could use a good meal. Lea waited stoically as they entered the yard and stopped a small distance from the house. They were dressed in the usual Seminole assortment of bright colored shirts and scarves. Two wore single silver gorgets around their necks, others had two or three knotted kerchiefs above crossed leather strips decorated with beads and shells. The one in the center had a profusion of black feathers crowning his turban and three silver gorgets against his colorful shirt—the Chief, Lea supposed. A short stick, painted bright red, protruded from the sash at his waist and he was holding a pole nearly as tall as himself, decorated with feathers, shells and rattles. Lea recognized it as the Chief's war lance, every item on it a symbol of some brave dead. Standing behind him was a black man wearing a drab shirt and canvass trousers, a battered felt hat pulled down over his eyes. Lea had seen enough men like that at Fort Brooke to recognize him as an interpreter.

"What do you want?" she said in as steady a voice as she could muster. She was not surprised when the little black man stepped forward.

"Chief Otulkee Thlocko, the Prophet, he want to speak to Ben Carson."

The Prophet. She had heard of him. But his camp was near the Peace River and he did not usually venture this far north. "My husband is not here," she said. "He's working in his fields. If the Prophet wants to talk with him, let him go there."

The Negro rattled off something in Seminole to the man with all the turban feathers. The Chief's eyes fastened on Lea. For almost a minute he didn't speak then said something in his own language.

"Chief Otulkee Thlocko will wait," the interpreter said. Lea's heart sank. What was she supposed to do? Invite them in for a cool drink? "There's no need," she started then broke off as she saw Ben galloping in from the fields on Buck's pony, his mount kicking up the dust. He came tearing up the road to the house, swung off his horse almost before it stopped and ran to stand beside her on the porch.

"Are you all right?" he asked as he looked over the row of Indians.

"Yes. They want to talk to you."

Ben recognized the interpreter right away. "All right, Sanchez. I'm here now. What do they want? Why does the Prophet come riding onto my land wearing his red war stick?"

The Chief spoke for several minutes. When he finished the Negro interpreter leaned forward and dug his heel in the sand. "Chief Otulke Thockle say you got somethin' that belong to him. He want it back."

Ben chose his words carefully. "If the Prophet means this land then he is wrong. This land was given to me by Chief Miconopy and his son-in-law, Ote Emathla. I have the map with his mark on it. Otulke Thockle can see it if he wants."

The Prophet had obviously recognized Jumper's name. A faint smile played about his thin mouth but it was quickly gone. He spoke again to his interpreter.

"Chief Otulke Thlocko know about Miconopy's map," Sanchez said to Ben. "He say he don't like it none but since the Chief made it, he let you live here and work the land in peace. Till you took what was his."

Ben searched his mind but he could not think of anything he had that could possibly belong to the Prophet. "I don't know what he means," he said to Sanchez. "Tell him I don't have anything of his and I don't know what he is talking about."

Before Sanchez could speak Chief Otulke Thlocko broke in. Pointing a long finger, he proclaimed in English, "That man mine."

Ben and Lea both turned to look toward the left corner of the house. Ulee was standing there, with Buck behind him holding the reins of his pony. They must have followed Ben, Lea thought almost prosaically. None of this made any sense.

"Ulysess?"

"That is right, Capitano," Sanchez said. "That black man, he belong to Chief Otulke. He his slave for five year then he run away. He Chief Otulke Thlocko's slave. Chief Otulke Thlocko his master."

Ben shook his head. "There must be some mistake. Ulysess is a free man. He has papers to prove it. He's nobody's slave."

The Chief spoke angrily then waited for Sanchez to translate. "Chief Otulke Thlocko, he say white man's paper don't mean nothin' to him. He capture this big black man and take him back to his village. Five year this man be his slave. He want him back."

"Captured him? Where? When?"

"On the St. John River, a little fight there. An' I tole you, five year ago."

"A fight? A massacre more like," Ben muttered. He turned and motioned Ulee to come closer. "Is any of this true, Ulee? Were you the Prophet's captive and his slave?"

Ulee tore his eyes from the Chief who was staring at him impassively. There was anger in the Negro's gaze, and a little fright as well. It was the first time Lea had ever seen Ulee look even a little scared. He had not shown this much concern even when the snake bit him.

"Tweren't no fight, Capt'n. I be workin' for a fambly name 'o Proctor. Him Indians come out o' night, sack de place, kill all de fambly and taken all us black folks back to he camp. Dey call us slave but I be free. I tole dem I be free."

"Chief Otulke Thlocko obviously thinks he owns you by right of conquest," Ben said quietly. "What about it? Do you want to go back with these Indians? I've heard that they treat Negros pretty well."

Ulee looked squarely at Ben. "I be a free man, Capt'n. I don't wants to be no slave, not to no white man and not to no Indian."

Ben glanced at Lea. They both knew what the other was thinking. It would be wiser to turn Ulee over to the Prophet and be done with it. To not do so could only mean courting trouble. Ulee and the Chief stood waiting while Ben quietly turned over every possibility in his mind. Lea reached out and squeezed his arm and he covered her hand with his.

"Buck, go inside and bring me my rifle."

Lea swallowed as Buck darted in the house and returned with Ben's long army carbine. He cocked it and sat it casually in the crook of his arm. "Sanchez," he called. "Tell the Chief that this black man is free and will not be a slave again. And if any of his men try to take him I will kill them on the spot."

Sanchez smiled crookedly and leaned over to spit into the dirt. "*Capitano,* you a crazy man. You want the Chief tell his warriors to kill all your women and your son? You can't shoot everybody."

"Otulke Thlocko will get the first bullet. Be sure and tell him that."

Sanchez spoke to the Chief. His black eyes flared pure hatred at Ben as he strode forward, pulled out the red stick from his sash and threw it in the sand before the porch steps. Turning away, he started from the yard with the rest of his party following on his heels. The last one to leave reached to retrieve the stick before hurrying after the others.

Lea let out a long sigh and sank to the steps. "Thank God," she breathed.

"Don't thank him yet," Ben said. "We may be all right now but that red stick told us we've unleashed a storm. It's bound to come back at us and probably soon."

Ulee turned to walk away but thought better of it and stopped, turning back to Ben. "I thanks you, Capt'n," he said. "Dem Indians, dey don't treat black man any better dan white man do, and sometimes not so good. My ole masta, he be a gentl'man. Dat Prophet, he jus' a savage."

"I know," Ben sighed, keenly aware that he would pay for this days kindness. He expected Ulee to hurry off but he did not. He stood as though weighing his words.

"I don't wants to cause no trouble for you, Capt'n. Maybe it better I jus' go. I be out of here by evenin'."

Ben shook his head. "No, I need your help now more than ever with the cotton nearly ready. You stay. We'll deal with Otulke Thlocko."

He was not as assured as he tried to sound. He smiled at Lea and slipped his arm around her waist as they walked back into the house.

"Have you had dealings with this 'Prophet' before?" she asked.

"No, but I know about him. He's a renegade Creek who has a reputation for occult powers. The Indians look on him almost as some kind of messiah. And he is dead set against any of his people leaving Florida for the west."

"I wonder what the Prophet will add to his war lance for this day's work? Still I'm glad you didn't turn Ulee over to him."

"Don't be glad yet. Let's see what he does about it first."

At first it seemed he would do nothing. After watching anxiously for several days, expecting a band of angry Indians to swoop down on them any minute, Lea and Ben both began to relax a little. They still kept their guard up but they began to hope that perhaps the Army's influence would prevent the Prophet from trying to steal Ulee or take his resentment out on the farm. Though Ben hated doing it, he told his workers about the Prophet's threat and said he would not hold them if any wanted to leave. Only two did—two of the men Ben had brought from Tampa Village who were not worth their wages anyway.

Lea put her foot down and absolutely forbade Buck to go far from the house. The boy was half-hoping for the excitement of an Indian attack and so gladly agreed. Ben kept his rifles loaded and nearby, and Lea practiced improving her aim. They discussed what they would do in case of a surprise attack until they had every precaution firmly in their minds. Yet the days went smoothly by one after the other in a comforting routine.

When Lea heard Buck hollering she threw down the bowl of batter she was stirring and ran to the kitchen door. A horse was galloping at breakneck speed up the road to the house. Fearing the worst she hurried out on the breezeway porch. Ben, who had been working on his financial records at a table in the front room, followed on her heels.

"Who do you suppose," Lea said warily.

"It's a white man. Whatever he wants he's in a big hurry."

As the rider drew closer Ben recognized Rob Snyder, one of the men who worked for Henry Lindsey in his Tampa real estate office. Any relief he felt when he knew this wasn't an Indian quickly faded. Lindsey would never send all the way up here unless it was something bad.

Snyder yanked his lathered horse to a stop near the porch steps and slid from the saddle. He was a lanky man with long, thin arms and legs. His face was thin as well, and always wore a stubble of blondish beard. He threw the reins to Buck who had come running up and asked him to see to his horse.

"Well, Snyder," Ben said, walking on to the porch. "What brings you up here so far from town?"

"Town! Ha!" Snyder pulled off his hat and slapped the dust from it against his legs. "Tampa's a little bit bigger than when you saw it last but it still ain't more'n a few stores and houses. Good afternoon, Ma'am," he said, nodding to Lea. "You wouldn't have a cool drink for a hard travelin' man, would you now?"

"Of course, Mister Snyder. Come inside and sit a while. You look like you could use a rest."

"That I could. It's a long way up here from Tampa, and Mister Lindsay said I was to make it fast. He sent this for you, Captain." Snyder reached inside his shirt and pulled out a long folded paper which he handed to Ben. Ben opened it and scanned it quickly.

"Come along inside, Rob. We can attend to business while Mrs. Carson gets some food ready for you." Ben refolded the paper and looked over at Lea, silencing her questions. The two men went to sit at the table while Lea and Josie removed dishes from the kitchen safe, fixing a plate from the left-overs from an earlier dinner. There was no way to avoid hearing the men's conversation and by the time she brought the tray of food and beer to Rob she already had an inkling of what brought him.

Ben motioned her to sit beside them. "Lindsay sent me this, Lea," he said, handing her the paper. She tried to read it but it was in so smeared by frequent handling she could make no sense of it so Ben explained. "It says that Ramon de Diego contends this land is his by virtue of his Indian deed and a pre-emption claim and has asked for a court settlement. There's to be a hearing tomorrow afternoon."

Lea's heart fell. "But you have the same claims."

"I know. And I also have Colonel Worth's directive but whether that will be enough to override Diego, I just don't know."

"But tomorrow…"

"Yes, that isn't much time. I can just about make it."

"Ben, you can't leave right now. I mean, it isn't safe, not for you or for us."

"I have to go. I can't let Diego contest me out of this land after all I've, we've put into it. It's mine and I intend to keep it. Diego is only doing this because he knows the cotton is almost ready to be brought in and because this war is ending. Soon this whole territory will open up and we'll all be fighting over who owns what. I can't let that happen here."

"But your crop," she said lamely, even though the Prophet was uppermost in her thoughts. "Can the men care for it without you?"

"Ulee knows as much about it as I do. Maybe more. As long as he stays on, it'll be cared for." He reached over and took her hand in his. "I know what worries you, Lea. But I don't think Otulke plans to attack us or he would have already done it. I don't want to leave you right now, God knows, I don't. But what else can I do?"

Take me with you. Yet she would not say those words. If they both left, they would be abandoning everything they'd worked for. Someone had to be left in charge. Their men were free laborers, not slaves. A few of them were white. They would never work for a black overseer, no matter how skilled he was.

"I should have hired a foreman long ago," Ben muttered. "That will be the next order of business once we get this cotton in."

Snyder lifted his face from the plate where he was shoveling in food. "You had Indian attacks up here?"

"No, not recently."

"Be glad. We heard that a family homesteading near the Peese River was hit by a band of renegades last month. A grandmother and two young daughters, one not three years old, was murdered. The son escaped by hiding down a gopher hole. When the rest of the family returned they found pieces of the old grandmother's skin hanging on the bushes near the door. The house had been plundered and burned."

Lea stared at the cold hearth, trying to keep her fear from bubbling over.

"Shut your mouth, Rob," Ben said angrily. "We don't need to hear stories like that right now."

Snyder took a long swig of the beer. "You may not want to hear 'em but you sure as hell need to, livin' out here by yourselves like you do."

"Mister Snyder is right, Ben," Lea said. "We have to be prepared. Although I thought the war was pretty much over and the raids had slacked off a lot."

"They have and that's a fact, ma'am. And more and more of these heathens leave for Arkansas territory every month. But there's still some left who would rather fight than move. And with Indians you just never can feel safe."

Ben turned to his wife. "If you would feel better moving back to Fort Brooke I won't try to dissuade you. I can take you and Buck and Josie with me and the men can fend for themselves. You decide."

She thought over his words. Every part of her longed to say yes! Take us back to the fort where we can feel safe. But what would she be leaving? Their farm, their people, their hopes for the future. And Ulee, Rafe, Primus, and Tom, how would they cope? If Chief Otulke and his band swarmed down on them, they might all be taken as slaves.

"No, we'll stay here," she said. "We can manage until you get back. Only please, please hurry."

He squeezed her shoulder, silently thanking her for her bravery. "I promise. Rob, what do you know about Clay Madrapore? Any idea where he is? He can vouch for me to the Judge if we can find him."

"I heared he was in Newmansville. I'm on my way there though I was hopin' to rest me and my horse first. If'n I find him I'll send him on to Tampa."

"Thanks." He turned to Lea. "I'd better go throw some things in my saddle bags. At least my horse is fresh. Snyder, can you face heading out again right away?"

"I can if you give me a fresh mount."

"You can take Buck's pony and return it on your way back south."

Half an hour later Lea stood watching as Ben and Rob cantered down the road away from the house. She looked over at the rim of trees where the afternoon was waning. The heat hung like a pall over everything, wilting the leaves and turning the grass brown. Even the birds seemed to lie sleepy and still. The dust churned up in the road by the two horsemen was the only moving thing on the whole landscape.

Let it stay this way, she prayed. *Until Ben comes back, please God, let it stay this way!*

CHAPTER 16

▼

In spite of what Rob Snyder told him Ben expected to see some changes and improvements in the village of Tampa when he rode in the next day. The place had always been little more than an appendage to Fort Brooke, the sprawling army camp at the mouth of the river, but now that the war was over and open land was becoming available he fully expected to see the village taking on an identity of its own. And in fact there were a few new houses fronting the streets Augustus Steele had laid out where before only pine barrens and oak groves had enlivened the sandy scrub. There were some new piers along the river and more ships out on the bay, their masts jutting upward like a de-nuded forest. The streets were still noisy and crowded with wagons and drays carrying supplies or household goods and there was a staccato of hammering where one or two new frames were being put up. Yet the overall impression was one of stagnation and lethargy, as though the Florida heat had drained life from the village itself.

Evidently most of the people who arrived with every new ship had decided to move on into the interior, Ben thought. With the war gone south and good land just waiting for settlement, they seemed to have little interest in putting down roots in a town.

He hurried to the courthouse after stabling his horse at the new hotel. There was half an hour to spare before the hearing and though Ben felt he needed to get a briefing from Lindsay, he didn't want to risk being late by visiting his store first. He was both surprised and gratified when he ran into the man himself walking up the wooden walk to the courthouse.

Lindsay's long face broke into what passed for a smile as he gripped Ben's hand. "Thank God you got my message. I only heard about this by the sheerest luck. That son-of-a-bitch Diego tried his best to keep it a secret."

"He can't do that. It's a contested claim that I've worked for nearly four years. I have the right to present my side."

"Ramon is not particularly concerned about anybody's rights but his own. However, since I wrote that note I've learned one thing that might be in your favor. Diego's pre-emption claim is based on a deed he got from Robert Hackley, Richard's son. And since Richard's Alagon claim has been ruled invalid, it can't hold much weight. You look pretty beat. Are you sure you can face this?"

Ben brushed the dust from his coat sleeves. "I've been traveling as fast as my horse could go. But yes, I want to get this settled. I know about the Hackley deed but remember, that invalidation was based on Florida becoming a State, which hasn't happened yet. What about Judge Steele? Is he here?"

"Already in the courthouse. We've got a few moments." Lindsay pulled a long cheroot from his coat pocket. "Have a smoke. It'll ease you for the ordeal."

Ben sank down on the low wooden steps. "No thanks, but you go ahead."

He would have welcomed a good stiff drink but he knew it was more important to keep his head clear. He watched as Lindsay blew smoke into the air and tried to focus on the arguments he had to make before Agustus Steele. The Judge was an unknown factor in all this. In the past he had been hand in glove with William Bunce and Robert Hackley and Diego's primary claim would rest on his purchase from Hackley. The treaty made with wily Ote Emathla would have little bearing in a United States court of law but old partnerships might count for a lot. Then there was also the fact that more than anyone else, Augustus Steele had worked to establish the village of Tampa and at almost every step he'd met barriers thrown up by the military at Fort Brooke, especially by Colonel Worth. Would he hold it against Ben now that he had once been part of that military establishment?

"Still trying to grow cotton up there to the north?" Lindsay asked, jarring Ben from his thoughts.

"Yes. My first crop is almost ready to bring in. I ought to be up there taking care of it instead of fooling around down here with this business."

"Don't know why you're risking so much on cotton. Prices aren't that good."

"I heard they'd rebounded."

"From a few years ago, sure. The panic of '37 sent them through the floor and they're a lot better than that now. But if you want a fortune, cane is the way to go. You wouldn't believe the numbers of planters ready to claim land down on the Manatee River to farm sugar cane. Buying up all that rich hammock land, building mills, planting acres and acres…"

"And bringing in plenty of slaves to do the work, I suppose."

"Of course. That's another thing, Ben. You refuse to own slaves and that makes it almost certain you won't get the amount of bales you need to really make money. Lose some of those principles and join the rest of us."

Ben gave a wry smile. "I'll stick to my principles, thank you. There must be a few others who feel as I do."

"Oh a few, but they're decidedly in the minority and they're mostly interested in dealing cattle. Besides, I hope you realize that if you want to build a future in politics your views on slavery won't help you."

"I'm not an abolitionist troublemaker, Henry, and my friends know that. I just don't take to owning another human being. I saw too many injustices in the practice growing up in South Carolina. If others want to live that way, well, that's their privilege. I ought to be allowed the same."

Lindsay shook his head. "Feelings are growing too strong for that kind of tolerance, Ben. You got to make up your mind what you want and go after it, principles or no principles. You'll need a lot of money to dabble in politics and buying and selling slaves is one way to get it. It's what our whole economy is built on. For the same reason you ought to think about planting sugar cane."

"The truth is, Henry, I don't know anything about cane while cotton is something I've wanted to farm for years. My first crop is small, I admit, but if I get a decent return on it the next one will be a lot bigger."

"Have it your way." Lindsay pulled his gold watch from his fob pocket and flipped the lid with a grimy nail. "About time to go in, I expect." He dropped the half smoked cigar in the sand and ground the tip under his boot. "After you, sir."

The courthouse only had two rooms. Ben followed Lindsay into the one that served as Judge Steele's court and stood against the back wall surveying the room. Sitting down in front, Ramon de Diego turned and saw him. If Ben expected some kind of hostile reaction he didn't get it. Diego gave him a dignified nod and smiled like he was greeting an old friend.

The cheeky bastard! Well, if he thinks this is going to be an easy win he's in for a surprise.

It was another hour before their case came before the Judge. Diego spoke first, laying the deed he had made with Hackley in front of Steele and placing the large piece of parchment he claimed Chief Miconopy had signed beside it. He called the Judge's attention to the dates on both.

"You will see, Sir Judge," he said with studied politeness "these dates precede those of Mister Carson's claim. That alone should give them precedence."

"Your honor," Ben interrupted but Steele waved him down. "You'll get your turn, Ben," he drawled. Thrusting aside the parchment, Steele picked up the deed and carefully read it while Ben seethed. He was very conscious of the nattily dressed figure Diego cut while he sat there with a day's growth of beard and his clothes covered with traveling dirt. He only hoped that wouldn't influence the Judge. The old man had been around Tampa Bay for years. Perhaps he put more store in the law than appearances. Ben could only hope so.

When his turn came he stalked to the front of the room and spread out his own claims. "Your honor," Ben began, "I call your attention to the fact that I have an agreement made last year with Colonel Worth and a pre-emption agreement based on the Territorial law of 1824. Further, I have a treaty made with Miconopy which in effect nullifies that made by Diego here. The Chief's spokesman, Ote Emathla, told me Senor Diego violated the agreement made with Miconopy by delivering worthless merchandise and he felt since Diego had not lived up to his part of the bargain, the original gift of land was invalid."

Ignoring the Chief's map, Steele focused on the two government papers for several long minutes. Then he picked up Miconopy's agreement in one hand and compared it with the other, shaking his head. "I don't see where it says that, Ben."

"It may not say so in writing but he did say it. That was the reason he called me to his camp in the first place. Ramon de Diego knows that."

Diego smiled. "Your honor, if you please, I know no such thing. Chief Miconopy never told me our agreement was invalid and I assumed it was as good as the day it was made. Mister Carson here has been homesteading my land for several years now and I demand redress."

Ben bit back the rejoinder he wanted to make. He was reluctant to be drawn into an argument about Miconopy's agreements since he felt sure they would not have a bearing on the Judge's eventual decision. He had long ago become convinced that the wily Chief broke his original agreement with Diego and signed away the same land to Ben in the hope they would fight over it.

Judge Steele shook his head again. "I'll have to look over both sets of deeds. Senor Diego. I'm sure you are aware that Mister Hackley's claim to ownership is questionable but since I myself have purchased land from him, I'll give it due consideration. As for the Indian treaty, I have nothing but your word, Ben, that the Chief made the second one because he thought the first was broken. Senor Diego, you say he never communicated that fact to you?"

"Senor Judge, never. I could only assume the agreement was still in place."

"Of course he'd say that, Judge," Ben snapped. "It's his word against mine."

For the first time Ramon de Diego's smile faded. "Are you calling me a liar, *Capitano* Carson? Those are harsh words. I hope you are prepared to back them up on the field of honor."

"I don't fight duels, Diego. And you know damn well I'm not lying."

Lindsay stepped up to keep Ben and Ramon apart. "Your honor, can't we at least postpone this until Ben Carson has time to find proof of what he claims?"

"He doesn't need proof."

Ben turned quickly at the voice at the back of the room and saw Clay Madrapore striding toward him. A sense of relief flooded through his body.

Clay looked as disheveled by hard riding as Ben. He threw a dusty saddle bag on a chair and took his place beside Ben. "I was there, Judge, when Jumper, as Miconopy's spokesman, gave this land to Ben. I can vouch for every word he spoke. It happened just as Ben said. The Chief felt Diego had swindled him and he wanted retribution."

Diego's face was a mask but his eyes burned with resentment. "Judge, these men are friends. They would of course back each other up. Is it fair that the two of them should put their case before you when I have no one to vouch for me?"

"Judge Steele knows Clay wouldn't lie."

Steele laughed. "Well, I wouldn't go quite that far, Ben. The truth is whatever that foxy Indian said to the two of you doesn't really have a bearing on this case." He ran his hand down Ben's parchment map. "The land is not surveyed and there is only the vaguest reference to where it lies. These other deeds are more important but even then there is some difficulty in deciding which ones carry the most weight."

While the Judge went on almost as though talking to himself, Ben studied Diego's aristocratic face. He was clearly seething but his control was so tight that his anger was only apparent in his hooded eyes. Everything else, from the casual stance, the easy inspection of his nails, the light brushing of lint from his immaculate black coat, all gave an impression of almost bored disinterest. Ben knew that wasn't true.

He heard Steele speaking and came out of his reverie. "I'm going to need time to look over these claims," the Judge was saying, "and I don't want to decide ownership without carefully considering everything. I'll see both of you again tomorrow morning."

Ben groaned inwardly. "But Judge, I've got to get back home. I left my wife and son there and things are unsettled. I planned to start back this evening."

Diego drummed his fingers on the table. "If things are so unsettled perhaps you should have waited before squatting on my land."

"It is *not* your land."

"Now that's enough, both of you," Steele intervened. "I'll give you my verdict tomorrow and that's all there is to it. If it weren't safe to leave, Ben, then you should have stayed. Besides, one night won't make that much difference. You could use the rest anyway. You'll be that much fresher before starting back."

Ben started to reply but Clay laid a hand on his shoulder and turned him toward the door.

"Come on. I'll buy you a drink."

The 'grogery' was new, carved out of a space where Ben remembered a huge grove of oak trees shadowing a stretch of level ground near what used to be the northern edge of town. It had the customary raw wood walls, a porch reverberating under a cacophony of heavy soled boots, one swinging door, a long rough pine bar along one wall, and several tables scattered opposite the bar, one of them covered with green baize. Several men were grouped around the table, playing a noisy game of loo. A tattered satin drape over the gilt frame of a large mirror above the bar was the only attempt at elegance in an otherwise drab, utilitarian, strictly functional room devoted to the pleasures of whisky and gambling.

"Cyrus Noble," Clay said to the man behind the bar. He threw a few coins on the counter then picked up the bottle by its neck, two glasses in the other hand, and led Ben to one of the tables as far away from the noisy game as he could get.

Ben downed the glass Clay half-filled, then shoved it across for a refill? "I take it Rob caught up with you," he said.

"I was in Newnansville at the Land office when he took me aside. I'd heard about Diego's claim just before from a man who knew I was a friend of yours."

Ben ran his finger around the top of his glass. "I wonder why Diego took this to court just now. I've been working that land for nearly four years without anyone questioning my right to it."

"I have a notion why. Rob found me just as I was about to head out to your plantation to tell you that Congress has finally passed the Armed Occupation Act. If you can get your claim in before Diego you'll have your land officially. He won't be able to bother you after that."

Ben leaned closer. "Are you certain this is true? There have been rumors about it coming for months now but it never happened."

"It's true. A courier arrived from Washington two days ago. One office will be in Newnansville but deeds can be filed in the mail before it opens."

"What are the terms?"

"One hundred and sixty acres free to anyone with a gun who builds a house on the land and develops at least five acres for five years."

"Well, it may be an answer. If the courts won't give me justice then I'll get it myself. I've worked too hard to develop that land to let Diego steal it from me."

Clay's eyes narrowed. He had seen that look on Ben's face one or two times before and he knew it meant trouble. "You can't be surprised by this. You must have known someday Ramon would try to claim ownership because he thinks it's land Miconopy promised him. That it interferes with your plans is just a bonus."

Ben reached for the whisky bottle. "That wily old fox, Jumper. He counted on us quarreling over that land even as he talked Miconopy into promising it to us. That's one reason I went ahead and cultivated it even before the war ended. I have the right of pre-emption even if they throw out Miconopy's treaties."

"And now you've put so much of your life's blood in the soil you can't give it up."

"Not to mention most of whatever money I used to possess."

Clay lounged back in the chair and studied his friend's face. This was not his fight and except for his long friendship with Ben and the respect he had for him, he knew he would be wise to wish him well and go offer his services to the commandant at Fort Brooke. The Army still needed scouts for the forts in South Florida where the Seminoles were not so quiet recently as they had been up this way.

But there was Lea. Always there was Lea. Could he really trust Ben to be as concerned for her safety as he was to hold on to his dream of owning a plantation?

"Look, Ben," he said, leaning forward, his arms on the table. "Judge Steele was hand-in-glove with Robert Hackley for several years and he won't throw out his deeds lightly because it might affect the ones he himself made. But whatever Steele decides tomorrow, don't be too rash about taking justice into your own hands. It could backfire on you. You have your family to consider and your future. It might give you a lot of satisfaction to kill Diego but it would ruin any possibility you have of someday being someone important in this territory."

Ben smiled. "Clay the Cautious." He started to fill his glass again then thought better of it and pushed the bottle away. "But you're right. Florida is going to be declared a State soon and there are ample opportunities for enterprising men to build a reputation and a political future. I want to be one of them. I *intend* to be one of them. And I won't allow Roman de Diego to ruin that for me. But don't worry. I'm not going to go off half-cocked even if the Judge rules against me. Diego would love to provoke me into a duel, which is his way of set-tling quarrels, not mine. And much as I would like to see him have some kind of 'accident' that's not my way either."

Ben leaned back in his chair, absently running his finger along the edge of the table. "I consider my homestead to be the first step toward my goal of earning a name for myself in this territory. My cotton crop is just before being ready to bring in. One good yield this year means two the next, and five the year after that. It's my future, Clay, and no Spanish fisherman like Diego is going to cheat me out of it."

Clay reached for the bottle and refilled both glasses. "Don't underestimate the man, Ben. He's not one of those indigents with an Indian wife eking out a living near Spanishtown Creek. He's an aristocratic Spaniard with business enterprises in Charlotte Harbor, Key West and Cuba. He has money and ambition. Rein in your anger at him and concentrate on your options in case you lose."

"I'll consider them but I won't stop being angry," Ben answered, picking up the glass and swallowing its contents in one gulp. He wiped his sleeve across his mouth. "Let's see what happens in the morning."

The hot afternoon wore on with a lazy, sleepy quietude. The air seemed heavy, the trees burdened under it. The sky was a hazy chalk-white, with a few dispirited clouds hovering near the horizon. Even the birds were subdued, as though they had lost the energy to sing or quarrel. A kind of breathless quiet hung over every-thing.

Too quiet, Lea thought, as she sat rocking on the porch. With a start she became aware that her fingers were gripping the arms of her chair, as if it might fly from under her. All quiet and calm on the surface, she chided herself, all seeth-ing anxiety within. And for no reason. Ben had been gone for days now and everything at the farm still moved along at an orderly, smooth pace. Ulee had less to say than ever yet she noticed he got more work out of the other blacks than anyone had before—even Ben. Only one white and one black man had opted to leave after the Indian's visit but they weren't much missed. And when that slat-ternly Nattie left with them it brought a peacefulness to the place which her divi-siveness had never allowed.

No, on the whole things were perking along without Ben almost as well as with him. Even Buck continued to be more cooperative, offering to help before he was asked. And he still stayed close by, much to her relief.

Why then was she so filled with this disquiet, this dread that hovered around her? Why else? Because the Prophet could pounce at almost any moment just when you least expected it, when you were the least ready for it.

"Missus…"

Lea jumped, startled from her thoughts by Ulee's quiet voice. He was standing near one end of the porch and she hadn't heard him approach from the road. She sat up, suddenly aware that the sun had sunk lower in the sky and it was almost time for the evening meal.

"What is it, Ulee?" she said, rising and smoothing down her skirts. "Are the men in from the fields yet?"

"Yes, ma'am."

"Good. Tell them to come up to the house and Josie and I will have their supper ready to dish up in ten minutes. I'm just waiting now for the bread to cool."

"Yes, Missus." When he didn't turn to lope off toward the cabins Lea waited. Ulee stood, turning the brim of his hat in his big hands, his dark eyes looking everywhere but directly at her.

"Is there something else?"

"Yes, Missus. You oughta know Miz Carson, Tom, he seed one o' them Indians around this mornin'."

Lea's hands went to her waist to still the sudden dread in the pit of her stomach. "Around? Where?"

"Tom, he say dis man hangin' close to dem trees ober der. When he seed Tom watchin', him slip back underneath. He be lookin' at the house, watchin'."

Spying. The word leapt into her mind. *Calculating. Making sure Ben wasn't here. Oh, Lord…*

She ran her tongue over her dry lips. "It probably doesn't mean anything, Ulee, but thank you for telling me. I think maybe tonight we should all keep our guns nearby and loaded. Just in case…"

"We done been doin' dat anyway, Missus." Ulee's broad lips turned up slightly at the corners in what for him passed for a smile. Lea found it reassuring for all that he would never tell her in so many words not to worry.

"You'd best go call the men," she said. and watched him turn away to lope off back toward the cabins. She glanced over at the woods beyond the corn fields, straining for a sign of movement in the dark shadows, a glimpse of bright colored shirt or turban. Of course, there was nothing. Just the deadly, dark calm.

Maybe Tom was wrong.

Ben expected to spend a sleepless night—that was one reason he had downed so much of Clay's whisky. He could barely remember the times in his life he had passed out cold from too much to drink but this was one night he would have welcomed the prospect. However, he wanted to be clear headed in the morning. So he reluctantly left the saloon and his friend with only a mild buzz of good feeling to buoy him.

The Tampa hotel was another disappointment. The previous owners, the Kilgores, had suffered bankruptcy and sold out earlier in the year. Now the new owner was struggling The place was falling into disrepair and kept going on a minimum survival level. Still, it offered a reasonably clean bed and the dining room still functioned.

He decided to take supper then spend the evening reading until he thought he could sleep but his plans took an unexpected turn when he heard someone calling his name in the dining room and looked up to see William Ferris coming toward him. Ferris was a New Yorker who had come to the area as a sutler at Fort Brooke a year ago. Ben was surprised to see he was still around.

"Mr. Ferris…how are you," Ben said, rising and extending his hand.

"I heard you were in town," Ferris said, pulling up a chair to sit at the table. He was a big man with receding black hair, a long nose and ears that jutted out behind thick sideburns. He laid his straw hat on the table and motioned for a waiter. "You won't mind if I join you?"

"Of course not. I'm glad to have a chance to catch up on how things are going. How is the military store doing?"

"Not worth spit since they cut back on the garrison after Colonel Worth declared the war over." He leaned toward Ben. "I tell you, Captain, if it weren't for all those crackers coming though here on their way to the interior, this place would be down-right dead. I guess you saw how the town's gone down."

"Oh, I don't know. I just left Clay Madrapore in one of the new saloons."

"Oh well," Ferris waved a big-fisted paw. "You'll always have those pleasure houses as long as you have soldiers around. We get too many drifters, cowmen, gamblers and their women passing through not to have places for them. But that's not what makes a town, Ben and you know it It's houses, streets, shops, respectable people."

"Surely there are a few left."

"A few but nothing compared to what was planned or even what was here a year back." William Ferris' eyes glistened. "My dream was to help build a real place here on the Bay, streets to be laid out where there's nothing but palmetto scrub and weeds now. Someday there would be a formal survey but I can see it right now, here in my head. This whole area for two miles north of Fort Brooke would be a grid with street names and divided lots. The lots near the river, they'd be very valuable for warehouses and docks. Speaking of which, how about letting me sell the ones you're holding while there's still a chance someone will buy them."

Ben shook his head. "Is that why you were looking for me? Sorry, but you're wasting your time. Maybe I'll just hang on to them till your grand vision comes to pass."

"You'll be a long time waiting then. I heard just today that Colonel Worth has decided to expel any and all settlers from the village. He wants to create a no-man's-land for one solid mile around the garrison. That'll be the death knell for Tampa."

"But what about the Colonel's colonization plan? I thought he wanted settlers."

"In the interior, along the Manatee, anywhere away from his God-damned fort. If he has his way there won't never be a town here at all, much less a city someday."

Ben laughed. "City? Tampa? Why, I remember when it was nothing but a collection of shacks and a post office."

"Looks like that's what we're going back to, at least until we get rid of this damned Colonel. What are you eating anyway? Is it any good?"

"Oyster stew, made from the local catch. I recommend it."

Ferris gave his order to the waiter and turned his attention back to Ben. "I'm serious, Captain. Why, it's so bad even Judge Steele is thinking of pulling up stakes."

Ben rubbed a finger along his lip. "He's been threatening to do that for some time. Truth is, I was thinking I might want to improve my house here in town and move my family here once the farm is established. Lea would probably prefer town living and it would be better for my boy. He's getting pretty wild out in the country. But that won't be for a while."

"There may not be any town to move to by that time. Let me sell that water land for you now and use the money to improve your farm. It makes better sense."

Ben thought for a moment. "You make everything sound pretty grim, Ferris, but I'm not ready to give up on the village yet. I think I'll just hang on to those lots."

Ferris dipped a spoon in the bowl of oyster stew the waiter placed before him. "Suit yourself. But don't be surprised if Colonel Worth takes them right out from under you and sends you packing."

After finishing their supper the two men decided to walk around the village. Ben wanted to check on the state of his house while Ferris was anxious to show him the places he had figured on building for the future—a future that now looked like it would never come. It was beginning to get dark but there was still enough light to find their way. With Ferris as a guide, they walked beyond the existing stores and houses and out onto trails that snaked across land newly cleared. Remembering the lush tropical scrub that used to be there, Ben gazed in awe at the lumpy ground dotted with tree stumps and cut weeds lying like wheat tares across the earth.

"You really thought to build here?"

Ferris stretched out his arm, his enthusiasm bounding back. "I tell you, Ben, I already had the streets named. Right along there, that's Layfette. Over there Steele crosses it. Polk runs east and west, and Franklin intersects north and south."

"Where's Ferris Street?" Ben said, laughing.

"I haven't got one with my name on it yet but I bet you recognize the others. Anyway, Franklin was going to be one of the choicest sections. Here at the north end you could build a fine house in one of the better areas of town. Mrs. Carson would love it."

"And what happens when the shops and grogeries and bawdy houses begin to move this way?"

"Come now, that won't happen. They'll all be confined to that area near the fort. The outskirts is the place for upstanding citizens. We need men like you here in Tampa, Ben. Look at William Bunce. He came here in the twenties, built a ranchero down on the Manatee, made himself a reputation, and now he's a Judge. There's careers to be made here and now's the time to do it. You're wasting your energies out there in the wilderness trying to build a plantation. We've got to show Colonel Worth that Florida's future is here, not out there."

Ferris' vision was intriguing but Ben was not yet convinced it was practical. "Remember General Armisted burned Bunce's Manatee ranchero to the ground for consorting with the enemy. It sounds as though that's what Worth may have in mind for the rest of us." He looked out over the darkening expanse of ground, desolate in its emptiness, and tried to envision houses, neat yards, trees. But the image was dimmed, not by Colonel Worth's determination to create a wasteland around Fort Brooke but by his vision of rolling fields and crops swaying in the wind. "I don't know, William. Let me think about selling those lots. I'll let you know before I start back north."

Ferris pulled a plug of tobacco from his vest pocket, bit off an end and chewed thoughtfully. After a moment he spat a long stream of brown juice onto the sand. "Why don't you try talking to Colonel Worth. You're a military man. Perhaps he'd listen to you."

"I doubt it." He didn't add that he was too preoccupied at the moment with his own problems to care much about the village.

By the time they walked back again night had descended. The lanterns bobbing outside the log theater building threw long shadows on the wide sandy street. Ben tried not to notice the crowds around the porches and along the walkways, swelling now with soldiers, farmers, cowhustlers and idlers eager to be swindled out of the little money they possessed. The men near the hotel were more respectable and he knew many of them. Several were officers he had known at Fort Brooke. He stopped briefly to speak to them before starting up the hotel steps. With one boot on the first step he looked up to see Ramon de Diego standing above him, blocking his way.

Ramon had one hand in the fob pocket of his embroidered vest, the other pushing aside his jacket to where a pistol might hang on a gun-toting man. His expression was as black as his eyes.

Ben had no intention of stepping aside. "Are you planning to move or do I shove you out of the way?"

Diego smiled thinly. "That is a provocative comment, Captain. But coming from one who is accustomed to shoving aside better claims than his, I should not be surprised."

"You are no stranger to provocation, Diego. And you should know by now that I will not be drawn in. Our differences will be settled in court."

"Oh, indeed they will, Captain Carson." He moved languidly down the two steps to stand directly in front of Ben. "At least, they will tomorrow."

Ben glared at the dark face so near his own. "What's your problem, Diego? It seems which ever way I turn I always find you there, trying to block me. What have I done to earn this avid interest you have in complicating my life?"

Diego smiled thinly. "Many men try my patience, Captain. Others simply offend me."

"And I take it I am one of those."

"At the top of the list."

Ben struggled with the urge to yank this foppish, interfering, infuriating man by his satin collar and knock out a few of his even, white teeth. He did not do so because he could see that was just what Diego wanted. He had known a few men like Ramon before—men who got their pleasures from provoking other men to the point where they lost all reason and struck out blindly. Well, he would not give Ramon de Diego that much satisfaction.

"I'll say one more time. Either you move out of my way or I'll shove you aside. You'll have no one to blame but yourself if your nice coat gets rumpled."

Diego smiled, stepped to the side and waved a hand to Ben to pass on. Without another word Ben left him standing there and marched into the hotel. Someday, he knew, there would be a point beyond which he could not go and then Diego would get the confrontation he wanted. But not tonight. Tonight he had to think about those river lots and whether or not to sell them. Tonight he had to try to face what he was going to do if the Judge ruled against him tomorrow.

Ramon stood on the steps watching Ben disappear into the hotel. Anyone watching would have seen the smile on his aristocratic face fade to a cold grimace. Why did he hate this man so much? Captain Carson—the soldier everyone respected, the army officer renowned for his bravery and wisdom, the kind friend of the Seminoles, the shrewd entrepreneur using his accumulated savings to buy property and develop it, the handsome white man with the pretty wife who had insulted and rejected him, Ramon de Diego!

These arrogant Anglos! He had seen the contemptuous looks they gave men like himself. He heard the derogatory comments and insulting names whispered behind his back. Even though he, Ramon de Diego, had the blood of Spanish noblemen running through his veins, in their eyes he was no different than one of those dirty fisherman raising half-breed children and eking out a living in a Spanishtown shack.

Well, he would show them. One day they would court his favor like they now did Judge Steele. When he owned most of the town and held high office, wielding power and influence, they would grovel before him, Ben Carson most of all. Tomorrow morning would be the first step toward that goal. Then one day Lea Carson would come crawling on her knees to him, offering herself in exchange for mercy for her husband. Oh, the satisfaction that would give him. He might even spurn her offer and send her packing.

But probably not.

Yesterday afternoon Buck had found three broken sticks, each about seven inches long, lying on the porch, neatly laid out in parallel lines. Lea paid little attention to them, thinking they had blown there accidentally. But such was her anxiety that she made Buck leave them until Ulee could inspect them later that afternoon. She could tell by the expression on his face and the way he suddenly looked toward the woods that they were no accident.

"Do they mean something?" Lea asked quietly after sending Buck off to help bring in the horses.

Ulee spoke softly, glancing toward the kitchen where Josie hummed a song as she worked. "I don't know how they's done it, Miz Carson, but them's the Prophets way of saying we gots three days."

Lea caught her breath. "The Indians left them?" Dear God, they had walked up on her porch and she hadn't even known it. "Three days? Before what? Before they attack?"

"Yes, missus. Dat's what it mean."

Lea sank down on the rocker, gripping her hands and thinking hard. Three days! And one already nearly gone. "But why would they tell us this, Ulee? I mean, don't they usually just surprise the people they raid?"

Ulee shook his head. "Sometime dey lets peoples know. Maybe de Prophet, he like you, Miz Carson. He don't wants you gets killed."

"Perhaps he wants us to leave, is that it? But I can't do that, walk away from all this and let them destroy it. Ben would never want me to do that."

Ulee stared out at the trees. "I thinks I oughta go, Miz Carson. I is the one he wants."

"Give yourself back to them? Be a slave again? No, I won't let you. Besides, we need you to help us if they do attack. I could never fight them off by myself."

"Maybe de Prophet, he wouldn't come if'n I be gone. He chase me in de woods and lets you alone."

Lea had a brief image of this big man fleeing through the scrub with the Seminoles in hot pursuit. "No, I won't hear of it. And anyway, maybe the Captain will be back before the day after tomorrow." She didn't add that she had been searching the horizon every day looking for Ben to ride down the road toward the house. Four days at the most he said he'd be away and it was now nearly two weeks. Her mood bounced back and forth between fury that he had left her alone so long and fear that something might have happened to him on the trail. That thought was just too horrible to dwell on.

"We won't say anything about this to the others, Ulee. But I think we will increase the guard at night. Let two more of the men keep watch even if they have to cut back on their work during the day."

Ulee nodded and picked up the sticks, balancing them in his hand. Then with a sudden angry gesture, he broke them in half and threw them out into the yard.

Lea watched as he went off toward the cabins, holding in the sense of dread that filled her. She had almost begun to hope the Prophet had given up wanting his slave back, it had been so quiet. And now this. Three days, that was all the time they had left. What could she do if they actually raided the farm? Could she hold them off with a handful of black former slaves, a few white drifters, two women and a child? She would do her best but she had no illusions about what the outcome would be. If only Ben would return!

Lea barely slept that night. The three days respite had heightened her sense of dread and she listened through the long hours for any sharp cry or unusual sound that might signal an attack. By the next morning she was moving mostly on nervous energy. In between her usual chores she got Josie to help her add to the goods stored in a pit near the house and smooth sand over the top. As an added precaution, she filled a canvass knapsack with a few provisions and what money she possessed. It was probably a foolish gesture for once the Indians swept down on them, she would be lucky to get out with her scalp intact, if at all. Twenty times she checked the rifles in the house, making sure they were primed and ready. She kept Buck always in sight, making sure he stayed busy with the horses, the one thing he really loved.

She got through that night by falling into a drugged sleep out of sheer weariness though every far off howl of a wolf, or nearer shriek of a panther jarred her awake. In the morning she dragged out of bed dreading the coming night as though it was Armageddon waiting to drag her down into darkness. *I must be calm. I must be ready*, she told herself over and over as she went about her work and in between prayers to the Almighty to please bring Ben home quickly. It was late morning when three Indians walked into her yard and stopped before the kitchen breezeway.

They stood there quietly watching her, their faces absolutely blank. Lea thought over at least ten ways to respond before deciding to act as though seeing them standing there was just an ordinary occurrence. "What do you want?" she asked as Buck came to stand behind her and Josie cowered behind the kitchen door. From the corner of her eye she saw Tom hurrying off toward the fields to warn the other workers.

One of the Seminoles motioned to his lips. "Food?" Lea asked. "You want food?"

The man nodded and grunted a reply she did not understand. She racked her mind trying to remember if he had been one of the men on horseback that day with the Prophet. The two with him did not look at all familiar but there was a glimmer of recognition about the middle man. Was it the patterns of his shirt? The colors?

"Josie," she called. "Fill three plates for these men. They can eat here on the porch."

The Indians seemed to understand her words. They walked forward to sit on the steps, laying their long rifles beside them. Lea went into the kitchen to help with the plates, taking them from Josie whose eyes were pale with fright. Her hands trembled as she carried them outside but she fought not to let her fear show. The three men shoveled the food into their mouths with fierce concentration, ignoring her. Lea moved back beside the door and waited, her arms tight against her waist. She motioned to Buck who slid inside the room and quietly lifted Ben's rifle in the crook of his arm. Once the plates were empty the Indians threw them into the yard and rose. Lea held her breath.

"That," one of them said, motioning toward a sack of corn ears on the table clearly visible through the open door.

She wasn't sure how to answer. Would it be better to give it to them in the hope they would leave? Or would that be an invitation to take more? "You can't have them," she finally said. "We don't have enough left to give you any."

The man shoved her aside, walked into the kitchen and grabbed up the sack. Heaving it over his shoulder, he walked out again, pausing long enough to cradle a sack of sweet potatoes in his other arm. Lea saw Buck lift the rifle to his shoulder and shook her head at him. "All right, you can have the food. But go away. We don't have anything else to give you."

A second man pushed by her to pick up her sun bonnet hanging on a peg near the door. Walking back out on the porch, he jammed it down over his head, laughing while the other two chuckled. Lea felt a slow burn of anger seeping through her. She grabbed for the bonnet but the man gripped her hand in an iron vise, twisting her arm so badly she fell to her knees.

"You let her go!" Buck screamed, raising his rifle to peer down the barrel.

"No! Get back, Buck," she shouted. "I'm all right." Working her arm free she got to her feet and leaned against the porch wall while the three Indians loped down the steps, picked up their rifles and started across the yard. Across the tobacco field she glimpsed Tom hurrying toward the house while far behind him, several small figures followed.

Oh, God, please make them go away, she prayed. She could hear Buck scrambling up beside her, his rifle poised. Together they watched as the three Seminoles crossed the yard and started along the garden patch toward the line of trees. They were nearly abreast of Tom who had stopped to stare at them, not sure whether to go forward or retreat, when one of them casually lifted his gun and shot him. Lea screamed as she saw Tom crumple to the ground. Beside her a blast of Ben's rifle reverberated in her ears. One of the Indians clutched at his back and sank to his knees. She reached out and grabbed the gun from Buck then dragged him back inside the house. Even as she slammed and barred the door she could hear the high piercing cries of several more Indians who bolted from the woods shouting and screaming.

"Put up the shutters!" Lea yelled, and began running from window to window. Buck raced to help her but Josie, overcome with fright, sank to the floor in the corner, her hands over her ears. Lea was trying to throw the last bar over the shutters when there came a frantic battering on the door. She cracked the door just far enough to see Ulee pushing against it, then pulled it open to let Ulee, Primo, two of the hired men and Rafe, half dragging the wounded Tom, slip inside before she slammed it closed and locked it again. Lea leaned back against the door and watched as the men quickly moved to positions at the window holes with their guns. Outside the shrieking noise grew in intensity. There were more Indians now swarming from the woods, blasting their rifles and screaming their heathen cries. The sharp thud of bullets hitting the wooden shutters drove her to the floor where she pulled Buck down beside her. Smoke from the gunblasts choked the room. The air was acrid with saltpeter.

It had finally come.

CHAPTER 17

▼

The noise was almost worse than the fear. Lea scrunched down near one of the windows and poked the end of her rifle through the small opening between the shutters. She couldn't see the Indians outside but she could hear them howling like banshees as they dodged for cover to attack the house. The blasts of the guns, the stifling smoke, the oppressive odors of powder, the heat with the windows tightly shuttered—she could hardly breathe but was too frightened to care. She took turns with Buck, one standing, the other reloading, while Primus and Ulee covered one window, the two hired men the other. Tom, wounded but not incapacitated, and Rafe loaded rifles from their places on the floor.

"How many of them are there?" Lea asked Rafe as he handed her another rifle.

"Couldn't tell. More come out of the woods when they heared the gun."

"Do you think we can hold them off?"

He looked bleakly at Ulee. "We's gonna try."

Though he didn't say it, Lea knew what he was thinking. They might hold them off for a while but if the Prophet's force should be augmented by more warriors they would never stand a chance. She glanced over at the powder supply. Enough to last until evening, anyway. Then maybe they could slip out to a hiding place in the woods.

The 'ping' and 'thunk' of the bullets hitting the window shutters and outside walls resounded like blows in her head. But bullets were better than arrows. Seminole arrows were apt to be four feet long missals, often with fire attached.

She wouldn't think about that. How long had the firing gone on? Fifteen minutes, maybe half an hour. Beads of sweat rolled down her neck and under the collar of her dress. They would never be able to stay in this kitchen until night.

"Aunt Lea, I got one!" Buck cried, his eyes glistening with excitement. Lea didn't answer. Let him get some satisfaction from this. He'd learn soon enough the danger they were in.

"Missus Carson...look..." Lea turned at Ulee's excited cry. "No, no, don't nobody shoot," he shouted as he ran toward the door. Lea leaned back against the wall, cradling her long rifle. She stared in disbelief as Ulee lifted the bar to open the door.

"Ulee, don't!" she cried even as she heard someone banging on it, calling her name. The door inched open and two men shoved their way through. White men!

She gasped as she recognized Ben then flung herself at him. He grabbed her, swinging her around briefly before putting her away.

"Hello, wife," he said jauntily. His hat was gone, his coat was white with dust from the road and he had a days growth of beard. He had never looked more beautiful to her.

"Ben! How...? Where have you been!"

"We can talk later. Right now it looks like we've got more on our hands then we can handle. Buck, move. Let me stand there. You go help Ulee."

Lea sank down on the floor and slouched back against the wall. Everything would be all right now. With Ben here everything would be all right. She looked up and saw Clay Madrapore watching her from across the room where he had already replaced Primus at the north window. "Hello, Clay," she said, trying to smile. "Nice reception we managed for you."

Clay grinned at her before turning his attention back to the outside. It was another ten minutes before the howling grew quieter and the marauders faded into the woods. Lea scrambled up and peered through the peephole.

"Have they gone?" she asked her husband.

Ben wiped his arm across his face, smudging the black powder that covered it. "I doubt it. They're just planning the next assault. God, but it's hot in here. Get some water, Lea. We could all use it."

She ought to have thought of that herself. Where was her mind? After trying to drag a trembling Josie from under the table, she gave up and took the water bucket around herself. Once that was done, she began looking for any food they might eat while the Indians allowed them time. She spied the saddlebags she had filled earlier and dragged them near the door, just to have ready. She threw her cloak on top of them, piled the rest of the powder and shot boxes beside the cloak, then added a wooden canteen filled with as much of the water as she felt they could spare.

Ben looked around the kitchen wondering if they wouldn't be better inside the house where they could fire from four sides instead of three.

"We'd be too separated in the house," Clay said, reading his thoughts. "Better we stay concentrated here."

Even as he spoke the howling and the gun fire started again more strident than before. It seemed to go on for hours though Lea knew it was not nearly so long. Her clothes were damp with exertion and the heat of the room. With three windows and nine people they could spell each other from time to time. She spent the least time with the gun since she was the poorest shot until Ephraim, one of the hired men, caught a bullet in his arm. Lea tore off part of her underskirt and bandaged the arm then took his place at the window. When she smelled smoke she cried in alarm.

"It's the barn," Ben said grimly. "They've run off the stock and now they've set fire to the barn."

"Are we next?" she whispered. He looked around. "We can't stay here. If we wait to be run out by fire we won't stand a chance."

"I agree," Clay said quietly. "We'll have to try to slip away."

Lea couldn't see how that was possible with all those Indians outside but she had faith in Ben's judgement and Clay's experience. She pulled Buck over close to her and laid her arm around his shoulders. He seemed to appreciate the gesture. His earlier excitement had long since given way to wondering if they were going to get out of this alive.

Ulee spoke up. "Me, Primus and Rafe, we can keep shooting' long enough fo' the Capt'n and the Missus and Buck to try for the woods back of de corn. Dat corn, him high and can hide you afore you gets to de fence. We foller you wid Josie and Tom."

"Me and Ephraim will do the same," the hired man added.

Ben shook his head. "I'm not running away leaving all of you to face certain death."

"For God's sake, Ben," Clay said, "Lea and Buck can't go into those woods by themselves. They wouldn't stand a chance. You've got to go with them."

"You go. You know more about making your way through the woods than I do."

"I need to help these men cover you. The rest of us can take care of ourselves."

"We'll all go," Lea said firmly, "or none of us will. I agree with Ben. I'm not running away leaving the rest of you to face that savage mob alone."

The howling had subsided again. Clay turned and sank down on the floor, his arms resting on his knees. He wiped at his face, leaving a pale streak along the black gunpowder residue. "All right. We'll all go. But those who run first must have the cover of our guns. That's you and the boy, Lea. And Ben, just in case the rest of us don't make it. Primo, you take Josie, and Ulee, you take Tom. I'll help Ephraim."

"I don't like it," Ben muttered. But he knew there was no other choice. "Even if we make it into the woods we'll have to get back to the road eventually, assuming we don't get lost."

Buck spoke up. "I know a trail. It comes out about a mile and a half beyond here, right on the road to Turner's."

Of course he would, Lea thought. He'd spent more time in the woods than on the farm.

Ben clasped his son's shoulder. "Good boy. All right, Clay. We'd better go now before they come back again."

There was no time for good-byes. Lea pulled Buck close to her and hovered near Ben while Clay and two other men took their stations by the door. "Now!" Clay shouted. Ben threw the door open and lunged through, followed by his wife and son. Lea grabbed up the hem of her skirt and scrambled down the steps while Buck went flying by her. Together they streaked toward the cornfield as fast as they could go, ignoring the guns that began blasting behind them, hurling themselves among the tall rows of corn and pounding toward the other end. With the husks scratching at her face and clutching at her dress she hunkered down, keeping her head low and following in Ben's wake. Her fear was made worse by the knowledge that, once out of the cornfield, they would have to cross an open clearing to reach the protection of the woods. Her breath was beginning to hurt her chest. The fading light turned to twilight amid the corn rows but she could see light at the end and hear Buck crashing through the row alongside. The shots grew louder along with the howling that told them the marauders were in pursuit. Ben was getting ahead of her and she pushed to catch up.

They were nearly across the cornfield when she remembered the fence. Out in the open they dashed to it. Ben paused to give her a hand up while Buck went sailing over in one leap. Lea threw herself over to the other side but her skirt caught on a jagged edge of wood and she fell in a heap. Ben jumped back long enough to yank her to her feet and they both tore toward the dark line of hammock just across the clearing.

From the frantic howling of the Indians Lea guessed they were just behind. It put more thrust in her legs as she dashed after Ben into the darkness of the trees. She ran straight into a pine tree and clutched at the truck, leaning against it and gasping for the breath that tore at her lungs.

"No time for that," Ben cried and yanked her away. Grabbing her hand he pulled her through thickets that ripped her skirts, dragging her deeper into the woods. Buck was far ahead, running. He knew his way well but Lea had never been this far inside the forest. She pushed through thick palmetto fronds, shoved aside long, sinewy vines that clutched at her ankles and dodged the narrow pines that grew in thick stands. The ground was soggy, in places and her shoes went ankle deep in mud yet she pushed on. The howling was beginning to grow fainter, the darkness growing so thick she could barely see Ben ahead.

When they reached a short space of level ground Lea hit her foot against a decaying log half submerged in the mud and went flying. She landed on wet grass unhurt but without the strength to pull herself up. She lay, collapsed, struggling for breath. Ben moved back to kneel beside her. From the corner of her eye she saw Buck hurl himself down on the grass, gasping.

"Have...to rest..." Lea tried to speak.

He nodded. "Just for a moment. Got to keep moving."

It was heavenly to sprawl there and let her tortured lungs ease a bit. She could no longer hear the howling behind them but then the blood was pounding so loudly in her ears she could hardly hear anything. She rolled over on her side, clutching at Ben's hand.

He squeezed her fingers tightly. "It's over ten miles to the Turner's place. Can you make it?" His breathing was ragged too.

"I'll make it," she gasped. They had to make it. They had no other hope. But ten miles! So far!

"We must be near the road," Ben said, between deep breaths. "Shouldn't be so bad after that."

"I know the way," Buck spoke up. "I done it lots of times. But it's hard going, Aunt Lea. Will you be all right?"

"I can go anywhere you can, Buck," she said, trying to smile. "But Ben, is it safe to follow the road?"

"We'll have to risk it. If we try to reach Turner's place through these woods we'll be lost in no time." Ben stood and pulled her up. "Let's get going, then. The longer we rest the better chance those savages have of catching up with us."

That was all Lea needed to force herself back into the thickets. The pace was slower now. With Buck leading the way, she waded through the spongy ground, grateful that at least the thick woods had slowed their progress to a hurried walk. Night would be around them soon. Already the racket of the night creatures was growing in intensity yet she still thought she could occasionally catch the high yowling of their pursuers. In the darkness that grew deeper with every minute Lea could barely make out Ben's form ahead of her. She followed blindly, guided by the noise of his footsteps until they finally reached the road, a wide, yellowish thread through the darkness of the forest. Buck was waiting there for them to catch up but before moving out they all three clustered in the shelter of the trees, watching. The road lay quiet, lonely, empty, silvery in the moonlight, yet Ben would not venture on it until he was reasonably sure there were no Seminoles nearby.

Lea leaned against Ben, so tired she felt she couldn't take another step. "Thank God we made it this far," she sighed, pushing her straggling hair back from her face.

"We're not out of this yet, not by a long shot," he whispered. "We'll be in more danger out there in the open than under these trees." He listened, conscious that there were no sounds of Indians yet acutely aware that did not mean they weren't there. "We'll try the road but be ready to duck for cover when I say so."

She nodded. She had begun to think they were safe until Ben's cautionary words dispelled that comforting thought.

"I wish we didn't have to take the road at all," Ben whispered, still not moving. "Buck, you knew the woods we came through so well. Couldn't you find the rest of the way to Turner's place through them?"

Buck shook his head. "I never took the woods this far from home before, Pa. I reckon we should stay with the road."

"Or close to it anyway," Ben answered. "But it's the first place they'll look."

He ordered them to stay put while he moved out to the edge of the trees to make sure the trail was empty. When he suddenly appeared beside them Lea jumped nervously.

"It looks clear. Come on."

Her fear gave her renewed strength to scramble through the thickets to the open ground. Lea followed behind her husband and stepson, stumbling often on the rutted, uneven trail. The scratches on her face and arms stung like fire and every muscle in her body screamed in protest but anxiety and fear kept her slogging ahead. They had walked along the darkened road nearly an hour when Ben stopped, listened, then gave a muffled cry that sent them scrambling back into the cover of the trees. Looking around frantically, Lea spotted an uprooted tree whose circular root system lay tilted up on the ground like a huge black mill-stone. She dived beneath the tangled roots and squirmed into the husk as far as she could go. Behind her, Buck went slithering into a large gopher tortoise hole. Ben hunkered down behind Lea's tree, holding his breath as a group of Indians came loping down the road. Moonlight glimmered off the barrels of their long rifles and the bobbing feathers in their turbans. Inside the tree trunk Lea closed her eyes and prayed there would be no sudden shrill cry and thrashing into the underbrush. When all grew quiet again Ben waited a long time before whispering it was safe to come out. Lea and Buck emerged from their holes, filthy dirty but relieved to be safe.

"We'll have to stick to the woods," Ben muttered. "We'll never make it on that road. If the light had been better they surely would have seen our tracks."

Lea groaned inwardly but didn't object. She could see Buck had fallen half-asleep and she herself felt she had never known what tired was before. But they had to keep moving or all was lost. She pulled herself up, half-dragging Buck with her.

"Can you keep going, child?"

Buck wiped his arm across his face and nodded. "I'll keep going."

Ben smiled at his son. "You've done splendidly, Buck. Just a little farther and we can risk taking a break to rest." He pushed ahead, moving cautiously through the underbrush, keeping in the shadows of the trees but following the line of the road. It was so dark Lea felt as though she was shoving her way through a black tomb. Their progress was much slower and, to Lea's dismay, much louder in spite of the way Ben tried to cut down the noise by making a way for his wife and son.

There was a lot of movement in the woods around them but Lea tried not to think about what caused it. She was more afraid of snakes than any other creature, but she told herself the noise of their footsteps would scare them away. Far off they could hear the frightening howl of a panther or bobcat and the frantic scream of an animal in the clutches of some predator. The roaring of the tree frogs was incessant and ear-splitting but soon she was too tired to even care. Her hands, face, arms, and skirt were torn by the clutching thickets, her shoes were soaked yet she was too weary to notice. She felt they had been tramping their way through the darkness for hours when Ben finally let them stop.

They'd come to a small patch of grassy hammock sheltered by several huge old blackjack oaks. Ben ordered Lea and Buck underneath the low sprawling tentacles of one of the limbs while he kept watch. Lea fell to the ground, grateful just to stop, but still concerned. She could not see his face in the darkness but she knew he was as weary as his wife and son.

"What about you?"

"I learned to cat-nap on army duty. I'll be all right."

She lay down beside Buck, sure that she was too tired and anxious to sleep. Yet she'd hardly curled her arm around the boy's thin body before she dozed off, waking in what seemed only a short few minutes later when Ben shook her shoulder.

"It's nearly dawn. We have to be off."

The light was better now and she could see that he looked terrible. She knew she did as well, besides shivering from sleeping on the chilly, damp ground. She was thirsty and hungry and she thought longingly of the Turner's warm kitchen, of the heady aroma of coffee brewing, biscuits, thick slices of ham...

Ben ran his hand down her cheek, streaked with thin welts from the branches. "We should be at the Turner's soon," he said to encourage her. He didn't add, *if their place is still there* but Lea knew he was thinking it. She refused to believe the Prophet might have attacked Turner's place too. The Indian war had been declared over last August. Surely he would not risk starting it up again with a widespread attack on settlers.

They found a creek nearby with water to slack their thirst. Hunger was another matter. A small coontie plant offered a half-withered root which, with a few berries, helped to take the edge off their need for food. Lea pushed on, berating herself for forgetting that saddle bag which would have sustained them. Though Ben still had his rifle he had only a small supply of powder and shot and he feared trying to kill game for the noise it would make.

By afternoon Ben had to admit he was lost. By keeping to the woods they had somehow missed the road. It meant they were safer but it ended in their not knowing where they were. Lea fought down her disappointment and renewed fear. By now she was almost more afraid of starvation than Indians. And she was increasingly filled with a growing panic of the woods themselves. This thick Florida scrub, this jungle of thorny grasping, thickets, of huge leafy plants and jagged palmettos concealing who knew what, these wet bogs of cypress, these stands of pines clustered so closely you could barely squeeze between them, these towering old oaks and hickories trailing spidery tendrils of dead moss, their lush primeval growth untouched by the centuries—it all began to take on the face of the enemy. The clouds of insects, the thick vines whose lovely flame red, delicate orchid, or virginal white flowers concealed thorny, tangled barriers, the sandy ground that gave way unexpectedly to clumpy weeds, the deceptive tangles of reeds disguising what looked like solid ground but was actually foot-deep muddy water—the wilderness itself was an impenetrable wall, a fortress that challenged them to struggle through. She thought longingly of the clear road.

They kept going until darkness fell like a blanket around them once again. This time Ben stopped at the first fairly open spot he could find and there they spent the night.

All three fell into a drugged sleep from which, had the Indians stumbled upon them, they would never have known it. They woke the next morning refreshed and more hungry than ever. Ben decided if they didn't find the road by afternoon he'd have to risk using his gun just so they could keep going.

It was nearly noon when Clay found them. Once again Ben, hearing something in the woods, cried to them to dive for cover. He had his rifle primed when he heard his friend's familiar voice.

"By God, Ben, if I was Otulke Thlocko I'd already have your scalp hanging from my belt."

Lea gave a cry, relief flooding through her aching body. Ben lowered his musket and laid his head down on it, as relieved as his wife, though he wouldn't admit it. Buck jumped up and darted toward the voice.

"Clay! Clay!" Clay's big form rose up out of a patch of tall grass to clasp Buck as he jumped at him. He swung the boy around before setting him on his feet and putting him away with both hands on his shoulders.

"You look worse than a wet bobcat. I bet you haven't eaten in two days. Come on. I've got some jerked beef with me. We'll share it with those two scared rabbits if we can get them up out of their hidey-holes."

Ben and Lea leaned on each other. "I don't think I've ever been as glad to see you," Ben said, clasping his friend's hand and gratefully taking a piece of the dried jerky Clay handed him. "I admit I got us lost. Guess I've just grown too used to trails, maps and compasses for these woods. I'm still not sure we ought to be making all this noise."

Clay watched as Lea sank down and began chewing on the meat. She looked completely done in, but her eyes showed her gratitude. "It doesn't matter," he said. "The Prophet's gone back south to the Peace River area. I went to Turner's place first and when they hadn't seen you, I knew you'd be floundering around out here. It wasn't too hard to pick up your trail."

"You've been to Turner's? Is it still standing?"

"It's still there. Seems the Prophet only wanted to get even with you for not handing over his slave. He's not after starting the war up here again, though I confess I was worried he might be."

Lea spoke quietly between chews of the delicious meat. "Did he get Ulee?"

"I don't know. Primo and Rafe showed up with Tom and Josie at Turner's just before I left. They don't know what happened to Ulee either or the two other men. But they stuck around long enough to know about your farm."

He looked at Ben, his face revealing the bad news before he spoke of it. Ben stopped chewing his jerky and steeled himself for Clay's news. "The Indians

burned the house, the outbuildings and the fields. And they drove off the livestock."

Lea gave a cry. "Everything? Pigs, oxen, horses, my milk cow?"

"I'm afraid so. They took everything they could move."

Ben looked away into the darkness of the trees. "And the cotton?"

"Burned. Down to the last plant. I'm sorry to be the one to tell you this, Ben,
but there's nothing left. The Prophet's warriors did a very thorough job."

Lea caught back a sob. "But why? All this over one slave? It doesn't make any
sense!"

Clay shrugged. "Maybe it wasn't just the slave. Maybe it was all the years of
fighting, of being forced into exile and away from their homes. I think the
Prophet just wanted an excuse to vent his anger and he didn't dare carry it further
or he would have burned all the farms within fifty miles. Instead he just did a real
complete job on yours."

She looked at her husband. He continued to stare into the trees, a muscle in
his jaw jumping, his teeth clenched. But he said nothing. She longed to put her
arms around him and comfort him but she knew he would hate that. Instead she
sat dumbly, hurting for him.

"I'm not sure we can deal with this right now, Clay," she finally said wearily.

"No, nor should you. You can face it all later. Right now we must get all three
of you to the Turners where they're expecting you. They'll have a bed and a good
meal ready for you."

It sounded heavenly in spite of the pain in her chest when she thought of their
farm. Clay stood and reached down a hand to pull Lea up. Buck was already on
his feet, galvanized by the thought of food waiting.

"Right, Ben?"

Ben nodded and dragged himself up. "Right."

It took the rest of the day to reach the Turner's farm. Althea Turner took one
look at Lea and put her straight to bed where she slept for over nine hours. She
woke rested, sore in every muscle, and famished. While she sat at Althea's kitchen
table wolfing down fried eggs and biscuits, she learned that Ben had already set
off to visit what was left of their farm.

"Is that safe?" Lea wondered aloud.

"Mister Madrapore said he thought so. And Cory went with him, along with
them two black fellows, Rafe and Primo. They should be all right."

Lea nodded, hoping silently that Althea was right. If the Prophet's only purpose had only been to get even with the Carsons for keeping his former slave then

the Indian threat should pretty much be over for now. But she was not yet convinced that the raid on their farm was just one isolated event. She finished her breakfast then walked out on the porch and sat in the rocking chair staring at the road until two hours later when she saw the men riding in.

The first question she asked Ben was answered in such dismissive fashion that Lea knew he didn't want to talk about what he'd seen. In a few curt words he told her he'd found exactly what Clay warned him he would find and didn't feel the need to explain it in more detail. Lea didn't push him, partly because she could see how difficult it was for her husband to accept the ruin of all his dreams and partly because she didn't want to know. They were her dreams, too.

But after two days of watching Ben sitting and brooding Lea felt she had to speak.

By the second day her fear had begun to subside and she had stopped starting at every strange noise. Their Negroes hung around waiting to see what Ben was going to do and though they helped work around the farm, she knew the additional mouths to feed would quickly become a strain on even the best run household, not to mention one as casual as the Turner's. Once she felt up to it she began to take part in the chores which Althea and her young daughters were constantly engaged in. Clay left for Fort Brooke but to Lea's surprise, Ben chose not to accompany him. Instead, her husband stayed at the Turner's farm, sitting, staring absently at the road and the fields, cleaning his gun, occasionally helping with the chores, and now and then rousing himself long enough to go look for game in the woods. She had never seen Ben like this in all the time she had known him, not even when Rachel died, and her fear for him soon eclipsed any worries about the Prophet coming back.

When Cory Turner set out to hunt wild turkeys and Ben refused to go with him, Lea knew this terrible apathy had to be faced. She walked out on the porch as Cory and Buck went striding toward the woods and saw Ben amble to a fence overlooking the Turner's garden patch. He leaned against it, his back to the house, unaware that Lea had followed him. He stood resting his arms on the fence rail and looked up in surprise when she touched him.

"Ben, I want to talk to you."

"There's nothing to talk about."

She could tell he was annoyed but she didn't care. "There's everything to talk about. This isn't like you, all this brooding and doing nothing. It worries me."

Ben shrugged. "You don't need to worry about me. I just need some time to reorganize my thoughts. To make plans."

"What plans? What did you find at the farm? Is there anything we can salvage?"

"I found exactly what Clay told me would be there," he said bitterly. "And no, there's nothing to salvage." He pounded his fist lightly on the wooden rail, the first tentative sign she had seen of the anger he had to be feeling. "The house is gone, the barn, the outbuildings. The stored hay, the cornfield, the crops. The livestock is missing, and…" his voice almost broke, "…the cotton decimated. Burned to the ground. Nothing left but acres of blackened cinders."

The enormity of all that destruction was like blow to her stomach. She felt as though she could see it herself, and the horror of it raised a terrible hurt in her chest. "It's so unfair," she murmured.

He gave a sharp, bitter laugh. "Unfair? Yes. A bad hand dealt us by God, or fate, or by Otulke Thlocko, if you will." He turned to her, crossing his arms over his chest. "Let me tell you just how unfair it is. Did you never wonder why I was so late getting back home after that trip to Tampa Village? Why I only arrived at the last hour? It was because I went from Tampa straight to Newnansville. When Judge Steele ruled against Ramon Diego and for me, I knew I had to file my claim right away or I might not keep the acres he had awarded me. I rode straight to the Government office at Newnansville and filed for my 160 acres."

"160? But that's only a fraction of what we have."

"Yes, but it's all that is allowed by the U.S. government, and then only if you agree to work it for five years. I got 160, Clay got 160 and we both got the promise of more when we can bring in people willing to get it and then sell it to us at one dollar, twenty-five an acre. I figured it was a good deal because at least it was mine. No one like Diego can take it away from me, ever."

Lea's body sagged against the fence. "Oh, Ben."

"Yes," he said bitterly. "I got back just in time to see everything I've worked so hard for go up in smoke. There's nothing left of my hard won 160 acres. The wild creatures of the woods can have them. Ramon Diego can have them!"

She looked up at him. "What do you mean?"

"I mean that without that cotton crop we have nothing to base next year's profits on. Or to pay off this year's debts. I still have a little of my capital left but certainly not enough to begin over again. Not enough to rebuild all the buildings and restock all the animals. Nor do I have the heart for it."

Lea studied his face, the features she so loved. There was a depth of bitterness in his eyes she had never seen before. The lines along his cheeks were deeply drawn, his lips narrow and tight. She watched him turn back to rest his arms on the fence, his body sagging with weariness.

"I saved and worked and planned so long, Lea. I can't do it again. I've spent these last days wondering just what I should do, and now I've decided. I'm going back into the army."

She caught her breath. "But your dream, your plantation? You can't just give it up because of one setback."

He laughed, cold and humorless. "A rather complete setback, wouldn't you say? I banked everything on that cotton crop. The Prophet doesn't know it but he could have just burned that and it would have ruined me."

Lea pursed her lips. Down deep within something bent with sadness suddenly stiffened and strengthened, bolstered by anger and a fierce determination. "No!" she said. She caught his sleeve. "No, we're not ruined. We can rebuild."

He looked down at her, a terrible sadness etching his face. "I told you, I don't have the means or the heart."

"Maybe not the means to grow cotton but, Ben, there are other ways of making a successful plantation. You can grow food crops or sugar cane. Lots of planters have done well with cane."

"You need a mill for sugar cane and lots of money and lots of help."

"No more help than you need for cotton." Her grip tightened on his arm, forcing him to face her. "Listen to me, Ben. People have told me more than once that this land is not suited to cotton. You'll never be able to get a big plantation going here like the ones in Georgia or Mississippi or South Carolina or even Middle Florida. This soil is not suited to it."

She could see he was growing annoyed with her but considered that a good sign and pushed doggedly on. "You only need to readjust your sights."

"I tell you, Lea, I have no interest in sugar cane. Nor food crops either. And I don't have the capital to begin either one."

"Then try cattle."

He turned angrily away. Then, after a pause, turned back. "Cattle?"

"Yes. You already have a small herd with your registered mark wandering around these woods. The Indians can't have possibly stolen all of them. And there are a lot more wild animals out there to be brought in and branded. Bring them in, import new strands, buy a valuable breeding top-cow. There's always a market for cattle, Ben, either with the army, or Key West or in Cuba. The native breeds thrive on this scrub."

"Thrive? They're scrawny, stringy and disease ridden."

"Then improve them to make them better. I'm sure it can be done. And it wouldn't take nearly as much capital to begin over again with cattle as it would with a sugar plantation, not to mention cotton."

He waved a hand as if to dismiss her ideas. "You sound just like Clay." Then he stopped, staring at her a moment before turning back to look at the distant woods. "Just like Clay." A long silence fell between them which Lea dared not break.

"It might be possible."

His words were so soft she almost didn't catch them. But they brought a renewal of hope. She reached out and grasped his hand, entwining her fingers in his. "It *is* possible, Ben. I know it is."

"Of course we're talking about a cattle ranch now, not a plantation."

"So we build a big roomy ranch house instead of a fancy mansion with white columns. I won't mind and I'm sure Buck would prefer it. He's much more at home on a horse than in the fields. He's always said he hates farming."

Ben looked down into her eager face. "It would be a way of holding on to the land until we got the place going again. That is assuming Otulke Thlocko doesn't take it in his head to enjoy a little more revenge."

There was a sparkle back in his eyes. Lea felt a tentative swell of happiness to see it as she smiled up at him. "He won't. The Seminoles are finished, Ben. Everybody knows it. They know it too but they won't accept it. And even if the Prophet does come back, we'll just rebuild again. With a cattle ranch he won't be able to do as much damage."

In a sudden gesture he gripped her shoulders, then wrapped his arms around her in a fierce hug. "By God, Lea, you've got spunk. Here I am ready to quit and you inspire me to keep going. After all you've been through, all that work to do over again, and you're ready to plunge in."

Lea hugged him tightly to her. Joy. gratitude and relief, all mixed together, soared back into her heart. "You won't quit, Ben. I won't let you quit. Whatever happens we'll keep building, keep trying. With both of us working together, nothing can get us down!."

BOOK III

1847

CHAPTER 18

▼

"You smell like the inside of a privy!"

"Maybe you'd like me to walk ten paces behind you. Or better yet, on the other side of the street."

Lea smiled at the tall young man striding along beside her. In the five years since the Prophet's raid, Buck had shot up like a weed until he was taller than his father and towered over her. He was handsome, too, in a rugged, rough-hewn kind of way. She could see Rachel's fine lines in the long planes of his face and the pale, thick lashes framing his blue eyes. The strong jaw, wide shapely mouth and dark creases along the cheeks were all his father's.

His pretended offense was belied by the teasing mischief in his eyes. "No, I'll just keep my head turned down wind," she said. "But promise me you'll never do anything so foolish ever again."

"I promise. The next time I'm challenged to a duel I'll find someplace less pungent than a smelly cowpen to fight it out in. Look at that," he said, gesturing across Whiting street. "Isn't that another new house going up?"

"Yes, it's the Henderson's new place. They just started it last month and it already looks ready to move in. Flora Henderson will be relieved. The one they've been living in for the past year is pretty small for five children. It's going to be a nice house, but not as nice as mine."

"I swear, I never saw a town so crazy to grow as this one-horse village," Buck exclaimed, shifting Lea's basket to his other hip. "Every time I come down here I don't know the place. Stores, houses, and now even a new courthouse. It wouldn't be so bad but they keep tearing down the good old saloons and grog shops to make room for these newfangled buildings."

Lea stepped around one of the large oaks that blocked the walkway in front of McKay's store. An ox-drawn wagon lumbering along the sand trail that was Whiting Street wobbled drunkenly, nearly careening into them. Buck drew her back closer to the pine log building until it passed. "I declare, traffic is getting downright dangerous in this town," he muttered.

"Actually, the village is growing less now than it was a few months ago," Lea said, adjusting her hat as they turned north on Monroe Street. "Judge Turman and the Commissioners had some grand plans in place until they learned President Polk had failed to sign the order separating the town from the garrison. Until that's settled real progress can't start."

"Well, however much progress it makes, Tampa will still be a backwater little village on the edge of nowhere. Even at that, it's too crowded for me. I guess I've just grown too accustomed to wide open spaces. Look, Aunt Lea. There's a fat lady across the street waving at you."

"That's Mary Stringer. Mornin', Mrs. Stringer," she called. "Fine day, isn't it?

"It is, Mrs. Carson. Fine day for a little shopping and a stroll."

"Tip your hat, Buck," Lea spoke under her breath, jabbing Buck with her elbow. He dipped his head, touched the brim of his hat and smiled weakly at Mrs. Stringer who nodded back and waddled on.

"Mornin', you old biddy," Buck called softly. Lea jabbed him again.

"For shame. She's a nice lady. You don't even know her."

Buck grinned. "I know she could stand to lose a little of that lard. Let's face it. I'm just naturally shy of matronly ladies—all except you."

"I'm not matronly! And you're only shy of proper ladies because you spend so much time in the company of horses and cows, not to mention those painted hussies at the saloons. How am I ever going to get you married to a nice young girl if you won't be civilized."

"Now you sound like Pa."

"Well, your Papa and I would both like grandchildren someday. Morning, Mister Kennedy," she said, as a gentleman coming toward them stepped aside to allow her to pass.

"Mrs. Carson. Buck. Good day to you both."

Thomas Kennedy had put on weight this past year. Unlike most men in the town he was beardless when in fact his large jutting lower jaw could have used some camouflage. He tipped his tall black hat as they passed on, sniffing the air as he caught a whiff of Buck.

"Now there's a predatory fellow," Buck whispered. "Owns half the town by now, I suppose. Or if he doesn't, he soon will."

"No more than many another gentleman of the village, including your father. Really, Buck, you ought to be kinder to people. How do you ever expect to marry well? No self-respecting woman will want you if you don't put on polite airs and show decent manners. Not to mention getting rid of that constant aroma of horses and leather."

"Now I thought it was the privy you objected to."

"That too. Of all the hare-brained things to do, to fight a duel with cow chips in Mrs. Chumbley's cow bin! What can you have been thinking of."

"Would you have preferred pistols at ten paces? Or swords? I thought it was a brilliant move."

"I would have preferred you didn't get into these fights at all. However," she added grudgingly, "if I had to choose between cow dung and bullets, I'll take the dung every time. If only the effects didn't linger so."

Buck shoved the brim of his hat up on his thick blonde hair, bleached now to the consistency of straw by being out in the sun so much. Lea shook her head as she studied him. His once fair skin had tanned to a leathery bronze and he was as skinny and rangy as one of the Florida longhorn steers he tended—and nearly as wild.

And with it all, he is completely oblivious to how attractive he has grown, Lea thought. He has no inkling of how the respectable young women of the area primp and preen to attract his attention—or how appalled their mothers were at the thought they might be successful. Ben might be the owner of a fast growing and successful cattle ranch, but Buck was still too addicted to the out-of-doors to be accepted in polite society. It grieved Lea, yet she wouldn't change that boyish, delightful quality of his for all the foppish young blades in Tallahassee or New Orleans. They might know what wine to choose and what color cravat to wear but Buck, who at nearly nineteen practically ran the family ranch by himself, was already more self-sufficient and tough. As a cowman working Florida's flatwoods, hammocks and swamps he'd confronted his share of snakes, alligators, panthers and bears. She'd been told by Rick MacAlister, one of the men he worked with, how he had once killed a wolf with no weapon but a stirrup iron.

Yet, she sighed, she did wish he could learn to make his way in both worlds. His wild streak worried her, and Ben, too.

A noisy hammering drew her gaze across the street to where Mister McKay's new County courthouse was going up. It promised to be a handsome building, two stories high, gleaming white in the Florida sun and set in the middle of a wide empty block. There were plans for a picket fence to be built around it someday but that would have to wait. At the moment, unless the conflict between the fort and the village was resolved by Congress once and for all, it might never even be used.

Still, the new court house was just one of the new structures rising amid the old scrub and beautiful scattered oaks of the village. Citizens with any capital, and some without, were eager to build new sprawling homes on the city blocks laid out in Mister Jackson's town map survey of last December. New streets—little more than wide sand trails—new houses, new stores, it seemed that everyday the boundaries of the town pushed a little farther north and even across the river to the west. The Fort Brooke garrison still sat at the entrance to the bay, though much shrunken and not as militarily important as it was a few years ago when the war was raging. Florida was mostly peaceful now, and those Seminoles who were left came to the village in small groups of thirty or so to trade and hold their pow-wows at the shacks that made up their camp. Since Florida became the 26th State of the Union two years ago, new settlers had poured through the village on their way to establish home and farms in its central and southern sections. Tampa had expanded from the tiny, struggling village that once was an appendage to the fort into almost a town. The old groceries and shanties which served the military were fading, though a few of them still survived near the village outskirts. But there was trade and traffic now in Tampa, and that meant money to be made. Ben was taking advantage of it, along with a lot of other men who had staked out an early claim.

"You really like it here, don't you," Buck commented, bringing her thoughts back.

"Yes, I do," she smiled. "I love the ranch, but I never felt so much at home there once it was rebuilt as I had before it burned. Maybe that was because it became more of a ranch than a homestead. At any rate, I was glad to move back into town."

"Pa rebuilt his house here for you, you know. He sure didn't do it for me. I wouldn't ever want to live in a town like this. It's too confining. Too many buildings, too many people," he added, with a shiver.

"I'll admit it's growing. We have a new church now, or a minister anyway, though the congregation has to meet in the parlor of the Palmer House. As for the new house, Ben built it for himself as much as for me," Lea added dryly. "He may claim he likes the country, but he's as much at home wheeling and dealing in the village as I am among the other housewives. He hopes someday to be a County Commissioner, you know."

Buck stopped, staring in surprise. "He doesn't!"

"Oh yes. He wanted to run in the first election but decided to wait. Now he's thinking of making a try for the State Assembly. The Commissioners like him and he thinks he might be able to get the nomination and so do I. I encouraged him to try for it."

Buck pulled his hat down closer to shadow his eyes. "I suppose that means he'll turn over the ranch to me. Well, that's all right. I won't mind that."

Lea paused as they turned down Lafayette and headed toward the river.

This was pretty much the northern boundary of the village and traffic was thicker here than when they started from the other end of town near the garrison. She stepped back to avoid the splatter of mud as a wagon loaded with timber rolled by. "He'll keep a hand in the running of the ranch, but he'll probably give you more responsibility."

Buck frowned. "I ought to have known he'd never turn it over to me completely. He wouldn't trust me that much."

Lea grabbed her skirt out of the way of splattering mud as a large domestic pig scurried across her path. "He does trust you, Buck. He's already put you in charge of most of the day-to-day running of the place. Someday it will all be yours. Don't be so anxious."

"You don't have to make excuses for him, Aunt Lea. I know what he thinks of me—or doesn't think, I should say."

There was too much truth in his comment for Lea to deny it. Instead she paused at the corner and gazed down Water Street past Judges Steele's old blockhouse, smiling with satisfaction. "Look at that pretty house. Isn't it just the loveliest thing you ever saw?"

Buck's mood shifted with the change of subject. "I agree," he said. "It's really nice. I wonder who designed it."

Lea laughed with delight. It was her dream, this house. Ben made it possible when he decided to rebuild the simple log home they had owned for so long on the river. At least, they hoped Ben owned it. Until the United States government made the official transfer of land from the army to the village, everyone who built anything in Tampa could be considered 'squatters'. Still, her vision had shaped and planned the new house, and she never tired of gazing at it, delighting in how well it turned out.

It was a two story building—that in itself set it apart—with the small upper story lying under a long, sloping roof. The house was built around a central chimney providing heat for cooking and the occasionally needed winter warming upstairs and below. The windows were large and airy to allow breezes off the river to cool the inside and to offer a sweeping view of the silvery river from the parlor and the upstairs bedroom. A porch at one end trailing thick flame vines offered a place to sit in the cool of the evening. A neat fence enclosed the whole, and both fence and house were whitewashed to present a finished appearance. Green shutters at the windows could be closed when heavy rains warranted it and gave a bit of elegance to the whole. A walkway from the street to the front door was bright with native lantana and gaillardia blossoms she had planted herself.

Of course, Ben had wanted something smaller, with a wide central hall and a tin roof. But Lea was having no part of the kind of house homesteaders in the scrub were building up and down Florida. She wanted a town house similar to the ones she knew at home in New York. She finally got her husband to agree by appealing to his pride. An up and coming gentleman of some wealth and distinction ought to live in a distinguished house, not a log box that any cracker would be happy to call home.

Her house was as dignified as it was comfortable and she loved every board and nail of it.

"If you're done admiring your new house, we can cross the street now."

Lea giggled, not in the least perturbed by Buck's sardonic comment. "I still can't quite believe it's mine," she said, starting across the sandy street. "Once I get some shrubbery around it, and plant some more flowers, it'll be the best looking place in town."

"Suitable for a State Assemblyman," Buck added, steering her past a green leather curricle that was parked in the sand near the front walkway. "What I don't understand is how you ever got Pa to spend the money. I can't get him to do half the things that need doing on the ranch."

"He has a lot of obligations, Buck. But there are a lot of the newcomers in town building new homes and I think he wanted one to be proud of." She started up the walk to the side porch. "I'm sure he wouldn't deny you anything that was really needed."

"Yes, but we seldom agree on what's really needed. You sound as though you've been listening to him complain about my spend-thrift ways. Of course I want to do more than he does, but some things are just necessary. They ought to come first."

"Like that new chestnut racer?" Lea opened the door and walked into her large, bright hall. Though she wouldn't say so to Buck, she was well aware of how often Ben stormed over the tall stack of bills accumulated by his ranch, and how his son needed to be more circumspect in his spending. At the same time, no one knew better than Ben that the bulk of their income depended on the ranch. He'd never withhold what was needed to keep it running successfully. And Buck was still too often inclined to use poor judgement.

"Just set those things on the dining room table, dear," Lea said to her stepson. "Sukey will sort them out and put them away." She reached up and unpinned her straw hat. "How about a cool drink?"

"No thanks. I'm going back out into the village. I just came along here to help you carry your parcels. Who's Sukey?"

Lea laid her hat on the table and primped her hair in the mirror above it. "She's one of our two new slaves. The other is Ulee."

Buck's jaw dropped. "Pa owns two slaves? And Ulee—I thought he was free."

Lea walked to the dining room and began removing her parcels from the basket. "Your father had to become a slaveowner when the Legislature voted all free Negroes must leave the State. Ulee agreed just to stay with us. He's very loyal, you know, and I think he feels obligated because Ben lost his first farm for not turning him over to the Prophet. And Sukey knows she can have manumission anytime she wants it. So far she's seems content enough to stay. That's what it has come to here in the South. If you want help you are forced to own slaves even when you don't want to."

Buck pulled out a chair and draped his rangy frame over it. "I never thought I'd see the day. But seriously, Aunt Lea, it's one thing to pass up a perfectly beautiful chestnut mare who would be bound to bring in money at the races, but it's quite another not to invest in a breeding top cow that will upgrade your stock. Pa won't do either one."

"I thought he just bought a top cow."

"A second rate breeder whose only advantage was he came at a cheap price. But just last week Chapman told me he's got a strong South American Brahman going to be delivered next month. Sure, he'll come high, but he'll be worth it in the long run. I told Pa he ought to buy him but he paid me no mind, as usual."

Lea caught up several strands of hair which had come undone in her walk and pinned them in the bun at the nape of her neck. She hardly knew how to answer Buck. The last thing she wanted was to be involved in these wretched arguments between father and son. She studied her stepson. His long, lean face was so eager, so focused. Yet in some way, underneath that tanned, rugged exterior he was still just a boy.

"I can't help you, Buck. I'm sorry but I know nothing about running a ranch."

"But you got him to agree to this house."

"Only because he wanted it too. Instead of trying to convince him to do things your way, be a little more tactful. Help him see that it's for the good of the business."

"I've tried that and it doesn't make any difference. No matter what I want, he doesn't want it just because I do. He's always been like that."

"I'm sorry you feel that way."

"Oh, Aunt Lea, you always defend him. Even when he spends half his time staring at that old portrait of my mother in his watch, you still defend him. Why can't you face the truth?"

She felt her cheeks flame with warmth. Words of denial rose to her lips but she refused to speak them. "That has nothing to do with this," she muttered, and turned away, starting toward the hall. Pausing at the entrance she stopped long enough to call over her shoulder, "You'll be back in time for supper, won't you?"

Buck walked over to her, almost laid a hand on her shoulder, but withdrew it. He loved Lea, whom he'd long considered his mother, and he knew he'd hurt her. Yet he refused to apologize for what, after all, was only the truth. "Not, tonight. I'll get something in the village. Keep a light in the window for me."

Lea managed a weak smile. "All right. I'll do it for tonight. But don't forget, tomorrow you're supposed to take supper with the Davenports."

"Ugh! I haven't forgotten."

"And no more fights in the cow bin, you hear!"

He laughed. "Okay."

She watched him bound out of the door and on to the porch, then walked through the hall and into her sunny parlor. It was a lovely room, with lace curtains at the windows, a new flowered aubasson carpet on the floor, a mahogany secretary from New Orleans against one wall, comfortable chairs upholstered in a chinese patterned fabric, and two fancy oil lamps imported from New York sitting on round cherrywood tables. A few minutes earlier it would have filled her with pleasure just to enter it.

But not now. Not after Buck's comment.

How clever of her stepson to know just how to strike her where it hurt most. He was a boy who gave little thought to anything he did, yet he had an instinct for knowing just where to throw his barb so it hooked the victim in the heart.

Did he think she was not aware of how often Ben pulled out his gold watch, flipped open the lid and stared at that old picture? Did he imagine she wasn't hurt by the way her husband resorted to that portrait as though it were some kind of fetish. How when, after an argument between them, or a disagreeable encounter in the village, or when studying a pile of receipts to be paid, he would walk off somewhere alone, sit thoughtfully for a moment, then take out his watch and flip open the lid. She couldn't count the number of times she had stood in the shadows watching, wondering why Rachel's portrait should be a comfort when she was there, alive, to be touched and held. When she would give anything to console, advise and encourage him.

Why still Rachel? Why, after all this time, not me?

Usually she ended up telling herself she was being silly and thin-skinned. Usually she put it aside, reminding herself that no matter how dear her picture, Rachel was dead, while she, Lea, was alive, sharing his life, his home, his bed. Let him have his moments with his dead wife, she told herself. They are only a brief interlude in a busy life.

Most of the time she pushed down the hurt, determined to ignore it. Until a few well placed barbs from her foolish stepson reopened the wounds. She sank into one of the chairs, wiping her hand across her brow. Get busy! Do something. The garden…the mending…

It took her a moment to hear the soft knock on the front door. With sudden relief, she rose to her feet, tucked her disturbing thoughts away in the tidy cupboards of her mind, smoothed down her skirt, and walked into the hall to open the door.

The woman standing in her doorway was tall and unsmiling. Her dark eyes fastened on Lea's with a smoldering intensity.

"Mrs. Carson?"

Lea stood with her hand on the door frame, almost too stunned to answer. "Senora de Diego. What a surprise."

"Might I have a moment of your time," Costa de Diego said with curt formality in her lightly accented, carefully enunciated English. "I won't keep you long."

"Of course. Please, come in."

Lea stepped aside as Costa de Diego swept regally by to stand in the hall. "Come into the parlor, please," Lea gestured. "Sit down. May I take your coat?"

Foolish! The woman wasn't wearing a coat, though at first it was difficult to tell, she was so swathed in black bombazine. Lea watched as Costa sat primly on the edge of a tufted velvet chair facing the window, then took one opposite. She, too, sat on the edge, her hands clasped in her lap, trying to get control of herself at this unexpected presence in her house.

Why?

"Can I offer you something? A cool drink, or a cup of tea or coffee, perhaps?"

"No, nothing, thank you."

Lea watched as Costa's black eyes swept the room, then lingered on the blue waters of the river beyond the window. "Your home is lovely," she said, with more surprise than admiration in her voice. "It must give you great pleasure."

"It does, very much. My husband had once thought to sell this land near the river but I particularly wanted to hold on to it. I thought it would be so pleasant here, watching the boats and the birds…"

She should not be saying so much to this woman who was the wife of a man neither she nor Ben could trust. Stop talking and relax, Lea adjured herself. It's *my* house, after all.

Abandoning the customary polite formalities, Costa became all business. "Senora Carson, I know I surprise you coming here today, but I especially want to speak with you. I am going away, you see, back to Havana, to live."

"Oh?" To live? Did that mean she was leaving her husband? Lea waited, forcing herself to be quiet and let Costa explain.

"Yes. My husband has many interests and several homes. I prefer Havana to all of them and I choose now to live there. My children have been there for some time in school."

"And is…your husband, is he going to live there as well?"

Costa bent to pluck at an imaginary speck of dust on the folds of her wide black skirt. "No, he is not."

That was a disappointment. The Carson's life in Tampa would be so much easier if only Ramon de Diego moved somewhere else, somewhere away from Ben and their presumed rivalry. She glanced at Ramon's wife who had turned her lovely face back toward the window, staring through the lace curtains at the river beyond.

Once again, Lea thought she had never seen any woman quite as perfect in her features as Costa de Diego. Her white cheeks, long black lashes, aquiline nose and shapely pink lips would have been perfectly at home on a Greek statue. Her shining black hair was piled high below a perky hat trimmed with jet beads and gauze. She wore a high necked dress with long sleeves, fashionably full at the top then tapering to her wrists just above knitted mitts. Tiny jet buttons down the bodice set off a full, sweeping skirt that hid all but the tips of black kid shoes. She looked the picture of composure even though Lea knew she had to be sweltering under those heavy clothes. One thin bead of perspiration above her sculptured lips was the only sign of discomfort.

"That is why I come here today," Costa added, as though the words were torn from her. "It is not easy to make the decision to come see you. I think about it long and hard. But I finally decide I cannot go back to Havana without speaking to you. For my husband's sake as well as yours."

"I don't understand."

"You know how my husband feels toward your Captain Carson, of course."

"Yes. I know there has been some rivalry there."

Costa gave a brittle laugh. "Rivals, yes. Ramon, he does not take any rivalry casually. He has only got where he is by cutting down other men who get in his way. And your husband has got in his way very often."

"I'm sure Captain Carson never intended to. He is only interested in building a name and a living for himself. He feels no animosity toward Senor de Diego."

"Come now, Senora Carson. We both know better. It seems to have come about that our husbands want the same thing too many times. Ramon does not like that."

"But I don't understand. Senor de Diego has many business interests and is very successful. He owns fishing rancheros all up and down the coast—why, his largest is right here on Cabbage Key. He is a man of wealth and substance. Why should he even care what Ben does?"

Costa's narrow smile was full of disdain. She might have been speaking to an idiot.

"I never try to see into my husband's mind. Whatever the reason, he has come to think of Captain Carson with bitterness. I fear for what may come of it. I do not want my husband to seek trouble, nor do I want to see trouble forced on others. That is why I come to warn you."

Lea's realized she was twisting her hands and willed them to be still. "Warn is a rather strong word, Senora. Just what is it that your husband plans to do about this supposed rivalry."

Costa's eyes flickered to the other side of the room. "I cannot say exactly. I only know that he has for a long time set his sights on representing this County as a…what you call, *commissionar*. When that became not possible, he turn his attention to the State Assembly. Now I hear your husband intends to run against him. We both know who is likely to win such a contest and I am much afraid of what will happen when Ramon loses."

Lea felt the first small surge of anger. "It is true my husband wants very much to serve the State, but first he must win the nomination and it is by no means certain that he will. Forgive me, Senora, but your husband has substantial wealth and has been active in Central Florida affairs for a long time. He is as well known to the Commissioners as Ben. There is no reason why one should be more successful than the other."

"Ah, but you have forgotten one important thing. He is *Espana*." For the first time since Costa arrived she appeared to feel as uncomfortable as her hostess.

"I beg your pardon?"

Costa gave a cold, humorless laugh. "Please do not do me the disservice of pretending you do not know what I say. In any contest between a Spaniard and an Anglo, the Anglo is sure to win."

"I don't think that's necessarily true. Manuel Olivera was elected Clerk, after all. And Joseph Elzuardi has had several distinguished appointments."

"Oh, I grant you a few enterprising gentlemen have won some success. And in an election there are many *Espana* voters who were here long before the Anglos came with their army and their settlers. But many of the ranchero workers are not interested in voting and have no idea how. It is not part of their culture. They may wish my husband well but they cannot support him in the same way you English will support Captain Carson."

Lea's anger began to simmer in a slow boil. "Senora, perhaps your husband does not receive the support he needs because he has not cultivated it. Pardon me for speaking so frankly, but he is a man with few friends, a man with a reputation for taking anything he wants. I do not believe it is prejudice against his native origin so much as perhaps because of his…"

She almost said 'character' but did not wish to insult the woman's husband when she was a guest in her home.

"…personality?" Costa offered.

"Yes. Personality."

Costa gave another of her humorless chuckles. "I knew you were naive, Mrs. Carson, but I did not realize to what extent. Clearly it is of no use to try to enlist your aid." She rose abruptly and draped the ribbon of her reticule over her arm. Lea got to her feet as well.

"If you intended to ask me to try to talk my husband out of running against yours, it would be a waste of time. I could never do it, any more than I suspect you could."

"Of course." She swept into the hall and to the door. Lea followed leisurely, taking her time to reach for the knob while Costa waited. Even as she opened the door, Senora de Diego stood, hesitating.

"I talk with you about this because I do not wish to leave for Havana without speaking of it. When my husband is pushed too far, his honor requires vindication. In this case, I feel that is what he very much wants as well as what he will seek."

Lea looked at her quizzically. "Are you talking about the *Code Duello*?"

"Exactly," she answered, smugly.

"Oh, for heaven's sake, Senora, we are living in the nineteenth century. Duels are not only stupid, they are against the law. Ben…Captain Carson would never consider getting involved in such a thing."

Costa's black eyes bored into her own. "And is there not a point at which Captain Carson feels his honor must be vindicated?"

"Why, I suppose so, but it would certainly not be by means of such an idiotic thing as a duel."

Finally Costa tore her gaze away. "Very well. I have said what I wanted to say. You may do with it what you will."

Expecting her to leave, Lea pulled open the door. She was surprised when the Senora still did not move.

"Oh," Costa said, as though recalling a long-forgotten memory. "There was something else, a minor matter. I am closing my home here and taking most of my servants with me. However, I have a girl, a young kitchen maid, whom I do not wish to take to Havana, yet whose welfare has become important to me. I wonder whether you might have some useful work for her?"

Lea, still dwelling on the crazy idea of a duel between Ramon and her husband, barely paid any attention to Costa's new concern. "I have only one woman who cooks and helps in the house," she said absently. "And an occasional man for the yard."

Costa smiled. "Surely with a house this large you could use the help of a strong young girl. I assure you she is a good worker and of sound moral character."

When Lea still hesitated, Costa spoke up again. "My concern, you see, comes from the fact that I knew her father. He was a Cuban fisherman who married an English woman. That makes poor Emeline welcome neither in Cuba or these United States. You have a reputation for…er, compassion, Senora Carson…"

"Why, thank you. But I really don't need…"

"You would be doing a deserving young child a good turn."

It was obvious to Lea the woman was not going to leave until she got her way, and it was suddenly important that she did leave. In fact, it was rather a shock for Lea to realize how much she wanted the Senora out of her house. "Oh, very well. Send the girl around and I'll talk to her. If my husband approves, I'll ask her to give Sukey a hand."

Costa gave Lea one of her regal smiles. "You are very kind. I don't imagine we shall meet again, Mrs. Carson. Thank you for receiving me. Good day."

She swept out the door and down the walk before Lea could answer. Lea stood at the door, watching as a little Negro boy jumped up from the porch to follow Senora de Diego, while a man dressed in dark livery stepped away from holding a beautiful black horse harnessed to a green curricle. He handed the Senora inside, climbed up on the seat beside the boy and flicked the reins to send the carriage rolling briskly off down the street.

Only then did Lea slam the door, swirl around and lean against it. "Well, of all the crazy, arrogant, insane ideas…"

She stalked down the hall into her parlor, grabbed up the chair which Costa had been sitting in, and deliberately moved it back against the wall, vigorously brushing off the seat as if to remove all traces of her guest.

"Arrogant woman! And I am *not* naive!"

CHAPTER 19

▼

By the following afternoon Lea was still seething over her haughty visitor. "You should have seen her, Ben. She swept into my parlor like Queen Isabella, as though she was doing me some kind of favor by paying me a call."

Lea dug her spoon into her blancmange and twisted it. Across the table Ben sat studying his dessert with a detached air, his mind far away.

"I told you, Senora de Diego is like that with everyone. She's a beautiful woman, but a cold one. I suppose she'd have to be, living with such a husband."

Lea glanced quickly up at him. She had said nothing about Costa's preposterous talk of duels, preferring to let Ben think her annoyance came from the woman's arrogance alone.

Ben pushed his dessert dish aside. "I don't understand why she called on you anyway. You're not exactly friends."

"She's moving back to Havana and I suppose she's saying her farewells to everyone. It seemed to be that kind of a visit."

"Still it's surprising she'd bother to come here when she must be well aware of how I feel about her husband. And how he feels about me."

Lea chose her words carefully. "I think she had some idea that I might be able to influence you more favorably toward Ramon."

"That's ridiculous. The problems between Diego and me are strictly political and will have to be resolved on the political front."

"I told her as much. Coffee?" She picked up the Hammond family silver urn and poured him another cup. "Actually, I might have been pleased that she called on me if her highhanded attitude had not been so obvious. I have no quarrel with her."

"My dear, I'm afraid my quarrels will become your quarrels. It can't be helped."

Lea watched him pour milk into his cup and stir it around. He looked tired and tense, more so lately than ever before. Even the hard work and worry of rebuilding the ranch after the Seminole raid had not shown so severely on his long face. Of course they were both older now. Perhaps time was just taking its toll. But she suspected it was something more.

"What exactly is this quarrel with Ramon, Ben? I know you've never liked each other and that business of the deed to the ranch caused a lot of bitterness. But why is it so much worse now? Florida is a State and Tampa village and Hillsborough County are growing. Isn't there room enough for everyone's ambition?"

Ben sipped his coffee, frowning. "You'd think so, wouldn't you. Unfortunately, my ambitions and those of Diego too often seem to be focused on the same prize. When one of us loses it, the other grows more bitter. I had barely put about my intentions of running for the Assembly before he was in the running as well. It's not the first time that's happened, either."

"Do you think he only went after it because of your interest?"

"It's possible. Though why he should seek such an obvious confrontation is beyond me."

"If he had announced first, would you have backed off?"

Ben drummed his fingers on the table. "No, I would not have because I believe I am the better man for the job."

He didn't add that he saw this election as the first step in getting ahead politically but Lea knew that was true. Probably it was just as true for Ramon de Diego. She was startled from her thoughts when Ben abruptly changed the conversation, asking about Buck.

"He's having supper at the Davenport's. They've asked him so many times he finally agreed because he was embarrassed to refuse them again."

Ben smiled. "Good. He might as well get to know that daughter of theirs. The more I think about it the more convinced I am it's the best match he can make."

"Oh Ben, he really isn't interested in Matilda. Everytime I mention her to him I get such a cold response."

"Buck is not really interested in any woman, other than those floozies down at the saloons. Respectable women bore him."

"He's happy at the ranch, riding his horses, tending the cattle."

"I didn't raise my only son to be a cracker cowherder! He's got to marry and it might as well be into a family with money." His voice softened as he saw how his harshness startled her. Yet he would not apologize. "It's only the truth, Lea, and you know it. If Stephen had lived or if we had been able to have children…"

He stopped as her face went white. These oblique references to her childless state were rarely made because he knew they cut deeply. Yet it was a fact that all his hopes for the future rested with his only son. They might not be important to Buck, but Ben cared far too deeply about them to indulge his son's cavalier attitude toward life. He pushed back his chair and rose, throwing his napkin on the table.

"We won't talk any more about this tonight. But Buck will marry that Davenport girl and he might as well get used to the idea."

Lea watched him leave the room then drained the last of her coffee and followed him. At the door of the little study she saw him pull up a chair to the secretary and pull out his watch. She felt her throat tighten as she walked to the stairs and started up them. She would get ready for bed, read a while and force any disturbing thoughts from her mind.

"Miz Carson?"

Lea looked back to see Sukey standing at the foot of the stairs.

"We've finished supper, Sukey. You can clear up now."

"Yes, ma'am. But there's somebody here to see you, Missus. In the kitchen."

"In the kitchen? Who is it?"

"I don' know. Some white gal. Says she was tole to come round and talk with you."

Curious, Lea followed Sukey back to the kitchen where she found a young girl standing apprehensively near the table, her hand resting on a large bundle tied up in a checkered cloth. It took a second look for Lea to realize the girl was not as young as she first appeared. Though not tall, the makings of a striking figure were apparent beneath her shabby clothes. Below a short kerchief masses of black hair fell nearly to her waist. Her thin face was white, almost pasty, but her eyes were large, very dark and lined with thick lashes. With a little more color and a decent dress she would be a very pretty girl indeed.

Her voice was low and soft. "Miz Carson, I'm Emmy."

Lea looked at her in confusion. "Emmy?"

"Emeline Fresca. Miz Costa told me you were gonna hire me."

"Oh, now I remember." Emeline. The girl of good character whom Senora de Diego did not want to take with her to Havana. "I'm afraid you're mistaken. I said I would talk to you but I really don't have a need for another servant right now."

The girl's face fell. "But…she said…"

Immediately Lea regretted her harsh words. "I explained to the Senora…oh, dear," she exclaimed as the girl's eyes filled with tears. "Don't cry. Is there no place you can go? Don't you have a home?"

Emmy shook her head. "No, ma'am. I lived at the Diego's place but they're closing up the house now and told me to go elsewhere."

"Have you no relatives nearby where you can stay until you find another position?"

"No, ma'am." She was silent for a moment then rushed on. "My Ma lives here in the town but she's left now and I don't know where she went. My Pa is dead."

Lea thought a moment. "Is your mother Delia Fresca?"

The girl's head sank lower, as though she knew the name brought unkind recognition. "Yes, ma'am," she muttered.

Lea looked away. She had heard of Delia. She worked mostly as a washerwoman and had the reputation of an easy woman of small virtue. "Well, we can certainly offer you a place to sleep for a few days. You can't just be turned out on the street."

The girl brightened, looking up at Lea with brimming eyes that added a shimmering brilliance to their brown depths. "Thank you, ma'am. You are kind."

Lea found herself softening to the child in spite of her determination not to. "I'll tell you what. You can stay here for a week and help Sukey with the housework and in the kitchen. At the end of that time, if Captain Carson approves, we'll discuss whether or not you can stay on."

Sukey glared at the girl. "I don't needs no help, Miz Carson."

"Now Sukey, in truth this house is big enough for two servants. And there is the possibility that Captain Carson may be doing a bit of entertaining in the near future. We'll give her a try."

Emmy threw Sukey a glance full of naked triumph, then picked up her bundle of clothes off the table. Lea, who had felt rather magnanimous in letting her stay, was shaken a bit by the glint she saw in the girl's eyes. For the first time she realized this was no trembling, obsequious child grateful for any crumbs thrown her way.

But perhaps that was all to the good. She preferred a girl with spirit to one who would fall apart at the first scolding. "Sukey, help Emmy make up a bed in the parson's room. If she stays, we can figure out a more permanent place for her later." She turned to the girl. "Once you're settled you can give Sukey a hand clearing up the supper things."

Grumbling, Sukey led the way off the kitchen to the adjoining shed reserved for traveling clergy. Emmy gave Lea a little curtsey before following her. "Thank you, ma'am," she muttered. Lea watched her go, frowning to herself and wondering if she was doing the right thing. Yet the girl came highly recommended and was certainly in need of work and a home. If she turned out to be lazy or insolent she'd just have to be palmed off on one of Ben's friends with a bigger house.

A light rain had turned the muddy streets to the consistency of churned butter. Buck cursed quietly and pulled his boot from a hole that sucked at his heel like quicksand. Unlike the streets where the saloons held forth, there were no casual boards laid down for walks here. The weeds and stubby grasses of the Florida scrub gave better footing closer to the houses but here, where the sand was inches thick, it was hard slugging, especially after a rain. He muttered damnation for the name of every prominent gentleman he could recall who had been instrumental in building up the village while ignoring the walkways.

It was so dark he could barely make out where the street left off and the front yards began. If only he could see maybe he could keep his balance. Perhaps he shouldn't have had quite so much of that beer and Green Head whiskey.

Yet what was a man to do when he had spent the most boring evening of his life in the company of self-important local snobs and their pasty-faced, straight laced daughters. That girl! She was such a fraidy-cat she barely had the courage to look at him, and when she did, he felt like a bull going on the block. It was no surprise that such a horrible evening was enough to drive him to Reid's afterward. Primitive as it was, the grogshop at least had happy people laughing and drinking, and smiling women as well who never tried to be anything but what they were. It had taken some of the bad taste out of his mouth. Yet the dregs still lingered.

His stomach gave a lurch. He grabbed at the nearest fence and waited for the nausea to subside before weaving his way on down the street. Just a little farther now and he'd be home. At least, he'd be at his father's house. He'd never be able to think of it as his home.

Yet suddenly the thought of sinking into a chair and laying his head on a table seemed heavenly. He lurched forward, taking three quick steps until the world went swimming around him again, forcing him to grab for the fence. Somewhere across the road a dog began barking hysterically.

"Sh..h…h…" Buck exclaimed, trying to put his finger to his lips and not quite finding them. "Mush be quiet…wake…the…neigh…the neigh…everybody!"

He giggled as he pictured himself clutching the fence trying to shush a barking dog, then groaned as the hammering in his head began anew. He needed something to stop this terrible pain. More whiskey, that would do the trick. Using the fence as a guide he edged along the road to the house, stopping long enough to take his bearings before weaving down the graveled path that led to the kitchen door. He had just enough presence of mind left to know he did not want to wake his aunt and his father. The house was dark but for one small dim lamplight in the kitchen.

What was the name of his aunt's new slave? "Sukey…" he mumbled. "Sukey'll know what to do for a headache. Good old Sukey…"

Staggering down the walk, he lurched toward the porch, grabbed at the wooden post, steadied himself and pushed open the kitchen door. The blinding light shot up the hammering in his head to horrendous levels. He groaned, squinted, then looked back once he could see.

Sukey was not there. Instead a child stood at the drysink working the long handle of the pump. She turned and looked over her shoulder at him, her eyes huge in her white face.

"Sukey? You're not Sukey. Where's Sukey?" Buck mumbled, clutching the door jamb.

Emmeline Fresca jumped back from the sink and wiped her wet hands on her apron. "Who are you? What do you want?"

"Who am I? Who're you? I'm Buck Carson. I b'long here. Where'd you come from? What'cha done wi' Sukey?"

The floor of the room began to undulate beneath his feet. He gripped the door, leaning forward and peering at the child. When the door frame began to waver as well he made a dash for the table, falling over one of the chairs before finding his seat.

"Are you drunk?" he heard her say with something like relief. Whether that was because she was not afraid of drunks or because she recognized his name, he couldn't tell. Probably both. He couldn't look much of a threat in his present pitiful condition. He gingerly folded his arms on the table and slowly lowered his head down on them.

"Not drunk!" he muttered. "I'm jus'…jus' sick."

He couldn't see her smile. "I can see you are." She walked around the table and laid her cool hand on his brow. "No fever. Sick to your stomach, are you?"

For an answer Buck lurched over the table, heaving. Emmy grabbed a bucket and stuck it under his face, holding his head with her other hand. It wasn't pleasant, all that second-hand beer and whisky, and she turned her face away, wrinkling her nose. When at last there was nothing more to come up, Buck groaned and fell back on the table. Emmy walked to the door to dispose of the bucket, leaving the door open to help disperse any lingering odors.

"What you need is some strong coffee. The water's already hot. Now if I can find where Sukey keeps the coffee beans, I'll stoke up the fire and brew you up some."

She went bustling around the kitchen while Buck gingerly opened one eye to watch her. His stomach seemed easier but his head was pounding. "Got anythin' for a achin' head?" he mumbled.

Emmy laughed. "I just bet you've got a good one. The coffee will help." She found the sack of coffee beans and ground up a few. "It won't take long. You'll feel better once you've got some hot coffee in you."

Buck's stomach turned over at the thought. "Who're you, anyway? What'ave you done wi' Sukey?"

Emmy looked over her shoulder at him as she got down a large white cup from a cupboard over the dry sink. "I'm the new housegirl. Sukey went to bed and left me to finish up in the kitchen. And a good thing she did, too."

Buck raised his head, very slowly and gently. "How come a little girl like you knows so much about helpin'…sick people?"

She laid the cup on the table in front of him, looking down with eyes full of smiles. "'Cause my old Daddy used to come home drunk as a skunk more nights than he was sober. Ma would get mad and leave so I was the one who had to help him. I got pretty good at it."

Buck leaned his head on his hand, giving her one of his boyish, crooked smiles. "So you knew right off I wasn't really sick."

"Oh, you were sick all right. Too much rotgot whisky and too much carousing, I suspect. Here," she said, using a cloth to lift the coffee pot and pouring the hot liquid into his cup. "Drink this and you'll feel better. Then go to bed and sleep it off. There's nothin' else that works as well."

"Can't drink it without sugar."

"No, no sugar nor anything else. Black, hot and strong. That's what the doctor orders."

Buck grinned and struggled to lift the heavy cup. "You ain't no doctor. What's your name anyway?"

"Emmeline, but most folks call me Emmy." She took the chair opposite him and watched as he struggled to get down a few sips of the strong brew. "And you're Buck Carson, ain't you. Miz Carson's son."

"Stepson. Though God knows she's more of a Ma to me than my own flesh and blood Daddy is a Pa. And I wasn't ca…carousin'."

"I just bet you wasn't."

"You don't understan'. I had to spend a whole evenin' listenin' to a pompous old stuff shirt blather about his business deals while his simperin' homely daughter made cow's eyes at me. It was awful! After that I had to have somethin' to take the bad taste outta my mouth."

"And that somethin' was whisky and beer. Well, at least it's different from some of the excuses my Pa used to make. I've heard 'em all at one time or another." She sat back in her chair and watched him struggle to get down the coffee. He was a good looking young man, long and lean and with the sun-burned, leathery look of the out-of-doors about him. He must have looked like a fish out of water in a fancy parlor trying to balance a tea cup on his knees. She smiled to herself at the foolishness of people with money and standing. It seemed to her that sometimes they had no idea at all about the ways of the world.

"What're you laughin' at," Buck commented dryly, pushing the cup aside.

"At you," she said smiling at him. "I was trying to picture you sitting in a stuffy parlor among fancy folk. You don't seem to fit there."

"You're right. I don't. Give me a good horse and an open range any time over parlors and houses and chitchat. None of that's for me." He looked closer at her through blurred eyes, surprised at how perceptive this slip of a girl seemed to be. She wasn't a child at all if the neat figure beneath her apron could be believed. A kerchief held back her hair but below it long strands of jet black waves fell to her waist. He reached out and touched a strand. It was soft, like feathers beneath his fingers.

"How old are you anyway, Emmy?"

"Seventeen, going on eighteen. And you need to be in bed. Come on, I'll help you up the stairs."

"Bed. Hmm. Maybe you can join me there…"

She was not surprised at his invitation, indeed she was expecting it. Two years of fighting off the none too welcome advances of Ramon de Diego had taught her what 'gentleman masters' expected from their female servants. Well, she had never succumbed to Senor Diego and she was not about to give in now. She had long ago determined she was not going to be a younger version of her mother. She would save herself for something better.

"No thank you, sir. Not for anything. I just got this job and I'm not about to lose it for a toss in the hay with the drunken son of the Carson family."

With her shoulder under his arm she helped him to his feet. "Not drunk…" Buck said indignantly. "Jus…a little tipsy."

Emmy laughed and half-supported him toward the hall door. "All right, the tipsy son of the Carson family." Lurching their way to the stairs she helped him get a grip on the railing then stepped aside.

"Good night, son of the family."

Buck gave her a mock bow that nearly sent him toppling. "Good night, new house girl."

She watched him wobble his way up the stairs, then went back to the kitchen, still smiling.

It was mid-afternoon of the following day before Buck finally stumbled back downstairs. Though he passed the new housegirl in the hall he barely noticed her. His eyes were still blurred and his head was still pounding almost as violently as the night before. Lea met him in the hall, took his arm and led him into the dining room, ordering Emmy to bring a pot of hot coffee.

"And some of Sukey's fresh rolls and butter too, Emmy. This poor hung over boy looks as though he needs some food in his stomach."

Buck, who wasn't at all sure his stomach could handle food of any kind, slumped into the nearest chair and leaned his head in his hands. "No food," he muttered. "But coffee sounds good."

Lea took a chair opposite him. "Bring the rolls, too, Emmy," Lea ordered. The girl scurried off to the kitchen while Lea studied her nephew. "That must have been some kind of evening social Sam Davenport threw last night."

He gave her a sharp glance. "It was."

"Somehow I can't picture Matilda Davenport in the middle of the kind of wild party which would leave you looking as bad as you do right now. It doesn't fit."

Buck smiled at the thought of straight-laced, quiet Matilda sitting amid the cavorting characters in Reid's grogshop. "You have a point, Aunt Lea. The truth is I left the Davenport's with such a rotten taste in my mouth I simply had to wash it out at one of the saloons."

"It appears you did a bit more washing than was necessary. I suppose that means you are not any closer to considering Matilda as a potential bride."

Buck groaned. "I'd rather marry one of my cows. Look, I know I messed up all your nice plans. Let me sober up and ease this raging headache, then I'll be off. I'm needed back at the ranch anyway. I'll slip quietly away and no one will be the wiser."

Lea sighed. "If you think to avoid your father by quietly fading back up north, you couldn't be more wrong. Last night's affair was important to him. He hoped you would make a good impression on the Davenports and they on you. He's going to be disappointed."

"I don't give a damn how disappointed he is. It's my life, isn't it? He's not my 'Commanding Officer' and I'm not one of his groveling Privates. I won't be shackled to some ninny for the rest of my life just because he thinks it would be good for his career."

Lea raised her finger to her lips to quiet him as the door swung open and Emmy came through bearing a tray. Once it was set on the table Lea sent her off again, barely noticing how the girl's eyes lingered on Buck or her disappointment when he failed to return her gaze. Lea had always felt strongly against airing family problems in front of servants and she wasn't going to start now. Especially with a young girl who was still a stranger.

"Don't go back right away," she said quietly to Buck. "Your Papa is having a little social of his own in a few days to try and get a feel for whether or not he should offer to run for the Assembly. I know he'd like you to be here for it. And it will give us time to try to make him understand how you feel about Matilda."

Buck felt the heat of the liquid all the way down his gullet. "When has time ever made a difference? He'll never understand."

It seemed perhaps Buck was wrong that evening when Ben came home and the three of them sat down to a quiet, congenial supper. Though Ben asked about the party the night before he had little to say once Buck commented on how dreary it had been. He knew polite social events did not appeal to his wilderness-loving son and was not surprised that it had gone badly. After the meal he and Buck spent some time in the small office off the parlor going over the ranch's financial records. Lea sat in the parlor crocheting a table cover and listening to the quiet murmur of their voices. It was all so pleasant that she was beginning to think she had underestimated her husband's good common sense.

That satisfied feeling changed swiftly once the two men joined her. Buck barely sat down before he was up again, saying he thought he'd take a walk before bed.

Ben stood at the marble mantel filling his pipe. "I'll be obliged if your walk doesn't take you as far as Reid's groggery tonight."

Buck threw Lea a quick glance that shouted 'you told him'. She shook her head silently. "I thought I was very quiet last night," he said to his father.

"Oh, I didn't hear you. But I was told all about it by several acquaintances today. It seems you made quite a spectacle of yourself. If you're going to get drunk, Buck, why can't you do it in private?"

His tone of voice set his son bristling. "Because that would be no fun at all. I was no rowdier than anyone else who was there, including your lawyer friend, Magbee."

Ben lit his pipe and took several drags on the stem. "Perhaps not, but everybody knows Magbee drinks too much. And the rest of those gamblers, whores and wild crackers don't have fathers who are trying to make an impression on this growing town."

"Trying to win elections, you mean."

Lea felt a sense of dread growing in her chest. "Ben, for goodness sake, let him go. He's young. He has to sow a few wild oats."

Ben made an effort to keep his voice calm and unemotional. "I'm not trying to argue with you, son. I only want you to be conscious of how important it is to me to win this nomination. I have earned some respect in this County and I don't want to lose it because my only son disgraces me."

"Ben..." Lea said as she saw Buck's face go white with sudden rage.

"Disgrace you! I run your damned ranch, and very well, too."

"Don't curse in front of your aunt! I know you've done a good job with the ranch. Didn't I just say so when we were looking at the books?"

"Faint praise that doesn't last long."

Lea rose to lay a hand on her nephew's arm. "Buck, please. Can't we have one quiet evening without a quarrel? Your father has made a perfectly reasonable request."

Buck's face hardened. "And haven't I been reasonable in answering it? Didn't I spend three boring hours yesterday being picked over like a steer at auction at the Davenports? I work long and hard when I'm up at the farm and I can get drunk if I want to when I come to town!"

Ben's strained calm broke. "Then you can damn sure go somewhere else to sleep it off!" he roared, his carefully reined anger giving way to his rage over his son's obdurate ways. "Go down to Reid's or O'Reily's if you want. Make a spectacle of yourself again. But stay there the night. Don't come lurching home to parade before all my neighbors the fact that I have a drunkard for a son."

"You don't know what a drunkard is, Papa dear. You know what's the matter with you? You can't bear any criticism from your straight-laced friends. I can carouse, fight and drink all I want so long as I don't let any of your neighbors know about it. That's the worst hypocrisy I ever heard. You're nothing but a hypocrite!"

"That's enough!"

Lea's shrill voice silenced them both. She lost her temper so seldom that they both turned toward her in stunned surprise.

"That's enough," Lea repeated more quietly, having got their attention. "For once I've had enough of your quarrels. Go on, Buck. Take your walk, and if you have too much to drink, stay at the saloon to sleep it off. Your father needs the support of men in this town, some of whom might be offended by your behavior. There's nothing wrong in trying to keep in their good graces. It won't kill you to try to make a decent impression until this matter is settled. Then you can go back to the farm and do whatever you please."

Buck glanced at his father. "Lea is right," Ben said, tapping his pipe on the mantle. "Go on."

Turning to leave, Buck paused beside the hall door. "I'm sorry," he said quietly. "You know my temper. I'll sleep at Reid's tonight and be gone for the farm in the morning."

She took a step toward him. "No, don't leave tomorrow. The next three weeks will be crucial for your father's plans and we'd both like you to be with us. This is a quiet time for the ranch and you can afford to stay in town a while longer."

Buck's glance moved between the two of them. "All right," he said with a shrug. "Three more weeks. But that's all the good conduct I can manage."

Lea gave him a weak smile. She didn't turn back to her husband until she heard the front door close. "He doesn't mean half of what he says. He takes your criticism so much to heart because he wants your approval so much."

Ben gave a bitter laugh. "I hadn't noticed he cared about my opinion at all. But he has done a good job with the ranch. If only he would settle down."

Lea picked up her crocheting and resumed her seat. "He's nineteen, Ben. That's very young."

Ben leaned on the mantle looking down at the open grate. "I was engaged to be married at nineteen. And a husband the next year and a father the year after that. Ah well, he'll come around eventually."

"I don't think it will be to Matilda Davenport."

"Oh, I'm not discouraged about that. I never thought he'd take to her right away. But he'll come to see how advantageous a marriage it would be. I'll make sure of that."

CHAPTER 20

▼

Ben selected a long seegar from a mahogany humidor and handed the box to Judge Turman sitting next to him. He clipped the end, bent to light it, then leaned back in his chair and looked around the room. Satisfaction like a slow warmth spread through him.

"How did you get these?" the Judge asked as he blew a puff of gray smoke. "I've had an order with the Constant for three months and got nothing."

"The Constant has an unreliable captain," Ben answered. "You should have gone with Jameson on the Westerly Wind. He docked two days ago with hogsheads of oil, claret, tobacco and Cuban coffee. These were just a little extra something I had him pick up for me."

"Trust Ben Carson to know the right ship," Micah Brown commented from the other end of the table. "He's been in these parts longer than any of us."

Ben smiled. "You forget most of my beef is shipped to Key West and Cuba. I'd be pretty negligent if I didn't know the best captains to trust."

Still, the compliment pleased him. The men sitting around his table were part of the new Hillsborough County Board of Commissioners and, as such, were some of the most influential leaders of the growing community. It gave him much satisfaction to see them at his table. The whole meal had gone well. Lea had done a first rate job of making the room comfortable, the food excellent, the atmosphere congenial. Though she had left the room shortly before, her lovely presence still lingered on in the faint scent of lavender she always wore. She had looked especially pretty tonight in her green satin dress with her hair delicately braided and curled. He must remember to compliment her.

She had even done a good job with the new little serving girl who was as prim and proper as he could have hoped as she went around the table serving the meal. The table linens were starched to embroidered perfection, the cherry wood sideboard and chairs were polished to a reflective sheen, the oil lamps threw shadows on the gleaming old Hammond family silver and the new Turkish rug, the gilt mirror over the sideboard reflected a scene of comfort, maybe even luxury. The only thing not as perfect as he would have wanted was Buck, who had sat stiff and silent through most of the meal before excusing himself. Still, he hadn't disagreed with anyone or tried to pick any arguments so Ben guessed he should be grateful for that. On the whole, with Lea's help, he felt he had done his part. Now if only these gentlemen would do theirs.

"Well," Judge Turman said, leaning back in his chair, a smile creasing his broad, flat face. "A good meal followed by a fine seegar—what more can a man ask for? We are indebted to you, Ben."

"My pleasure, sir."

"The only other thing one might ask for is that the Whigs lose the election next November," Benjamin Moody said dryly from his place opposite the Judge. It was a typical remark, Ben thought, for Moody was always a worrier. It showed in the long furrows creasing his face from nose to chin and the perennial outthrust lower lip. "Which brings us to the matter at hand."

The Judge smiled, relieved that the subject which had lain underneath the polite dinner conversation was at last out in the open. "Yes, the matter at hand. There's not much doubt that the Whigs will run General Taylor on their ticket in this next presidential election. He's such a popular figure here in Florida that he's sure to sweep a lot of other men into office with him. We can't allow that to happen." He turned to Ben. "We need a good slate of Democrats who can carry the party to victory even if the General wins the national election. We need you to represent Hillsborough County in the Assembly, Ben, and we want you to run."

Ben looked around the table at the eager faces watching him: Micah Brown, the New Hampshire Yankee who had come to Tampa to open a clothing store and ended up going into partnership with Kennedy; Benjamin Moody, the former Georgia farmer now commissioner; Thomas Kennedy, Brown's partner and Town Treasurer; James Goff, former Territorial Representative; and Judge Simon Turman, an Ohio native who settled originally on the Manatee but moved to Tampa after being elected County Commissioner. All of them except the older Turman were of an age with him. All as ambitious and eager to build their fortunes in this burgeoning town and fledgling State as he was.

"Gentlemen, I am honored," he said, carefully picking his words. It would serve no purpose to pretend he hadn't sought this offer when they all knew he had. "I would like nothing better than to be elected as the Democratic representative in the lower house. However..."

"I know what you are going to say," Moody interrupted, frowning. "The Whig ticket is formidable and possibly will be difficult to beat, especially if they choose Cabell to stand for Congress. We expect our party to nominate William Bailey as Governor and DuVal for Congress, but should the Whigs carry both offices, that may adversely affect our other candidates." He sat back in his chair, his face slumping into his high collar points, the furrows from nose to chin deepening. "Still, we have to put forth the best men we can. We think that with your familiarity with the area, having been in it so long, and with your success as a cattleman, you should be one of them."

"My 'familiarity', don't forget, was because I was part of the military."

"So what," Goff spoke up. "That's where General Zachery Taylor got his fame. Counter a military man with a military man, I say."

Judge Turman leaned forward on the table and tapped the ashes off his seegar. "Besides, right now we need to walk carefully with the military. Until the Congress and President Polk officially transfer garrison land to the village we don't even have the legal right to a town! That must be settled and quickly or none of us will be re-elected."

"What's being done about that?" Ben asked, cringing inwardly as he remembered how all the plans for a sale of land last April had to be dropped when it was learned that President Polk had failed to sign the order.

"I did my best last spring and summer to light a fire under them," Micah Brown muttered. "But the current of politics runs exceedingly slow. However, I was assured the matter would be taken care of. Once Congress acts, we will be a legal entity and can move forward from there."

"And if they don't?"

Kennedy reached for the claret decanter. "They will. The military know they don't need all these acres for Fort Brooke. That boundary was set years ago when there was nothing but wilderness here. Now, with all the settlers moving into the outlands, the town is poised to grow. We need this land and we'll get it."

Ben leaned forward, resting his elbows on the table. "Gentlemen, I am sincere when I tell you I am honored and eager to run. However, I have two questions which must be addressed before we can settle this, neither of which have anything to do with the Whig slate. The first is Ramon de Diego."

"Oh, Diego." Kennedy dismissed Ramon with a wave of his hand before smoothing back his thinning hair over his high forehead. "He won't be any trouble. He's been running around courting both Democrats and Whigs trying to get his name on the ballot but he'll never succeed. We don't want him and for certain the Whigs don't."

Ben pressed the issue. "He has some support. He's worked hard at cultivating it."

Judge Turman reached across the table to take the claret bottle from Kennedy. "He could bring in the Spanish vote but we don't need that. It is our belief we can win without it."

"He has money, ambition, connections," Ben went on.

"But my dear Ben, he doesn't have character. His wife is living apart from him in Cuba, he is a known womanizer, and his ambitions often seem more important to him than the methods by which they are realized. We don't think he is our man."

Kennedy added, "And his connections are primarily with the Spanish rancheroes. We don't need them to win." Kennedy's large prominent chin and small pursed mouth bespoke his determination. "Believe me, Ramon de Diego hasn't got a chance of running on our ticket. I've had enough business dealings with the gentleman to know first hand how ruthless and ambitious he is. It's a dangerous combination."

"And we all remember his treacherous dealings with the Indians," James Goff added. Kennedy nodded. His own trading post on the Peace River lay in Seminole reservation lands and while he was on friendly terms with the natives at the moment, every man there knew how quickly that could change.

Ben sat back and hooked his thumbs in his vest pockets. "All right. That takes care of one question. The second is actually more important. Before you agree you want me to run on your ticket, you must determine whether or not my views on slavery will be a detriment. On the whole, Democrats are so pro-slavery and pro-annexation that I am going to appear out of place. You know that for years I refused to own slaves, and still find the system repugnant."

Moody frowned. "But you can manage without a lot of slaves because you are not a planter. Cotton and sugar cane require them in order to be viable."

"I never used them when I was trying to be a planter."

"But that's what I mean. Had your plantation grown as large as the ones which are now scattered all over middle Florida, you might have been forced to. You avoided the issue by concentrating on cattle. Perhaps without realizing it your distaste for slavery even led you to do so."

Ben shook his head. "That had nothing to do with it. I simply don't believe human beings should be bought and sold like animals. Nor owned like them."

"Gentlemen, gentlemen," Judge Turman broke in. "Let's not get into this issue. Even the Whigs try to avoid being pinned down on the question of slavery from fear of agitating the subject." He turned to Ben. "We know your views, Ben, and we respect them even though they are not practical. You dislike the institution of slavery but you call yourself a Democrat, right?"

Ben nodded. "Yes. And have ever since the party was named as such seven years ago."

"And you certainly do not accept the precepts of the other party."

"I distrust financiers and banking interests even more than slavers, if that's what you mean."

"Exactly. We believe you will be a first rate addition to the Assembly and we're willing to do all we can to get you elected. What do you say?"

Ben looked at the eager faces turned toward him and smiled broadly. "I would be honored, gentlemen."

"How do you think you would like living in Tallahassee?" Ben asked.

Lea looked up from her dressing table where she sat in her nightgown brushing out her hair. Across the room Ben stood in his shirt sleeves, removing the studs from his cuffs. The painted globe of an oil lamp threw rainbow hued shadows over the bedroom, leaving deep caverns of darkness in the corners.

"I don't know. I've never been to Tallahassee." She peered closer at her reflection in the mirror, the smile she could not suppress teasing the corner of her lips. "I take it the meeting went well then."

Ben laid his cuff links on the highboy and walked over to stand behind her, slipping his hands over her shoulders. Their eyes locked in the mirror. "My dear, there is a possibility you might just be the wife of the distinguished Democratic representative from Hillsborough County! Would that make you happy?"

She reached up and laid the palm of her hand along his cheek, smiling at his reflection. "Not as happy as I think it makes you." She could not suppress a delighted laugh. "Oh, Ben. It's really quite an honor, isn't it."

"They want me to stand for the office, Lea. That in itself gives me great satisfaction. Of course…"

She turned in his arms and lifted her face for his kiss. "Of course what?"

He kissed her lightly then turned away and began matter-of-factly undoing the buttons on his shirt. "There are still a number of obstacles. This was only a select committee after all. I still have to win the nomination from the larger constituency. And even if I do, I'll have to face stiff opposition from the Whigs and a hard campaign. But I don't mind that. In fact I look forward to it."

"What Whigs?" She hesitated. "Not Ramon de Diego?"

"No, no. The Democrats don't want Diego and I doubt the Whigs do either. Rumor is it will be somebody like Magbee."

"That scalawag! Who would ever vote for him. He's a notorious drunkard."

Ben smiled and removed the starched collar from his shirt. "I don't know if it will be him. It could be anybody. But it won't be me running against him until I get the party's endorsement. By the way, Lea, everything was very nice tonight. You did a good job."

Lea caught her long hair inside the lacy folds of her night cap. "Thank you. I knew it was important. Emmy and I have been working for days to make everything perfect. Once I saw that Buck intended to behave himself I breathed a little easier." She threw back the bedcovers and climbed into bed. "Speaking of Buck, how do you think he will take to the campaign?"

Ben slipped off his shirt and trousers and climbed in beside her in his long johns. "I'll keep him so occupied up on the ranch he won't have time to get involved. I doubt he will want to anyway." He slid down in the bed and settled back on the pillow, lacing his fingers behind his head. "What about you, Lea? A political campaign can be a ruthless business. I remember vaguely the one back in the twenties when General Jackson's wife suffered such vilification she lost her will to live. This one might become brutal in its own way."

"I don't think Mrs. Jackson's situation and mine are in the least comparable. After all, I was not married before I married you. And my sister was already dead before we made our vows. There can be no impropriety in that."

Ben frowned. "Only that our marriage took place in some haste, if you remember. And you were my sister-in-law."

"Only the most rabid puritans could find fault with that." She leaned over to turn out the lamp then slipped underneath the covers to nestle against him. "If this campaign is what you want, I'll bear with anything. I'm proud of you, Ben."

Reaching his arm around her, he pulled her close, leaning over to smooth back her hair and kiss her forehead. "Thank you, my dear. I feel rather proud of myself tonight."

Lea's knew she had not told her husband the exact truth. Though she was happy for Ben that his ambitions seemed on the verge of becoming reality, at the same time she dreaded facing a political campaign which, if it were like others she had seen, might quickly turn vitriolic and scandal ridden. She could think of no glaring 'sin' in the Carson family background that opponents might exploit, yet she was well aware that in a political battle, sins which had no basis in truth sometimes grew into ugly accusations. In this day and age political campaigns tended to be ugly, vicious and unfair. There was no reason to believe this one would be any different, especially if Ben ended up running against Ramon de Diego.

However, the Christmas season was almost upon them so she pushed her mixed feelings about Ben's plans into the background and threw herself into enjoying the festivities. She was both surprised and pleased that Buck stayed with them for the holidays. After one flying visit to the ranch he returned to Tampa and seemed in no hurry to leave. Both he and his father were in such good humor that there were no arguments to mar the pleasantness of the season. Looking back later she remembered it as one of the happiest times in her married life. One of the last for a long time.

The first hint that something was different occurred early in January. Buck came home one day bleeding from a long gash on his cheek and with one eye swollen nearly closed. As Lea doctored the cut she scolded him for fighting in the streets like a common ruffian, probably over some woman or a gambling bet gone bad.

"It was nothing like that," Buck muttered under his breath. Yet when she urged him to tell her what had caused the fight, he pursed his lips and refused to say any more. It took ten minutes of wheedling before it all came out.

"Have a look at this," her stepson said, handing her a grimy torn handbill. She spread the paper on her lap with a sinking feeling in her chest. Her worst fears were confirmed as she ran her eyes down a long list of accusation against Ben made up of half-truths, entire lies and hints of even worse revelations to come.

Lea spluttered: "Hoarded funds stolen from the army…responsible for his first wife's death…married his second before his first was cold in her grave…illegally bought up public lands…this, this is…why, this is…"

"A pack of half-truths and lies," Buck offered. "Unfortunately some people will believe it."

"No one who knows your father would believe such trash. Rachel died of camp fever, Buck. To say your father was responsible for her death is the worst kind of slander. Where did you get this?"

"One of my acquaintances at Reid's shoved it in my face this morning. They're all over the village."

"Is he the one you fought?"

Buck turned his face away. "No. That was one of Diego's men."

"Oh, Buck. Don't tell me Diego is responsible for this."

"Who else would be? Who else has the most to lose?"

Lea studied her stepson's long face. "So you accused the man then tried to get even by beating him up."

"Well, he didn't deny that Diego had paid him to pass them around. You wouldn't expect me to just shrug that off, would you?"

She felt the beginning of a cold despair. Everything she had feared was starting to come true. This scurrilous paper was only the first step. There would be much more, much worse.

"We mustn't let your father see this," she said, crumpling the handbill in her hand and throwing it in the grate. "He's been so happy about this chance to run for office. This could ruin everything."

"You can't keep it from him, Aunt Lea," Buck said, frowning at her. "He knew things like this were bound to happen when he went into politics. It goes with the territory."

"I don't think he expected you to have to defend him in the streets of the village."

"That happened because I was there. Besides, I'm going back to the ranch the end of this week so it won't happen again."

Lea felt a sense of relief that her hotheaded nephew would be out of the turbulence that was sure to come. "That's probably for the best. It wouldn't be so bad, Buck, except that it comes from Diego, and there is already so much bad blood between your father and him. I confess it worries me."

"Papa must have known you'd be exposed to some harsh accusations when he took on this campaign. Did he even ask you how you felt about it?"

"Of course," she said quickly. "Naturally, he knew I would support him in anything he wanted. And he wants this badly."

Buck got to his feet, holding the bloodied rag against his damaged cheek. "Well, he would never have subjected my sainted mother to this kind of trouble. She would have told him to forget it and forget it he would have."

Lea ignored the sudden flush on her cheeks. "I'm not Rachel," she murmured.

Buck paused by the door, looking back at her with sympathy. "No, you will do whatever he wants no matter how much it hurts you. I think Papa is very wrong to get you mixed up in this filthy business."

"I can take their lies, Buck. I worry more about what this kind of thing will do to Ben."

"You would, Aunt Lea. Sometimes I wish you were more like my mother."

Lea watched him go then sat for a moment thinking over his words. More like Rachel? That fragile, doll-like creature who only thought of her own comforts and needs? But Buck was right about one thing. Rachel would have refused to be involved in anything as grubby as a political campaign and for her sake Ben would have given up his dreams. No, she was not like Rachel. She would fight and claw and do anything possible to help her husband realize his ambitions. And if she got hurt in the process, she would bear that too.

And maybe someday, when it was successfully over, Ben would realize how much he owed her. Then it would all be worth it.

By the next morning Ben had also seen the handbill circulating against him but, to Lea's surprise, he did not explode with anger or bitterness. "In politics you don't fight lies by trying to deny them," he said evenly. "You fight them with other lies."

"What does that mean?" she said, her heart sinking.

"It means that two can play at this game. Diego has a past much more checkered than mine, with so many questionable business dealings it would take ten handbills to detail. By this evening he'll have a broadside leveling charges against him that make mine pale by comparison."

"Oh, Ben. Do you really think that is the way to go?"

"That is the only way to go, Lea. Pride demands it."

He left the house before she could try to talk him out of it. By that evening the men and women lounging on the porches of their homes, the soldiers and gamblers and drinking men in the taverns, the pedestrians ambling along the wide sandy streets of the village could talk of nothing else but the circulation of a second broadside against Ben and two new ones against Diego. For the most part they found them highly entertaining.

The battle of the handbills went on for the next three weeks. To Lea's disgust they grew ever more vitriolic and accusatory yet both Ben and Diego as well as the public at large seemed to relish them. What ever small dregs of truth had been involved in the beginning were soon eclipsed by the rampant wildness of their accusations. When she tried to talk to Ben about what was happening he waved her away, saying that was the nature of politics. Lea soon decided if this was the nature of politics she would just as soon Ben had never dreamed of seeking office.

In the beginning she had been hurt a little by some of the veiled insults Diego threw at her. As the days went by, and the decision as to who would be the candidate drew closer, she began to ignore the campaign altogether. Ramon was driven to such excesses that she felt certain anyone who knew her would only laugh at them. She just wanted the whole thing to be over.

Yet when it finally came, it was a blow. She first heard of the party's decision while browsing along the shelves at Kennedy's store. Thomas Kennedy saw her from his perch on a ladder at the rear and came hurrying over.

"Mrs. Carson," he said, his long face severe as he took her gloved hand. "I hope you are all right."

For a moment Lea wondered if there had been a death in her family that she didn't know about. Kennedy's funeral manner certainly implied it. "I'm very well, thank you, Mister Kennedy," she said. Her surprise must have shown in her face.

"Oh, dear. I see you haven't heard. I do hope you'll forgive my speaking out precipitously."

"Speaking out? About what?" A slow sense of dread began to darken what had been a bright afternoon.

"The campaign. Here," he said, pulling her back into a corner. "Let us speak privately. It's about the Captain. I hope you won't hold it against us, Mrs. Carson. We have the greatest respect for him and we tried very hard…"

Lea fastened her gaze on his face. "Mister Kennedy, I don't know what you are talking about but I suspect a decision has been made about who will run for State Assembly."

He dropped her hands and smoothed back his thinning hair. "Yes, yes. A decision has been made. Unfortunately…"

"Are you trying to tell me Ben will not be in the running?"

"We wanted him to be. Judge Turman, Micah Brown, Goff, we all pushed hard for it. But the larger group, mostly the men from the Manatee area, they thought, well, they figured someone who could represent the whole County would have a better chance of winning."

"I see." She turned her face away for a moment to regain hold of her emotions. Surely she felt relief. Yet that was eclipsed by disappointment for Ben. This was going to be hard for him.

"Tell me, Mister Kennedy, did their decision have anything to do with the meanness of the campaign so far?"

He shrugged. "Well, that might have had some effect. It's been pretty bad around here what with your husband and Diego both going at each other tooth and nail. It would have been hard for Ben to put all this behind him and start a new campaign, especially when the public has been choosing up sides. We can't afford to lose any votes in this election and perhaps it was thought a third candidate might be a compromise everyone could accept. I'm really sorry, Mrs. Carson. I know how much the Captain wanted this."

She felt a sudden urgency to get home. "Yes, he did," she said, turning to leave. "I thank you for telling me, Mister Kennedy. Good day to you."

She hurried out of the store, purposefully avoiding any acquaintances, and almost ran the few blocks to her house. Checking the rooms downstairs she saw that Ben was not there. Possibly he didn't know yet. No, he would have had to learn of this before she did. He had too much riding on the nomination of the party not to be there when the decision was made. But why hadn't he said anything?

She sank on to one of the chairs, absently remembering it was the same one Costa de Diego had taken in this very room so many weeks ago. The though of Diego was like a bitter taste in her mouth. Damn the man! Always a spoiler. Always in the way. And now what? How much more bitter would he be toward Ben, for he had been denied the chance to run just as surely as Ben had.

The front door slammed. Lea jumped to her feet and ran into the hall. Ben stood there, calmly pulling off his hat and hanging it on a peg by the door. He looked up and saw her standing by the parlor door, her face white against the dark paneling.

They stood watching each other. Ben tried to smile but couldn't quite make it. "I see you've been told," he finally said.

Lea ran to him, throwing her arms around his waist and holding him close. His arms tightened around her so strongly they squeezed the breath from her lungs. Then they eased and he put her away.

"It's quite all right. I'm not devastated. We'll all live."

"My dear..."

He slipped his arm around her shoulder and led her back to the parlor. "Please, no consolation, Lea. I tried and I failed and that's all there is to it. I've suffered losses before. I've failed before."

"But you wanted it so much. I know what a disappointment this must be."

He sank into one of the more comfortable chairs. "It's a disappointment, I grant you that. How about pouring me a glass of Madeira, there's a girl. It's good to get home."

Lea lifted the glass decanter on the sideboard and filled his glass. Handing it to him, she pulled up a tapestried stool and sat next to him, her skirt spilling out around her. She caught his hand and entwined her fingers with his.

"It's probably just as well," Ben said between sips of the wine. "This would have been a bitter campaign. It had already become that, in fact. At least you'll be spared any more insults."

"What about you? He only made hints about me. You, he vilified."

Ben gave a short laugh. "His accusations were so preposterous they were almost comic. Anyway, it's all behind us now."

"I doubt Diego will think any of this is funny. Watch out for him, Ben. He's a dangerous man and he's likely as not to blame you for both parties not wanting him. Promise me you won't let him drag you into anything foolish," she added, remembering Costa's warning.

He reached out and stroked her hair. "I'm not afraid of Ramon de Diego. Besides, he published the first handbill that got this thing going. He has no one to blame but himself."

"I don't think he will see it that way. Are you sure you're all right?"

"I'm fine. And I'll be better once I get used to the idea. That reminds me, how would you like to take a little trip?"

She sat up. The sudden change in conversation was almost jarring. "A trip?"

"Yes. It might not be a bad thing to get away for a time. Help both of us to reorganize, so to speak. Micah Brown is going to put our petition for the land belonging to Fort Brooke before the Congress again but first he has to consult with the Legislature in Tallahassee and he's asked me to accompany him. It's rather a sop thrown to the loser but I'm not too proud to take it up. The thought of getting away from this village right now seems rather appealing. Besides, it will give me a chance to look up Clay Madrapore. It's been too long since we've seen him."

"Tallahassee," Lea said, smiling. "I've never been there. I'd like to go. But do you think Mister Brown will mind me trailing along?"

"I told him I'd only go with him if I could bring my wife. I'm certainly not going to leave you here to bear the sympathy of well meaning neighbors alone. You'll need to bring some nice gowns, and you should take along a maid."

Suddenly the room seemed brighter to Lea, the dead weight inside her chest eased a little. "I could take Emmy. She learns quickly and is very agreeable. And she'd probably love a trip as much as I would. When would we go? Do I have time for some sewing?"

"Next week. Do what you can before we leave and then perhaps you can do some shopping up there. And now, my dear, I think I would like to be alone for a while. Do you mind?"

Lea rose from the stool then bent over to kiss his cheek. "Of course not. I have to see to supper, anyway. Thank you, Ben, for thinking of me."

He squeezed her hand without answering. Walking to the door, Lea looked back, some of the delight she felt about the coming trip fading as she saw his dejected figure. He seemed to have slumped farther into the chair, his chin leaning on his chest. The glass in his hand glimmered in the afternoon light as he set it on the table beside him. When she saw him reach into his vest pocket and pull out his watch, she turned and fled the room.

CHAPTER 21

▼

Two weeks later, on a gray, overcast morning, Ben and Lea boarded the lighter that would take them out to the schooner, John T. Sprague, moored in the Bay and ready to set sail up the Gulf to St. Mark's. Emmy followed close on her mistress' heels. She was carrying a flowered hatbox and had a dark woolen shawl draped over her arm in case the wind proved cool. Her dour expression deepened as she followed Lea up the ladder to the deck. Lea noticed but didn't mention it until Ben left them in the cabin.

"I declare, child," she scolded as she fussed around the small room which was to be their home for the next two days. "Ever since I told you about this trip you've acted like a hen with an egg busted in her. I thought you'd be as excited as I am to go to Tallahassee."

Emmy carefully stowed the bandbox on a shelf with a bar along the front. "I don't much care for boats, ma'am."

"You should have said something. I could have brought Sukey. I remember so well how miserable my sister Rachel was on the trip to Fort Brooke years ago. The sea doesn't bother me at all. I love it."

She paused beside the small cabin window to glance out at the turquoise water. How long ago that was, and how young and naive she had been. Now Rachel was long dead, Buck seemed like her own son, and Ben, dearest Ben, was her husband of many years. She would never have thought it possible those long ago days when they sailed into Tampa Bay. Or *Espirito Sancto,* as the old ship's carpenter had called it.

Emmy's querulous voice broke into her thoughts. "Do you want me to unpack, ma'am?"

Lea glanced over at the girl's white, pinched face. She was really frightened of the water. How selfish that she hadn't noticed just because her own excitement was so great.

"No, we won't be at sea that long. Just leave everything and go up on deck. The fresh air should help you."

"Thank you, Ma'am," Emmy muttered and slipped from the room. Lea wasn't long in following her up the hatchway. She wanted to stand at the railing and see Fort Brooke fade into the distance just as she had stood watching it draw near so long ago. The breeze was fair and the clouds lifting. It was going to be a fine, fine day after all.

There had never been a question of going to Tallahassee overland with the roads so undeveloped and the threat of Indian attack still possible. Lea was glad, for she had warm memories of the sail from New York and looked forward to another pleasant trip on the Gulf.

She wasn't disappointed. The ship was seldom far from land and the seas were smooth and gentle. There was only one brief spell of threatening weather but that soon blew over. By the time they arrived at St. Mark's she was sorry to leave the boat, and even Emmy's cheeks seemed more rosy and fair than when they left Tampa.

A horrendous train carried them to Tallahassee. Pulled along by mules on tracks that seemed more like one of the old corduroy roads in New York, Lea was so bounced around she feared she might at last succumb to the sea-sickness she had avoided on the ship. A pleasant, round faced conductor assured her that soon there would be a 'real up-to-date train' to replace this primitive conveyance and Lea was glad to hear it. Still, by the time they came pulling into the station at Tallahassee she had regained her buoyant excitement at visiting a new town. She stood on the little platform waiting for Ben to commandeer a horse and buggy, trying to take in everything at once. She was struck right away by how beautiful the countryside was. Flowers seemed to be everywhere, growing in colorful profusion. There were real hills, rolling and green, and lush trees dangling spanish moss. That raw, tropical wildness so common farther south seemed tamed here. This was a countryside reminiscent of the lovely Hudson valley, the first echo of her old home she had experienced since leaving it.

Some of that memory faded as they rolled along the wide street leading to the City Hotel. Crowds of people strolled along the boardwalks and lounged on the wide porches of houses and hotels. Vehicles jammed the roadway, creating a fearsome cloud of dust—four-wheeled pleasure carriages, loaded wagons, black leather buggies, sulkies, shays and ox carts, with single horse and riders jostling among them. Small flocks of bleating sheep pushed through, making their way toward the market to the accompaniment of stray dogs, loose chickens and rooting hogs. Many of the men wore dignified frock coats and tall hats, others spats and checkered trousers. A few women were scattered among the crowd, some in country poke bonnets, others in fashionable feathers and wide, swirling ruffled skirts. It seemed Tallahassee was as much of a magnet for questionable denizens as Tampa had always been.

Because the Assembly was in session their hotel was jammed, yet somehow Ben managed to get them a decent bedroom with a small adjoining sitting area. Emmy at once set about unpacking her valise but Lea, seeing the girl's thin, gray face, took pity on her and made her lie down on the cot in the dressing room instead.

"There's plenty of time for that," she assured her. "Right now I'm more interested in going outside and seeing the town. The Captain will be back in an hour, so you rest until then. I'm told a proper lady in this town always has her maid along when she strolls the streets. So, you see, I can't go out without you."

The grateful servant did as she was told while Lea changed her traveling dress and spruced up her hair. She had noticed a millenary shop not far from the hotel and she intended to stop in this very afternoon and examine some of the delicious looking hats in the window.

The smoke filled taproom of the City Hotel was almost as popular a meeting place for the gentlemen of the Assembly as the new Capital building, just across the street. It didn't take long for Ben to discover that his time in Tallahassee would be about equally divided between the two, perhaps more than equally since Micah Brown, before leaving for Washington City, found the tavern just as convenient for conducting business as the Capital.

But Ben didn't mind. Though in a perpetual fog from the prevalent seegars smoked there, the taproom was a warm, congenial place with polished wood, small, discrete tables, a liberal sprinkling of brass spittoons, and sawdust on the floor. And the whiskey served was the best Kentucky bourbon. He enjoyed watching the stream of important men who wandered in and out. He had met most of them before during his long years in Florida territory, but only briefly. Now he found the opportunity to discuss and argue at leisure very stimulating. There were renowned gentry everywhere you turned—Richard Call, David Yulee, Thomas Brown, who, it was rumored, was certain to be the new Whig candidate for governor, and wealthy planters, the Gambles and the Bradens whose sons were building huge sugar plantations on the Manatee River. Every day some new luminary showed up. It made him realize for the first time how limited his vision had become by living in the outlying territory of a very young state.

While Ben smoked and argued in the taproom, Lea ventured out into the town. In the late hours of the morning she would tether her carriage at the Washington Square market and begin visiting the shops. The fashions intrigued her. They were so new, so feminine, so pretty that she gave in to purchases much more often than she should have. Broad skirts, cascading ruffles, layers of ribbons and laces, shimmering satins and delicate ribbed calicos—she was enthralled by the beauty of them all. There was something new to spark her interest every day—a ruffled parasol in the deepest lilac, delicately crocheted silk mitts, a paisley shawl, big as a tablecloth and with a long silken fringe, a cameo from Italy with the divine profile of a goddess—before she knew it she had gone far over her self-imposed budget. But it was so much fun she couldn't resist. She consoled herself with the thought that it didn't seem to bother Ben in the least. And when he informed her that the next day they were invited to an afternoon tea, and the following evening to a dinner at the home of Archibald Clarey, one of the wealthiest men in Tallahassee, she felt all her expenditures were justified.

There was a bonnet she had been admiring for two days which she now convinced herself would be just the thing to wear to the tea at the Capital. Dragging Emmy, who had still not completely recovered from the sail up the Gulf, she took herself off to try it on.

It was the latest thing—pink uncut velvet trimmed with a silk fringe and a band of braided velvet in the same color. Its fashionable brim framed the face and hair, rather than poking out far over them in the manner of the older styles. Cascades of satin pink flowers adorned the velvet band and trails of darker rose ribbons tied in a bow under the chin.

Lea allowed the milliner to put it on her head and tie the ribbons. Delighted with the result, she preened in the mirror, turning this way and that.

"Oh, it's lovely," she sighed. "Really lovely."

A man's face appeared beside her in the mirror. "Not as lovely as the face it frames."

Lea gave a startled cry and turned to look up into Clay Madrapore's smiling face. "Clay! As I live and breathe! So you *are* here in Tallahassee. We were hoping to see you."

Clay raised her fingers to his lips with a courtly bow. "This is an unexpected delight for me. I saw you through the window and could hardly believe my eyes."

"I'm here with Ben. He came north with Micah Brown who has business with the Assembly. I'm so glad to see you, it's been ages since you were down our way."

"Ben's here too? We'll have to have a drink together. Don't tell me he's finally got into politics."

Lea frowned. "Well, that's another story, I'm afraid. I'll tell you all about it. But first, what do you think of my new hat?" She turned back to the mirror. "Is it the right thing for a tea at the capital?"

Clay pretended to examine the question even though they both knew he approved. "Well, it might have a little more vivid color but, yes, I think it will have all the ladies green with envy and all the men rushing to pay you their favors."

"Oh pooh," Lea laughed. "It's not that grand. But it is pretty and it will go nicely with my new gray satin dress. I'll take it," she said, pulling the ribbons free and handing it to the milliner. "Put it in the bandbox and give it to my maid. She can carry it back in the carriage." Rising from her chair she slipped her arm through Clay's. "I'm going to walk back to the hotel with this handsome gentleman."

The bonnet disappeared into reams of tissue inside the flowered box while Emmy waited near the counter. "Are you sure you don't want me to go with you, Miz Carson," she murmured.

Lea waved to her as she left the shop on Clay's arm. "No, you ride back. You're still not feeling well and it's perfectly respectable for Clay to escort me."

Once outside on the crowded walk, she leaned close to his shoulder and said in a low voice, "See how concerned I've become about the proprieties. I won't even venture out on to the streets without a proper maid or a gentleman escort. Why if these people rushing by could have seen me a few years ago running through the woods in my shift with the Indians breathing down my neck, they'd be horrified."

Clay laughed. "It wouldn't surprise me if half the people in this town hadn't gone running through the woods with savages howling behind them at one time or another. Tallahassee might seem like a big city compared to Tampa, my dear, but it's still very much a frontier town. But what is this about Ben that you wouldn't speak of in the shop?"

The buoyant delight on Lea's face dimmed as she moved to step around a Negro boy sitting on a wooden crate against the wall of a tobacco shop. Beside him was a box filled with assorted brushes, rags and jars of shoe-polish. Lea pulled in her wide skirt and answered in a lowered voice: "Ben nearly won the nomination for member of the Assembly from Hillsborough. He wanted it very much and thought it was his, but at the last minute the commissioners decided to run someone else. They thought enough of him to offer him this trip with Mister Brown, but it didn't help his disappointment much."

"Ben would have made a very good candidate. Whatever led them to drop him?"

"I'd better let him tell you about that. Suffice it to say, Ramon de Diego wanted the same nomination and between them, they cancelled each other out."

They paused at the corner, waiting for the traffic to thin so they could cross. Between the carriages, wagons, men on horseback and assorted drays that jammed the road and raised the dust, it was going to take quite a few minutes. "All right," Clay said. knowing there was a lot more to Ben's losing the nomination than her brief explanation. "I won't press you on the subject. Ben can explain it all when I see him." He grabbed her arm, pulling her back from a wagon that leaned into the walkway. "I'm too pleased to see you, Lea, to talk about anything unpleasant."

He smiled down at her. "Do you know how pretty you look in that green gown and fetching little bonnet? I can barely remember the last time I saw you all gussied up. Those drab country dresses you lived in on the farm may have been practical but they did nothing for you. Now you look like a picture in a fancy ladies book."

Lea felt her cheeks burning even though his compliment gave her great pleasure. "Now don't look at me that way," she said, ducking her head. "I know I look freakish in all this get-up."

"On the contrary. It's very becoming. I don't think I've ever seen you look nicer."

She blushed again and gave him a beaming smile. "Thank you, Clay. But you know, I could say the same about you. I believe this must be the first time I've ever seen you without your fringed buckskins."

And indeed, she had almost not recognized him in the hat shop because of his civilian clothes. They sat rather awkwardly on him, yet the effect was pleasing. He was dressed to the nines in a flowered vest, biscuit-colored trousers, a long brown frock coat, and a floppy silk neckcloth tied in a large bow at the collar. His long hair was pulled back and tied in an old-fashioned queue which disappeared beneath the high collar of his coat. The coat was wrinkled but nicely tailored and clean.

"I feel like a fish out of water," Clay said with a snicker. "You can't take the woods out of a man by dressing him up. But as I needed to make a good impression on a few grasping bankers, I had to try."

Seeing a break in the traffic, he grabbed her hand and pulled her across the street. They scurried around several vehicles and horses to reach the other side where they took up their leisurely pace again, Lea's arm in his.

"I think you look very handsome," she said lightly. "Civilization becomes you."

Clay laughed. "Well, now that we've got the requisite compliments out of the way we can move on to more important matters. Such as, how about joining me for a little lunch at the hotel. I'm presuming you're staying at Browns."

"Isn't that what they used to call the City Hotel? If it is, yes we are. And I'd love to have lunch. I want to hear all about what you've been doing since we saw you last. But I warn you, you'll not get many words in edgewise. I've been dying to tell someone all about the interesting things we've planned to do on this trip and you're elected."

"That's all right," Clay said, guiding her on to the porch of the hotel. "We'll take turns fighting for the right to talk."

And talk they did. They were still chatting over coffee when Ben walked in the dining room and joined them. The conversation did not end until time to go up and dress for the afternoon tea at the Capital.

Though Clay wasn't at the tea, Lea was pleased to learn he would be one of those invited to supper at the Clarey mansion the following evening. As she and Ben took the carriage from the hotel, Ben explained that this was a posh dinner for a select group of people from both the Democrat and the Whig camp, hosted by one of the wealthiest planters in the area who liked to ingratiate himself with all sides just in case it might prove valuable later. A road lined with arching oak trees led to the house with its front of white columns across a long porch. Once inside, Lea had to force herself not to gape. The graceful entrance with its curving stairway, the luxurious paneled drawing room, the long dining room ablaze with candle and lamplight that set silver and crystal sparkling like diamonds—it was like entering a fairyland. An elegant dinner was served to a group of twenty people, most of whom she had never met before. The ladies were distant but polite and the men gracious. As she had expected, Ben moved easily in such circles but she had to watch him closely to make sure she did not commit some social faux-paux. The evening was nearly half over before she began to really relax.

But it was Clay who surprised her the most. There was still something a little unsettling about seeing those elegant evening clothes on his large frame, though this time they were carefully pressed and very stylish. Beyond that, however, he seemed perfectly at home, joining in the general conversation both at the silver laden dining table and in the more formal drawing room. To her astonishment, he spoke as knowledgeably about Thackery's latest novel, *Vanity Fair,* and the early death of the composer, Mendelssohn, as he did about the end of the Mexican war and the likelihood of Zachery Taylor becoming the next President. Lea had known for years how reluctant he was to talk about himself and his background, but now she found herself wondering about him in a way she never had before. Where on earth had he come from? Over the years from time to time she had asked him about his former life but he had always been reluctant to talk about himself. She decided to try again, and later, when the men re-entered the withdrawing room after their cigars and port, she was grateful he joined her in a quiet corner a little apart from the others. The talk at the supper table had included a long discussion about expanding slavery to the new territories, something which Ben and Clay were the only two people against. Lea raised the subject again and to her surprise, Clay, for once, began explaining why he was so opposed to it.

"My father was a successful Virginia planter," he said, leaning back in his chair and crossing his long legs out before him. "And, of course, he expected me to follow in his footsteps. But as I grew up my antipathy to the abomination of slavery created a very high wall between us. My father believed in it with his whole heart and soul. He was convinced, you see, that he could not run a successful plantation without it. And he wasn't a bad owner. For the most part he treated his Negroes fairly and responsibly.

"But even at that, I saw enough bad owners and witnessed enough heartbreaking sights to come to hate the whole rotten system. With feelings on both sides running so high, well, you can imagine…"

He looked away, studying the heavy brocade drapes on the window near his chair. "You couldn't work it out?" Lea asked quietly.

"I was always the restless sort anyway, so one day I simply walked away—or he threw me out, difficult to say just which. I've never gone back and, as far as I know, he's never tried to find me."

Lea sat stunned, unsure how to reply. There was a quiet, half-smile on Clay's lips but no humor in his eyes at all. She sensed a poignancy beneath the surface of his studied complacency, or perhaps a nostalgic regret. "I'm sorry," she murmured.

"Oh, it was probably for the best," he said, shuffling off any vestige of his private feelings. "Enough about me. Tell me more about what you've got planned for the rest of your visit."

That night she pressed Ben for more information but he was non-committal. "I know he comes from an aristocratic Virginia family, Lea, but I can't tell you anything more because I don't know. Clay doesn't talk about himself."

"But didn't you ever ask? Surely he must have mentioned something. He's so well educated and has such impeccable manners for a woodsman scout. I've always thought the world of him but I never wondered about his background so much until I saw him at ease among all those wealthy people."

"Did you ask him? No, because it isn't polite to press a man about his background when he doesn't want to speak of it. Especially in a territory like Florida where many a man comes seeking anonymity. I'm not even sure 'Madrapore' is his real name. It sounds like a type of coral, you know, and he may have taken it on purpose to make a break from his old life."

Lea took a deep breath, glad to be free of the confining corset in which she had spent the evening. She was already in bed, settled back with her long hair spilling on the pillow as she watched Ben undressing. He caught her reflection in the mirror and came over to sit beside her on the bed.

"Forget about Clay. Did you enjoy tonight?" he asked, taking her hand.

"Oh yes, it was a revelation. I never knew people could live so grandly. Those rooms were like a king's palace. The grand furnishings, the wonderful food, all those servants just standing there waiting to hand you anything you want."

"Mister Clarey owns two plantations and nearly four hundred slaves."

Lea's eyes widened. "Four hundred! What does he do with them all?"

"Most of them work the fields in his very profitable cotton plantations. He's dead set against any talk of abolition, as you might guess." Ben frowned, stroking her hand absently. "Most of the men I've met up here are dead set against abolition, Lea. And it is a subject more on their minds than any other. They are almost obsessed with it."

Lea shrugged. "It's been an obsession in the Southern States for the last ten years, hasn't it? And there's never a solution."

"I never liked slavery and now I hate it even more. Those horrible markets where men and women are bought and sold like cattle, and treated even worse. I've seen more sympathy given to mules than to some of the poor creatures who go through those places. Sometimes I wonder if the South won't bring retribution down on itself someday for its support of slavery."

Lea took his hand, entwining her fingers in his. "You've done everything you can, Ben. You wouldn't own slaves at all until you were forced to. And look what you've done for Ulee. One man can only do so much."

"Perhaps if I had been given a chance to help make the laws I could have done more." He slid his palm up her arm to her chin and drew her face to his, kissing her lightly. "You've enjoyed this trip?"

"So much. In fact, I've had such a good time that I'm almost afraid to speak of it for fear something awful will happen."

"Don't worry about that," Ben said, rising and pulling at the buttons on his shirt. "The worst happened before we took this trip."

They were to leave two days later. Lea decided to spend her last hours in Tallahassee buying up everything she might need which could not be found in Tampa Village. Emmy was still not feeling well, so she decided to finally brave convention and go alone. She dressed early and set off downstairs filled with the happy anticipation of the born shopper.

In the lobby of the hotel she ran into Mrs. Brown who for ten long, boring minutes regaled her with the details of her coming trip to Washington. Once Lea finally extricated herself she stepped onto the porch of the hotel and frowned as she saw a bank of dark clouds over the trees of the square.

"I'd better bring my parasol," she mumbled and hurried back up the stairs to her room. Stepping inside, she had grabbed up the umbrella and started back to the hall when she was struck by strange noises coming from behind the closed door of the bedroom. Lea stood quietly, listening to the unmistakable sounds of retching and coughing, followed by long, wailing sobs. Distressed, she threw aside her gloves, bag, and parasol and opened the door to the bedroom. The sobbing was loud now and it was coming from behind the dressing room door. Quietly Lea turned the latch and stepped inside.

Emmy lay stretched out on the cot, her head buried in her arms. On the floor beside her a porcelain chamber pot gave off the noxious odors of recent vomit. Stifling the urge to cover her mouth, Lea pushed the pot beneath the bed and knelt beside the girl. Emmy looked up at her, her face swollen, her eyes red rimmed. Lea recognized fear, not fever, in their dark depths.

"Emmy, child, what on earth is wrong?"

"It's nothing, nothing. Just the ague. I can't shake it off."

"I don't think so," Lea said quietly, wishing she could believe her. As she laid her hand on the girl's cool forehead there was a sinking sensation in the pit of her stomach, an intuition she could not explain of trouble to come. "Sickness would not cause this kind of distress."

"Yes it would. I hate to be sick. I've always hated it."

"Look at me," Lea said, gently turning the girl's stark white face toward her. "This is not like you. Something is very wrong, I know. Can't you tell me what it is?"

Emmy's lips folded inward into a stubborn line. She jerked her head away from Lea's fingers and stared down at the bed covers.

"Have you been sick like this often?" Lea asked.

"Nearly every day," the girl mumbled in reply.

Lea began to feel sick herself. "Is this what has kept you cooped up here in your room? Does it go on all day?"

Emmy turned a defiant, fierce gaze on her. "No, usually just in the mornings."

"Oh, no." It was more a sigh than a comment. Lea pulled herself up. "We have to talk, you and I, but not here. Come out into the bedroom."

For a moment she thought Emmy would refuse to obey. Then reluctantly the girl dragged herself off the cot and followed Lea into the next room. The buoyant, pleasant girl Lea had known was utterly vanished, replaced with a brooding, resentful young woman whose tear stained cheeks were as pale as the ecru background in the flowered wallpaper behind her. Lea closed the door and turned to face her.

"You are with child, aren't you?"

"Yes, maam. I wanted to tell you but I didn't know how. I was afraid of what you would do."

Lea's mind became a jumble of terrible thoughts all tangled up with each other. She eased herself to the nearest chair and sat down. "And the father?"

"What about him?"

"I want his name. I think you owe me that much."

Emmy gave a sharp laugh, more characteristic of a hardened woman than the child Lea had thought her. "It's not the Captain, if that's what you're thinking."

Something deep in Lea relaxed. Though she had feared to hear Ben's name, at the same time something in her could not believe it of him. It was not unusual for masters to seduce their servants, especially when those girls were as young and attractive as Emmy. But Ben had too much integrity for that, she felt sure.

"Then who?"

The stubborn lines around Emmy's mouth grew more rigid. "I can't tell you."

"But child, don't you see. If there is a chance he would marry you…"

"He will never marry me. We're too far apart, too different. I don't even want him to marry me."

"I can't believe that. You realize you'll be an outcast. Captain Carson can hardly allow you to stay on with us in this condition and no other family will take you on. The best thing for everyone, including your baby, would be to give the…the child a name."

"The bastard? Is that what you meant to say?"

"Please, Emmy, you may not believe it but I'm trying to help you."

Emmy's face softened as a sense of Lea's genuine concern got through her defenses. Yet something hardened within her at the same time. "You've been good to me, Miz Carson, I'll give you that. When that snobby Diego woman dumped me on your doorstep you took me in, taught me how to be a lady's maid and gave me a home. I won't deny I'm grateful. But now I'm in trouble, you'll want to throw me out. Like all smug, respectable people, you won't want to have me around. I know all the names. I'm a 'fallen woman', a 'soiled dove'…"

"I never said any of those things."

"You don't have to. It's in your face, your posture, your voice. Well, don't worry about me. I want to see something of the world before I die and I figure this is as good a time to strike out as any. If you'll just ask Captain Carson to give me the wages he owes me, I won't bother you ever again."

"Emmy, don't talk nonsense. You can't go traipsing off on your own when you're expecting a child. You need care, and so will your baby when it comes. We may not be able to keep you on as a servant but we certainly won't throw you to the wolves."

"I don't want your charity!" The pure hostility in Emmy's voice sent Lea's hand to her throat. Some reservoir of anger had transformed the girl into someone Lea had never known existed. It took her a moment to realize how much hurt was beneath all that anger.

"I don't want your charity," Emmy repeated more quietly. "Just give me my wages and let me go. I've had enough from your family, all of you. It will be better if I never see you or your son again."

Lea caught her breath as Emmy's pale face blanched even more white. "I mean, the Captain. It would be better if I never see you or the Captain again. That's what I meant."

A dawning realization sent Lea's stomach turning over. "Emmy! Is Buck the father of this baby? My Buck?"

Emmy turned her back, mumbling, "No, no, that's not true. It was…one of the fishermen at Spanishtown Creek. Yes, it was one of them." But the tears that began to flow made her words sound hollow. Lea gripped the arms of her chair and held on for dear life. One of the Spanishtown fishermen was too absurd to believe. Besides, since Emmy came to live with them she had almost never spent time away from the house. But Buck?

"But when? There was no time."

But there was, of course. All those weeks around Christmas when Buck lingered in Tampa far longer than expected, far beyond time for him to head back to the ranch. All the nights he came home late, long after she and Ben had gone to bed. The gentle, teasing politeness he showed the girl as she served him at table, the pleasant smiles, the little spontaneous gifts of flowers or ribbons—now they all made sense. Everything fell into place, and in her stupid, gullible way she had never suspected a thing.

Anger welled in her heart. She wanted to rail at the girl for seducing a young, impressionable boy, for ruining his life as well as her own. Yet she caught back the hard words because she knew they were not fair. Buck had a mind of his own and he might well have been the one who did the seducing. "How did it happen?" she managed to murmur.

It took Emmy so long to reply Lea began to wonder if she was going to admit it. "I didn't mean for it to happen," she finally said very softly. "But he would come home late at night, terrible corned…hung over, and I guess I just got in the habit of soothing the ache. He was gentle and kind to me and he treated me…like a person, not like a servant. I guess I fell in love with him right from the first."

"And Buck? Did he fall in love as well?"

"He never said so. I don't think he really thought much about it. He was happy with me and that was enough."

Oh yes. That would be enough with Buck. He was never one to worry about consequences. Lea looked up at the girl's taut back. With sudden insight she realized that she was keeping Emmy standing—a servant being reprimanded by her mistress. Yet she was too sick at heart to tell her to sit.

Emmy turned suddenly. "Look, Miz Carson, I didn't want you to know about Buck but there it is. It doesn't change nothin'. If you'll just get me my wages I'll go away and you can be done with all this."

"You foolish girl! It changes everything. We're not just talking about an illegitimate baby, we're talking about a grandchild. Buck will have to marry you."

"No!" Emmy took an involuntary step backward. "No! He'd hate me for it, and the baby too. Besides, I know how much the Captain wants him to marry well. He's never going to let his only son throw himself away on a servant girl like me."

That was true. It was going to be very hard for Ben to give up his dreams of a good marriage for Buck, much less accept this girl of questionable morals as the mother of his grandchild. But what else could they do? It was the only honorable thing. There was no other way.

"I'll talk to the Captain today, while we're having lunch. Somehow I'll make him see reason. In the meantime, I think you'd better continue to stay in your room until we leave to return home. We can say you're still not well."

"And my wages?"

"You'll have them at the regular time as usual. Perhaps I should have a doctor look in on you, just to be sure everything is all right."

Emmy gave a grim smile. Now that the dreadful bastard child was known to be a grandchild, of course have the doctor look in.

"No, thank you, ma'am. I don't need no doctor. I remember my mother having babies. This sickness is normal."

Lea forced herself to her feet and walked over to lay a hand on the girl's shoulder. "I'm going down stairs now, Emmy. I need to do some thinking before I approach the Captain. You rest, and we'll talk again later."

Emmy looked up at her, her large eyes dark with a mixture of emotions. "Yes, ma'am," she answered docilely.

Lea walked into the hall, closed the door and leaned against it, breathing hard. And they thought the worst had already happened!

"No! I won't hear of it!"

Lea cringed as Ben slammed his rolled newspaper down beside his plate. The china wobbled noisily while several of the startled diners at nearby tables turned to look quizzically at him.

"Ben, please," she whispered, glancing around. "Not so loud."

"If you didn't want me to make a scene then you should not have sprung this news on me in a public place."

She did not answer that she had chosen this place on purpose, hoping his reaction might be a little tamed by the surroundings. If the price of a lesser tantrum was to be stared at, then so be it.

Ben lowered his voice, still choked and strained. "I won't hear of it. The girl's a trollop, a strumpet, just like her mother. She will be put away until she has her child and that will be the end of it. I'll pay for that much but if she thinks she'll get another penny out of me then she's sadly mistaken. We'll have nothing more to do with her."

"But Ben, it's your grandchild."

"I refuse to believe that. It's easy for her to accuse Buck. Who's to prove her story false?"

"He might."

"He will never know anything about this!" Ben's face hardened. "I won't see all my plans for his future thrown away on a tramp of a girl who abused our trust—your trust. We'll see she's cared for until she has this bastard child and that will be the end of it. That's all I'll say about the matter, Lea, and I'll thank you never to raise the subject in my hearing again."

Lea sat back in her chair, sick at heart. "But if this is Buck's child, how can we turn our backs on it? That seems very mean, Ben."

"No meaner than what she's done. I thought you were assured she had character."

"That's what Costa de Diego told me. 'A good girl' who just never had the right kind of chances."

"Ha! Costa de Diego. It wouldn't surprise me to know this was her plan all along. She and her devil of a husband would do anything to ruin me."

That thought had also crossed Lea's mind but she dismissed it as too far fetched. After all, Costa couldn't know that Buck would come home drunk, find solace with Emmy and stay in Tampa far longer than he planned. She could never have supposed such unlikely events. Yet certainly she had assured Lea that Emmy was a girl of high moral fiber when she obviously wasn't. Nor had she mentioned that Emmy's mother was little better than a prostitute.

Lea toyed with her fork. "The girl is very distraught."

"As well she might be."

"You know how society looks on unwed mothers. It's a hard fate."

"Then she ought not to have got herself into such a fix."

Shoving his plate aside he grabbed up his newspaper and rose to his feet. "There is nothing more to be said, Lea. Go upstairs and tell this girl she has to leave as soon as we find a place that will take her. I'll pay for her care until her child is born and then she's on her own. That's all there is to it."

"You haven't touched your lunch."

"I'm not hungry."

She watched him stalk out of the hotel dining room. No longer hungry herself, she followed him and stood numbly near the newel post while Ben took a chair in the lobby, opened his newspaper and began to read. Then she dragged herself up the burgundy carpeted staircase to face Emmy.

Ten minutes later she came running back down the stairs and yanked the newspaper out of his hands.

"You needn't worry about paying for Emmy's care," she said bitterly. "She's gone. Taken all her belongings and gone!"

CHAPTER 22

▼

Emmy had indeed gone, taking nothing with her but her few clothes, a book of poems she had carried with her from Tampa, and Lea's large gold and garnet ring. The theft of the ring was the hardest to bear for it made the girl a thief as well as a wanton. She left a brief note for Lea explaining that she was taking the ring in place of her wages and that once she got settled in a new home she would send her the money for it. It was an old ring that had been in the Hammond family for years but it was too large for Lea to wear comfortably and she was more disturbed by Emmy's taking it than she was over its loss.

"I was never very fond of it," Lea said to the Constable whom Ben had immediately called in. "And we did owe her nearly a month's wages. I don't want to bring any charges against her for the theft of the ring."

The Constable was a tall man with a protruding chest and a deep, bass voice. He rumbled his disapproval into the large walrus type moustaches adorning his broad face. "I think that is a mistake, Mrs. Carson. Thievery in any form must not go unpunished. Otherwise it only encourages the perpetrator to try again."

"All the same, I don't care about the ring. The girl is ill and with child. She's in no shape to be running about the country trying to live on her own. I would just like to know she's all right."

Ben gripped Lea's shoulder with a force that warned her to be silent. "My wife is upset, Constable, and not thinking too clearly. Sometimes she allows sentimentality to overrule her good judgement. I want both the girl and the ring back, so please do your duty and set about finding them."

"I've already put one of my men on it, sir. We should have both of them back by evening."

Yet the evening passed with no word from the Constable or from Emmy. Late the following morning the officer came to the hotel and asked to speak to Mr. and Mrs. Carson in their rooms. Lea stood in front of the window, her arms tightly crossed at her waist, afraid to hear what he had to say.

"I have both good news and bad," he began in his most officious voice. "Such little time had passed between the time Emmaline left the hotel and you called us in that we were able to get a good trace on her. She went straight to St. Mark's and there boarded a ship bound for New Orleans. We have no doubt that she paid for her passage with Mrs. Carson's garnet ring and once we are able to get in touch with the ship's master, I feel confident we will get it back."

New Orleans! While Ben questioned the Constable further, Lea turned to push aside the lace curtain and stare out the window at the traffic in the street below, her thoughts racing. Emmy must have planned this out before hand. How else would she know about the boat leaving for Louisiana last night? She had asked her for her wages and when she knew she wouldn't get them, she took the ring, a piece of jewelry Lea had often said felt too large for her. But New Orleans! They would never be able to trace her among the throngs of people in that vast city.

"My wife and I are leaving for Tampa in the morning," she heard Ben say. "If you find this ring in the Captain's possession, tell him I will pay him for the girl's passage if he will give it back to us."

"You are a generous man, Mister Carson."

"I just want to be done with all this."

In the weeks that followed it often seemed to Lea that nothing had gone right from the moment she heard Emmy sobbing in her room at the City Hotel. If only she hadn't gone back for her parasol that morning. If only she had ignored the curious sounds coming from the girl's room and gone on with her shopping. Emmy would still have left of course, and would have taken the garnet ring with her. But at least Lea would not be dogged by the constant thought that somewhere in New Orleans wandered a woman carrying a child who was part of her family, a woman who might be hungry, homeless, or sick. At least there would not be this underlying bitterness between her husband and herself, a bitterness that eroded the edges of the love she had always felt for him and the closeness they had often shared. And perhaps their affection for Buck would not now be tarnished with unspoken resentment, a resentment the boy could sense without having the faintest clue as to its cause.

The voyage back to Tampa was miserable. Bad weather added to the silence and distance that lay between Lea and her husband. Though she tried to see his side of things, she could not forgive him for being so callous and cruel as to cast out a girl in trouble. She had been so sure he would swallow his resentment and care for Emmy's child because it was Buck's. Well, she had been wrong, terribly wrong, and now she clearly saw a side of her husband which she had never faced before. He had always been stubborn when convinced he was right, and she had learned early how hard it was to shake that stubbornness. Look how he had clung to the idea of a cotton plantation against all the indications that it would never work. How for years he had made up his mind that Buck's character was destroying everything he wanted for him. How he had clung to the memory of Rachel as his great love long after she was dead. Perhaps it was his old army discipline, or maybe just something in his character. Whatever the cause, it was obvious to Lea that he was never going to see poor Emmy as the mother of his grandchild but simply as a girl gone deliberately wrong. When, the second morning out, she came across him sitting on the ship's deck with his watch in his hand, her bitterness boiled to the surface stronger than ever. She said nothing, merely turned on her heel and went below, but she could not erase the image from her mind.

Ben put her silence down to moodiness. It wasn't like Lea, of course, but then when had he ever understood women. She'd get over it in time. It was just one more thing to blame Emmeline Fresca for. That girl! Sometimes he felt if he could get his hands around her throat he'd strangle her with no compunction at all. Just when things seemed to be going so well, she had to come along and ruin everything. Nor could he forget that it was Costa de Diego who had put her in his house by prevailing on Lea's soft heart and good nature. The more he brooded on it, the more he was convinced that Ramon Diego was behind the move and had cleverly designed it to bring disaster upon him.

It was two months before Ben finally received word from the Tallahassee police that the Captain of the packet Emmy took to New Orleans had finally returned to St. Mark's and denied ever taking a ring from the girl. The Constable believed he was lying and had probably already sold it. Since there was nothing more to be done, Ben made a mental resolve to put an end to the entire episode. For the most part it worked. He refused to discuss it with Lea, other than to chide her for her sullenness and declare that the best approach was to forget it had ever happened. It was only when he was around Buck and found himself resenting the boy's cavalier ways more than ever that he realized he could not put it out of his mind as easily as he wanted.

To Lea it seemed that nothing went smoothly that spring and summer. The weather was especially hot and dry, while the town was consumed with an election that grew more bitter every day. The bad feeling between the Whigs and the Democrats was made even more divisive by the boom in real estate that followed the approval at last by Congress of a bill granting to the town the land on which it sat. Now the area beyond Whiting street was out of the hands of the army and up for grabs, and the rush to make a profit set many entrepreneurs in conflict with each other. Ben had thought to do well out of the opportunity offered by the release of government land but he soon found that competition was fierce. That competition was made more complicated when he heard rumors that Ramon de Diego and his friends were the ones who were frustrating his efforts. Though he preferred to ignore Diego for now, the simmering animosity between the two men added to the growing sense of unease in the Carson household.

Looking back, Lea wondered if their shabby treatment of Emmeline Fresca and her baby might not have brought some kind of punishment on her family. As the summer wore on Ben and his son could never be around each other without quarreling. At first Buck seemed confused by his father's constant irritation and demands but as the hot months went by, his quick temper led to ever more angry arguments. Many times Lea wanted to explain things to Buck but she held back, knowing that Ben was absolutely determined not to tell his son about Emmy and her baby. Lea began to hate to see Buck come into town, whatever the reason that brought him. Usually it was some business concerning the ranch and that quickly became the excuse for another confrontation.

Today they were at it again. She had been sitting beside the river enjoying the peacefulness of its flow, the gentle wind off its gray surface, the soft billow of sails on the fishing boats heading downstream toward the bay. She had almost dozed off when the angry voices from the house jarred her awake. Buck's voice, rising to ever higher levels of frustration, followed by Ben's low, furious answers, quickly stirred a familiar agitation in her own chest. She tried to block out the voices and waited, hoping Buck would storm from the house as he usually did.

What was it today? Some wild scheme to buy another splendid horse Buck had his eye on? A plan to purchase more of the surrounding acres to expand the ranch? Or, like last time, Buck's attempt to talk his father into driving their cattle to the markets in Jacksonville or Savannah instead of shipping them to Key West or Cuba?

It seemed to Lea that most of the time Buck's schemes were not so far fetched, that they often made good business sense. She even wondered sometimes if Ben did not react so negatively because the ideas came from his son, and not because of their credibility. She had never shared that thought with Ben since she knew he would deny it, but she felt pretty certain it had occurred to Buck too. It was the old story of fathers and sons trying to work together. How seldom it went smoothly.

The voices died down. With a sigh, Lea picked up her parasol and the Godey Ladies Book she had been reading and started back to the house.

Buck jammed his hat down on his head and stalked through the front door, making sure it slammed after him. He was so focused on his fury that he almost didn't see his aunt before careening into her. One look at her face and he knew she had been listening to the argument with his father.

"Off again?" she said, a little too jauntily.

"Yes. Don't look for me for supper."

He tried to push past her but she caught his arm. "Don't work off your anger at the grog shops, Buck. Getting drunk won't solve anything."

"Getting drunk is the only thing that makes me feel better. But don't worry. I won't inflict myself on the family until I've sobered up. And I'll head back to the ranch tomorrow so neither of you will have to put up with having me around."

"Oh, Buck, you know I don't feel that way. And neither does your father, if he would only realize it."

"Aunt Lea, you're always trying to be the peacemaker between us. Why don't you give up? I'm through trying to please him. It's a hopeless job. If he would only let me do some things my own way, I could make this ranch ten times more successful than it is. It's not my ideas he's against, it's me, pure and simple. If he had anyone else running things, he'd go along in a minute. He already pays more attention to Ulee's ideas than he does mine."

"But Buck, driving cattle to Savannah would take months. What would happen to the ranch while that was going on?"

"You turn it over to someone you trust to take care of things. Ulee could do it easily. And it doesn't have to be Savannah. Other cowmen are already driving their steers to Jacksonville and we're in a good way to be left behind. But does that matter to him? God no! He's against the whole thing just because I suggested it. He's never wanted to listen to me much but lately he's just grown impossible. I don't know what's the matter with him."

Lea pursed her lips. The words were on the tip of her tongue but she knew she could not say them. "He's your father, Buck. He does care for you."

Buck was too angry to let the love he felt for his aunt modify his wrath. He shook off her hand and stalked down the walk.

"He has a very strange way of showing it."

"Buck, please don't go…"

He walked on without answering, striding down Water Street, past Steele's decaying blockhouse, to turn up Lafayette, knowing Lea was watching him and not caring. This was one time too many. He had suffered for years under his father's heavy hand and now it was time he got out from under it. Time to try his own wings, to build something up from the bottom himself. Let Ben Carson find another servile foreman to run his ranch. He would go his own way without any help from his father at all. And he would be a success, too.

These comforting thoughts carried him all the way to Reid's Groggery. Though the streets were crowded and traffic heavy, Buck scarcely noticed. It was only as he pushed through the door to the familiar bar that his spirits lifted. He demanded a bottle of Monogahela whisky from Joe Morgan behind the bar, then took a chair at one of the nearby tables, poured himself a generous glass and gulped it down. The warm glow spread through his body, taking an edge off his anger.

Buck ran his tongue over his lips and looked around. The place was crowded for early afternoon and most of the men grouped around the card tables or standing at the bar were familiar to him. A few of them smiled and waved and Buck waved back, hoisting his bottle by the neck. That was a signal for some of the usual habitues of Reid's to join him in finishing it off, and he soon had Rick MacAlister, Jake Ellison and two others less familiar at the table with him. Rick and Jake, both crackers from Georgia, had worked at the ranch off and on when it suited them. Buck, who knew both their good humor and their indolence well, was nevertheless glad to share a bottle with friends. The other two men he recognized but could not remember their names.

He didn't pay much attention to the men near the back of the room who were deeply engrossed in a game of three-card Commerce or he would have recognized Ramon de Diego among them. Not that Buck was much bothered by the old rivalry between Ramon and his Papa. He had never liked Diego and made no secret of it, yet he had too many troubles of his own to get involved in an old feud that didn't involve him.

Ramon de Diego, on the other hand, had a habit of noticing everything going on around him, and he had not missed Buck's entrance. He was sitting with his back to the young man and he carefully stayed that way, not bothering to turn sideways and reveal himself. Buck's loud voice and forced good humor were enough to let him hear everything the foolish boy said anyway. He focused on the game, carefully weighing his chances and reading his opponents, all the while keeping one ear tuned to Buck's loud conversation.

The other men at the table were also focused on the game. The lawyer, Magbee, sat opposite Ramon, with Doc Roberts to his right and Lieutenant Slidel, a new arrival at Fort Brooke, opposite the doctor. Ramon had sized them up long before. Magbee was a decent enough lawyer but had a weakness for drink that made him easy to read. Doc Roberts always had one part of his mind reserved for a call to go assist some suffering soul in the village. Slidel seemed self-contained, his face a mask, but it hadn't taken Diego long to realize his skill did not match his blank expressions. It was not difficult for Ramon to tune one ear to Buck's noisy ramblings while scalping this bunch.

The bottle was almost consumed before that conversation moved beyond the idiotic bad jokes, loud laughter and inane comments of the men at Buck's table. Most of them were wastrel types who spent their days in the groggeries hatching get-rich-quick schemes that never quite came off. They knew Buck as someone who worked hard when he was out of town but became one of their own when he was back to visit.

"What brings you into Tampa, Buck?" Rick asked. His question carried through the room, causing Ramon to lean back in his chair and momentarily lose his focus on his cards.

"I bet I know," one of the other men spoke up before Buck could answer. "You came in to buy that wild bull old Conway is trying to sell. Ain't that right?"

"Buck Carson can't buy that old bull," Jake said. "Conway wants nearly one hundred and sixty dollar for that animal. Ain't no bull worth that much. And Ben Carson ain't the man to pay that kind of money for one, neither."

"You can say that again," Buck said bitterly. The whisky had taken some of the edge off his fury at his father, but now it came sweeping back. "That bull could be made of gold and shit silver ingots and still Ben Carson wouldn't buy it."

"Let you down, did he?"

"No more than I expected. Now, I wouldn't mind having that bull, and of course, I made the suggestion, but I knew he wasn't going to do it. And not because the animal isn't worth it."

"He ain't worth it. No animal's worth that much."

"Maybe so, but that wasn't the reason. It's because the suggestion came from me! I could tell dear old Papa that the sun will set tonight and he'd tell me it won't because I said so. That's how much confidence he has in my good sense."

"Now Buck, no son ever worked well with his Papa. It's the way of the world."

Buck exploded. "Don't tell me what it's like to work with a father. I could write a book on it. If just one time he ever said 'you've done a good job' I'd keel over from shock. He might say that to someone else of course, but never me. That's because he doesn't think I do a good job of anything. Never did."

Buck sat back, amazed to discover his words were beginning to slur a little. He'd have to have another drink to correct that. "Hey, Joe," he called waving the empty bottle at the barkeep. "Another Monongahela, if you please."

"You'd better go easy, don't you think, Mister Buck?"

"Nonsense. I'm sharing it with my friends, aren't I? Bring me another and put it on my Papa's bill." He looked around at the other men, laughing. "That'll go over well, won't it. Another thing for him to add to the list of my sins."

Reluctantly Joe Morgan walked over and sat a full bottle on the table. He wasn't worried about the money for Ben Carson always made good on his son's tab. But as it happened, he thought a lot of the Captain and he didn't like hearing his son running him down this way.

Buck filled all the glasses round the table then lifted his own. "To the beloved Captain. May he have long life and prosperity!"

Though Rick MacAlister recognized the sarcasm, he drained his glass then wiped his sleeve across his mouth. "You're hard on your Pa, Buck. He's a good person. And so's your Ma."

Buck leaned across the table into Rick's face. "My Ma was the only person Ben Carson ever really cared about. She still is. He never cared about me, that's for sure."

"Oh come on. He put you up in business, didn't he? That's more than my Pa ever done for me. Drank himself to death in the gutter, did my Pa, leaving me to make my own way from the time I were ten year."

But Buck had no interest in any life story but his own. "A business he keeps firmly under his thumb. I've poured my life's blood into it but do I ever get any credit for it? Never! Am I ever allowed to use my own judgement or run it the way I think it ought'a be run? Not on your life!" The injustice of it almost brought tears to Buck's eyes. He filled his glass again.

"Your Ma is a good woman," Jake said. "Last winter when I was down on my luck and my kids were goin' without their supper, she brought a big basket of food to the house, not once but three time. And blankets and sweaters, too. Helped us get through a hard time, Miz Carson did."

"That's right," Rick added. "Everyone in town knows the good things Miz Carson's done. It's no wonder your Pa cares for her. But that don't mean he don't care for you too."

Buck struggled to clear the fog in his head. "You mean Aunt Lea. Oh sure, Aunt Lea is a jewel. You don't have to tell me that. But she's not my Ma. My Ma was her sister, Rachel. She died of the camp fever back in '35, along with my little brother. Now Rachel, she was the only woman my Pa ever really loved. Still does."

You don't mean after all this time Ben Carson don't appreciate his wife? 1835 was thirteen year ago."

"I do mean it. Oh sure, he gives lip service to me and Aunt Lea. But we both know where his heart really lies—down in that hole in the ground with Rachel. He never got over my Ma's death, and to this day…"

Buck turned as he felt a hand on his shoulder. "I think you've said enough about your Pa," Joe Morgan commented dryly. "Come on inside the kitchen and have some supper. You need a little ballast to go with all that liquid."

"I'm not hungry," Buck answered sullenly.

"You sure about that?"

"Well…maybe a little." In truth his eyes were growing a little blurred, and he remembered he had eaten nothing since that morning. The huge anger that had obsessed him was slipping into self-pity. Why not go ahead and have supper. The kitchen Joe kept to serve food to his customers was known for pretty good fare. Maybe afterward some of the women who frequented the taverns would wander in.

"Okay, Joe Morgan. I'll eat some of your supper. But I'm taking my old Monongahela with me."

He got to his feet and started toward the kitchen door, stiff legged to control the wobbling in his knees, paying no attention at all to the men at the round table near the back of the room, still absorbed in their card game.

Ben was relieved the next morning to learn that Buck had already left for the ranch without seeing anyone. He could not get rid of a nagging guilt about the quarrels that so frequently erupted between them, yet he could not be around his son without wanting to shake him till his teeth rattled. His sense of shame and disappointment over that disgraceful episode with the Fresca girl was just about the last straw. He knew very well where his impatience and anger came from, but he refused to face his son with the real reason. Knowing Buck, he'd probably go off half cocked to look for the girl and her bastard child, and that would really put an end to their relationship.

Once Buck was gone, Ben found it was easier to forget his son's problems and concentrate on the only thing that gave him real pleasure these days—business and politics in the growing village of Tampa.

CHAPTER 23

▼

And growing it was, even though the entire civilian population only numbered a little over one hundred. Streets plotted through the wilderness beyond Madison already had lots for sale along with plans for houses. New roads to the east and north were being blazed. A few homes had been established across the river in the old 'Tampa City', and a settler named Joseph Robles had an isolated homestead on a small lake a mile north of the village. The increasing numbers of settlers who rolled their wagons into town to buy supplies attested to the growing number of farms in the interior. More ships arrived stuffed to the gunwales with supplies to stock the warehouse near the wharf and the shelves of the Kennedy and Ferris store. The Palmer House Hotel on the river was often full, though not everyone who stopped there was considered desirable as a new citizen. The village, being adjacent to a thriving military garrison, had always attracted an unusual number of drifters, gamblers and unsavory women and even though the war with Mexico had shrunk the fort's viability and the number of its soldiers, its attraction for ne'er-do-wells remained high.

But the new County Councilmen who had been appointed after statehood became a reality were working diligently to make certain Tampa was a village on its way to becoming a town, and maybe someday, even a city. Once the United States Congress had ratified Micajah Brown's petition and the President signed it into law, building on the now legal land to the north and east began in earnest. Big profits were waiting to be made and Ben was determined to get his share of them.

Yet it was with a growing unease that Lea watched a muggy August give way to an even muggier September. Things were just not going well for her husband.

Rather than enjoying the new opportunities opening up in the village, he seemed more moody and depressed than before Buck had left. When she tried to ask him what was wrong he only replied in curt sentences that such and such a deal had not gone as expected, or that someone had got there before him. Even his friendship with the Council could not prevent many of his entrepreneurial activities from being stopped in their tracks. Lea had also heard the rumors that the person behind those obstructions was Ramon de Diego. The reason given was that he was even more bitter and resentful than Ben over losing last year's nomination for the Assembly.

What Lea sensed, Ben knew for certain. When Diego purchased a third lot on Franklin street right out from under Ben's fair bid, his irritation nearly drove him to confront the man. Yet again he held back, knowing that in the long run Ramon's hatred could not completely prevent him from expanding his interests in the village. There was too much land and there were too many opportunities. It was better to ignore him and look somewhere else for new lots.

Then his friend, Judge Turman, told Ben in strict confidence that the Council had decided to appoint him a Road Supervisor. Ben was delighted. The duties of a road supervisor were not onerous—they mostly consisted of seeing that roads were kept in passable condition—but it meant that finally he had a position in the political structure of the village. Surely this small beginning would lead to bigger and better appointments.

Ben knew the Council would not make their choice public until the next meeting because they were fully aware of the rivalry between himself and Diego and wanted to avoid any unpleasantness that might arise. Once the appointment was made, Diego could not do anything about it and Ben took some delight in knowing this was one accolade the cheeky bastard could not ruin.

A week before the Council meeting Ben, followed by Ulee, who was in the village to buy supplies for the ranch, accompanied Benjamin Moody from the new court house to one of the better class saloons fronting the wharf for a late afternoon drink. Leaving Ulee on the porch, Ben and Moody entered the building through the open doors. A ship had arrived that morning and the place was crowded, smoky and smelling of tobacco and beer. Ben did not recognize many of the faces of the men lounging over the bar or playing billiards at the tables, but that was not unusual. Though the denizens of the village knew each other well, their numbers were continually being swelled with new arrivals. A few of these wanderers set down roots but most moved on, either to another ship or into the interior. Most of the time the established citizens tended to ignore them.

When an acquaintance motioned from a back room for him to join a card game going on at the monte-table, Ben took out his watch and decided he had enough leisure time before going home for supper to gamble a few hands. Without being conscious of it, his gaze lingered on the lovely portrait of his first wife, her sweet face, delicate, rounded lips, the soft tendrils of yellow hair that set off her white brow. The familiar pang made him snap the lid shut and return the watch to his fob pocket, wondering how it was that after all these years Rachel's memory could still bring such a sharp stab of grief?

He pushed the thought away and pulled up a chair at the big round table. These were men he knew well, and he joined in the game with enthusiasm. He won the first two hands and enjoyed them so much he stayed in far longer than he had intended to. As his winnings piled up he decided his luck was really beginning to change. Then he heard a too familiar voice behind him.

"I trust there is room for another player, gentlemen?"

Ben did not have to look up to know Ramon de Diego was standing behind him. Immediately he began drawing the coins toward him to leave. Then William Ashley jumped up. "I was just going, Diego. Seems I can't do anything but lose this afternoon. You can have my place. Maybe it'll bring you better luck."

"Very kind, Mister Ashley," Ramon said, smiling as his slipped smoothly into the vacant chair.

Ben drew in the coins. "I'll be going too, gentlemen. Thanks for a good game."

A chorus of protests rose around the table. "You can't go yet with you winning!" "Give us a chance to get our money back." "It's not sportin', sir."

Ben hesitated, knowing full well the rules of a good game meant you play long enough to let the losers win back some of their money. Sitting at the same table with a smug, smirking Diego was utterly repugnant to him, yet why should he let this man's oily presence drive him away. He pushed the coins back. "All right. One more hand, then."

The game continued. Ramon was sitting close enough to mutter quietly as he focused on his cards. "Well, Captain. It seems congratulations are in order."

Ben glared at him without replying. "Two," he said to the dealer, laying his discards on the table.

"As Road Commissioner you will be in position to make a pretty penny on the side."

"I wouldn't know. Though I'm sure you do." He was pleased to see a slight flush darken Ramon's tanned skin.

Diego studied his cards. "Someone should enlighten the Council as to the character of the man they are considering for such an honor."

"Why not just send them one of the scurrilous handbills you used in the election. Except that of course they'd recognize it for the pack of lies it is."

The other men at the table, sensing the undercurrent of hostility that was beginning to eclipse the game, began to be uncomfortable. "Come, sir," one of them said. "We're here to play and gamble and win money. Other matters should be put aside for the moment."

Ramon smiled silkily. "Why, that's what I'm trying to do, sir. Though the Captain here takes every opportunity to insult me."

This was not working and Ben knew it was time for him to go. He laid his cards on the table. "Gentlemen, I must get home to my wife. I don't want my winnings. Spread them out among you if you wish. I'm out."

Ignoring the protests he rose to leave.

Ramon sat back in his chair, smiling up at Ben. "Yes, go home to your wife. The wife you wedded when your 'other' wife, her sister, had been dead only a day or two. An intriguing story, don't you think, gentlemen. What lies behind that, I wonder? Maybe you'd been carrying on behind the first wife's back, eh? Having the girl and her sister too. A pretty arrangement."

Ben's boots stayed frozen to the floor. *'Don't let him get to you'* something screamed in the back of his mind. *'He's trying to provoke a response. Don't give in.'*

Vaguely he heard one of the men across the table say softly: "Look here, Diego. Those are dirty accusations, not worthy of a gentleman."

Ramon looked around at the men who were staring at him with a mixture of fascination and repugnance on their faces. "Oh I'm certain all your friends here will defend Miss Lea's reputation right enough. We all know her. But what about her sister? Do any of us know what kind of woman she was? Ask yourself what kind of woman would allow a *menage a trois* in her own home? Or did she perhaps set it up herself, for her own entertainment. What does it say about the kind of woman who would stand by and watch her husband fool around with her own sister while he was having his wife too?"

Dimly Ben heard Lea's words: *'Promise me you won't be drawn into anything foolish'.* But they were drowned in the roaring rage that rose up like a blinding tide to send the room swimming around him.

"What was her name…Rachel. Was Rachel a whore too…"

He struck out, knocking Diego in his chair to the ground. In an instant he was on him, his hands squeezing the air from that swarthy throat. Growling, he dug his fingers into Diego's neck and squeezed with all his strength even as other hands grabbed at him, prying away his fingers and yanking him back.

"For God's sake, Ben, don't kill the man! He ain't worth it."

"Can't you see he was tryin' to rile you, Ben?"

Ben stood, held fast in the grip of his friends, while Diego, choking and coughing, raised himself slowly to his feet. There was still a smirk on his handsome face as he walked over to Ben and casually spit at him. Ben yanked one of his arms free and slapped Diego across the jaw with a force that sent him reeling backward.

"You saw, gentlemen!" Ramon cried, turning to the men who grappled Ben away. "You all saw the challenge." Coolly he turned back to Ben. "I accept it. You shall hear from my second tonight."

Clawing at his ruined cravat, Diego turned on his heel and stalked out of the saloon. Not until he was out of sight did the men release Ben. Then one of them picked Ben's hat off the floor and handed it to him. "You ain't really goin' to fight that man, are you, Captain? He provoked you pure and simple. He loves duels and has fought a lot of them."

"Killed a man or two with 'em, too."

"It's what he wants, Captain. You'd be foolish to give in to him."

Foolish. Don't be drawn into anything foolish

"For God's sake, he's insulted you before, your wife, your son, even your dog and your horse. Why on earth would you let him rile you like that!"

It was true. He'd taken all kind of insults from Ramon de Diego for years and not given in, knowing the man was trying to push him over the edge. But to hear Rachel's sainted name on the obscene lips of that lying bastard—that was too much. There was no way he was going to allow Diego to get away with insulting Rachel. Not his Rachel.

He stuffed his hat on his head and straightened his coat. "Good day, gentlemen," he snapped and pushed through the crowd on to the porch. Ulee was standing there staring at him, his eyes wide. His first words made it obvious he had heard everything.

"Capt'n, you ain't goin' to fight no duel, sure not?"

Ben stomped off down the street without answering, leaving Ulee, shaking his head in disbelief, to follow.

He was still seething that evening when Diego's friend, Juan Elzuardi, arrived to speak privately with him. Ben knew Juan slightly as a man of great dignity who was related to Joseph Elzaurdi, a prominent settler down on the coast near the

Manatee. Juan and Joseph had once both been associated with Diego in William Bunch's huge fishing ranchero. Now Elzuardi's extreme discomfort was plain to see.

"This is a bad business, Senor. A very bad business. I have tried to talk my friend, Ramon de Diego, from it but he insists the challenge was made and must be met."

"As do I," Ben replied. "Tell him I will meet him in three days time at Graves's tavern on the river at the Springs. That is far enough away to keep this business private."

"Three days? It is the custom…"

"I don't care about the custom. I'll need that much time to set my affairs in order." Ben's eyes flashed. "I would suggest Diego do the same."

"I shall tell him," Juan said sadly. "But perhaps an apology…"

"Any apology must come from him. He insulted my wife in the worst possible way."

"But Captain, I understood it was your deceased wife." At Ben's furious glare Elzuardi shrugged and moved to the door, having not even removed his hat.

"I assume pistols will be acceptable," Ben said after him.

"Pistols. Yes, Senor de Diego said as much."

"Good. You can find your way out."

As the door closed behind Juan Elzuardi Ben walked to the hearth and leaned an arm on the mantle. Now if he could just keep all of this business from Lea.

Ulee knew it was bad. He didn't quite know how it was bad but he sensed that nothing good could come of the angry fight between Capt'n Ben and that Senor Diego. Duels were white folks kind of fight and not something Uleee knew anything about or even understood. He'd been in plenty of fights, and with worse men than the Capt'n or Diego either, for that matter. But when you had it out with a man, you used your fists. If things got too rough, you whipped out your knife and that was the extent of it. You might get whupped, you might even get thrown in jail. But one of you came out the winner. When Capt'n Ben and Diego broke off after some hard words and a couple of blows, he didn't understand why. But he knew it was bad. Something was bound to come of it and it had to be bad.

Ben had told him to head back to the ranch right after the argument and he should have started off right away except that he thought maybe it was better to wait around long enough to find out what Capt'n Ben's next move was going to be. When he saw one of the Senors from the town visit Ben that evening, he slipped around the side of the house and listened outside the window. He waited restlessly until dawn and then set off, frustrated by the slowness of the mules and the wagon plowing the White Sand road. By pushing his team hard he was able to arrive at the ranch late that afternoon.

Buck was working at repairing a fence when Ulee found him. At once the black servant began blubbering incoherently about how he needed to set off right then to go help his father. When Buck was finally able to get some of the details from the agitated Negro he couldn't believe them. For a moment he was tempted to just shrug the whole thing off and go on with his work.

His anger at his father still smoldered and this foolish confrontation seemed just one more evidence of Ben's stupidity. Even if it led to something more deadly, why should he care? Since his father had so little regard for his ability, why not stay out of it completely and let his Pa deal with this in his own way?

Yet he had only to think of Lea to know he couldn't stand aside and let matters take their course. He knew Diego well enough to be fairly certain he had finally managed to draw Ben into this stupid duel. If he had, and Ben was killed, it would break Lea's heart.

He made Ulee sit down, then calmly went about trying to understand the situation. "Do you have any idea what they're planning?"

"No, Mistta Buck. Exceptn'..."

Buck waited while Ulee looked out over fields dotted with the blackened stumps of burnt trees. "What?"

"I stoods outside a window and I heerd Capt'n Ben talkin' with one of Mistta Diego, he friends. He say somethin' 'bout bein' in his grave in three days."

Three days? That could mean a duel But 'in his grave'? It took only a moment's hard thinking for Buck to make the connection. "Did you hear him say anything about a spring?"

"Yes, sir. I believe he done so."

Not 'grave' but Josiah Graves' Inn, situated near the spring with the noxious sulphurous water on the Hillsborough River. Not much time, but better than if his crazy father had gone out to meet Diego at dawn which would have meant it was all over and he could do nothing to stop it. Buck looked up at the darkening sky. The weather had been peculiar all day, heavy and still, like it often was before a storm. A storm, indeed.

"Ulee, I want you to ride to Newnansville right away and find Clay Madrapore. If he's in the town anyone can direct you where to find him. Tell him to meet me at Graves tavern at the Spring by dawn the day after tomorrow.

Go get some supper then take a good horse and get started right away. Rest along the road as you need to."

"Noonansville…?"

"Yes. I know it's a long way and you're tired but if anyone can do it, you can. I'll give you a note and you can stop along the way for fresh horses. You're likely to hit some bad weather but don't let that hold you back. It's absolutely necessary that you find Mister Clay."

Ulee had already started for the porch when he turned back. "Is the Capt'n goin' to get hisself killed?"

Buck yanked down the brim of his hat, his face grim with determination. "Not if I can help it."

Ben should have known he couldn't keep it from her.

Too many people had witnessed his argument with Diego. The rumor that a duel was in the making was soon bandied about by groups of men in saloons and on porches and, of course, word of it was carried to their women. In shocked whispers they passed it along until several of them decided it was only right that Lea should be told, especially after the wife of Captain McKay noted Ben leaving the house of lawyer Magbee. Lea finally heard the rumors at a meeting at the Palmer House on Friday afternoon before the duel was to take place the next morning. The women had gathered to set up for a service of the newly formed Methodist church when Sarah McKay took her aside and told her what was up. With a hot iron branding her chest she excused herself and hurried home.

When Ben looked up to see her standing in the doorway of his study, her face chalk-white, he knew there was no hope of seeing this thing through without her knowing. Well, so be it. He was finally going to have it out with Diego the following morning and Lea would just have to accept it.

They stared at one another across the room for a long silent minute. "Come in, Lea," Ben finally said, laying down the new will he had been reading over. "I suppose we had better talk."

How like him, she thought. No evasions or excuses. No questioning if anything was wrong in order to put off the subject. Stiff-legged she crossed the room and sat in the chair opposite her husband. "Then it's true."

"Yes."

"And everyone in the village knows about it but me."

Ben shrugged. "I thought it would be best you didn't know until it was over."

Lea caught her breath, fighting down hurt and anger. "How thoughtful of you. And what if I learned of it when they brought in your bleeding corpse? How did you suppose I would feel then?"

"I don't expect to be a bleeding corpse. It's just another confrontation with Diego. He's been asking for one for years and its time I had it out with him, once and for all."

"Confrontation? With what? Fists? A fistfight? Is that what you're planning?"

Ben looked away. "Not exactly."

"What then?"

"Pistols," he said angrily.

Lea exploded. "Pistols! You mean he's drawn you into a duel at last. That's the truth of it, isn't it, Ben? He's been trying for years to 'meet you on a field at dawn' and he's finally succeeded. Ben, you're…you're such a fool!"

"That's enough!" He slammed the will on the table and jumped up to stand at the window with his back to her. "You don't understand."

"Oh, I understand," she said, twisting her hands in her lap. "When? Where?"

"Tomorrow morning. Not here in town. At Grave's tavern, six miles north."

"Grave's Tavern—how appropriate!"

He turned back to her, stubborn lines etched on his face. "Now see here, Lea. I expected better of you than women's angry hysterics. I've taken care of some business I'd been putting off for years and had a proper will drawn up." He ignored Lea's stifled gasp. "I never made one you know, since that scribbled thing I wrote right after we were married and I went off to war. It was time for a better one."

Lea fought back stinging tears. "Just in case you don't survive."

Ignoring her, Ben went on. "I've left everything to you and Buck equally. And I've made Clay Madrapore my executor, with a small share in the ranch. I think his good sense will help reign in some of Buck's wild tendencies."

She jumped to her feet. "Stop it, Ben. Do you think I care about anything you leave behind? I love you. I want you here with me, as we've always been. Why would you go and put yourself in such danger, knowing how it would ruin my life as well as yours?"

"It's no more dangerous than when I went off to fight with the army. I came back from that all right, didn't I."

"Ben, Diego is an excellent shot. You know that. He's killed men in duels before. How could you let him draw you into this one? Don't you see what he's doing?" When she realized she was still twisting her hands together she deliberately forced them behind her back. "Dueling is against the law. It makes you both criminals."

Ben scoffed. "A law that's ignored more often than not. Everyone in town knows how Ramon de Diego has dogged me for years. They'll expect me to stand up to him."

"Not in this way. "There's another law, remember? If you take part in this duel, you can never hold government office. It will be just the excuse Ramon and his cronies need to force you out of the position of Road Inspector. That's probably what he intends or why else would he have provoked this just now. It isn't worth it, Ben. It isn't fair to me or to Buck, the people who love you most."

She had hoped this at least would make a difference but the stony stubbornness of his face told her she had failed.

"You don't understand, Lea. Diego has insulted me and those I love for the last time. I won't take it anymore."

Feeling drained, Lea sat down stiffly on the edge of the chair, gripping the arms with her fingers. "But why? He's said the most terrible things for years about all of us. Even me. It never drove you to such lengths before."

"This time was different. The last straw."

Lea's anger was beginning to subside, leaving her empty and lost. She hardly knew what she was saying anymore. "What could he possibly say that drove you to finally give in to his crazy desire for a duel? Was it something nasty about me?"

"No. It was Rachel."

"What?" The last vestiges of her hot anger turned cold, a creeping, seeping frigid numbness spreading through her chest. The room came into sudden focus, startling clear—the framed Hudson River print over the mantle; the glare of the matching ornate imported lamps; the intricate edging of the antimacassar she had crocheted herself.

"Rachel," Ben snapped. "He called her a whore. He said...I won't repeat what he said. It's enough to know that I would never tolerate it. The man hates me and it's time I took care of him."

"Rachel," Lea whispered. "I should have known." Now the coldness was turning to fury—not the white hot anger that clouded the brain and which had consumed her when she entered this room, but an icy steel fury that left her mind entirely clear and rational. "Rachel. Poor Rachel, dead these thirteen years."

Ben stalked the short distance between the window and his desk. Suddenly the sound reasoning that had led him to agree to this duel seemed to take on thin hair-cracks. The injured outrage that had burned in him since the quarrel wavered just a bit. "You know how I feel about her. How I've always felt."

It was a struggle to find her voice. "Oh, yes, I know. All these years I've loved you and done my best to build a life with you. And always the shadow of Rachel stood between us. Always you kept for her the love I wanted, even though she was long dead."

"Some things never die."

The sadness in his voice crystallized her coldness into a clear determination. "This is the last straw for me too, Ben. I can't fight a ghost any longer. I'm telling you now, if you go through with this foolish escapade, I won't even try anymore."

"What? What are you talking about?"

Lea rose, staring at him across the room. "You are prepared to sacrifice my well being and that of your son, and your own future for the sake of a dead woman's honor. Well, assuming you survive this duel, you can go on living with your great love for Rachel. Alone."

"What's this? A threat? If you think you can force me out of this by threatening to leave me, you're wrong. My honor is at stake now. I can't back out."

"I mean it, Ben. If you meet Diego tomorrow morning, you will come back to an empty house. That is, *if* you come back."

"And just where do you propose to go," Ben snapped.

"I'll go back home to New York. I haven't seen my parents since I left all those years ago and there are ships leaving from Tampa nearly every day. I'll take the first one north."

"Lea, you're being ridiculous. You ought to be supporting me in this. Rachel was your sister."

"I know that better than you. She was my sister and I loved her even though she was a self-centered creature all of her life. Beautiful, yes. Fragile, and loving in as pitiful a way as she was able. But self-centered all the same."

"That's enough!" He turned on her, his face florid with anger. "I won't hear anymore of this."

"Yes, for once you will! You've made some kind of saint out of my sister. You've held tenaciously to a dream that was never real. Think, Ben. How much time did you actually spend with her? Most of your married life you were off serving the army. Yet you've built her up into some kind of romantic image that walls off and keeps at arm's length all the people who really love you. Well, I can't fight it any longer. I've done all I can to be a good wife to you but this is too much. I tell you here and now, if you fight this duel, I *will* go back to New York."

"I can't believe you're acting like this. And if you do go back, then what?"

"I don't know. At least you'll know where I am if you ever decide you want a living woman instead of a dead one."

In frustration Ben waved his arm in the air. "I don't understand you. What are you talking about? Stop this nonsense!"

"Will you stop this duel?"

He faced her squarely, sensing this was a crossroad in their lives yet unable to retreat from the stubborn resolution that had brought him to this moment.

"No."

"Very well." She walked to the door, holding herself tightly, trying to keep together something that was breaking to pieces within her. With her hand on the doorknob she turned back to look at her husband standing near the hearth. There was so much she wanted to say. *Be careful tomorrow. Don't get hurt, don't get killed, oh my dear, my love.*

Without saying another word she walked out and closed the door behind her. She ought to start putting her things together. But no, wait through this evening. He might still change his mind. Tomorrow morning, if she woke to an empty bed, would be time enough to start packing.

CHAPTER 24

▼

Three days. And two almost gone. Still, Buck thought, enough time to get to Graves' if he didn't run into any unexpected trouble. Things were in place on the ranch, and if he got away by afternoon he ought to reach Graves' Tavern well ahead of Ben and Diego. If he could just get to his father before this foolish confrontation he might be able to talk some sense into his thick head. If not, well, he'd think of something else. Everything depended on getting there in time.

Clay was another matter. Though he'd sent Ulee flying off to Newmansville, there just weren't enough hours for Clay to get back soon enough to talk sense to Ben. But perhaps he could help pick up the pieces in case Buck wasn't able to stop this fight and the worst happened.

He hadn't figured on the weather but it had proved to be the hardest part about getting away since provision had to be made to protect the animals and the hay. It was well after noon before Buck was able to set off down the White Sand road under a sky growing steadily more threatening. Though he made good time it was after dark before he reached the Inn near the Springs in one of those sudden intense Florida showers. The river was an angry black and frothy with waves. The dark trees were thrown into grotesque silhouettes against bright, shattering lightning, their branches whipped by the lashing wind. Buck stabled his nervous horse in the shed next to the ramshackle building then hurried into the tavern. Once inside, he had to fight to close the door against the wind. The one large room was almost as dim as the night outside. Two feeble lanterns glowed in the darkness, illuminating a few tables at one end of a long, rough wooden bar. A rickety ladder led to a loft above.

Buck pulled off his soaked oilcloth cape and shook off the rain before hanging it on a peg near the door.

"Not much of a night to be out in," said Josiah Graves, rising from one of the tables to throw back a wooden flap and step behind the bar. "Not much in the way of customers, neither. Glad to see you, Mister."

"You'll have a free bed then, I trust," said Buck, shaking out his hat and hanging it beside the cape.

"Oh, it's you, Mister Buck. Well, come on in and let me fix you a toddy. I was hopin' I might get a traveler or two who don't want to try to make it down river. Sure I got a bed. In better weather you'd have to share it but tonight you'll probably have it all to yourself."

There were a couple of other men sitting at one of the tables. They glanced up at Buck then went back to studying their drinks. Possibly other travelers who had been caught on the road, Buck thought. He walked over to the bar and said quietly, "You haven't see my Pa, have you, Josiah?"

"Your Pa? No, not in a while. Not since the last time he was goin' up to your ranch and stopped in for a drink on the way. He wouldn't be out in this weather anyway. Even my regulars haven't shown up tonight, ceptin' for those two over there."

Buck took a long drag from the glass Josiah Graves put in front of him. It was cheap blackstrap whisky but it went down smoothly enough and was warming as well. "Anything particular happening around these parts," Buck asked, hoping maybe Graves knew something about the duel.

"Nah. Nothin' unusual. Always the same with us here in the woods. Without there's no Indians around, we stay pretty quiet. Even this little storm will probably blow itself out in a couple of hours."

Had he made a mistake? For a horrible minute Buck wondered if he had jumped to the wrong conclusion and this was not where the duel was supposed to take place. What if he lingered here while the whole affair was happening somewhere else? Yet what could he do? He couldn't go on in this weather. He'd have to try his luck and hope he was right. If God were merciful, he'd be here to save Ben for his Aunt Lea. If not…well, he wouldn't think about that now.

The wind woke her the next morning, sporadic gusts that rattled the window panes then died to ominous calm. Even before Lea opened her eyes she felt certain the other side of the bed would be empty. Ignoring the heaviness that had dogged her through the night, she dragged out of bed and went downstairs where Sukey informed her the Captain had left long before the sun was up. Lea forced down a cup of tea and a biscuit then set about filling her small steamer trunk and carpet valise with the minimum belongings she would take with her.

It was really over. Tears burned hot behind her eyes but she refused to let them fall, knowing they would drown her if she did. *Why leave?* The words rang like a tolling bell in her mind. Why *not just wait and see what happened?* If Ben came back whole, perhaps they could set about righting things between them, maybe even in a way that would be more honest than before.

And if Ben does not come back? Do you really want to be off sailing on a ship to New York while his body is laid in the ground beside your sister?

Perhaps he would at least be happy there near his beloved Rachel. Maybe he would finally be at peace.

But you won't know if you're a wife or a widow.

Does it matter? Haven't I been the same as a widow all these years, married to a man who is still in love with a dead woman?

Oh, come now, Lea. You know that's not fair…

"No!" Lea threw the dress she was folding into the trunk and slammed down the lid. Isn't that what this was all about? All these years she truly believed she had supplanted her dead sister in Ben's life because she was real, she was alive, she was *here.* Yet now he was willing to throw away all they had built, all they had shared, because of an insult to that same dead wife. It was not to be borne. It was the final hurt.

"I *will* go!" she said aloud. "And I won't return unless he comes crawling after me on bended knees, begging me to come back."

If he can come to you. Suppose he's badly wounded in this fight?

But that other voice was weakening under her grim determination. Lea moved to the bed and closed the lock on her carpet valise. She had decided not to wear the traveling dress so recently worn on the trip to Tallahassee for it had too many memories. Instead she put on a dark green bombazine, somber and neat, and with a skirt just wide enough to be easily managed on the ship. She fastened her bonnet under her chin, picked up the valise, and went downstairs to give Sukey instructions to send the trunk to the docks. Then, resolutely not looking back, she stepped from the house.

A sudden gust sent her skirts billowing. Lea glanced up at the gray, heavy sky. The day was overcast, sultry, oppressive, much like her mood. She noted the strong wind as she made her way past Whiting to the docks. With any luck she might find a ship that would sail before it and make good time.

She was relieved to see a schooner and two steamers at anchor in the bay, with two small lighters near the landing. Surely one of these ships would be ready to sail, if only to take her as far as Key West where she could find passage up the east coast. After two unsuccessful inquires, Lea located the Captain of one of the steamers, a man whom she knew slightly and who agreed to make room for her on his run to Key West. The ship was wobbling in the turgid water but Lea was able to make her way from the lighter to the deck where the ship's First Mate, a bearded man with leathery skin and deeply set eyes, welcomed her aboard. The young sailor who showed her to her cabin seemed preoccupied by the rolling waves. He laid her valise in a wall receptacle then, touching his hat, quickly left.

Lea stood looking around the tiny space that would carry her away from Florida, perhaps forever. The ship gave a sudden lurch and she lost her balance, falling with a thud across the cot. She pulled herself up and buried her face in her hands, overcome with such loss and sorrow as seemed almost unbearable.

"No. I won't give way. I won't!" she cried, jumping up and straightening her bonnet. "I won't hide down here either. I'll go up on deck and watch Tampa fade into the past." With the motion of the ship in the close cabin she felt an unaccustomed twinge of seasickness. At least on deck there would be fresh air.

By late afternoon the Captain informed the passengers that because of the fickle winds he did not think they would be able to sail until the following morning.

"You could put up at the Palmer House for the night," he told Lea and the three other paying passengers, "or you can stay aboard. If this blows over by dawn we'll sail at first light. Meantime, I'll have my crew take what baggage you need for the night over to the hotel."

Lea struggled to hide her disappointment. Any long delay worried her, not only because she was anxious to be gone before Ben got back—if he got back— but also because a delay would give her time to think. Maybe even time to change her mind. She didn't want to change her mind!

When the other passengers opted to stay on the ship she decided she would too.

It would have been more convenient to go back to her house but she refused to consider it. Even though she would have to get through the coming night not knowing if there had been a duel that morning and Ben was alive or dead, she would not go back. Sukey knew she had left to take a ship and there were not that many in the bay. If anyone needed to find her, they certainly could.

But no one came and she rose after a restless, sleepless night still not knowing if the duel had taken place or if Ben had survived it. She dressed and went up on deck hoping to see some sign that the wind had eased and to find the kind of activity going on which meant they were getting under way.

Instead she found a brooding, black morning with violent gusts of wind and sudden lashings of rain, sailors working to tie down everything on deck, and a worried Captain overlooking it all.

"Mrs. Carson, ma'am, I really must insist you go ashore. This has all the marks of a bad storm and you're not safe out here on the water."

It was disappointing but she understood the Captain's concern. The Gulf could be treacherous in the best of weather. To sail in a storm like this would be beyond foolish. Yet she could still not bring herself to return to her home.

"Do you suppose there is still room at the Palmer House?" she asked.

The Captain nodded. "The other passengers who stayed aboard last night are headed there. One of my sailors will carry your boxes for you, ma'am."

"And will you let me know the minute you're ready to depart?"

"You have my word on it."

Handing her valise to a waiting sailor, Lea fell in line with two other passengers who had hoped to be sailing at dawn. The wind almost scuttled the lighter before they reached the pier, and the gusts of rain had her shawl and skirts nearly soaked. With one hand steadying her hat and the other gripping her skirts she made her way to the nearby Palmer House hotel.

The hotel was situated on the river at the foot of Whiting street near Kennedy's store. It was a fairly new, large building of eleven rooms with a dining room across the length of the rear overlooking the river. The porch along the front usually held casual tables and chairs but today they had all been removed away from the strong wind gusts. When she entered the narrow front hall she saw that lamps had already been lit against the gray gloom. Then she heard the sound of singing from the parlor and remembered the Methodist service that was held there every Sunday morning. Glancing through the door she saw that the crowd was smaller than usual and was made up mostly of women and children.

"The men was all called away to help 'kedge' the schooner, John T. Sprague, to the wharf," the Palmer House manager, Hugh Fisher, told her. "It's just arrived from New Orleans with supplies and specie and nobody wants to see that lost. They'll have the devil of a hard time tying her down in this wind, I should think."

"This is just a summer storm, isn't it?" Lea asked.

"Well, that's what I thought, ma'am. But one of the gentlemen spread it around that all the Indians has left Tampa for inland villages, and he says that's a sign something worse is comin'. Now me, I think he was just talkin' through his hat."

"What's something worse?" the lady standing beside Lea asked faintly.

"Oh, you know, a bad storm. Maybe even a hurricane."

A Hurricane! Lea felt a quick chill. One or two hurricanes had come through Fort Brooke since she arrived here thirteen years before—a strong one just two years ago. In fact, it was that storm which collapsed the old hotel the new Palmer House replaced. Still, the damage had not been severe enough to cause much concern. A few trees blown down, a few ramshackle structures fallen, streets flooded, things like that. True, the winds were violent at times and the rain could be vicious. But if a hurricane was truly on the way now, that meant her steamer was certainly not going to sail any time soon. Maybe not for days.

She had already asked for a room but now she hesitated, wondering if perhaps she should go back to her house. How ironic that after being so determined not to return home, she should be forced to it by the weather. Yet some stubborn determination to cut herself away from this life and from Ben still kept her from giving in. Unsure about what she should do, she decided instead to step into the parlor and quietly join the service going on there.

She took a chair in the back row just as the congregation began to read the eighty-ninth psalm together. When the lady next to her offered to share her bible Lea halfheartedly joined in. At once she recognized the words which had sent Ben and his column off to war that long ago day just after they were married. She read perfunctorily the lines concerning victories and enemies. Then, passing beyond them, a later verse leapt out at her—*I will keep my love for him forever.*

She stopped reading as her throat constricted and tears sprang to her eyes. Of course the psalmist was talking about the love of God for his servant, David. Yet just a few days before she would have thought those words summed up better than any others her feelings for her husband and would continue to do so for the rest of her life. What was she doing going back on everything she had held dear for so many years? Of course she was hurt and angry about the way Ben had put his love for Rachel above what he felt for her, yet, if she ran off, never to see him again, what did that say about the depth of her love? At the very least perhaps she ought to use this enforced wait to think more carefully about leaving.

She slipped out of the parlor and ran straight into the hotel manager. "Perhaps I won't stay the night, Mister Fisher. On second thought, I think I'll go along home until this storm is over."

"As you wish, ma'am," he said, taking off in the direction of the dining room.

Lea picked up her valise and started down the hall thinking that with any luck she might get to her house before the weather grew worse. Just as she reached out to open the front door a gust of wind blew it against her, knocking her back. A young woman shrouded in a wet cloak blocked the doorway, trying to push her way inside. For just an instant, as she started past, the hood covering her head flew back and her startled eyes locked with Lea's. Then she quickly drew the hood over her face, backed out of the entrance and turned to hurry across the porch.

Lea stood in stunned surprise while the wind tore at her skirts. Throwing aside her valise she ran after the girl who had got no farther than the steps where she was pinned against the railing by the wind.

"Emmy!" Lea grabbed the girl's arm. "Emmy, is it really you?"

Angrily the young woman tried to tear her arm away. "Let me go. I don't know any Emmy!"

Could she be mistaken, Lea wondered? But no, it was Emmy. She had recognized that startled face almost at once.

"Emmy, please don't go. Come back inside. Talk to me."

Lea had to fight to keep her grip on the girl's arm. With an animal ferocity the young woman pulled from her trying to break free. Then all the strength seemed to go out of her and she sagged against the porch rail. Putting her arms around the girl's shoulders, Lea half-dragged her back inside the Palmer House. Once inside she pushed the hood back to reveal Emeline's thin, white face peering up at her.

"Oh, Emmy, it is you. And you look totally spent. Come sit down." Gently Lea drew the girl to one of the chairs that had been brought in off the porch and helped her sit. Though Emmy draped her wide cloak around her, Lea, kneeling beside her, got enough of a glance to see that her body was thinner than before except for the swollen belly. So, she was with child and pretty far gone. "And to think," Lea went on, trying to sound normal, "I might have missed you if I'd gone on home instead of coming to this hotel. I'm so glad to see you, Emmy."

"Are you?" There was bitterness in the low voice. "Why should you be glad? I stole your ring. I ruined your boy. Go on home and leave me be. I didn't come back to see you nor nobody in your family."

Lea gripped the girl's hand and refused to let go. "I don't care about the ring, and my 'boy' was as much at fault as you. I wanted to find you but we lost your trail almost at once. Why did you come back? When did you get here?"

"I came in on the Sprague. I came back to find my Ma, if you must know. I thought…maybe she could help me."

"You're near your time, aren't you?"

"No! Nowhere near. And even if I was, it's nothing to do with you."

"I don't know where your mother is. I haven't seen her for months. She may not even be in Tampa now."

"I'll find her. If not, I'll take care of myself like I always done. You just go on back to your house."

Lea sat back, releasing Emmy's hand, defeated by the bitterness in the girl's manner. Maybe she was right. Perhaps it was best that they not have anything to do with each other. "Is there anything you need?"

"Not from you." Emmy struggled clumsily to her feet then seemed to regret the brusque words. "But thanks for asking. You always treated me fair. I'm sorry about the ring. I'd pay you for it if I could. I always meant to."

"Oh, Emmy." Lea felt as though her heart would break as she watched Emmy start toward the door. The girl was so alone, so near her time to give birth. To see her walk away, with the weather growing worse by the minute, was hard to bear.

A sudden cry brought Lea to her feet. Emmy had reached the door and was nearly doubled over, clinging to it for support. In an instant Lea was beside her, her arm around her, holding her up. "Is it the baby?"

"No!" Emmy turned her face into Lea's shoulder. "Yes. At least, it may be. But it's not time yet."

"How long has this pain been going on?"

"Since this morning."

Hugh Fisher had been watching them anxiously from the dining room entrance. "Now see here," he said, as he started toward them.

"You see here," Lea snapped at him. "This girl needs a room and quickly."

"But Mrs. Carson, look at her state. We're not prepared to handle childbirth. Really, Mrs. Carson, I don't think Mr. Palmer would approve."

"You've got rooms and beds, don't you? Where else can she go with a storm outside. Give us a room and send someone for Doctor Roberts. And don't worry, you'll be paid. Well paid."

"Well, if you put it that way. The room you would have had is still available."

"I want an inside room. As far away from the wind as possible."

"All right. Take number three. Come along, I'll show you."

Emmy clamped her hand to her side as another pain doubled her over. Gripping her arm, Lea led her slowly toward the stairs, yelling back over her shoulder, "I'll find it. You go get Doc Roberts. And hurry!"

CHAPTER 25

▼

On Saturday morning, the day he was to fight Diego, Ben left his house an hour before dawn while Lea was still sleeping. He took nothing with him but his army pistol packed in his saddlebag and a lantern to guide his horse. It would have been quicker and easier to sail up the river but in this wind he might run the risk of being capsized. Above all he wanted to get to Graves' in time to get this thing over with. For years he had despised Diego and now he was going to finish with him. Whether he wounded or killed Ramon, this would be the last confrontation between them.

And if he should die? Well, it might be better for all concerned. Lea would then be free to pursue her life and Buck could go his own way. And he might finally be with Rachel again.

With a mental shake he spurred his horse on in the darkness. What nonsense! Common sense told him that neither of them would die but that facing Diego should finally free him of the man's meddling contempt. He was determined to come out of this in one piece. Remembering Lea's last words, he dismissed them out of hand. She didn't mean it when she said she'd go back north. They had built too much together. They had modest wealth, a nice home, good standing in the community and a fairly successful ranch. She wouldn't be so foolish as to give all that up just because he had refused to allow Diego to demean his first wife, and her sister at that. He didn't understand her thinking at all. Rachel was family and Lea should have encouraged him to seek revenge for Diego's insults.

Well, even without her encouragement he would stand his ground. With the wind at his back he ought to arrive at Graves' in plenty of time, maybe even before Diego. And the note he sent to Clay three days ago, asking him to be his second, ought to have him there waiting by the time he arrived. He hoped so, anyway.

It had been a bit of a shock to realize he had no close friend in the Tampa area to support him. Lots of acquaintances, some better than others, but most of them he didn't want to drag into this fight. So his thoughts had turned to Clay. If that friend didn't turn up then he'd just fight without a second. It had been done before. In a provincial backwater like Tampa the strict conventions of dueling seemed ridiculous anyway.

He arrived at the tavern just as the black sky should have been brightening. The air was heavy. What with the wind and the sudden light rain squalls, the day promised to be only a little lighter than the night. Ben stabled his horse in the lean-to adjacent to the Inn then made his way into the dim gloom of the tap-room. As he slammed the door shut against the wind he saw a tall figure rise from the table at the end of the room and start towards him. Expecting Clay, Ben came to a stop in shocked surprise as he recognized his son.

"What the hell are you doing here?"

"I came to stop this damned foolishness."

How like Buck to blurt out a challenge without even bothering to be civil. Ben slapped his saddlebag on the bar and nodded to Josiah Graves who reached under the counter for a bottle. "Mind your own business. This has nothing to do with you." He took the glass Graves offered and downed the whisky in one gulp.

Buck stepped up beside him. "Nothing to do with me! My Pa gets himself killed in some stupid gunfight and it has nothing to do with me! Even if you believe I don't care what happens to you, you might at least have spared a thought for Aunt Lea. What do you think this will do to her?"

"I'm not going to be killed. Lea understands."

Buck stared at his father's grim face. It was so apparent he was lying. "I don't believe you. Aunt Lea would never let you risk your life like this. She has better sense."

Ben slammed the glass on the bar. "Mind your own business, I say! Go away. You shouldn't have come here."

Buck fought back his anger and struggled for patience. "Papa, for once listen to me. Diego isn't worth this. He's nothing but a bully who's had it in for you for years. Giving in to this duel is just what he wants. There is nothing you could do that would give him greater satisfaction. Can't you see that?"

Josiah Graves set down the bottle he had lifted to refill Ben's glass. "Duel? What's that you say?"

Ben turned to the tavern owner. "Has Ramon de Diego showed up here yet?"

"No, but…see here, Mister Ben. I tole them fellows the last time I don't like that kind of lawless stuff going on at my place. I could get in a heap of trouble over it."

"It won't be at your place. We're to meet down at the river in one of the clearings. You won't be involved at all."

"All the same…"

Papa, listen to me." Buck gripped his father's arm but Ben shook his hand off angrily. "I told you, stay out of this, son." He grabbed up his saddlebags. "If you hadn't run your mouth off about your mother, this might not have happened in the first place."

Patience was swept away in the surge of familiar white-hot rage. "Oh, so now it's my fault, is it? Well, I'm not surprised. Everything is my fault and always has been. Of course you're not to be blamed at all. You're such a good father, such a fine husband."

"I've taken care of you for years, much good it's done me."

"I've worked my fingers to the bone for you. I've made that ranch everything it is."

"Yes, and fighting me every step of the way, when I wasn't getting you out of another scrape. But what should I expect from the kind of son who would father a bastard child on a servant girl!"

Buck stared at his father. Of all the familiar accusations he expected to hear, this one came as a complete shock. It made no sense. "What are you talking about? What child? What girl?"

Only then Ben remembered. He turned from his son and shoved his glass across the bar. "It's nothing. My anger got the best of my tongue. But I mean it, Buck. I'm determined to see this through. Go on back to the ranch and tend to your own affairs."

He started toward the door but Buck moved quickly to step in front of him. "What did you mean by that? What girl?"

Well, maybe it was time he knew, time he took responsibility. "That strumpet, Emmy Fresca that Diego and his wife fostered off on us. She was with child when she ran off in Tallahassee. Your child, so she said. Probably was lying. A girl like that could have had it off with plenty of men."

Buck was so stunned that for a moment he forgot why he had come. Emmy! A virgin the first time they laid together in the parson's room of his father's house. And it had taken plenty of time too, before she was willing. She was not a girl who'd sleep around, he'd bet his life on it. Wrenching himself away from his shocked thoughts, he saw his father had gone around him to reach the door and was pulling it open. "Papa! You're not going to do this," he cried. In two strides he was across the room to pull Ben away from the door.

Ben twisted to break his son's stubborn grip. "For the last time, Buck, get out of my way." He struck out but with a quick move Buck blocked the blow, swung his right fist with all the force he could muster and hit his father square on the chin, knocking him back against the wall. When Ben slid to the floor, Buck knelt beside him, thankful to see he had lost consciousness, even if briefly.

"Josiah, help me get him upstairs. Then I want you to tie him to the bed and don't let him loose until I come back."

"I don't know, Mister Buck…"

"You do it or so help me God, I'll tell the Sheriff you knew about this duel and arranged for them have it here. Where's some rope?"

Josiah grabbed up a loop of rope from behind the bar and between them they got Ben up the ladder and on to one of the narrow beds. Buck fastened the first knots then threw the rope to Graves and ran downstairs. He grabbed up his father's saddlebag and saw that the army pistol was inside. He was out the door when he heard Ben give his first startled groan. The yard was bathed in a gray gloom, light enough for Buck to see a horse and rider pulling up. A wave of relief washed over him as he recognized Clay Madrapore swinging down from the saddle.

"Thank God, I was afraid Ulee wouldn't reach you."

"Ulee? I haven't seen him. Ben sent for me to act as his second. His 'second' for God's sake! What the devil is going on?"

Buck took off at a fast lope with Clay following. "It's some crazy duel my father let himself to be drawn into. Down by the river clearing."

"Let me guess. Diego?"

"Of course. Who else would he let dog him into such an insane fight. Well, he's not going through with it. I've made sure of that."

They had nearly pushed through the palmettos into the clearing when Clay grabbed Buck's arm to hold him back. In the dim light they could make out two dark figures ahead. The wind still gusted around them and a light mist of rain laid a carpet of pewter fog along the ground. The sultry air was a yellow haze that hovered over the clearing.

"You don't mean to face Diego yourself, do you? That's crazy, Buck. He's one of the best shots in the area and he's killed men in duels before."

Buck's face hardened. "I'm not that crazy. I mean to finish what Diego started, but not exactly on his terms."

"For God's sake, boy, in this weather your powder might not even fire."

"Then neither will his."

Shoving away from Clay, Buck pushed through the palmettos to step into the clearing. Ramon de Diego and another man near him, whom Buck recognized as one of the Elzuardi clan, both looked up. With satisfaction Buck noted the surprise that crossed Diego's face.

"What does this mean?" Ramon said coldly. "Where is your father?"

Buck strode forward. "He's not coming."

"He must come or be forever branded a coward of the worst stripe. I don't believe he would do that."

"Believe it," Buck said, pulling out his father's pistol from the saddle bag and checking it to see if it was primed. "I'm taking his place."

A sarcastic smile flittered over Diego's' lips. "You! A boy?"

"Man enough to face you, Ramon de Diego."

"I have no quarrel with you, boy. Go back and send out your father. Or did he put you up to this in order to avoid facing me honorably."

"You don't know the meaning of the word honorable. For years you've goaded my Pa, trying every way you could to ruin his life. I don't know the reason, but I do know you've had it in for him ever since I can remember. Well, now you can finish it, only with me, not my Pa."

Diego drew himself up, staring down his nose at Buck. "This is ridiculous. It is against all the rules of dueling and I'll have no part in it. But I shall make sure the world knows what a baseless coward you have for a father."

From the corner of his eye Buck saw Clay enter the clearing off to one side, his rifle cradled in his arm. "I don't believe in old fashioned dueling, Diego. I say we have this out right now, face to face, like men." Buck raised his arm and pointed his pistol at Ramon.

"Pshaw! If I wanted a common gunfight I would have faced Ben Carson in front of a Tampa saloon. Go on home, boy!"

Through his anger Buck heard Clay's urgent whisper. "Don't do anything you'll regret, Buck."

"Don't call me a 'boy', Diego! I'm man enough to face you."

With utter contempt Ramon turned his back on Buck and strolled over to Juan Elzuardi standing behind him. The two of them spoke softly ignoring Buck who lowered the gun, his face a mask of angry perplexity. What was he to do if the man refused to fight him? All of a sudden he was unsure of what he had been so certain of an hour before. He had prevented Ben from taking part in a duel but at what cost? The threat of being branded a coward was not an idle one, not with a man like Diego. It would ruin Ben.

He looked over at Clay, a question in his eyes. "Come on, Buck," Clay said softly. "There's no more to be done here."

For a moment Buck stared at Diego's half-turned back. The man was running his fingers along the pistol in his hand, examining the elaborate filigree on the handle with a nonchalance that did not admit Buck was even there. Unsure of what to do next, Buck turned away to walk back toward Clay. He had taken only a few steps when a blast from a pistol exploded across the clearing. A white hot iron sank into his shoulder, knocking him to his knees. He clawed at his arm with his other hand still gripping the pistol as a second shattering explosion split the thick air. Acrid smoke seared his lungs as he fought against the most terrible agony he'd ever experienced. He pitched forward on to the wet grass and rolled over, groaning, trying to escape the searing pain.

Someone was kneeling over him. Clay's face swam before him. Something was being forced against his shoulder, intensifying the pain.

"You're hit. Lie still until I can see how bad it is." Not Clay. His Pa's voice. How did he get here? He was supposed to be tied up back at the tavern. Was his mind playing tricks? He looked up into his father's white face, trying to stammer.

"But…Diego…he turned away…"

"I know. Lie still, I say!"

Buck squirmed back and forth on the grass, trying to ease the hot flame in his shoulder. The rainy mist on his face felt cool but why was there smoke still rising from the grass? He turned his head and thought he could make out a dim outline of a figure lying crumpled across the clearing. Then the darkness closed over him, drawing him down into a black abyss that offered thankful release from the searing pain.

By Sunday evening it was obvious a hurricane was blowing in from the Gulf. Furious gusts rattled the windows, throwing broken branches against the panes. The rain was falling in sporadic squalls, almost perpendicular in the gale of the wind, biting like ice against everything in its path. The Hillsborough River had risen to the steps of the Palmer House and was threatening to flood the porch. Many residents who had sought refuge there now began to wonder if they shouldn't move to higher ground. The darkness and the oppressive weather was made more weird by a luminous phosphorescent glow on the water, gleaming like fire all the way to the horizon, so bright you could almost read by it.

Doctor Roberts was able to reach the hotel just as night fell. Lea was so grateful to see him she hardly noticed his worried demeanor after he examined the patient. As the long night wore on toward morning Emmy grew quiet, even sleeping for a while, and Lea was beginning to wonder whether perhaps this had been a false labor and it might be better to move the girl to her house. But when Monday's dawn came and she was ready to leave, the storm began to grow worse even as Emmy's pains became harder and more violent than before.

Yet still the baby refused to be born. As the morning wore on the storm grew in intensity. The rain came in steady, blinding sheets now, skewered by the unrelenting wind that set the wooden structure shivering and groaning. Inside the tiny bedroom Lea watched Emmy, her body bunched in agony on the bed, and knew there was no chance now of either of them reaching her house.

"I'm not going," she said to a frantic Hugh Fisher who came around eleven o'clock to urge them to evacuate the hotel for higher ground. "This girl is in no condition to be moved. It might kill her and her unborn child."

"But Mrs. Carson, it's getting dangerous here. The river is rising to serious levels and if the hotel is flooded you might all be killed." He turned to Doctor Roberts standing at the foot of the bed. "Talk sense to her, sir. Tell her you have to leave."

Doctor Roberts shook his head. "Mrs. Carson is right. Emeline could not survive a move in her condition in this weather."

"But will she survive if the building goes? Will any of you?"

Lea looked up at the doctor. He had thrown off his coat hours ago and was standing now with shirtsleeves rolled up to his elbows. His face showed age and weariness, determination and anxiety. Earlier he had informed her that Emmy's baby was in the wrong position for birth and that it was going to be a long, hard delivery. Since then, the mother's pains had grown in intensity but the child still had not come.

"I'm not leaving this room and neither is Emmy," Lea said curtly. "If you want to go, Doctor, I won't try to hold you back. But we'll take our chances here."

The big wooden structure shuddered in a sudden vicious gust. "And how could you, Mrs. Carson, manage to deliver this child into the world alive by yourself?" the doctor muttered. He turned to the frantic manager. "No, we'll all stay. We'll take our chances."

"But the hotel can't be responsible."

"I know that," Lea said, giving Roberts a grateful glance. "It's our decision alone. Please just go."

Fisher scurried out just as the wind began a fearful wail. As the door banged shut behind him Lea looked up at Roberts. "You're sure?"

"Yes, Mrs. Carson. We'll see this through together. Even then, you know, this little gal may not make it."

"I know. But if we leave now she'll have no chance at all. Nor will her child." All the outside noises of the hotel fell away, leaving only the screaming wind and the rasp of rain against the windows across the hall. "What do we do now, Doctor?"

Doc Roberts shook his head. We wait and pray, Mrs. Carson. We wait and pray."

Though a few worried residents left the hotel to move into the town, many others from the low-lying, flooded Fort Brooke area arrived to take their place inside the shuddering structure, all of them hoping the hurricane would soon blow itself out. In the small, dim upstairs room near the center of the hotel Lea barely heard the howling of the wind, so obsessed was she with the agonized moaning of the girl on the bed. She began to resign herself to the worst.

"Isn't there anything you can do?" she asked the doctor again.

"I'm doing all I can. It's really not up to me, you know."

By now Emmy's slight frame had begun to grow so weary that Lea doubted the girl could survive much more. Toward noon Lea took a break and walked down to the dining room to seek a cup of hot coffee. She found the tables being laid for dinner and most of the people who had taken refuge in the hotel milling about in a growing panic over the increasing wind and rising waters. The wind had shifted earlier and they had all hoped the worst was over. Instead its velocity had grown wilder and stronger. On one sudden howling scream Lea fancied she heard the cry of a baby. Abandoning the coffee, she turned and rushed up the stairs.

Doctor Barnes was bending over the bed. "Thank God you're back," he muttered. "Take her hand. I think something's finally going to happen."

Lea rushed to the bed and grabbed Emmy's hand. Emmy's grip was like iron but Lea held on, her prayers silent beneath the girl's screams. When finally Emmy fell back, and she heard a faint, pitiful cry from the foot of the bed, she realized tears were streaming down her face.

With deft hands the doctor tied off the umbilical cord and wrapped the baby in a soft blanket. Then he handed the tiny bundle to Lea. "It's a girl, thank goodness. A boy might have been larger and neither child nor mother would have survived this birth."

"She's alive then?"

"Barely, but yes. Show her to her mother. Maybe it'll give her something to keep fighting for."

Lea took the tiny child in her arms and looked down at the pale, wrinkled face. A powerful warmth like none she had ever known swept over her, a consuming love for this small creature who, like her mother, had suffered so much in order to come into this world. Buck's daughter!

And Emmy's. Lea carried the baby to her mother and laid her in her arms. A smile that was almost beatific crossed Emmy's ashen face. "A girl," she muttered, trying in vain to lift her arms to take the child. Lea held the baby's brow to Emmy's lips and she kissed her. "A little girl…"

Doctor Roberts bent over the bed again. "Wash off the child, Mrs. Carson. We've still got work to do here. You can let her mother hold her in a few minutes."

Lea carried the baby to a washstand in the corner and gently wiped her small body with a clean, damp cloth. The child was perfectly formed, though not as pink as one would hope. Her tiny features worked noiselessly until she was able to emit a cry that grew steadily stronger. Lea smiled with relief to hear it. It wasn't until she laid the baby back in Emmy's arms and the room gave a frightening shudder that she remembered their precarious situation. "I'm going to go see what's happening downstairs, Doctor, if you can spare me."

"Go ahead. As soon as I feel everything has settled here, I'll be off myself. They may need me in the town."

The dining room was in complete chaos. With the shifting of the wind into the southwest, the river had begun rising even more quickly than before. When Lea got near foot of the stairs she was astonished to discover that water had filled the lower floor of the hotel and the residents were stampeding for the exits. Through the dining room doors she could see the young Josiah Ferris swimming toward the porch, holding a young girl in his arms while tables and chairs floated like flotsam around them. Lea hurried quickly back up the stairs.

"My God, what have we done!" she thought. "Worked so hard to bring this child into the world only to see her swept out of it in a flood?" A loud crash sent her running faster to the upper floor. She expected at any moment the building would give way but it held. On the landing she ran to the room across the hall and threw open a shutter on the window. The angry river was streaming by beneath, carrying a mass of wreckage in its churning waters. Among the cluttered debris she recognized the jagged corner of a roof with a huge uprooted tree caught in its wake. What looked like a whole section of a wall bobbed on the torrent like a raft, with the shattered mast of a ship weaving back and forth across broken timbers. The rain fell in sheets against the building and the howling of the wind was like the cry of lost souls in hell. Lea slammed the shutter closed then clasped her hands over her ears before running back to the bedroom.

Of course Doctor Roberts was not going anywhere. She told him of their situation and they settled down to wait, expecting at any minute that the building would give way and sweep them into the roaring river. Lea held tightly to Emmy's hand, and stroked the baby's soft brow, praying they would get through this. She lost track of how long they stayed that way but it felt like hours. The lamp gave out, the room became dark and she thought Emmy must be sleeping. Then she heard her soft voice.

"Miz Carson?"

"Yes, Emmy, I'm here."

"If I...if I die, and you come through this, will you take my little girl?"

"Hush, Emmy. You're not going to die. You've come this far and you have a beautiful daughter. You must get well so you can care for her."

"But, if I don't, will you take care of her? There's nobody else. I'd feel better knowing. And someday, maybe, her father...You've been good to me, without much cause. I'm, I'm grateful."

"Now don't talk nonsense, Emmy. If this wooden hotel can make it through this storm, surely you can make it too."

"But will you? Will you promise?"

Lea fought back tears. "Of course I will, Emmy. Of course I promise. She's my grandchild, you know. I'll always love her and care for her. But you're going..."

Emmy held up her hand. "I want to call her Cecelia. I always thought, it's such a pretty name."

Something in Lea broke and she laid her head in her hands. "Oh, my dear."

A hand on her shoulder brought her around. The doctor pulled her away. "I don't like this," he was saying. "She's still losing blood." He took the baby from her mother's arms and handed her to Lea, then bent over the prostrate form on the bed. Lea walked to the chair near the door and sat down, gently rocking the whimpering baby.

Emmy died an hour later, just as the storm was finally beginning to subside.

CHAPTER 26

▼

Sucked up out of the darkness, Buck fought against the searing pain, desperate to fall back into the numb gray void where he had been wandering. A far-off voice speaking close beside his ear dragged him unwillingly to consciousness.

"Buck, Buck. Can you hear me?"

His voice was a gravely croak. "Clay? Is that you?"

But he knew it wasn't. Consciousness brought with it the recognition of his father's desperate whisper. "No. It's your Pa." A hand lightly shook his shoulder causing Buck to grimace and try to turn away. Another voice said, "He's coming round. That's a good sign."

Buck barely opened his eyes to see his father bending over him. Behind Ben he recognized Clay and Josiah Graves, their faces creased with worry.

He struggled to shake off the hand on his sore shoulder. Ben moved back. "Sorry, son. I just wanted to be sure you were still with us."

The ache was awful, but in spite of his will to sleep he was growing more aware with every minute. He turned his head to gaze up into Ben's face, surprised to see the concern written there. "Papa." He was amazed to find he had enough control to speak. "How long…have I been here?"

"Since you were shot on Saturday, three days ago. We tended the wound but you had a fever and were unconscious for a long time. There's been a bad storm and we couldn't get you to a doctor so we had to wait and hope."

"What happened?"

Ben glanced up at the other two men. Graves mumbled, "I'd better get back below and make this boy up some strong beef broth," and shuffled off. "I'll help,"

Clay added. He laid a hand on Ben's shoulder as he moved away. "Call if you need me."

Ben nodded and turned back to his son. "I'll explain it all but maybe it should wait. I don't want to upset you."

Buck's voice was halting but clear. "I'm already upset, Papa. And I want to know. Who did it? How bad is it?"

"The ball went clear through your shoulder. You're going to be pretty sore for a long time and you'll have to work to get back full use of that arm again. But in time, Clay thinks you will."

"But…Diego turned away. I saw him."

Ben's face hardened. "Yes, he turned away. But I guess his anger wasn't as much under control as he thought. Maybe when he saw me coming he thought he was aiming at me. On the other hand, maybe he thought he'd get even with me in the worst way possible by shooting you. Whatever he was thinking, he hit you, then turned his gun on me."

"In the back? He wouldn't! All that talk about honor…"

"Well, when it came right down to it, honor didn't count as much as getting even. When he raised his gun at me Clay threw me his rifle and I used it. To good effect, too."

A sickening wave swept over Buck, part pain, part misery. "Papa. You didn't kill him?"

Ben leaned forward, gripping his hands. "It looked like a clean wound and we thought he might be all right. They took him down to Grave's cousin's place but they sent word to us later he was dying. They're keeping him there until they can get him back to his people in Tampa."

"You'll be in bad trouble."

"I don't think so. His friend, Juan Elzuardi, is downstairs. He's an honest man and he saw Diego shoot you then turn his gun on me. Clay did too. They can testify that my shot was self defense. Considering what happened, I think you could call it more of a gunfight than a duel, and the law's more familiar with that and more lenient. The worst you get is some time in jail and a fine.

"It'll end your…politics."

Ben sighed. "Yes, I know. But somehow I don't much care anymore. Sitting here with you, wondering if you'd come out of this alive or not, well, it's helped me think through a lot of things."

Buck groaned with the throbbing pain in his shoulder. He knew his father's brave words were not completely true. Political ambitions that had been nurtured for years were not going to disappear overnight. It would take a long time. "What ever made him hate you so?" he mumbled.

Ben's voice was low. "Long ago I blocked him from building a trading post on the Alafia River. After that, we were rivals for almost everything we both tried to build. Then too, Spaniards have a tendency to want vengeance when they feel they've been injured. But I don't think that was all there was to it. Last night Clay reminded me of something I had forgotten. Years ago Diego made advances to your Aunt Lea and she would have none of him. It probably hurt his pride and that, added to all the other times we went up against each other, built up a proper hatred for me. Of course, I didn't like him much either, but I never hated him enough to shoot his son in the back."

Ben paused at the grimace on Buck's face. "Here, would you like a drink of water?"

Buck nodded and Ben carefully lifted his head and raised a glass of water laced with a little brandy to his lips. "We need to get you home but that can't be done until this storm is over. It's easing up now, so maybe the worst has passed."

Buck sighed as his head fell back on the pillow. "Aunt Lea. Who would have thought?"

"Your Aunt Lea was a fine looking woman. Still is a fine looking woman."

"I didn't think you noticed. You were always so busy staring at that picture of my mother."

Ben studied his hands. "Was it that obvious? It's true I loved Rachel dearly and I thought I'd never get over her death. And when Lea and I married, it was more for convenience than anything else."

"Oh, Papa, when are you going to see that Aunt Lea is twice the woman Mother was." He took a deep breath. "I remember her, you know. She was always sick, always complaining. She never had time for me or Stephen. It seemed like we were always in the way. It was Aunt Lea who took time with us…took care of us…loved us."

Buck's voice faltered, his breath became labored. Ben pushed back the hair from his brow and noticed the warmth that was still there, though not as high as before. He hardly knew how to answer his son. Truth was, he'd had a lot of time to think sitting beside Buck's bed wondering if his boy was going to die, and some things had grown clearer to him than ever before. Not just about the way he'd treated his son but about the way he felt toward Lea as well. "Don't talk now, Buck," he said, gently. "We can discuss all these things when you're stronger."

Buck reached up and gripped his father's hand. "Papa, remember this. Mother could never have worked beside you like Aunt Lea has. She could never have been as strong and helped you to build all you have. Don't let Aunt Lea get away, Pa. You need her more than you think. We both do." He gave a weak smile. "She's the one who keeps us from killing each other."

Ben tucked his son's hand under the cover and smoothed the blanket over it. "I know, Buck. Believe me, I do know. You rest now and we'll talk about it later. And don't worry about anything. It will all work out. I'm going down now and see how that broth is coming. It'll help you get your strength back. You try to sleep."

Ben was satisfied that Buck had already drifted off again by the time he climbed down the ladder. The darkened room was brightened by two circles of lamplight and the glow from a battered iron stove where Graves bent stirring something in a kettle, probably the broth for Buck. As Ben crossed the room Juan Elzuardi glanced up from one of the tables, then went back to staring in misery at a glass with a jug standing beside it. Ben walked to the window and lifted the oiled flap to push open the shutter just far enough to see that it was growing light and the wind had died down. Behind him Clay was already headed to the loft but he stopped when he saw Ben lift his coat and hat off the peg and start to pull them on.

"You're not going out in this?"

"It's not as strong as it was earlier. And now that I know Buck is awake I have to get back to town. It's important."

"Important enough to risk being blown into the river? It's still pretty dark. Why not wait until afternoon when things are more settled?"

"The worst is over. I'll be all right. But I'm not so sure Lea is. I've got to know."

Clay gave up protesting. "Yes, you should see about her. Don't worry about Buck. We'll take care of him and bring him back to the village as soon as he can be moved. We'll float him down the river if he can't ride."

"Thanks, Clay." He paused. "You're a good friend." He was out the door before Clay could reply.

One look at the river and Ben knew it would be a while before anyone could float a raft down it safely. It had become a raging torrent, cascading along with the current and spilling over its banks into the thickets and pine forests, almost up to the trail he had to follow back to town. There was still a wind but it was lighter now, almost gentle at times. The heavy, humid air soon had him dampened through but he pushed on. There was so much debris cluttering the trail—

downed trees and flotsam of broken branches—that it would probably take him most of the morning to make what in better weather was a relatively short trip. At one point he was astonished to see the dark looming shape of a ship tethered between the trees where the wind had swept it off the river. With growing alarm he spurred his horse on.

In between clearing a path and urging on his reluctant horse he had plenty of time to think. What had he said to Clay? 'To see if Lea was all right'? What he should have said was, 'To see if she was still there'. For it was entirely possible she had sailed before the worst of the storm hit. What would he do if she had gone? For that matter, what would he do if he found her still in the village? What could he say to ease the anger and hopelessness of their last confrontation? He kicked his horse to spur him on. Whatever happened, he had to get there as soon as possible, if only to know she was safe.

By Monday evening the wind had died down enough that Doctor Roberts felt it was safe to leave the Palmer House to see where he was needed in the village and make the necessary arrangement for Emmy's burial. Lea wanted to get the baby to higher, safer ground, but she was unwilling and too exhausted to set out in the dark so she decided to wait for first light. She found a large basket in one of the upstairs closets which she lined with blankets for the baby then sought out a little water and sugar in the kitchen which would have to do until she could find milk in the town. She spent a restless night, rising several times to check on the baby, then fell into a heavy sleep near dawn from which the Doctor shook her awake.

"I've brought old Martha to lay Emeline out, Mrs. Carson, and some milk for the baby. I think we should leave this place now," he said kindly.

She did not object. Aching in every muscle, she fed the baby, then pulled a comb through her hair and smoothed her wrinkled clothes. Once the baby was asleep she carried the basket down the stairs, pausing at the landing where the water still lapped inches deep. "I'll need to find a source of milk for this child." she said to the Doctor, as she lifted her skirts to wade to the porch. "A wet nurse, maybe, or at least someone whose livestock survived this storm." Gripping the basket handle, Lea shoved open the hotel door and stopped in shock, staring at what remained of the fort and the village she knew.

Swollen by the waters of the bay, the river covered everything, its surface littered with the debris of fallen buildings and trees. To the south, nothing remained of the familiar Fort Brooke buildings. The commissary, Mr. Ferris' warehouse, Mr. Allen's boarding house—all gone. The emptiness where their substantial bulk used to stand brought a sweeping sense of desolation. Far down the bay Lea made out an overturned building that looked to be the chapel, now flopped on its side. All that was left of the fort's barracks were scattered, jagged pieces of cedar logs bobbing in the river, jostling among the barrels, boxes and ruined supplies of Mr. Ferris' store. The boats that had been moored in the shipyard were gone. There was no sign of the Sprague or her steamer at all. Only an old abandoned hulk still bobbed near what used to be the west side of the river. The tiny islands out in the bay were completely submerged.

Doctor Roberts took her arm and they made their way through the shallow water around the building to look to the north. Lea gasped as she saw that the shoreline which used to be lined with houses now stood empty as a lake. The water had flooded so far inland that in places only the tops of some trees were visible. Had her own house been swept away, too? It almost made her heart stop to think so.

Making their way to the higher ground, they found some of the survivors huddled in the remaining houses between the court house and Kennedy's store. Almost none of the village's homes had escaped damage. Many had roofs and shutters missing, shingles and beams lay beside broken trees that littered the muddy streets. With the supplies gone from Mr. Ferris' warehouse, those left in the surviving stores were already being carefully rationed. Yet Lea was able to locate some milk for the baby along with a nursing bottle. With those most important first needs filled, she was able to listen to the tales of the survivors who had watched the tidal wave sweep most of the town away.

It had been an awesome sight. The river had risen twelve feet higher than normal, engulfing the islands in the bay and carrying away the buildings along its shore. There had been a horrible crash when the commissary went, though Lea had not heard it over the wind in the upstairs room at the hotel. The fact that the Palmer House had withstood the flood was considered nothing less than a miracle. Though the water on the eastern side of the river was beginning to recede now, the entire western shore was still underwater far inland. The Turman and Ashley residences were gone and the roof of the Spencer house was blown away. The Jackson house, where some of the survivors from the hotel had originally sought shelter, had been carried off its foundation by the force of the water. Yet when she heard that Captain McKay's house had somehow been spared she began to hope that perhaps hers had been as well.

Finally when she couldn't stand not knowing any longer, she took the baby's basket and made her way to Water Street.

Or as close as she could get. Leaving the court house she sloshed through the mud down Madison to Ashley. To the north she could make out the roof of Steele's old residence, but looking ahead where she hoped to see her lovely home, her heart sank as she saw only shallow water ebbing around a huge pile of debris. She had to force herself to walk closer. The house had not been swept off its foundations like the Jackson house. Instead the towering trunks and branches of two large oaks had fallen on to it, splintering the walls like a child's toy. Huge sections of the roof lay haphazardly jumbled among shattered furniture, broken walls, sodden cloth and jagged lattice work. She stood frozen, unable to force her feet against the muddy detritus that lay along what used to be the walkway to her kitchen.

How could she bear it! Her life was in ruins and now her home was as well. Nothing was left. She turned up a barrel lying on its side and placed the basket on it to free her hands. Then she began rummaging around in the debris, pulling away pieces of jagged lumber and broken furniture to get at what lay beneath. Lifting a wet slab of wood she found a shattered picture frame that held the painting of her home in New York. The print was soaked and torn. Broken pottery, every piece something she recognized from long use, lay haphazardly among the timbers. A limp bonnet, wet cloaks and shawls, Ben's old Army hat, all lay mangled among the debris of bureaus, chairs, the brass bedstead from Buck's room. Her rocking chair seemed to be still mostly intact but the lamps from Ben's study which she had ordered from New York and always loved were shattered beyond repair. She pulled Ben's soaked Captain's hat out of the wet sludge, and holding it in her hand she turned back to retrieve the baby's basket. She wasn't sure why of all the flotsam she should save this old army hat. Perhaps because it reminded her of when she first came here to Fort Brooke, silently loving its owner. Maybe it symbolized all the hopes she had felt when he asked her to marry him, all the joy she had expected to share with him in their years together. She tried to pick up the basket but found she couldn't move. Sinking down on the bench that used to frame her garden gate, she laid her head in her hands and sobbed.

How cruel of fate! Or God. Or something. Three days ago she had made the decision to put all this behind her and start anew, and God, or destiny, or nature had made sure everything was wiped out for her. The old slate was gone forever. There was nothing left of the years she had poured into building a life, a home, a marriage. She had never felt so empty, so devoid of any purpose in living, so hopeless.

And now there was no ship to sail away on and she had a baby to care for. However in the world was she going to manage!

"Lea!"

With a start Lea looked up to see Ben standing behind her. She tried to focus through her swimming tears. Was he was really there? Was she imagining? Hallucinating?

His arms went around her, lifting her to her feet, crushing her tightly to him. "Thank God you're safe. I was afraid I'd lost you."

For a moment she let herself lean against him, savoring the blessed comfort of being in his arms again. Then she pulled away. "Ben, Ben…our lovely home…"

He wiped the tears from her cheek with his rough fingers. "It was just a house. It can be built again. What matters is that you're all right. We're both all right."

His words brought everything back. With a deliberate effort Lea moved out of his embrace to sit back down on the bench, struggling to find the words to ask about the duel. She silently thanked God he was not wounded or dead, yet her still deep hurt loomed like a chasm between them.

"What happened?" she finally asked. He sat beside her, looking away.

"There was a gunfight but it was no duel in the regular sense. In the end Diego could not abide by his own rules. He shot Buck, and I shot him."

"Buck!" She felt the color drain from her face. "Is he…"

"He's alive. The ball went through his shoulder. It was pretty chancy for a while but he seems to be all right now. Diego was not as fortunate. I despised the man but I never meant to kill him. It just turned out that way."

"Oh Ben, how terrible. But how did Buck get involved? He didn't know about it."

"Ulee told him. Once he knew about it he hot-footed it down to the Springs determined to prevent me from going through with what he called this 'damned fool idea'. And he almost did. He got to Diego before I did but Diego refused to fight him. Buck started to leave and Diego shot him. He might have been aiming at me, or he might have done it deliberately to hurt me. At any rate, when he did aim at me, I got my shot in first."

"Poor foolish Buck. So like him."

:"Yes. It was a foolhardy thing to do, and incredibly brave. I had a lot of time to think sitting by his bed, hoping and praying he'd come through. I promised the good Lord if he'd save Buck's life, I'd try to think more about the boy's strengths in the future instead of coming down so hard on his weaknesses. Well, the good Lord did his part and I intend to do mine."

He leaned forward, his arms on his knees, clasping his big bony hands. "I have been hard on him in the past, I know that. Perhaps if Stephen had lived and I'd had two sons I might have been easier. But he was the only one and I wanted so much for him. I just couldn't accept that they were my ambitions, not his."

Lea ached to smooth back his hair, to touch him and comfort him. But she could not bring herself to raise her hand. "This is bound to put an end to your political hopes, Ben. I hope you realize that."

"I do. I can't say it won't hurt, and I know there will be times when I'll regret it. But it's done. And now there are other matters to attend to. And the first one is you."

"Me?"

He turned and forcibly took her hands in his own. "Lea, there were times coming down here today when I thought I couldn't bear it if I found you had gone, or been hurt or even killed in this storm. For the first time I began to realize everything you mean to me. You've been my touchstone, my mooring through all these years. Without you, I would not be able to start over, or rebuild. Without you I'd be lost and floundering. I'd be as much a ruin as what's left of our house out there."

She would not look at him. Her profile was like sculptured stone, as white and as cold. "I know I've never been good at showing you my feelings," he went on. "Maybe I wouldn't allow myself to recognize them. Perhaps we didn't get off to a good start, but we did well together. We built something good together. This storm has wiped away a lot of that, not just the material things but the old parts of our marriage as well. Can't we start over? Can you find it in your heart to stay and begin building it all up again?"

Lea tried to speak but the words choked in her throat. "I can't go on living with a dead woman standing between us, Ben. I just can't."

He dropped her hands and turned away. "I know. But I think now perhaps I can face the fact that Rachel is gone, has been gone for a long time. Sitting beside Buck's bed I realized what a warm, loving woman you are and how I've let my obsession with an old, first love keep me from appreciating you. I said another prayer there, Lea. If the Lord would let you stay with me, I'd do everything in my power to make you feel loved and happy."

Lea's face softened. "I have felt loved, Ben, many times. Yet whatever I did, I could never take Rachel's place in your heart. I tried to, perhaps sometimes I tried too hard. I always lost. Now I just don't have the heart to keep trying anymore."

"But you won't have to. Surely a man can love two women. And my heart is full of love for you. All I felt for Rachel hasn't gone away but I realize it's time to put it aside, along with the past. The future is ours. It's all we have and it's a gift not to be thrown away lightly. All the way down here today I promised myself that if I could just find you, I'd try to make it clear how much I need you with me, how much I depend on you. How much I love you and want you by my side. Don't leave me, Lea. Say you won't leave."

Did he really mean it? She finally turned and looked into his eyes, seeking an answer. He'd never said such words to her before. Were they really true? If she gave in now there would be no turning back. Would she find herself once again in the shadow of her sister's ghost if she gave in now?

Yet, studying his face, she knew she had no choice. She had loved him too long and too deeply. He was so much a part of her that without him she would never be a whole person. She didn't speak but raised her hand and laid it along his cheek in a gesture that had become lovingly familiar over the years. He moved her palm to his lips then, overcome with relief, swept her in his arms and kissed her.

"My dear old girl..." he murmured when he could speak again. "We'll get through this, you'll see. We'll build a bigger house, then we'll buy more new lots and build houses and sell them. This town will have to be rebuilt and we'll help do it. We'll help build this State, this Florida. It's all new and empty now, unformed and wild and just waiting to be settled and tamed. We'll be part of all that."

Lea laughed. "There's that ambition again."

"Of course, but not the same. No more politics. Buck can have the ranch to make what he wants of it, and we'll concentrate on our home and..."

He broke off at a faint cry from the basket. "Oh," Lea cried. "I forgot about the baby. That new home we're going to build already has a new resident." Lifting the basket she sat it in her lap and pulled away the blanket to reveal the pink face of the child stirring in her sleep. "Meet your granddaughter, Ben."

"What! My what? Grand-daughter?"

"Yes. Emmy came back to Tampa and I found her just as the storm hit. She was near her time and completely on her own. We waited out the storm at the Palmer House where Dr. Roberts and I helped deliver her baby. It was a terribly hard birth, so hard the poor girl did not survive it. My heart hurt for her, Ben. She was so proud and so alone. I only found her by accident and at first she didn't want my help. But everything got so bad that in the end I think she was glad I was there. Before she died she asked me to take care of her little girl. Look at her. Isn't she beautiful?"

A hard shadow passed over Ben's face. For a moment Lea felt her hopes die away as the old anger suffused his features. He barely looked at the baby. "Emmy! That slattern we took into our home who ruined my son! I thought we had seen the last of her."

Something hardened in Lea as well. "I don't believe she was a slattern, Ben. She told me Buck was the only man she'd ever been with and I believe her. She was incredibly brave having this child and facing her death and I tell you right now, if you want me back, you'll have to take this baby with me. I will never give her up."

She could see the struggle he was going through mirrored on his face and for a moment she feared all was going to be lost. Then he glanced up at her and managed a tight smile. "You know, Buck may have something to say about that. He's the father after all."

Relief sent her spirit soaring. "Well, he's in no position right now to protest. She's lovely, isn't she, Ben? Emmy named her Cecila but I think I'll call her 'Cissy'. While she's little, anyway." She smoothed the soft blonde hair. "At least one good thing came out of this terrible storm."

Ben put his arm around her shoulder and drew both her and the baby into his embrace. "A lot of good things, I'd say."

Lea leaned against his chest and breathed in the warmth, the familiarity of this man she had loved for so long. She knew his faults—his stubbornness, his dogged insistence on what he felt had to be done, the way he tried to bury his feelings, his sudden, quick temper. Yet she knew even better his other side—his decency, his loyalty, his willingness to take risks, his capacity for sympathy and loving. He was so much a part of her that she knew now she could never leave him. Surely God must have meant for them to be together.

"I will keep my love for him forever," she thought. *And stay beside him as long as the Lord allows.* It was all right. Everything was all right again.

Lea sighed, nestling her head in the hollow of his shoulder. "I guess we ought to start trying to salvage what we can from all this."

"And we'll have to find a temporary place to stay," Ben said, resting his cheek against the softness of her hair. Neither of them moved.

"There's so much to be done."

"We're not alone. Many others here are facing the same problems. We'll all help each other." His arm tightened around her. "There's time."

The wind was a whisper now, the birds subdued and quiet. From the village in the distance they could hear the soft cries of a cow lowing, the bark of a dog, children calling. Reluctant to move, they stayed, drawing strength and comfort from each other before rising to begin re-forming their broken world.

Above the sluggish river huge piles of towering gray clouds reflected on its silver surface. Lifting her head, Lea turned her eyes to the sky where, between the dark, towering banks she could make out a thin streak of blue breaking through. By tomorrow the clouds would be blown away and the hot sun and ethereal blue bowl of the Florida sky would engulf them.

A shaft of golden light broke through the clouds to caress the basket in Lea's lap. At the sudden brightness on her face the baby stirred from her unformed dreams and lifted her tiny new hand to the sun.

END

9 780595 364688